## Someone to Trust

"The balance between sweet and bitter produces a complex and winning love story."  —*Publishers Weekly*

"The sheer perfection of Balogh's prose in the fifth superbly written installment in the Westcott series marries her rare gift for crafting realistically nuanced characters to produce another radiant Regency historical romance by one of the genre's most resplendent writers."

—*Booklist* (starred review)

"With tenderness, humor, and infinite finesse, Balogh turns the classic younger woman / older man pairing on its well-worn ear in another sigh-worthy [novel] that readers are sure to savor."  —*Library Journal* (starred review)

"The quiet, authentic intensity of the characters' emotions is a hallmark of Balogh's work, and it is a pleasure to experience each heart-wringing moment in this romance made for warming a winter night."  —*BookPage*

## Someone to Care

"A love story nearly perfect in every way."

—*Booklist* (starred review)

"A story that is searing in its insight, as comforting as a hug, and a brilliant addition to this series. Another gem from a master of the art."  —*Library Journal* (starred review)

## Someone to Wed

"With her signature voice and steady pace, Balogh crafts a thoughtful, sweet Regency-era love story to follow *Someone to Hold*."
—*Publishers Weekly*

"Balogh's delightful ugly duckling tale may be the nonpareil Regency romance of the season."
—*Booklist* (starred review)

## Someone to Hold

"Written with an irresistibly wry sense of humor and graced with a cast of unforgettable characters, the second in Balogh's exceptional Westcott series, following *Someone to Love*, is another gorgeously written love story from the queen of Regency romances."
—*Booklist* (starred review)

"This 'Cinderella' reversal story seethes with desire, painted paradoxically in the watercolor prose that is the hallmark of this author."
—*Kirkus Reviews*

"This Regency romance dives deeper than most and will satisfy fans and new readers alike."
—*Publishers Weekly*

"Balogh is, and always will be, a grand mistress of the genre."
—RT Book Reviews

# Someone to Romance

## A Westcott Novel

## MARY BALOGH

JOVE
New York

A JOVE BOOK
Published by Berkley
An imprint of Penguin Random House LLC
penguinrandomhouse.com

ISBN: 9781984802392

Printed in the United States of America
3  5  7  9  10  8  6  4  2

Cover photographs by Richard Jenkins
Cover design by Katie Anderson

# Someone to
# Romance

# The Westcott Family

(Characters from the family tree who appear in *Someone to Romance* are shown in bold print.)

Stephen Westcott m. Eleanor Coke
Earl of Riverdale  (1704–1759)
(1698–1761)

Andrew Westcott m. Bertha Ames
(1726–1796)  (1736–1807)

David Westcott m. **Althea Radley**
(1756–1806)  (b. 1762)

George Westcott m. **Eugenia Madson**
Earl of Riverdale  (b. 1742)
(1724–1790)

**Mildred** m. **Thomas Wayne**
Westcott  Baron Molenor
(b. 1773)  (b. 1769)

**Boris**    **Peter**    **Ivan**
**Wayne**   **Wayne**   **Wayne**
(b. 1796)  (b. 1798)  (b. 1799)

Louise m. John Archer
Westcott │ Duke of Netherby
(b. 1770)  (1755–1809)

m. Ava Cobham
(1760–1790)

**Jessica**
**Archer**
(b. 1795)

Humphrey Westcott
Earl of Riverdale
(1762–1811)

m. Alice Snow
(1768–1789)

**Matilda** m. **Charles**
Westcott  **Sawyer**
(b. 1761)  **Viscount**
**Dirkson**
(b. 1761)

**Viola Kingsley**
(b. 1772)

m. Marcel Lamarr
Marquess of Dorchester
(b. 1773)

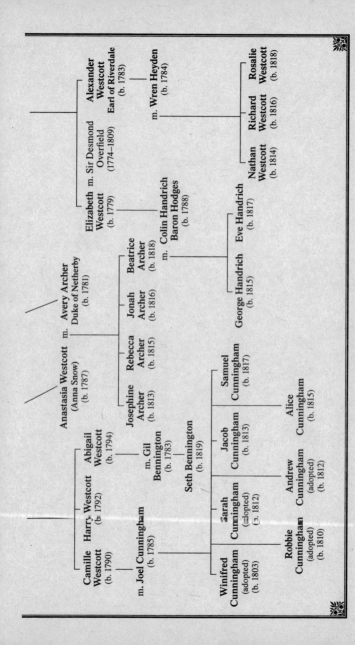

# One

L ady Jessica Archer was traveling alone across England
toward London. *Alone* was, of course, a relative term.
If she had been born male, she could have left Rose Cottage
in Gloucestershire that morning astride a horse or perched
upon the high seat of a sporting curricle, ribbons in hand,
and no one would have batted an eyelid. When one had
the misfortune to be a woman, however, there were always
enough people and enough eyelids to bat up a storm.

She was seated inside the carriage of her brother, the
Duke of Netherby, the ducal crest emblazoned upon both
doors, with Ruth, her maid. A brawny footman was seated
beside a burly coachman up on the box, both men clad in
the ducal livery, which was not subdued in color, to say the
least. It blared upon the eye like a clarion might upon the ear.

And then there were the two carriages bowling along behind her. The first conveyed Mr. Goddard, the duke's personal secretary, who had the whole of the duke's authority
vested in his person when he was acting on behalf of His

Grace, as he was currently doing. The coachman and foot-man upon the box of that carriage were hardly less impres-sive in girth than the first two.

The third carriage bore all the baggage, which could have been squeezed into and upon the other two convey-ances with a little effort—but why crowd them when there had been the spare carriage taking up room in the ducal carriage house? There was only a coachman upon the box of the baggage coach, but that might have been because he was a former pugilist and so broad and so fierce-looking with his once-broken nose and one cauliflower ear and sev-eral missing teeth that no footman fancied climbing up beside him.

And then there were the outriders, also in the ducal liv-ery, all of them large men upon large horses and appearing as though they might also have been professional fighters in the not-too-distant past. There were eight of them, two for each carriage and two to spare.

Any highwayman seeing the cavalcade make its colorful way east along the king's highway, not even trying to hide itself or tiptoe past any dangerous stretch without being noticed, would have either died laughing or else taken mor-tal fright and moved his business permanently to another part of the country.

And *this* was what *traveling alone* meant when one was a lady.

This was how it had all come about.

Abigail Bennington, née Westcott, Jessica's cousin and best friend, had given birth to a son, Seth, her first child, in late February, a little less than two years after her marriage to Lieutenant Colonel Gilbert Bennington. The Westcott family had been invited to the christening, a month later, in the Gloucestershire village outside which Abby and Gil lived at Rose Cottage, fortunately *not* really a cottage but more a manor. Even so, when a number of the Westcotts showed up, it was filled to the rafters, to use the phrase of Uncle Thomas, Lord Molenor. And it was a good thing, Aunt Viola, Abby's mother, the Marchioness of Dorchester, had said, though a little sad too since neither Camille nor Harry, her other two children, had come, having decided to visit later, after the weather had warmed up a bit. Camille and Joel's numerous children alone would fill a tent that would take up the whole lawn.

Jessica had gone with her mother, the Dowager Duchess of Netherby—and a Westcott by birth—and with her brother and sister-in-law, Avery and Anna, the duke and duchess, and their four children. It had been a jolly week, the only real frustration for Jessica being that it had given her scarcely a moment to be alone with Abby. She had not seen her best friend for an age, though they exchanged long letters at least once a week. Abby had been a bit disappointed too, but it was Gil who had suggested that Jessica stay on for a few weeks after everyone else returned home.

*Simple, right?* Jessica silently addressed an invisible someone seated opposite her in the carriage.

Wrong!

She would remain at Rose Cottage to give Abby her company awhile longer, Jessica had announced to her family. She was twenty-five years old, after all, and no longer needed to be coddled like a girl. Gil would hire a post chaise for her when she was ready to leave, and she would have her maid, Ruth, for company.

Her family, alas—at least the vocal part of it (which, interpreted, meant the female part)—saw things quite otherwise. Jessica, for all her advanced years, could not *possibly* be allowed to remain behind, since that would mean her returning alone. Poor Ruth, apparently, counted for nothing. All sorts of harm might befall Jessica in the form of footpads or highwaymen or rude hostlers at inns or wild beasts or broken axles or torrential storms.

"Besides which," her grandmother, the Dowager Countess of Riverdale, had pointed out as though to clinch the matter, "it simply is not done for any lady to travel alone, Jessica, as you must be well aware. Even someone my age."

Grandmama was well into her seventies.

Jessica's protests had gone unheeded.

"You cannot possibly stay here," Jessica's mother had said at last, a note of finality in her voice, "as much as I understand your longing to spend more time with Abigail— and hers to have you. I cannot possibly remain here with you. The Season is about to begin and I will need to get ready for the removal to London. So will you, Jessica. Perhaps we can arrange something for another time."

Jessica had cringed at the very thought of going back to London in order to participate in all the glittering entertainments of yet another Season—her sixth. Or was it her seventh? She had lost count. It was not that she hated balls and picnics and concerts and all the other parties and such with which the *ton* amused itself during the months of spring, while Parliament was in session. But these entertainments could very quickly become repetitive and tedious. And one tended to see the same people year after year and wherever one went.

Her continued single state was always more apparent in London than it was in the country.

"Oh, Mama," she had protested. Aunt Matilda had been smiling sympathetically at her, but it was not sympathy she had needed. It was a defender.

That was when Avery—her brother, the duke—had come

to her rescue. He had listened in silence to the family conference, sitting in one corner of Gil and Abby's sitting room holding Beatrice, the newest addition to his family, while she sucked partly on her thumb and partly on one formerly pristine fold of his elaborately tied neckcloth. When he had spoken, it had been with what sounded like a sigh, as though he had found the whole proceeding excruciatingly tedious, as no doubt he had.

"I daresay," he had said, "you would all consider Jessica both safe from harm and properly preserved from scandal if she were to travel home in the ducal carriage with her maid while Edwin Goddard followed close behind in another carriage, each conveyance manned with a coachman and a footman upon the box, and half a dozen outriders to serve as escorts."

The Marquess of Dorchester, Abby's stepfather, had chuckled. "All of them clad in the brightest ducal livery, I suppose, Netherby?" he had said.

"But of course." Avery had raised his eyebrows as though surprised that the matter could even be in doubt.

"It is a splendid idea," Anna had said, beaming at her husband and her sister-in-law. "Avery will send them whenever you are ready to leave, Jessica. How lovely it will be for you and Abby to enjoy some time together after the whirlwind of the celebrations during the past week."

And that had settled it. Though Avery spoke only rarely during family gatherings, when he *did* speak no one ever seemed to question his pronouncements. Jessica had never quite understood it. He did not look like an overwhelmingly powerful man or even behave like one. He was of only average height. He was also slight and graceful of build, with very blond hair and a face of angelic beauty. He might have looked . . . well, effeminate. But he did not, and somehow he wielded a great deal of power without ever having to bluster or bully or even raise his voice. Jessica suspected that most people outside his immediate family feared him but did not understand why any more than she did.

The result of those few words he had spoken after the lengthy discussion that had preceded them was that now, three weeks after everyone else had left, she was on the road back to London, at the very heart of a cavalcade that drew astonished stares and awed scrutiny in every town and village or hamlet through which it passed.

Being a woman—or, rather, being a *lady*—certainly had its frustrations despite the luxury of cushions that wrapped her in comfort and the springs that made the passage of the carriage over English roads almost a smooth one. She knew she was being treated as a child, although she was not one. Mr. Goddard, Avery's extremely efficient secretary, transacted all the business along the way, with the result being that Jessica had scarcely opened her mouth since the flurry of hugs and tearful goodbyes that had accompanied her departure that morning from Rose Cottage. Ruth was no real companion. Though excellent at her job and loyal to a fault, she had always insisted upon keeping a proper and respectful distance from her mistress. She never prattled on about anything and everything the way it seemed other ladies' maids did. She rarely spoke at all, in fact, unless spoken to.

It had been a very quiet journey.

It had given Jessica far too much time to think.

She had never dreamed, growing up, that she would still be unwed at the age of twenty-five. Like most young girls, she had dreamed of growing up and falling in love and marrying and beginning a family of her own, all long before she was twenty. But when she was seventeen and within a year of making her longed-for come-out into society, the

Great Disaster had happened. She always thought of it as though the words would have to be capitalized if written down. Her uncle, Humphrey Westcott, Earl of Riverdale, had died, and twenty-year-old Harry, his son, had succeeded him in title and property and fortune. Until, that was, the ghastly discovery had been made that Uncle Humphrey had already been secretly married to someone else when he wed Aunt Viola, Harry's—and Camille's and Abigail's—mother, more than twenty years before. Aunt Viola's marriage, unknown to everyone except Uncle Humphrey himself, had been bigamous. Harry was stripped of his title and everything else, and Camille and Abigail lost their titles and their dowries. All three lost their very legitimacy. They no longer belonged in the *ton*.

The whole of the Westcott family had been thrown into turmoil. But it had always seemed to Jessica that she suffered more than any of the others, except for Aunt Viola and Camille, Harry, and Abigail, of course. For Abby was her very dearest friend. They had always been more like sisters than cousins. They had dreamed of making their come-out together, even though Abby was one year older than Jessica. They had dreamed of falling in love and marrying at the same time, perhaps even in a dazzlingly grand double wedding. They had dreamed of living happily ever after, always as the dearest of friends.

The Great Disaster had put an abrupt and cruel end to those dreams.

Avery, Harry's guardian at the time, had purchased an officer's commission in a foot regiment for him, and Harry had gone off to Spain and Portugal to fight in the Peninsular Wars against the forces of Napoleon Bonaparte. Camille, in addition to everything else, had been rejected by her fiancé, the dastardly Viscount Uxbury. Abby never did have a come-out Season but went with Camille to live in Bath with their maternal grandmother. Aunt Viola had fled for a while to live with her clergyman brother in Dorsetshire.

And Jessica, untouched in all material ways by the disaster, had been left bereft. Alone and desolate, with crushed hopes and lost dreams. She had been uninterested in continuing with anything to which her privileged status as Lady Jessica Archer, sister of the Duke of Netherby, entitled her. She had lost all interest in a come-out Season of her own, in courtship, and in marriage. For Abby could not share any of the glitter and excitement with her but was rather incarcerated in her grandmother's house in Bath. *Incarcerated* had not seemed too harsh a word.

Perhaps worse for Jessica, though, than the lost dreams and the desolation had been the inexplicable sense of guilt, as though everything that had happened to her cousins, and particularly to Abby, was her fault. As though she had somehow wanted to assert her superiority over them. She had hated the fact that she remained unscathed, that her life and her smooth path forward to a dazzling future remained what they had always been. There was nothing to stop *her* from making her come-out as planned. There was nothing to stop *her* from making a brilliant marriage or from living happily ever after. She could still expect to live a life of luxury and privilege for the rest of her days.

Unlike Abby.

It had seemed so, so, *so* unfair.

She had never been able to do it, in fact, in the eight years since then. She had never found a man to tempt her into being selfish. She had chosen instead to stand in solidarity with her cousin, whom life had treated so unfairly. If Abby must be forever unhappy, as surely she must, then the least Jessica could do was be unhappy too. She had never fallen in love. Now she doubted she ever would or could.

Yet two years ago Abby had found both love and happiness with Gil Bennington. She lived in that spacious manor with its lovely name and its flower-filled garden on the edge of an idyllic English village. She had a husband she clearly adored, a stepdaughter she loved as her own—Katy, Gil's daughter by a previous marriage, that was—a new baby who was plump and gorgeous, and . . .

And Jessica had nothing. Even though she had everything. A strange paradox, that, and ridiculously self-pitying. Even more ridiculous was the fact that in unwary moments she found herself feeling a niggling resentment of Abby. As though her cousin had betrayed her by finding love and happiness when Jessica had sacrificed both for her sake.

How foolish she had been. And how very immature, something from which she had never quite recovered. She had made the sacrifice even against the pleas of Abby herself, who had a number of times right from the start tried to persuade Jessica that what had happened to her was hers alone to bear, that she would deal with it and find a new, meaningful path forward. As she had. The past few weeks had convinced Jessica, even if she had still had any doubts, that her cousin had not simply settled for something second best, but was actually deeply happy. As was her husband. They were both devoted to their children.

Jessica had greatly enjoyed those weeks—and found them hard to bear at the same time.

She had been left behind. By her own choice.

Well, no longer. She had made a decision while observing the quiet glow that seemed to emanate from her cousin. *This* year, *this* Season, her sixth—or was it the seventh?—she was going to choose a husband. She did not expect it to be difficult, despite her age and the fact that London would be flooded with a new crop of pretty young girls fresh from the schoolroom and eager to snatch up the best prizes the great marriage mart would have on offer. She had acquired a rather large number of devoted admirers during her first Season despite the fact that she had made no effort to attract or encourage them, and those numbers, against all reason, had swelled with every passing year, up to and including last year.

All those gentlemen would not necessarily be eager to offer her marriage at the first sign of interest on her part, of course. Some remained in her orbit, no doubt, only because it was fashionable to sigh over Lady Jessica Archer and always be on hand to fetch her refreshments or dance with her or converse with her or simply be seen with her. It never hurt, after all, for a man to be seen in company with a duke's sister and someone who had been dubbed for several years a diamond of the first water. Their interest did not necessarily mean they wished to marry her.

But surely a few of those men would become serious suitors if given half a chance. She was, after all, extremely eligible. And rich. And although she was not vain about her appearance, her glass told her that she still had whatever looks she had had as a girl—no wrinkles or gray hairs or faded complexion yet. She was *only* twenty-five, after all.

She smiled slightly as she glanced at Ruth, who was still sitting very erect in her corner of the seat opposite, her head still turned toward the window. She was going to end up with a crick in her neck if she was not careful.

One of the outriders rode past the window as though on a mission while Jessica was still looking. He remained in her line of vision for a few moments, apparently having a word with the coachman.

If only, Jessica thought, her mind returning to her newly made resolution, there were someone among her admirers whom she *wanted* to marry. But there was no one, alas. There were several she liked. Indeed, she did not *dislike* any of them. But . . . Well, she was going to have to make her choice based upon practicalities rather than partiality. Upon common sense. It was, after all, the factor upon which most *ton* marriages were contracted. Birth and fortune, followed by age and disposition.

So much for the dreams of youth. So much for love and romance and happily-ever-after.

Abby had been horrified. For of course Jessica had told her of her new resolution, assuming she would be pleased. And as usual when they were together, her cousin had urged her to *please* find some happiness so that *she* could be finally and fully happy herself.

"Birth and fortune, Jess?" Abby had said, frowning. "Age and disposition? What about love?"

"I might wait forever," Jessica had told her. "I have never felt even a spark of what other people describe as falling in love. I do not doubt them, but I do know that romantic love is not for me. Not at my age. So I—"

"Jess." Abby had leaned across the space between them and grasped both her hands. "It *will* happen. It happened to me. I fully believed it never would. And when I first met Gil, I considered him the very *last* man with whom I might fall in love. But I did, and—oh, Jess, you *must* believe me—it is the most wonderful thing in the world. To love and be loved. You must not become jaded and give up hope. Oh, please do not. You are *only* twenty-five. And you were made for love. Wait until you find it. It *will* happen."

"Promise?" Jessica had asked, and laughed, though part of her had been silently weeping.

"I *promise*," Abby had said with fervent conviction.

As though anyone had the power to promise such a thing for someone else. It was simply not going to happen, Jessica thought now. And she was tired of her single state. She wanted a husband and home and family—and those things were not beyond her grasp. Quite the contrary. She wanted to *grow up*. It was past time.

Her thoughts were interrupted when the carriage turned abruptly and unexpectedly to the right, and Jessica could see that it was pulling into the cobbled yard of a respectable-looking inn, though surely not the one at which they were scheduled to spend the night. Their journey had been delayed by a couple of hours after they had stopped for refreshments and a change of horses. There had been some issue with one of the wheels on the carriage in which Mr. Goddard was traveling. The delay would mean they were still a few hours away from their destination for today, a wearying thought. Darkness would surely be upon them before they arrived and there would be no time left for anything but a late meal and instant retirement to bed. Was it possible Mr. Goddard had decided they would stay here instead? She could not imagine why else they had stopped. Grooms and hostlers were hurrying into the yard. Mr. Goddard was descending from his carriage and moving purposefully toward the inn door.

Jessica sat back and awaited developments. For the duration of this journey, whether she liked it or not, Mr. Goddard stood in place of Avery. Her brother had made that clear in his usual quiet, half-bored manner as he took his leave of her a few weeks ago.

"I would be obliged, Jessica," he had said, "if when you look upon Edwin Goddard during your journey to London, you would see me, and if when he speaks, you would hear me."

She had smiled at him. "Mr. Goddard neither looks nor sounds anything like you, Avery," she had said.

He had raised his jeweled quizzing glass almost to his eye. "Quite so," he had said softly, and she had laughed.

But they had understood each other. If Mr. Goddard said now that they were to stay here for the night, then stay they would. If he said they were to proceed to the inn at which accommodation had been reserved for them, then proceed they would. There was no point in expressing a preference or throwing a tantrum. Mr. Goddard would merely nod respectfully and carry on with what he had decided. It was better not to humiliate herself by expressing a contrary opinion. Jessica closed her eyes and rested her head against the cushion behind it. On the whole she hoped they would stay, though then tomorrow's journey would be longer, of course.

The wait seemed interminable but was probably no longer than ten minutes. Then Mr. Goddard reappeared from the inn and opened the door of Jessica's carriage to inform her that they were to stay. The best chamber in the house, facing away from the noise and bustle of the innyard, had been reserved for her, he explained, and a truckle bed was to be set up there for Ruth. He would have one of His Grace's men stationed outside her door during the night lest she need anything or have any fear for her safety. The only private parlor the inn boasted, next to the public dining room on the main floor, had been secured for her use so that she would be able to dine and partake of her after-dinner tea in peace and privacy.

And without the rude masses gawking at her, Jessica supposed with an inward sigh. She would dine in grand solitude, then, since Mr. Goddard, though he occasionally dined with Avery when there were just the two of them, never sat at table with any other members of the family. Although he was a gentleman by birth, her brother's secretary was quite scrupulous in his observance of the niceties of social etiquette. He was lowering the steps now, and then offering a hand to help her descend before escorting her inside.

The lobby into which they stepped was empty though not silent. A hum of voices and laughter and the clinking of glasses, as well as the distinct odor of ale, came through the open doorway of what must be the taproom, to their left. Next to it was the dining room. Through the panes of the windows on either side of the closed door Jessica could see tables set with white cloths and silverware. It was empty at this time of day, too late for tea, a little too early for dinner. The registration desk was to their right. A stairway to the upper floors was beyond it.

It looked like a perfectly decent place. Not that it was Jessica's concern to discover whether it really was. That was Mr. Goddard's business, and he was perfectly trustworthy. He would not have survived in Avery's employ if he were not. Jessica looked forward to being upstairs in her room, where she would be able to take off her bonnet and gloves and wash her face and take the pins from her hair at least for a short while and perhaps even stretch out upon her bed before getting ready for dinner. What she would really love to do was go outside and walk through the village or out along a country lane. It would not matter which. It would feel lovely to stretch her legs and breathe in some fresh air. But she knew that if she decided to act upon her desire, a whole train of those burly riders as well as Ruth would be obliged to accompany her and she would be unable to enjoy a single moment. So would they, at a guess.

Mr. Goddard indicated the staircase with one respectfully outstretched arm and then moved to precede her up it—lest there be bandits waiting to leap out at her at the top, she supposed. He would also, she knew, unlock the door of her bedchamber—which he had no doubt already inspected—and step inside to look around before stepping out again to allow her and Ruth in before closing the door upon them.

Before she had taken more than a step toward the staircase, however, a closed door facing her across the lobby opened suddenly and two men stepped out, the first scurrying backward, both hands raised, palms outward, as though to stop the second man from stalking after him.

"It was quite unforeseeable—I do assure you, sir," the first man was saying. "But how could I—" He had turned his head and seen that he had an audience. He stopped talking abruptly, looking considerably agitated. His hands fell to his sides and he bowed from the waist. "My lady. I do beg—"

But Mr. Goddard had taken one firm step forward and cut him off. "There is a problem?" he asked curtly.

The second man was holding a book. It was closed, but he had one finger between the pages, presumably holding the place he had reached before being interrupted. He was a tall man, probably in his thirties, broad shouldered, solidly built, his brown hair overlong for the current fashion, his complexion noticeably sun bronzed, his features not quite handsome, not quite ugly or even plain. He was dressed decently but without any flair of fashion. His clothes seemed designed for comfort rather than elegance. His boots were well worn. He was looking annoyed. And that look was sweeping over Jessica, from the crown of her bonnet to the toes of her lavender kid shoes. What he saw did not appear to improve his mood.

"This is the lady for whom I am expected to vacate the private parlor for which I paid handsomely?" he asked, presumably addressing his question to the first man, who must be the landlord.

"I do beg your pardon, my lady," the landlord said with another bow and a smile that stretched his lips but did not register upon any other part of his face. He made a sweeping gesture toward the stairs. "Your room is ready for you. I trust it—"

Mr. Goddard cut him off again. *"Thank you,"* he said, his voice cold and firm. "I believe this matter can be left safely in your hands, Landlord." He indicated the stairs to Jessica again.

So this gentleman had reserved the private parlor, had he, but was now being evicted from it on account of her? It was the sort of thing Mr. Goddard would be able to arrange with ease, of course, having all the weight of the ducal authority behind him. Whether the guest would go meekly remained to be discovered. He did not *look* meek. He did not look quite like a gentleman either, or behave like one. What gentleman would speak openly of money in the hearing of strangers? Or look a lady over from head to toe quite so boldly or with such obvious disapproval? Middle-class, Jessica guessed. A cit, perhaps, a businessman of some means. He must have money to be staying at an inn, even of this not-quite-superior quality, and to be paying for a private parlor.

Jessica inclined her head to him with cool courtesy. "Thank you," she murmured before moving toward the stairway and the sanctuary of her room.

The unknown guest bowed to her in return, a slight, surely deliberately mocking gesture involving a small flourish of the hand that was not holding his book and a dipping of the head.

"I beg your pardon, Lady Jessica," Mr. Goddard said

when they had reached the top of the stairs. "I shall have a word with the landlord, who does not appear to have proper control of his house."

He led the way to her room.

Being a woman had frustrations in plenty, Jessica thought again as the door closed behind her and Ruth. But being a man had its annoyances too. What would that guest do? Would he flatly refuse to vacate the parlor and then find himself confronted by Mr. Goddard himself? Would the landlord bribe him, perhaps, with a free dinner in the public dining room? Money was something he seemed to understand. It was none of her concern, however. Mr. Goddard would sort it out to her advantage.

"Tell me that is warm water in the pitcher, Ruth," she said.

"It is, my lady," her maid assured her after cupping her hands about the water jug.

Of course it was. Why had she even asked? Mr. Goddard would have seen to it before coming to escort her inside.

# Two

Gabriel Thorne waited for the newly arrived guest to disappear up the stairs with her minions and move out of hearing before he spoke again.

She was Lady Jessica Archer, daughter of the late Duke of Netherby, sister of the present duke. She was exquisitely lovely and expensively clothed in what was no doubt the very height of female fashion. She was almost without doubt rich, privileged, pampered, entitled, and arrogant. She was surely accustomed to getting her way on any and all issues with the mere lifting of a finger. Everyone in her sphere would scurry about to satisfy her every whim. She had been delayed in her journey, the landlord had informed him. That must surely have provoked some temper. She had been forced to stop for the night well short of her planned destination—almost certainly an inn or a hotel far superior in quality to this one, though this was no hovel. And, having arrived at a substitute stopping place, she had made the inconvenient discovery that it boasted only one private parlor—*which was already taken.*

Such a fact would not disconcert Lady Jessica Archer for one moment, of course. She would merely have her major-domo oust the guest already in occupation of the room and install herself there instead. The fact that she would be inconveniencing that guest would not have crossed her mind—any more than would the possibility that he might refuse to go.

He was very tempted to do just that.

It was fortunate for him, perhaps, that according to his usual custom he had taken a room overlooking the innyard so that he could more easily keep an eye on his horses. The best rooms, the ones she would demand, would be at the front of the inn. If there had been no such thing as a private parlor, she would probably have demanded that the dining room be appropriated for her exclusive use while all other guests would be forced to eat in discomfort in their rooms.

Oh, it was probably unfair of him to judge the woman on such little evidence and no acquaintance. It was unfair to be hugely irritated by her and take an instant dislike to her. It was also virtually impossible not to do either. Even her "Thank you" had been spoken with the sort of frigid condescension that made it meaningless.

His irritation, even anger, had taken him by surprise. For really, what had provoked it had been slight. Perhaps the real cause of his annoyance was being back in England. He had forgotten what English ladies could be like. He had forgotten how obsequious the lesser classes could be when dealing with the upper classes, especially the aristocracy. The landlord had infuriated him. So had his understanding that really, the man had had no choice. He was regretting coming. Though he had had little choice beyond turning his back upon someone he loved.

"You will move out of the parlor, then, sir?" the landlord asked, his voice still anxious. "I shall reserve the best table in the dining room for you, the one between the fireplace and the window. And your dinner and all the ale and spirits you care to drink will be free of charge tonight. I will refund your payment for the private parlor in its entirety, even though you have had the use of it for the past couple of hours."

"Yes, you will," Gabriel said, his tone clipped.

The landlord visibly relaxed despite the curtness with which Gabriel had spoken. "It is very generous of you, sir, even though—" The rest of the sentence died on his lips when Gabriel fixed him with a steady gaze.

"Yes," Gabriel said. "It is."

For he could have contested the issue. Was there not some saying that possession is nine-tenths of the law? He would almost have enjoyed confronting that superior-looking majordomo. Unfortunately, he possessed an innate sense of courtesy that told him a lady who was traveling alone, except for her servants, really ought to be allowed the privacy of a parlor. Even a cold and arrogant lady.

He made his way up to his room, where he placed a folded handkerchief between the pages of his book to hold his place.

Lady Jessica Archer. Sister of the Duke of Netherby. In all probability she was on her way to London. Easter was over and the spring Season must already be heating up with all its myriad balls and soirees and garden parties and other fancy entertainments. The great marriage mart. He wondered why she was still unmarried. She was no tender young girl. If she were, she would hardly be on the road with only a majordomo and a maid for protection.

But even as he held that thought he wandered to the window of his room to look down upon the innyard. He smiled and shook his head in amused disbelief as he witnessed all the bustle. There were two grand carriages, one of them with a crest—the ducal crest?—emblazoned boldly upon the door that was visible to him. A third, somewhat more humble conveyance—though it was merely a relative point—must belong to the group too, since Gabriel was not aware of any other arrival within the past hour. The yard was teeming with large men, all clad in the same gaudy livery. The cavalcade must look like a traveling circus when it was strung out along the road.

Lady Jessica Archer had more than a majordomo and a maid for protection, then. She was as well guarded as a queen. She was a precious commodity. And she had all the accompanying haughtiness one might expect of such a woman. The inclination of her head when she had said thank you had spoken volumes about a life of aristocratic privilege and entitlement. He might have been a worm as easily as a man under one of those fine kid leather shoes.

How shockingly indiscreet it had been of the landlord to reveal her full identity in order to persuade him to give up the private parlor for which he had paid. If the man had only realized it, Gabriel would have been far more willing to relinquish it to a Miss Nobody-in-Particular than to the privileged daughter of a duke. It was what came of having spent the last thirteen of his thirty-two years in America, he supposed.

Lady Jessica Archer.

Sister of a duke.

Arrogant. Entitled. Unlikable, at least upon first encounter. But . . .

But considered another way, she was perhaps perfect.

So perfect that he might marry her.

He chuckled aloud at the absurdity of the thought.

It felt strange, unfamiliar, to be back in England. Of course, he had been gone all his adult life—since he was nineteen, in fact. But he liked America and had had no intention until recently of leaving it. When he had arrived in Boston, using his mother's maiden name of Thorne, he had had no more than the clothes on his back, one small bag, and only enough money to pay for room and board for a couple of weeks if he found somewhere cheap. He had called upon Cyrus Thorne, a widowed cousin of his mother, and the man had given him employment as a junior clerk in one of his warehouses and a dark little room in the cellar of his home in which to sleep. From those lowly beginnings Gabriel had proved his worth and risen to become his cousin's right-hand man by the time he was twenty-five. He had also been moved upstairs to a spacious room of his own. Most important, Cyrus had officially adopted him as a son since his marriage had produced no children before his wife died. Gabriel's name had been legally changed to Thorne, and he had become the official heir to everything Cyrus possessed.

It had been a dizzying rise in fortune, but Gabriel had given hard work and gratitude in return, and affection too. He had come to understand why Cyrus had been a great favorite of his mother and why her heart had been broken when he had decided to go to America to seek his fortune. Gabriel's father had told him about that. His mother had died giving birth to his stillborn sister. And Cyrus had had fond memories of her too.

A little over a year after adopting Gabriel, Cyrus had died from a fall at the dockside during the loading of one of his ships. It was an accident that ought not to have been particularly serious but had in fact proved fatal.

Shockingly, Gabriel was a very wealthy man by the time he was twenty-six and had huge responsibilities for one so young. He owned a large home, a thriving import-export business, and what amounted to a small fleet of ships. He had several hundred employees. He was a *somebody* in Boston society and much sought after, particularly by matrons with daughters in search of successful young men of fortune and industrious habits.

He had enjoyed the attention. He had dallied with a few of those daughters, though never to the point at which he felt committed to offering for any of them. He had enjoyed his life in general. The work suited him and filled his days with challenge and activity. Boston was bustling with energy and optimism. Within a few years he had expanded the business, added another ship to his fleet, and made himself wealthier than his cousin had ever been. In addition, he had raised wages for all his workers and improved working conditions. He had given his employees, even the lowliest of them, benefits to cover doctors' fees and lost wages when they were sick or had been hurt on the job.

He had been happy, though he had never thought to use that exact word at the time. He had been too busy living the life that hard work and sheer good fortune had brought him. Yet he would have given it all to have Cyrus back. It had taken him a long time to recover from the grief of losing him.

He might have forgotten about his life in England, or at least let it slide into distant memory, if it had not been for the letters that came two, sometimes three, times a year from Mary Beck. She was the only person to whom he had written after his arrival in America. He had known she would worry about him if he did not. And he had felt too the need to keep some frail thread of connection to his past.

Despite himself, he had read her letters avidly for the snippets of local news she passed on. He had looked, though he had never asked, for some hint, *any* hint, that the truth of what had happened before he left had become generally known and had not continued to be falsified. He had sworn Mary to secrecy in his first letter, though it had been unnecessary. She had said nothing about him to anyone, she had assured him in her return letter, and would never do so under any circumstances. He had trusted her word at the time and still did.

Perhaps he ought not to have begun the correspondence. It might be better to have known nothing, to have broken all ties, to have been content to be dead to everyone and everything he had left behind. Even Mary.

The year after Cyrus's untimely passing, Mary's spring letter had brought word of three other shocking deaths. Her sister and Julius—her brother-in-law—and nephew had died the previous summer, just after she had written him her last letter of the year. An outbreak of typhus had taken a few other people from the neighborhood as well, though it had not touched Mary herself, living as she did, almost as a hermit in her small cottage on one corner of the family estate.

That had been astounding news in itself, but there had been repercussions that were eventually to complicate Gabriel's life and force his return to England. For Mary's brother-in-law and Gabriel's uncle, Julius Rochford, had also been the Earl of Lyndale. Philip, his only son and his heir, though married, had had no sons of his own—no legitimate ones, at least. And he had predeceased his father by one day. Gabriel, son and only child of the late Arthur

Rochford, Julius's younger brother, was therefore his uncle's successor.

He was the Earl of Lyndale.

He had *not* been happy about it or about the death of his aunt, who had been sweet though dithery and a person of no account in her husband's household. He had regretted the death of his uncle too. He had not grieved the loss of his cousin at all.

He might have ignored his changed status for the rest of his life, and had done so for six years after receiving word of it in Mary's letter. No one knew where he was—except Mary herself, and she would not tell, having given her promise. If a search had been made for him, and he did not doubt that there had been some halfhearted attempt to discover the whereabouts of the new earl or whether indeed he still lived, then it had failed to turn up any trace of him. When he had taken passage for America, it had seemed a bit of an unnecessary precaution to use his mother's name instead of his own. As it had turned out, though, it had been a wise thing to do. After a certain number of years—was it seven?—he would be declared officially dead and the next heir in line would succeed him to the title and inherit everything that went with it. That would be his second cousin, Manley Rochford, whom Gabriel remembered with no more fondness than he had felt for Philip. But . . .

May Manley and all his descendants live happily ever after. Or not. Gabriel did not care either way. All that had happened was ancient history. He wanted nothing to do with the title or the property or the pomp and circumstance to which he was now entitled as a British peer of the realm. He was perfectly content with his life as it was and wanted nothing to do with England.

Except that there was Mary. His aunt's sister. Mary, with

her clubfoot and crooked spine and deformed hand and plain looks. Mary, with her little thatched cottage and her flower garden of breathtaking beauty and her vegetable patch and herb garden and her cats and dogs—all of them strays that she insisted had adopted *her*. Mary, with her books and her embroidery and her incomprehensible contentment with life.

Mary, now facing the threat of eviction.

Manley Rochford, heir to the title after Gabriel, was already acting upon his prospects. He had within the last year moved his family to Brierley Hall, as though by right, and taken over the running of the estate. He had dismissed the longtime steward, though he had no legal right yet to do so, and more than half the servants, indoor and out, in order to replace them with his own. His son, apparently a vain young man, was lording it about in the neighborhood. All of which facts in themselves would have elicited no more than a shrug from Gabriel. They were welcome, as far as he was concerned.

*But* . . . Manley had gone a step too far. He had given Mary Beck notice to leave his property by the time he became earl. She was not a member of the Rochford family, he had pointed out to her, and she had no claim whatsoever upon his charity. She was, moreover, a detriment to the neighborhood, where it was generally believed she had used witchcraft to bring the plague of typhus down upon her sister and brother-in-law and nephew, and upon a number of her neighbors too. He must consider the safety of his own family, he had informed her. And he must think of his neighbors, who were afraid to set foot upon Brierley land while Mary lived upon it.

*None of which is true except the fact that I am not a Rochford, Gabriel,* she had written in a letter to him. *I know it is not. The neighbors are not so superstitious or cruel. But I must leave anyway. Please come home.*

It was the only time she had ever put any pressure upon him to do anything at all. She might have exerted much further pressure, of course, by divulging her knowledge of where he was to be found in order to protect herself. But Gabriel knew she would not do that. Not Mary.

He had considered bringing her to America, setting her up in a comfortable apartment of her own in his home, giving her a part of his sizable garden, or even all of it if she wished, for her own use. But the journey might well kill her. And he could not imagine her being happy anywhere but in her own little cottage, where she had lived for as long as he had known her. And what would she do with all her strays? It might seem a trivial consideration, but they were Mary's family, as dear to her as husband and children would be to another woman.

He had considered finding a good agent in London and putting a new steward of his own in at Brierley, someone who would be capable of making sound decisions and exerting his authority while reporting to Gabriel once or twice a year. But doing that would mean revealing that he, Gabriel, was still alive. And if that was revealed, then he would be allowed no more peace in America. He would be expected to return home to England to take up his inheritance and fulfill his duties and responsibilities as a peer of the realm. Even if he held firm and refused to go, the truth would surely be found out in Boston, and everything in his life would change. Probably not for the better. He enjoyed being respected, even courted. He would *not* enjoy being fawned upon.

That last letter from Mary had turned out to be life altering. He had realized it from the moment he had broken the seal and read it. It had forced him to make the choice between the life he had built in America and the life he had left behind in England. The choice ought to have been ridiculously easy to make.

But there was Mary.

He had reluctantly put the business in the hands of Miles Perrott, his assistant and close friend, whom he would trust with his own life—*and* with the running of the business. He had made him a partner, leased out his house for two years, made numerous other arrangements, all within a couple of months, and sailed for home with no more than a few months to go before he was officially dead.

A strange choice of word, that—*home*. His home was in Boston. Once he had established his authority in England and made some sort of arrangements for the smooth running of all he owned there, he could return, he had told himself as he watched America disappear over the horizon, to be replaced by endless expanses of ocean. But *making arrangements*, he had admitted to himself during the endless days and nights of the voyage, was going to entail far more than he wanted to believe. For though even in Boston he would wish for an heir to inherit the business and the fortune he had amassed, here the need was of far more urgency. For in England he would not have the option of making a will and leaving everything to anyone he chose. In England there were rules and laws, at least for the aristocracy. If as the Earl of Lyndale he died without male issue—and both his father and Cyrus had died suddenly and early, not to mention his uncle and cousin—then the title and entailed properties and any fortune that went with them would go after all to Manley Rochford and his descendants: specifically that son who was already lording it over all who lived in the vicinity of Brierley.

Gabriel had not known Manley well when he was a boy—he had always kept his distance. But what he had known he had abhorred. The feeling had been mutual. The son sounded like a conceited ass. Gabriel did not know him. He had been a mere boy when Gabriel sailed for America.

His need to marry was an urgent one, and he had come to realize it long before the voyage was at an end and he set foot again upon English soil. It was not a happy thought. Nothing about this whole business was happy. But he no longer had the leisure to look about him for as long as it would take to find that one woman who would suit him and offer the expectation of a life of contentment. He needed to marry—and soon.

And his bride must be someone unexceptionable. An earl was not at liberty to marry a scullery maid or a shop-keeper's daughter or . . . Well. He must choose someone who could fulfill the duties of Countess of Lyndale as though born to the role. She must be someone wellborn, well connected, refined; able to deal with difficult relatives, difficult servants, difficult neighbors . . . difficult everything.

As far as Gabriel knew, his name had not been cleared all those years ago, though he had never asked Mary outright. He might be facing hostility at Brierley, to say the least. He certainly needed a woman who was no timid mouse, one who would command respect by the mere expectation that it would be accorded her. It would help too, and not just for his personal gratification, if she had some beauty, grace, and elegance. And a few more years of age and experience than a young girl fresh from the school-room would have.

More important than anything else, he needed someone

who could give him sons. Though that was the one thing that could never be guaranteed, of course.

And now it had struck him, as though as a joke, that Lady Jessica Archer might well be the perfect candidate.

*Was* it a joke?

He really had *not* taken a liking to her. But he would admit that his hasty judgment might not be a fair one. He knew that from his professional life.

She was almost certainly on her way to London.

And so was he.

Perhaps he would have the chance to get a second look at her.

# Three

Jessica rather enjoyed being back in London now that she was here. The weather had warmed even though it was not officially summer yet, and so far there had been more sunny days than wet ones. There had been shopping to do, since fashions changed with dizzying regularity, and last year's gowns would look sad if worn to this year's most glittering *ton* events and last year's bonnets would stand out like a sore thumb if worn to the daily parade in Hyde Park. There were friends to be called upon and a winter's worth of news to be caught up on.

There was family to visit and be visited by. Some of the Westcotts had been in Gloucestershire for Seth's christening, of course, but others had not. Either way, it did feel lovely, as it did every year, to be surrounded by so many family members in close proximity to one another.

This Season would be more special than any other, if everything went according to plan. She would marry and be settled at last. But . . . Well, what she had so sensibly planned while she was at Rose Cottage seemed a little cheerless now that she was about to put her plan into action.

Lady Parley's ball in honor of the coming out of her eldest daughter was to be the first truly grand entertainment of the Season, and Jessica was pleased that she had arrived in time to attend it. There had even been time to have the first of her new ball gowns finished and delivered to Archer House, Avery's home on Hanover Square. It was also her favorite, its narrow yet flowing lines both elegant and flattering to her figure, she believed, its color a deep shade of rose pink she had been looking for in vain for years. Her hand had already been engaged for three sets of dances— the opening set with Mr. Gladdley, who could always be relied upon to make her laugh; the second with Sir Bevin Romley, who for all his large girth and creaking corsets was light on his feet; and the first waltz with Lord Jennings, who despite having no conversation whatsoever beyond his horses always performed the steps with flair.

Jessica had kept all other sets free. There was always the hope, after all, that a new Season would bring new people to town—specifically new gentlemen. And there was always the chance that one of them would be tall, dark, and handsome. *And* eligible. *And* interested in her. This year in particular he would be very welcome indeed, this mythical man who would sweep her off her feet and rescue her from sensible plans.

Besides, if she did not keep at least a few sets free until the ball was already in progress, she would never hear the end of it from her disgruntled group of admirers, who would collectively feign heartbreak and heartache and any number of other silly woes. She derived great amusement from them all. It was impossible to take them seriously when they tried so hard to outdo one another in their ardor—most of it deliberately theatrical and not really meant to be taken seriously anyway. Which left the question: *Were* any of them serious about her? Was she in danger of being left on the shelf after all? But she would not believe that any such ghastly fate awaited her.

She looked forward to the Parley ball with some eagerness, just as she always did at the start of a new Season.

Gabriel arrived in London two days after disembarking from one of his own ships in Bristol. He was unfamiliar with England's capital, having spent a total of perhaps two weeks there during his growing years. He expected, moreover, that he would know absolutely no one, though there was Sir Trevor Vickers, his father's friend and his own godfather, who had been a member of Parliament at one time and might still be. Regardless of any reluctance on his part, however, he had chosen to come to London rather than set out immediately for Derbyshire and Brierley Hall. There was business to be done here.

He took a suite of rooms at a decent hotel and spent a busy week interviewing and engaging a good lawyer and a land agent. He was obliged to be frank with them about his identity, of course, though he did not want it generally known yet. He wanted first to get a feel for the situation he might find himself in when he was no longer merely Mr. Gabriel Thorne. He spent many more hours transforming himself into a respectable-looking English gentleman. He endured a tedious time with a reputable tailor and a barber the tailor recommended, along with a boot maker and a haberdasher and a jeweler. He interviewed a number of men sent him by an agency and chose a superior sort of individual named Horbath—no first name was provided—

to be his valet. He acquired a horse after being directed to Tattersalls. And he discovered that Sir Trevor Vickers was not only still a member of Parliament but was also a senior member of the cabinet now.

Gabriel called upon him and Lady Vickers one morning and was fortunate enough to find them both at home.

"Rochford?" Sir Trevor said when he and his wife joined Gabriel in the salon where he had been put to wait. The baronet gazed at his visitor in open astonishment. "*Gabriel* Rochford? But bless my soul, you must be he. You look just like your father."

"I go by my mother's name of Thorne now," Gabriel explained as he submitted to a very firm and prolonged hand-shake, though it was the name *Rochford* he had sent up with Sir Trevor's butler. "But yes, sir. I am Gabriel." He bowed to Lady Vickers, who had also looked astonished at first, though now she was beaming at him, her hands clasped to her bosom.

"Everyone has long assumed you are dead," Sir Trevor said bluntly. "It is about to be made official. But bless my soul, here you are, looking very much alive. Where the devil have you been hiding all these years? Ah, I beg your pardon, my dear. It seemed after the death of Lyndale and his son that you had fallen off the face of the earth. No one has been able to find any trace of you."

"I have been in America, sir," Gabriel told him.

"America. As bold as can be," Sir Trevor said, shaking his head slowly. "Yet no one found you there. You are going by your mother's name, you say? I suppose no one thought to search America for a Gabriel *Thorne*. But whyever would you do a thing like that?"

"My name has been legally changed," Gabriel told him, and explained how it had come about. He did not say that he had been using the name even before Cyrus adopted him and even on his passage to America.

"Good God," Sir Trevor said, suddenly struck by a thought. "Young Rochford has recently arrived in town—the son of the man who is expecting to be the Earl of Lyndale by the end of the summer. *Manley* Rochford, is it? Or Manford? No, Manley. His son is busy introducing himself to society as the prospective heir, and it is my understanding that society is opening its arms to him. I believe he is a personable young man. The father is expected to join him here soon. I understand grand celebrations are being planned for later in the Season, are they not, Doris?"

"Indeed they are," his wife said, "premature as it may seem. I have not met Mr. Anthony Rochford yet, but he is said to be very handsome and charming. He is being invited everywhere. But, goodness me, Mr.— My lord— Oh, *may* I call you Gabriel since I remember you well as a small boy? Goodness me, that young man is about to have the shock of his life. He is going to be overjoyed when he discovers that you are alive after all."

Gabriel very much doubted it. So, from the look on his face, did Sir Trevor. Well, but this was interesting. Manley Rochford's son was actually in London, and he was waiting for the arrival of his father and getting ready to celebrate his accession as the new Earl of Lyndale? He should, Gabriel supposed, save them some embarrassment, not to mention expense, and take steps without further delay to disabuse them of that notion and make his identity generally known. But he had hoped first to discover for himself if the prospective new earl and his heir were as bad as Mary had made them out to be. Not that Mary was prone to either exaggeration or spite.

"I would rather he not be told," he said. "For a short while, at least."

They both looked at him in surprise.

"But—" Sir Trevor began.

Gabriel held up a hand. "If the mere arrival of my cousin in town is causing a stir," he said, "one can only imagine what my sudden appearance here will cause, as though I had risen from the dead. Have mercy on me, sir, ma'am. I have only recently arrived from America, where I have spent the past thirteen years. I am already bewildered at the strangeness of being here. I need some time to find my land legs."

And perhaps . . . Well, was there a chance, however remote, that what Mary had told him really was distorted, exaggerated, a bit biased? Could even the Manley he remembered be cruel enough to evict her from her precious cottage when she had nowhere else to go? Her nieces, her sister's children, had never had anything to do with her, as far as Gabriel remembered. Now it seemed he had an unexpected opportunity to observe Anthony Rochford for himself, the young man who had supposedly been throwing his weight about and making himself obnoxious at Brierley. A charming, personable young man, according to what Sir Trevor and Lady Vickers had heard. Was it possible that before winter came on he would be able to return home to Boston and forget about this whole unwanted distraction?

He was very willing to grasp at any frail straws.

"I do, however," he added, "need some entrée into society. It seems unlikely the *ton* would afford even a passing glance at Mr. Gabriel Thorne, merchant trader from Boston."

"Is that who you have been all these years?" Sir Trevor asked, frowning and shaking his head again. "When you ought to have been here for almost seven years past as the Earl of Lyndale? There is clearly something I do not understand about your way of thinking. I suppose we can introduce you to the *ton* as our godson. My name carries some weight in this town."

"You forget, Trevor," Lady Vickers said, "that I had some family connection to Gabriel's mother. I never did understand quite what it was and neither did she. We had a good laugh about it once, I remember. Third cousin twice removed, I believe it was, or something absurd like that. But without having to resort to any outright lie, Gabriel, we can present you to society as our godson and my *kinsman*. And I do boast a viscount as a second cousin. Trevor, of course, has his own credentials—a baronetcy *and* an influential position in the government. Leave it to us. You will be accepted by even the highest sticklers before we are done with you."

"Thank you, ma'am," Gabriel said, grinning at her. "I would much appreciate your help."

"It will not hurt that you are also a handsome figure of a man," Lady Vickers said. "But why are we standing here in the visitors' parlor, Trevor, just as though Gabriel were a passing stranger instead of our godson and my kinsman? Your arm, if you please, Gabriel. We will go up to the drawing room. Albert is still at home, I believe—our son, that is. I will send up and ask that he join us. You were three years old when he was born, I remember. It was not long after the death of your poor mother. He is a dear boy, but he has a large circle of friends and acquaintances and I think it will be safer if we introduce you to him *just* as our godson and my distant cousin. Do you not agree, Trevor?"

"Whatever you say, my dear," Sir Trevor said as he followed them up the stairs.

Albert Vickers—*Bertie to my friends and long-lost relatives,* he told Gabriel with a hearty laugh as he shook his hand—was delighted to make Gabriel's acquaintance. Even before his mother could ask it of him, he insisted upon taking Gabriel about town and showing him what was what and introducing him to a few capital fellows.

During the coming days Bertie did just as he had promised, with the result that Gabriel visited White's Club and Tattersalls again and Jackson's boxing saloon and a fencing school among other places and made a number of male acquaintances, none of whom questioned his right to be one of their number.

And the ladies had not been excluded. Lady Vickers enjoyed herself enormously—or so she informed Gabriel—spreading word of the arrival in town of her handsome young kinsman and godson, who had recently returned from America with a sizable fortune. Gabriel began to receive invitations to *ton* events, most notably a ball being given by Lady Parley in honor of the coming out of her eldest daughter.

"The first grand ball of the Season," Bertie explained to him when Gabriel told him of the invitation. "It is gratifying that you have been invited, Gabe. Everyone who is anyone will be there. You can count on it. It is bound to be a dreadful squeeze. But once you have put in an appearance there, you will be invited everywhere. Wait and see."

Gabriel accepted the invitation. And if Anthony Rochford was in truth the darling of the *ton*, which was one term by which Lady Vickers had described him, then it was altogether probable that he too would be in attendance at this grand squeeze Bertie predicted. He must put himself in the way of meeting the man, Gabriel thought. He had no fear of being recognized. They had never met.

But the knowledge that Rochford was in town had been a mere distraction from Gabriel's real reason for wanting an in with the *ton* and a chance to attend the more select social events of the Season. His primary focus while he was here in London during the Season must be to find himself a wife—assuming, that was, that he would not really find it possible to slip off back home to America and put this all behind him like a bad dream.

He found himself wondering if Lady Jessica Archer was indeed in London and if she would also be at the Parley ball. On the whole he hoped she would not be. He had *not* liked her at all.

At last Jessica was at the first grand ball of the Season, standing at one side of the ballroom close to her mother, who was in conversation with a couple of older ladies, waiting for the dancing to begin. It would not be just yet. Sir Richard and Lady Parley and their daughter still stood in the receiving line, welcoming more and more new arrivals. Some gentlemen had begun to gather about Jessica, all of them familiar members of what it amused Avery to call her court. The ballroom was filling, and looking and smelling very festive indeed with the myriad colors of ball gowns and banks of flowers and one mirrored wall to multiply them all to infinity. Crystal candelabra overhead, each holding dozens of candles, cast a rainbow of light over the newly polished wooden floor and the gathering guests. Conversations were growing louder and more animated. The orchestra members were tuning their instruments.

This was often her favorite part of any ball, this eager anticipation of music and dance and feasting and forgetting the cares of everyday life. How very privileged she was to be here and to belong in these surroundings and with these people, Jessica thought as she flicked open her fan and plied it slowly before her face.

And how very old she felt.

There were a number of people she had not seen before, mostly young girls making their first appearance in London society, gowned almost exclusively in white, and some fresh-faced young gentlemen newly down from Oxford or Cambridge or up from the country. One such gentleman was Peter Wayne, Aunt Mildred and Uncle Thomas's middle son, who was across the ballroom with his older brother, Boris, trying unsuccessfully to look like a jaded veteran. She smiled and lifted a hand in greeting as she caught his eye. He grinned back, forgetting his chosen role for a moment. She met the glance of one of the young girls and thought she read envy in her expression. Well, that was cheering. Perhaps she did not look quite like a fossil after all.

Sir Bevin Romley reminded her that he had reserved the second set with her, to the loud complaints of those gentlemen who had not. Mr. Dean asked for and was granted the third set. Compliments meanwhile were being lavished upon her, many of them deliberately outrageous and provocative of laughter from the other men, and sharp retorts from her. Comments were being made also about other guests, some of them kind, some not, some witty, some not. She did not contribute any of her own.

It was all very familiar and really rather endearing. She might just as easily be a wallflower at her age and must be very thankful she was not.

Was one of these gentlemen going to be her husband? Oh, she really could not imagine it. She liked all of them to varying degrees and for varying reasons. But there was none she liked more than all the others. Sadly.

She laughed lightly at something that had just been said, fanning her face as she did so and glancing toward the door to see if the flow of new arrivals had slowed. There was still a trickle of guests moving along the receiving line.

And there was one man between Jessica and the door, his shoulder propped against a pillar, his eyes gazing very directly at her. He was not a member of her usual court. Indeed, he was a stranger. He did not immediately look away, as most people would when discovered staring. Neither did he move.

Jessica raised her eyebrows and fanned her face a little faster. He was an extremely good-looking gentleman, tall, broad shouldered, slender hipped, long legged, and elegantly and fashionably clad in black and white, his tailed evening coat looking rather as though he must have been poured into it, his neckcloth very white and arranged in a perfect, intricate fall. His silk breeches and stockings hugged shapely legs. His curly brown hair was short and expertly styled to look fashionably disheveled. His features were more harsh than perfectly handsome, perhaps, and his complexion was sun bronzed. But it was an attractive face nevertheless. Everything about him was attractive, in fact. Jessica felt an unexpected frisson of awareness and interest.

But his manners were not all they should be. He was still staring at her. Or, rather, he was gazing lazily, as though he had been doing it for some time. His whole posture was lazy, in fact, or perhaps *relaxed* was the more appropriate word. And informal. One did not lean one's shoulder against pillars at *ton* events. Jessica raised her chin and looked haughtily back at him, just as another gentleman approached him and he looked away and straightened up to give the other man his attention.

Strangely, bizarrely, it was only at that moment that Jessica recognized him—the man who had been staring at her, that was. He was the man from the inn. The one she had taken for a cit, a member of the middle classes, with his overlong hair and unfashionable, ill-fitting clothes and inelegance of manner. He had looked at her boldly then too, from her head to her feet, with an expression that had bordered upon the contemptuous. And he had been ungracious about vacating the private parlor for her use. He had spoken openly in her hearing about the money he had paid for it. He had made her a mocking half bow.

She must have been mistaken on that occasion. No mere cit would have received an invitation to a *ton* ball. Not even if he was a wealthy man. But how very rude of him to have stared at her as he had just now, even if he had been as surprised to see her here as she was to see him. Who on earth *was* he?

"Jessica?" Her mother was approaching, and Jessica turned her attention back to the scene immediately before her. Mama was bringing someone to introduce to her.

The man from the inn was forgotten. For standing before her, dazzling in a dull gold evening coat with sparkling gold waistcoat, lace foaming at his neck and over the backs of his hands in this age of far more sober evening attire and darker colors, was the man of Jessica's long-dead dreams. He was handsome beyond belief—of slightly more than average height and perfectly proportioned build, with handsome facial features that included slumberous eyes of a decided blue and very white, even teeth, which were fully on display now in a wide smile. Even his thick hair was perfect, though red-haired men had never figured in the romantic dreams of her girlhood. They ought to have.

"Jessica," her mother said. "Mr. Rochford has applied to me for an introduction to you. My daughter, Lady Jessica Archer, sir."

"Charmed, Lady Jessica," the gentleman said, making her an elegant bow while not removing his eyes from hers.

Oh, and so was she. Charmed, that was. Fortunately, she did not say so aloud. "I am pleased to make your acquaintance, Mr. Rochford," she said, inclining her head to him. She did not curtsy to any man below the age of fifty or below the rank of earl.

Her court had fallen silent about her. She was hardly aware of it.

"Mr. Rochford is heir to the earldom of Lyndale," her mother informed her. "Or soon will be, after his father succeeds to the title later this summer."

Jessica raised her eyebrows in inquiry.

"My cousin, the present earl, has not taken up his title in the almost seven years since the demise of the late earl and his son," Mr. Rochford explained. "He disappeared before that unfortunate event and has not been heard from since despite an exhaustive search. It has been very distressing to my father, who was dearly fond of him. Alas, the present earl is about to be declared officially dead. Both my father and I will be brokenhearted, but . . . Well, as the saying goes, life must go on."

Ah. It was one consequence of being later than usual to London, Jessica supposed, that she had missed this tidbit of news—and really quite a sensational one. It was rather a romantic story too—for Mr. Rochford and his father, anyway. Not so much for the dead earl, she supposed. So this veritable Adonis standing before her and still smiling was about to be an earl's heir, was he? And he was looking at her as though *she* were the fulfillment of all *his* dreams. She hoped her own interest in him was not so apparent. She fanned her cheeks slowly.

"I am sorry for your loss, sir," she said.

"Thank you." He bowed to her again. "Her Grace, the dowager duchess, your mother, has informed me that you have already granted the first two sets of dances to other gentlemen, who I trust are fully aware of their great good fortune. May I beg for the third?"

Dash it, Jessica thought. "That too is spoken for," she told him. "And the set after that is a waltz, which I have promised to Lord Jennings."

"Perhaps I will challenge him to pistols at dawn," he said with another wide smile as his sleepy blue eyes continued to gaze into her own. "Better yet, I will beg for the fifth set."

It would be the supper dance, she believed. Perfect. That would mean she would also sit with him at supper.

"I shall be happy to reserve it for you, sir," she said with an inclination of the head, and this time she noticed that her court did not erupt with the usual grumbles but maintained what might have been a sullen silence.

By then the receiving line was breaking up as the last trickle of new arrivals moved into the ballroom, and Mr. Gladdley was stepping up beside Jessica and pointedly clearing his throat.

"The dancing is about to begin," Jessica's mother said, and Mr. Rochford, with a final bow, moved away. Mr. Gladdley crooked his arm for Jessica's hand, and she placed it inside his elbow.

The gentleman from the inn was joining the end of one of the lines of dancers with a thin girl who looked not a day over sixteen. He was regarding his partner with what could only be called a proprietary smile. Then he looked up, caught Jessica's eye, and gave her a curt nod.

Mr. Rochford was also leading out one of the white-clad new debutantes, who was blushing and looking nervous and very much in need of reassurance while he smiled and gazed at Jessica. But he dipped his head at last to say something that drew a grateful, worshipful glance from his partner.

Well, Jessica thought as the orchestra struck a chord and the dancing began, this Season was already showing considerable promise.

# *Four*

Gabriel had come to the Parley ball alone, though he had been invited to join Bertie Vickers and a group of his friends for dinner at White's Club before proceeding here with them later. But he had not wanted to be late arriving. Rather, he had wanted a chance to look about at his leisure. This was not just entertainment for him, after all. He needed a wife—or, rather, the Earl of Lyndale needed a countess—and what better place was there to look than the first grand *ton* ball of the Season? Lady Vickers had suggested a few young ladies she knew to be both eligible and available. She had promised to make sure Bertie introduced him to any that were at the ball, since she was unable to be there herself.

In addition to that main motive, though, Gabriel had hoped the ball would afford him a chance to catch a glimpse of Anthony Rochford, his second cousin once removed, if he remembered the relationship correctly.

Coming here alone had not been a comfortable thing

to do, since he recognized only one or two men and no women. He was half hoping Lady Jessica Archer would be here. It would be interesting to see her again, to assess whether she was as perfect for his needs as she had seemed at their first brief meeting—and whether it might be possible to like her a little better than he had then. He was not even sure that she had come to London, however.

Numerous young girls had arrived even before he had, Gabriel saw—and *girls* seemed a more appropriate word than *women*. He must be getting old if he found them so alarmingly young. And all of them, almost without exception, were dressed in virginal white, as was Miss Parley, who looked all bright and flushed and pretty standing between her mother and father in the receiving line, greeting her guests. All of them looked pretty to him, though some were admittedly lovelier than others. All of them looked hopeful and eager, though a few tried to hide the fact behind unconvincing expressions of ennui. He felt an unexpected tenderness for them all and the dreams and aspirations they had brought to a London Season and what was undoubtedly their first grand *ton* ball. An almost avuncular tenderness.

He *must* be getting old.

A young debutante would certainly not do for his purpose, though all the young ladies Lady Vickers had suggested were in their first Season and almost certainly no older than seventeen or eighteen. He had been older than that when he went to America, for the love of God. A lifetime ago.

And then his eyes came to rest upon one particular woman. She was wearing a gown of vivid rose pink, startlingly noticeable even though she was half hidden within a cluster of men—or perhaps because of that. The men

were all talking and laughing, but it was very clear that it
was being done for the benefit of the woman and was designed to draw her looks and her smiles. She was very
definitely the focus of their admiring attention. They were
all vying to outdo one another. What popinjays, Gabriel
thought. Did they have no pride? Then one of the men
moved slightly to his right at the same moment as another
moved slightly to his left, and Gabriel had a clearer line of
vision to the woman herself.

She was of average height, slender, graceful, elegant,
beautiful. Not pretty, but *beautiful*. She was definitely not
a girl. Neither was she clad in virginal white but in that rich
rose he had noticed first about her. It was a low-cut gown,
short sleeved, high waisted, the Grecian lines of the skirt
hugging her hips and slim legs and yet flowing about her at
the same time. It was undeniably the handiwork of a
skilled—and expensive—dressmaker. Her dark hair was
piled high and arranged in intricate curls on her head, with
a few tendrils of ringlets over her temples and along her
neck. She was fanning her face slowly with a lacy fan, looking half amused, half bored.

*Lady Jessica Archer.*

She was every bit as exquisite as he remembered her.
More so, in fact. And every bit as haughty too. She was doing nothing deliberately to attract the men clustered about
her. There was no sign in her manner of flirtation or teasing. There were no provocative glances or enticing smiles.
Yet she was doing nothing to discourage them either. It was
as though she considered herself entitled as by right to their
adulation. She would condescend to stand there and listen,
her manner seemed to say, but she would not favor any one
of them with particular attention. She would certainly not
display any *need* to attract them. Yet she must be several

years older than all the pretty, eager, anxious girls in white. Did she feel no urgency to attract an eligible husband? Apparently not.

But why should she? She was a duke's daughter.

She was aristocratic hauteur itself.

She was perfect.

Gabriel propped his shoulder against a pillar that was conveniently next to him and settled in to watch her for a while. The dancing had not yet begun, Bertie had still not arrived, and he knew almost no one else, though Lady Parley had smiled upon him with particular graciousness as he passed along the receiving line earlier. *Another eligible bachelor,* her look had said. It was what her ball was all about, after all. She had a daughter to marry off.

He wondered how many of those men were seriously courting Lady Jessica Archer. If any of them held out any hope of landing her, they were fools. She obviously cared not a toss for any of them. Although she looked amiably enough at each in turn while they talked, she did not show any obvious partiality or any heightened awareness of any one of them. He wondered if they realized it. If they did, why did they remain? Did they not understand that they were making idiots of themselves? Or were most of them not serious about her and gathered about the lovely sister of the Duke of Netherby merely because it was the fashionable thing to do?

What fools.

And then, while she was smiling over something one of those men had said and fanning her face, she turned her head to look toward the receiving line, and in doing so saw *him.* Her eyes paused on him and held. She was assessing him. There was no sign of recognition on her face, a not-surprising fact, perhaps, as he had only very recently stepped off the boat the last time she saw him and had not yet subjected himself to the untender mercies of an expensive London tailor and boot maker and haberdasher and barber. Not to mention the tyrannical ministrations of a superior valet. Gabriel had hardly recognized himself by the time they were all done with him.

Perhaps he ought to have looked away. It would probably have been the polite thing to do. One did not stare at strangers. But he was interested to note that *she* did not look away from him or blush or appear in any way flustered. Indeed, she responded to his continued gaze exactly as he would have expected and rather as she had behaved at that inn. She lifted first her eyebrows and then her chin as though to ask him how he dared be so bold as to raise his eyes to *Lady Jessica Archer.*

He was the first to look away. Bertie Vickers had arrived and had come to gather Gabriel into the fold of his particular group of male friends. Though not for long.

"Come along, Gabe," he said, slapping a hand on his shoulder after the flurry of greetings had ended. "There is a young lady I want you to meet." He shrugged and pulled a face when his friends made jeering noises. "M'mother presented me with a list this morning—the names of daughters and nieces and granddaughters and whatnot of all her acquaintances. She made me promise to present Gabe to any of them who are here tonight. Don't look at me like that, Kerson—there's a good fellow. Gabe is in search of a leg shackle but he don't know anyone. He just came from America."

Kerson winced. "I'll say a prayer for you, Thorne, next time I go to church," he said.

"Next Christmas, will that be, Kerson?" someone else said. "It will be too late for Thorne by then. He will be caught right and tight in parson's mousetrap, and he will have Bertie to blame. I mean, to thank."

"I shall keep it in mind," Gabriel said with a grin. "Who is this young lady you want me to meet, Bertie?"

But someone else had joined the group of young men, and Bertie, distracted, was shaking him by the hand and exclaiming that he had not seen him in an age and a half, and where the devil had he been keeping himself?

Gabriel was not particularly interested in dancing, even though that was why he had come here. None of the young girls he had set eyes upon thus far attracted him. The only woman who did was surrounded by an army of devoted followers and did not need another idiot making a fool of himself over her.

He glanced across the room toward her while he waited for Bertie to finish slapping his long-lost friend's back and having his own back slapped in return. Ah. It looked as though after all there might be room for another admirer in Lady Jessica Archer's orbit. A man was being presented to her by an older lady of regal bearing, clad in royal blue. He had gone there to pay homage and was making her an elegant bow he must have practiced for hours before a looking glass. Someone ought to advise him to change his tailor or his valet or both. His gold evening coat, excellently cut and of a perfect fit, was a touch on the flamboyant side but might have passed muster if it had been worn with the right accompaniments. A waistcoat that was so covered with glittering gold sequins that it might have stood up on its own if set on the floor was *not* the right accompaniment. He had a thick head of dark red hair carefully shaped into the very Brutus style Gabriel himself had recently rejected.

Lady Jessica Archer, Gabriel was interested to notice, responded to his deep obeisance with a haughty inclination of her head, just as she had responded to *him* at that inn. A queen honoring a lowly subject.

Bertie had finished with all the back slapping. "Lady Jessica Archer," he said, noticing the direction of Gabriel's gaze. "Netherby's sister. The Duke of, that is. There is no point in wasting your time on her, Gabe. She will have no man, though if she does not change that attitude soon, she will be so long in the tooth no one will want her any longer."

"Who is that with her?" Gabriel asked.

"That is a trick question, right?" Bertie said with a guffaw of a laugh. "Half the male guests here tonight are with her, as they almost always are. Or do you mean the woman in blue? Her mother, the Dowager Duchess of Netherby?"

"The man in gold," Gabriel said.

"Don't know." Bertie shook his head, but one of his friends provided the answer.

"He is Lyndale's heir," he said. "The Earl of Lyndale, that is. Or soon-to-be earl. The ladies cannot get enough of him. They think him a handsome devil."

"Ah," Bertie said, "so *that* is Rochford, is it? I have been hearing his praises being sung all week. Mr. Perfection. Mr. *Charming* Perfection. One would think someone would change the subject once in a while."

"*Soon-to-be* earl?" Gabriel said, his eyes narrowing as he looked upon the distinctive figure of his second cousin once removed.

"The old earl died almost seven years ago," Bertie explained, "and his son with him. The nephew who got the title after him never claimed it and is almost certainly dead. If he is not found very soon, he will be called dead whether he is or not and there will be a new earl—that idiot's father."

"Idiot, Bertie?" someone asked. "Just because he is Mr. Charming Perfection?"

"Well, I ask you," Bertie said, "who but an idiot would wear that waistcoat in public? It is an abomination—that's what it is. Come along, Gabe—let me make that introduction, or the dancing will be starting and you will not have a partner for it and I will never hear the end of it after m'mother asks tomorrow."

The girl in question was the daughter of a dear friend of Lady Vickers, a viscountess. She—the girl, that was—was almost painfully thin and pale of both hair and complexion. It was nothing short of a crime that she had been clad in white, surely the worst possible color for her. And it was a shame that someone had tried unsuccessfully to powder over the outbreak of spots that plagued her chin. Gabriel bowed to her and her mother when Bertie introduced him, and he smiled and made conversation until, when the time finally came, he led the girl out to join the first set, still with that odd feeling that he was an uncle fondly humoring a beloved niece. He led her to the end of the line of ladies, took his place opposite her in the line of gentlemen, and tried to convey reassurance in the way he looked at her. He glanced away to see if the orchestra was about to start playing and found himself looking at Lady Jessica Archer, who was vivid and lovely among the delicate whites and pastels to either side of her in the line. She caught his eye, and he nodded to her. It would be disrespectful to his partner to look longer. But he did notice that her partner was not Rochford.

That one glance confirmed everything he had thought about her.

She was perfection.

He danced the second set with Miss Parley herself, her mother having summoned him with one white-gloved hand and an imperious nod of her tall hair plumes. It was during that dance that he realized he was no longer virtually invisible as he had been at the start of the evening. Word had apparently spread about who he was—Mr. Thorne from America, as though the *from America* was part of his name and perhaps the most fascinating part of it. Lady Vickers, it seemed, had done her work well and aroused interest in this man who was her kinsman and godson and who had made a fortune during the years he had spent in America before coming home.

After he had returned Miss Parley to her mama's side when the set was over, Lady Parley suggested she introduce him to someone else. "I know you are new to town and know virtually no one, Mr. Thorne," she said. "That will change after this ball, I do assure you. But in the meanwhile, perhaps I may present you to Miss—"

"Perhaps Lady Jessica Archer, ma'am?" he suggested before she could finish. He had spoken impulsively. There were even more men gathered about her now, after the second set, than there had been at the start. Why would he wish to swell their numbers? He did not wish it, of course. He had no intention of becoming one of her hangers-on, vying with a dozen others for one of her glances or—pinnacle of all happiness—one of her smiles. His only intention was to marry her.

But first, an introduction.

"Of course," Lady Parley said, and like a ship in full sail she set off across the ballroom, her hair plumes announcing her approach so that the cluster of men split apart to allow her access to the lady in their midst. *Ladies*, that was. There was another young woman with Lady Jessica, a very slender, dark beauty dressed in a gown of pale spring green.

Both watched their approach. Lady Jessica Archer closed her fan and slightly raised her chin. It was clear to

Gabriel that by now she had recognized him as the man who had given up the private parlor for her use at that inn, albeit somewhat ungraciously.

"Lady Jessica, Lady Estelle," Lady Parley said, "I have the pleasure of presenting Mr. Thorne, who has recently returned from America. Lady Jessica Archer and Lady Estelle Lamarr, Mr. Thorne."

"Lady Jessica. Lady Estelle." Gabriel bowed to them, though with none of the ostentation his cousin had displayed earlier.

Lady Estelle Lamarr greeted him with a smile and a curtsy before turning to a blushing young man who had touched her arm and seemed intent upon inviting her to dance the next set with him.

Lady Jessica acknowledged Gabriel with the same slight inclination of the head he had seen twice before. "Mr. Thorne," she said.

Lady Parley was hailed by someone to their left and hurried away with a murmured apology.

"For how long were you in America, Mr. Thorne?" Lady Jessica asked.

"For thirteen years," he told her.

"A long time," she said. "You must be delighted to be back home."

On the assumption, perhaps, that America was a wild and lawless land? "I suppose I must," he said.

Her eyebrows arched upward. "You only *suppose*, Mr. Thorne?" she asked him, and she looked slightly amused.

He thought about it. "I only *suppose*, Lady Jessica," he said. "I also suppose it is possible that I miss *being* home."

She tipped her head to one side and tapped her fan against her chin. "Ah," she said, "I catch your meaning, sir. America is your home too. Will you be returning, then?"

"Perhaps," he said.

The amusement in her eyes deepened and she drew breath to speak. But the blushing young man was leading Lady Estelle Lamarr onto the ballroom floor, and another man from Lady Jessica's court had stepped closer and was clearing his throat.

She ignored him for the moment, but she did not say whatever she had drawn breath to say. She looked inquiringly at Gabriel, perhaps waiting for him to ask for a later dance.

He did not do so. It seemed probable to him that every set was already spoken for and that it might give her great pleasure to tell him so. Or perhaps he was attributing to her a spitefulness that was not part of her nature. Anyway, it was too late now. Her partner had bowed to her and reminded her that the next set was his. He looked at Gabriel with a pointed frown, and it struck Gabriel that her whole court of admirers was viewing him with less than welcoming amiability.

"Your servant, Lady Jessica," he said, and turned to stroll away.

Bertie had not danced at all and apparently had no intention of doing so. "One attends balls because it is expected of one," he told Gabriel. "And because at the start of a Season it is always good sport to look over the new crop of young hopefuls come to market. The trouble is, though, that one is then expected to dance with 'em."

Gabriel chuckled.

"But come along," Bertie said. "I'll introduce you to old Sadie Janes's granddaughter. Third on m'mother's list. There is just time before the dancing starts."

Gabriel joined him again after dancing with the girl, a

pretty little thing who had a tendency to go tripping off in the wrong direction and then to giggle when she caused confusion among those performing the steps correctly.

"Lady Estelle Lamarr, Bertie," Gabriel said. "Who is she?"

"Dorchester's daughter," Bertie explained. "The Marquess of Dorchester, that is. She has a twin brother. He is over there with her now. The tall, dark one." He pointed inelegantly. "The marquess is with the Duke and Duchess of Netherby. The duke is the one with very blond hair and all the rings and diamond pins and the jeweled quizzing glass. I would give a great deal to get a look at his whole collection of glasses. It must be worth a fortune."

He looked very different from his sister, Gabriel thought.

"Lady Jessica is his half sister," Bertie said as though he had read Gabriel's thoughts. "Her mother was a Westcott. The duchess was also a Westcott, but there is a long story attached to that. I'll tell you one day, though I am bound to get all the details mixed up. Ask m'mother. She will tell you. The next set is a waltz. Do you know the steps?"

"You think they may not have crossed the Atlantic?" Gabriel asked.

"Well," Bertie said, "I have not learned 'em, and I have never done more than dip a toe into the Atlantic. Dancing face-to-face with the same woman, making conversation while avoiding treading on her toes, is not my idea of a good time."

"It might be," Gabriel suggested, "if you fancied the woman."

Bertie shuddered and then let off one of his guffaws.

Perhaps he would see if Lady Jessica Archer was free to waltz, Gabriel thought. But when he glanced across the

ballroom, he observed that someone else was already bowing before her and extending a hand for hers.

Lady Estelle Lamarr was still standing with her brother—
they looked very much alike, though he was a full head taller
than his twin—and two very young men. She was laughing
and patting one of the latter on the arm. A remarkably pretty
young lady, and the daughter of a marquess.

"I have this one, Bertie," he said. "You may take a rest
from your matchmaking duties." And he approached the
group and was introduced to Viscount Watley, the twin, and
to Mr. Boris Wayne and his brother, Mr. Peter Wayne, who
were, according to Lady Estelle's introduction, her sort-of
cousins. She did not explain in what sort of way that was.

"May I beg the honor of this waltz, Lady Estelle?" Gabriel asked. "If you have not promised it to someone else,
that is."

"There you are, Peter," she said while the whole group
laughed over a joke Gabriel had not heard. "The reprieve
for which you prayed no more than a few moments ago.
Thank you, Mr. Thorne. That would be delightful. Peter
claims to have two left feet, but I do not believe it for a moment."

She was not a young girl, Gabriel thought as he waltzed
with her. He would put her age at twenty-one or twenty-
two. Here was someone else, then, who was in no hurry to
make her choice and marry. She was the daughter of a marquess. She was prettier and livelier than Lady Jessica Archer. More approachable. Perhaps . . .

But he had the strange feeling that though he had come
here tonight in order to look about him for marriage prospects, his mind was already made up.

Really?

When he did not know the woman and did not much like what he saw? When it seemed to him she did not like what *she* saw?

Yes, really.

His mind was made up.

# Five

Louise, Dowager Duchess of Netherby, Jessica's mother, went the following afternoon with her sisters, Matilda and Mildred, to call upon their mother. Eugenia, the Dowager Countess of Riverdale, had lived for the past two years with her sister, Edith, who was celebrating her birthday today. It was not surprising, therefore, that the three sisters were not the only callers. Their former sister-in-law, Viola, Marchioness of Dorchester, and a cousin, Althea Westcott, were there too.

The conversation moved through a number of topics while they all sat about the dining room table, partaking of tea and pastries and cake. Inevitably the discussion included the Parley ball last evening. Four of them had been present for it—Louise, Mildred, Viola, and Althea—and those who had not were eager to hear all the news and gossip. There were always some newcomers to talk about this early in the Season.

"Peter danced four sets," Mildred said, speaking of her

middle son as she eyed a pastry that oozed cream before choosing a more sensible slice of seedcake instead, "including one with Miss Parley herself. The poor boy was very nervous about making his debut into society, though one rarely hears anyone talk about a man making his debut, does one? Thomas congratulated him this morning at breakfast for not having trodden upon anyone's toes. But apparently Miss Parley trod upon *his*, and he has the bruise to prove it."

They all laughed.

"It was gratifying to see that both Estelle and Jessica danced all evening," Viola said. Lady Estelle Lamarr was her husband's daughter by a previous marriage.

"It would be even more gratifying," Louise said, "if either one of them or both had shown any particular interest in any of their partners. It is disturbing that they are both well past the age of twenty without even the prospect of a wedding on the horizon, or even a betrothal. What is *wrong* with young women these days?"

"Perhaps," Matilda said, "they are waiting for love, Louise. And if that is so, then I can only applaud their good sense."

"That is all very well for you to say, Matilda," Louise said. "You do not have daughters to worry about. And do they have to wait until they are fifty-six to find love?"

The comment was a bit unjust. That was the age at which Matilda had married Charles, Viscount Dirkson, two years ago. It had been her first marriage.

"That is unfair, Louise," the dowager countess said. "Matilda would have married Charles—yes, the *same* Charles—at the age of twenty if her father and I had not stepped in, very ill-advisedly as it turned out, to stop her."

"No doubt you did what you considered the right thing

at the time, my lady," Miss Adelaide Boniface, Edith's companion, said soothingly.

"Jessica danced with Mr. Rochford before supper," Mildred said. "He was much in demand with the young ladies all evening. He is very handsome, and appears to be exceedingly charming too. Also well mannered. I noticed that he sought an introduction to Jessica before the dancing even began, and he did it the correct way, by applying to Louise. He was very attentive to Jessica while they danced. She looked as if she might be interested."

"Who is Mr. Rochford?" the dowager countess wanted to know.

"He is soon to be heir to the earldom of Lyndale, Mama," Louise explained. "As soon as the missing earl has finally been declared dead later this summer, that is, and Mr. Rochford's father becomes the new earl."

"Yes, of course," her mother said. "I know all about that. I had just forgotten the young man's name. He is as handsome as everyone says he is, then?"

"He is said to have red hair," Edith said. "I can never quite like red hair on a man."

"But his is a dark red," Cousin Althea said. "It is actually very attractive. *He* is very attractive. He would be a splendid match for Jessica, Louise."

"As she would be for him," Louise agreed. "But I begin to despair of her."

"Perhaps," Viola said, "something can be done to encourage a match with Mr. Rochford, Louise? He really is a good-looking man, though I did think last evening's choice of waistcoat rather unfortunate. Marcel, the silly man, commented that all the guests ought to have been issued with dark eyeglasses to avoid the danger of being blinded."

Matilda chuckled. "I must tell Charles that one," she said.

"The American gentleman caused something of a stir too," Althea said. "He is Lady Vickers's kinsman, Eugenia, and her godson—and Sir Trevor's. He is not actually American, but he has recently returned from several years spent there. He is a fine figure of a man. Very elegant. He also was introduced to Jessica—by Lady Parley herself."

"He did not dance with her," Louise said. "I am not sure he even asked. Jessica said nothing about him afterward."

"He waltzed with Estelle," Viola said. "She said afterward that she enjoyed his company, though she says that of most of her partners."

"Rumor has it he is very wealthy," Althea said. "Unsubstantiated rumors are not always to be trusted, of course. And no one seems to know a great deal about him or what he was doing in America—or what he did before he went there, for that matter. There is a certain air of mystery about him. I daresay that is part of his appeal."

"Are you thinking of him for Estelle, Viola?" Mildred asked.

"I am constantly thinking of *everyone* for Estelle," Viola said with a laugh. "But she has a mind of her own. She has yet to show any real interest in marrying."

"Girls are not as they were in my day," the dowager countess said with a shake of the head.

"I hear of both Mr. Rochford and the American wherever I go," Matilda said. "I assume it is Mr. Thorne you were speaking of, Althea? Lady Vickers has not been shy in putting it about that he is wealthy, so I daresay it is true. She would lose considerable face if it turned out that he was a pauper. I look forward to meeting both gentlemen. And I agree with you, Viola. Perhaps we really ought to start thinking of ways to throw Mr. Thorne into Estelle's path again, and Mr. Rochford into Jessica's."

"*We?*" Mildred asked, her eyebrows raised. She took the cream pastry after all, since no one else had removed temptation from her reach, and bit into it with slow caution.

"Well, if the past few years are anything to judge by, they are not doing much to help themselves, are they?" Matilda said. "What they need is a helping hand. Not to attract the gentlemen. Good heavens, they are both unusually lovely girls and could not possibly be more eligible if they tried, one of them the daughter of a duke and the other of a marquess. They need a helping hand to narrow their choices to one and to fall in love."

"I wish it could be done as easily as saying it," Louise said with a sigh.

"Alexander and Wren are expected to arrive in town tomorrow," Althea said, speaking of her son and his wife, the Earl and Countess of Riverdale. "Elizabeth and Colin are planning a small party to welcome them, though that is only an excuse, of course. Elizabeth loves entertaining and Colin does nothing to restrain her. I believe he loves it too. Perhaps I could suggest that both Mr. Rochford and Mr. Thorne be added to her guest list?" Elizabeth, Lady Hodges, was her daughter.

"Are we all playing matchmaker, then?" Mildred asked. "I thought we had stopped that after Matilda's wedding."

"It is not matchmaking when one arranges to throw together young people who may not have the good sense to throw themselves together," Edith said. "*Is* it? I daresay Jessica and Estelle have met so many eligible gentlemen since they left the schoolroom that by now they can hardly recognize a good catch when they see him. I agree with Matilda. And Viola. They *do* need a helping hand."

"Aunt Edith," Matilda said, wagging a finger in her direction, "you are talking *just* like one of us."

They all laughed.

"I am sure Elizabeth can be trusted not to be too obvious about it," Louise said. "But, Althea, can you make sure that Mr. Rochford and Mr. Thorne are not the *only* guests from outside the family? Jessica would realize the truth in a moment and she would be mortified. She would confront me with it too. She is very prickly about having her life interfered with."

Althea's eyes twinkled. "Elizabeth would never commit such a social faux pas, Louise," she said. "But yes, I will make sure there are other guests outside the family."

Louise sighed again as she surveyed the plates set out upon the table. "Oh," she said, "whatever happened to the cream pastry I have had my eye on? Did someone eat it? It was you, Mildred, was it not? You always did that when we were girls. You would wait until there was one slice left of a cake we all adored, and you would take it without any offer to share. My waistline thanks you, however. I hope something will come of Elizabeth's party, but I will not hold my breath. Behold a mother in the depths of despair. Hand me that plate with the jam tarts, will you, please, Aunt Edith?"

"It is a magnificent bouquet, Jessica," Anna, Duchess of Netherby, said, sounding a little doubtful. "It is also a little hard to see around, is it not?" She got up from her chair across the hearth from her sister-in-law's and sat on another. "That is better."

The bouquet, lavish and enormous, and surely containing at least one of every species of flower known to mankind, had been awaiting Jessica in the drawing room when she returned from a morning visit to the library with Anna and her children, Rebecca, aged four, and Jonah, aged two. Six-year-old Josephine had not gone with them, though reading was one of her favorite activities, because her father, Avery, had asked if she would like to ride her pony and accompany him to Hyde Park. Horses and riding were Josephine's passion.

The bouquet was from Mr. Rochford and was just the sort of thing Jessica might have expected him to send if she had thought about it. The dozen red roses from Lord Jennings, standing in their crystal vase upon the sideboard to one side of the door, were dwarfed in comparison.

"I wish it had been put somewhere else but here," Jessica said. "It is almost embarrassing." No, it *was* embarrassing.

Anna laughed. "I believe you have made a conquest," she said. "A *big* one. All the other single ladies in London would surely go into collective mourning if they could see it."

"He danced with me *once*," Jessica protested.

"Ah, but he had eyes for no one but you while he was doing it," Anna said. "And at supper he conversed with no one except you. I would swear he did not even look at anyone else. Then, after escorting you back to the ballroom, he left abruptly, never to return. He *strode* out, in fact. I would not swear that he intended to draw everyone's attention, but . . . Well, I would wager a modest amount upon it that he did."

"He wanted to dance with me again," Jessica explained, "and professed himself to be heartbroken when I informed him that the remaining sets of the evening were all spoken for."

"You have indeed made a conquest." Anna laughed again and poured them a second cup of tea. Luncheon was over and all the children except Josephine, who was still out with Avery, were in the nursery for their afternoon naps. Jessica's mother had gone with Aunt Mildred and Aunt Matilda to call upon Grandmama and Great-aunt Edith. It felt good to relax.

Jessica was not quite sure she liked Mr. Rochford. She *wanted* to. He had certainly seemed like the answer to all her prayers when she first set eyes upon him last evening. He was young, dazzlingly handsome, charming, amiable, and very eligible—or was about to be. He seemed in a fair way to becoming the darling of the *ton*. Certainly all eyes had been upon him throughout the evening. And though he had danced every set before theirs, it had been impossible not to notice that she was the focus of much of his attention. She had been the focus of *all* of it during their particular set, as Anna had just observed, even when the figures of the dance had separated them for brief spells. He had been visibly crestfallen when she had told him, untruthfully as it happened, that she did not have a free set to offer him for the rest of the evening after supper. When he left, he had succeeded in looking somehow tragic. Had it been deliberate?

What was it she had not quite liked? Oh, there was absolutely nothing. Perhaps for the first time in her life she was powerfully attracted to someone, was in grave danger of falling in love with him, and had taken fright. But no, that was absurd. That was not it. What *was* it, then?

Was it his waistcoat? Would a plain ivory one to match his silk knee breeches have looked more elegant with the dull gold evening coat? Her own brother was known for his gorgeous attire, morning, afternoon, and evening. He was known for his elaborately tied neckcloths, for the copious

and glittering pins and rings and fobs and quizzing glasses
he wore about his person. But . . . Avery was never, *ever*
vulgar. Had that waistcoat crossed a borderline into vulgarity, then? But what a trivial reason to dislike someone—to
*perhaps* dislike him. Ah, but then there was his smile. It
was a spectacular smile, given the white perfection of his
teeth, but did it always have to be quite so wide? He had
worn it practically all evening except when he was leaving.
Oh, and there was the studied elegance of his bow, which
he had demonstrated for her several times. And the lavish
and numerous compliments he had paid her.

She was being unfair, she told herself. He was new to
London. He was new to the social prominence of being heir
to an earldom, though his father was not yet the earl. Last
evening had been his first *ton* ball. He had told her so. He
had probably been horribly nervous and had overcompen-
sated for that fact. She must give him a chance to grow
more at ease in the new life that was about to be his. She
would like nothing better than to fall in love with him and
marry him and live happily ever after as the Countess of
Lyndale. The *future* countess. She must not consign his father to the grave just yet, poor man. *Or* the present earl, for
that matter, though it was surely almost certain that he really was in his grave and had been for many years.

Yes, she would allow herself to fall in love with Mr.
Rochford if she possibly could. But there was also this *bouquet*. There was something undeniably . . . ostentatious
about its size. Perhaps he had merely ordered it but had not
actually seen it. Perhaps if he had done so . . .

"What is amusing you?" Anna asked.

"Oh, nothing," Jessica said, startled out of her musings.
"Though I *was* thinking that if that bouquet was divided up

into smaller ones, we could fill every room in the house quite adequately."

Anna laughed again. "It was a very generous gift," she said. "Ah. Was that the door knocker?"

They both listened and heard the sound of the heavy front doors being opened below them. Visitors? They were not expecting anyone. But soon there was the unmistakable sound of the butler's footsteps approaching the drawing room.

"Mr. Rochford, perhaps?" Anna said, raising her eyebrows at Jessica.

The butler opened the door after tapping on it. "Mr. Thorne wishes to know if Lady Jessica is at home to visitors, Your Grace," he said, addressing Anna.

"Mr. Thorne?" Anna frowned and turned her gaze upon Jessica.

"Lady Parley presented him to me last evening," Jessica explained. "The American, Anna. Sir Trevor Vickers's godson. But how strange of him to call here today. He requested the introduction yet did not ask me to dance. Mr. Dean's set was about to begin, but there were numerous other sets after that."

"Ah yes, I remember the gentleman," Anna said. "Someone pointed him out to us. For some reason he appears to have caught the imagination of the *ton*. Perhaps because he is a fine figure of a man and there is some mystery about him. *Are* you at home to him?"

He had disconcertingly dark eyes. They made her uncomfortable. In two brief encounters she had been unable to identify the color of those eyes. Blue? Black? How could they be both? Yet they were. They were very penetrating eyes and seemed to look not just into hers but through them. Why on earth had he come here?

There was one way to find out, she supposed. Besides, she recalled that last evening Mr. Rochford had not been the only gentleman who had piqued her interest. Mr. Thorne had too, though surely only because of that earlier encounter when she had mistaken him for a cit. That was not altogether right, however. Her interest had been aroused last evening even before she recognized him. He was handsome. Well, sort of handsome. *Attractive* would be a more accurate word. *Very* attractive.

"Jessica?" Anna prompted.

"Show him up, by all means," Jessica said, addressing Avery's butler—and then wished, too late, that she had sent him back downstairs with a different answer.

A minute later Mr. Thorne stepped into the room, looking, as he had last evening, the epitome of elegance, in a dark green, form-fitting coat with buff pantaloons and shiny Hessian boots, both of which garments hugged powerful, shapely legs. His linen was white and crisp, the fall of his neckcloth neat and simpler than it had been last evening, as befitted daytime wear. A diamond pin of modest size winked from its folds. He looked larger, more imposing, than he had looked either last evening or back at the inn.

And yes, Jessica decided all within the span of the first second, he was very definitely attractive. More so than Mr. Rochford. But less handsome—if the two men were to be judged by facial features alone, that was. Facial features were not *everything*, though.

Anna had risen to her feet and was moving toward him, her right hand extended. "It is a pleasure to make your acquaintance, Mr. Thorne," she said. "I am the Duchess of Netherby, Lady Jessica's sister-in-law."

"Your Grace," he said, taking her hand and bowing over it—a slight bow, not a lavish one. He turned his eyes upon

Jessica, who had also risen, though she had not moved away from her chair. "Lady Jessica."

"Mr. Thorne," she said, watching him as he took the seat Anna had indicated.

"I trust you enjoyed the ball last evening," he said, addressing them both and holding up a staying hand when Anna lifted the teapot and looked inquiringly at him. "No, thank you, ma'am."

"We did," Jessica said. "Lord and Lady Parley must have been very gratified. They can boast in all truth today that their ball was a grand squeeze."

"And I hope you enjoyed it too," Anna said.

"Yes," he agreed.

This, Jessica thought, would clearly be hard going. But he had come for a specific purpose, it seemed, and he got down to business without further ado.

"I wonder, Lady Jessica," he said, turning his attention and the full intensity of that disturbingly dark gaze upon her, "if you are free tomorrow to drive out to Richmond Park with me. I have been told it is well worth a visit."

Oh goodness.

"Alone, Mr. Thorne?" Anna raised her eyebrows while Jessica regarded him thoughtfully.

"In an open curricle, ma'am," he said. "Ought I to have arranged a party? I have become unaccustomed to the English way of doing things."

But he looked slightly amused, Jessica thought, as though there were something a bit funny about her needing a chaperon if she stepped out with him.

*Would* she go? She knew nothing more of him than his name and the facts that he was a relative of Lady Vickers and had recently returned from a lengthy stay in America. Any other gentleman, if he made so bold as to call upon her the day after making her formal acquaintance, would ask no more than that she drive in Hyde Park with him at the fashionable hour of the afternoon or that she reserve a dance for him at the next ball. Or he would send her flowers. Her mother would certainly have something to say about this invitation if she were here. So would Avery.

But good heavens, she was twenty-five years old. And he was not asking her to go to the ends of the earth with him. Or the moon.

But did she *want* to go? That was the only question that signified. "It must be all of two years since I was last in Richmond Park," she began, but before she could say more the drawing room door opened and Avery strolled in.

He was still in his riding clothes, though he wore them, as he wore everything else, with a somewhat showy elegance. He had abandoned his outdoor garments. He was holding a quizzing glass in one hand, not as bejeweled as the one he had chosen last evening, though really there was no great difference. He wore rings on multiple fingers of each hand, and his nails were perfectly manicured. He might have been considered foppish, Jessica had often thought, had it not been for the air of authority and masculinity and even danger that he wore as surely as he wore his perfectly tailored clothes. And, as she had so recently thought, there was never anything vulgar about Avery's appearance.

His eyes paused upon Mr. Thorne for a moment before moving to Anna. "We have returned," he said. "No falls and no broken bones, you will be happy to know, my love. Merely a few sulks that we could not continue riding for yet another hour."

"You are sulking?" Anna asked.

"Ah," he said, raising the glass halfway to his eye. "Yes. I was not as precise as I might have been, was I? Josephine has gone upstairs to paint, because it is what she *wanted* to do all along. She did not *want* to go riding. It is stupid. She did it merely to humor me."

"Oh dear," Anna said, smiling. "May I make Mr. Thorne known to you? My husband, Mr. Thorne."

Mr. Thorne had stood to make his bow.

"You were pointed out to me last evening," Avery said, regarding their visitor with lazy eyes. "But there was no chance to make your acquaintance. You are a kinsman of Lady Vickers, I understand?" He looked steadily at Mr. Thorne, his quizzing glass halfway to his eye.

"Her second or third cousin, possibly with a remove involved," Mr. Thorne said. "I never was sure of the exact connection. We are a large, far-flung family."

"As far-flung as America, I understand," Avery said. "But you have returned."

"I have," Mr. Thorne said agreeably, and Jessica was again given the impression that he was amused. "And Lady Vickers has been obliging enough to make my return known to some of her peers, though I have been gone, alas, too long to remember any of them, if, indeed, I ever met them. I visited London only once or twice when I was a young lad."

"Quite so," Avery said, raising his glass all the way to his eye as he looked the bouquet over with a slightly pained expression. "Your offering, Thorne?"

"No," Jessica said quickly. "They were awaiting Anna and me when we returned from the library with the children. I believe they would look better broken down into several vases and distributed through the house."

"I will leave that to your judgment," he said, lowering his glass. "But I am happy to relinquish my mental image of you staggering into Hanover Square under the weight of such a floral offering, Thorne."

"Mr. Thorne has asked me to drive out to Richmond Park with him tomorrow," Jessica said. "In his curricle. I have not been there for at least a couple of years."

"A curricle," Avery said. "Without her mother or a maid to accompany her, then. It is fortunate, Thorne, that you have Lady Vickers to vouch for your respectability."

"It is." He inclined his head, and Jessica thought he *still* looked slightly amused. Most people, even men, meeting Avery for the first time were awed by him, even intimidated.

"Again," Avery said, "I leave the choice of whether she accepts your invitation or not to my sister's judgment."

Mr. Thorne had not sat back down since Avery entered the room. "I will not take any more of your time," he said, turning to her. "Lady Jessica, *will* you drive to Richmond Park with me tomorrow?"

There was, as everyone was saying, something of a mystery about him. He was a man who must surely have an interesting story to tell. But he was perfectly respectable, as Avery had just said. He was a gentleman, a relative of Lady Vickers. It was not, perhaps, quite wise to grant him such a favor upon a very slight acquaintance, but she could not resist the chance to learn more of that story. If, that was, he was willing to tell it. She wondered irrelevantly what her answer would be if it were Mr. Rochford standing there asking to take her to Richmond Park.

But there was a silence waiting to be filled.

"Thank you, Mr. Thorne," she said. "I will."

"At one o' clock?" He bowed after she had nodded, took his leave of Avery and Anna, and strode from the room.

"Well, this is an interesting turn of events," Anna said a few moments after the door had closed behind him. "I would have wagered upon Mr. Rochford's calling this afternoon, if anyone, but it is Mr. Thorne who came instead."

"I suppose, Jess," Avery said, "it was Rochford who sent the flowers."

"It was," she said.

"Yes," he commented, strolling closer and looking at them again, but with the naked eye this time. "It is as I would have expected."

He did not explain. He did not need to. Jessica had had the same thought.

"I wonder why Mr. Thorne went to America," Anna said, "and why he has returned—and to London instead of to his home, wherever that is, though he has hardly ever been here before."

"Perhaps Jess can twist his arm for information when she drives out with him tomorrow," Avery said, turning his lazy gaze upon his sister. "Were you even introduced to him last evening, Jess? I did not see you dance with him."

"I did not," she said. "Lady Parley presented him to me, but it was just before Mr. Dean claimed his set, and there was no chance to exchange more than a few words."

"Ah," he said. "But you made a significant enough impression upon him that he came today to lay his heart at your feet."

"How absurd," she said. "But the truth is, I had seen him before last evening. He was at the inn where I spent the night on the way home from Abby and Gil's, looking for all the world like a cit—nothing like his appearance last evening or today. He had already reserved the only private parlor at the inn, but Mr. Goddard arranged with the landlord to persuade him to give it up to me. I daresay I was not meant to come face-to-face with him, especially while he was arguing the point with the landlord, but I did. And he did eventually quit the parlor after Mr. Goddard had hustled me upstairs to my room."

"Edwin was uncharacteristically careless," Avery said. "I will have a word with him."

"Nonsense," Jessica said. "He was such a scrupulous guardian that I almost imagined, except when I looked at him, that he *was* you."

"But how romantic," Anna said with a laugh, "that when Mr. Thorne saw you again last evening, Jessica, he immediately asked Lady Parley to present him. And today he has come here to invite you to drive to Richmond Park with him. Perhaps none of it would have happened if Mr. Goddard had not been careless, Avery. Though I am sure Jessica is right and he was no such thing."

"Romantic!" Jessica said, tutting and shaking her head. "I do not believe *Mr. Thorne* and *romance* can ever be realistically uttered in the same breath."

Though she knew she would look forward to tomorrow. It was not often that she found any gentleman attractive *and* intriguing, yet she found Mr. Thorne both.

Her life had suddenly acquired color. Not one but *two* new gentlemen had arrived in town, and both of them were showing an interest in her. More to the point, she was feeling some interest in *them*. Had it ever happened before? She did not believe so. Perhaps there was hope for her this year after all, without her having to settle for someone who did not particularly attract her.

Perhaps by the end of the year she would be married.

*Happily* married.

Dared she hope?

# Six

The fine, sunny weather had held, Gabriel saw when he looked out of his hotel room window the following morning. In England one never knew what to expect from one day to the next, or even from one hour to the next. He had purchased a sporting curricle and pair the week before and hired a young groom. But a curricle, of course, called for fine weather, especially when one planned to share the high seat with a lady.

Horbath had put a letter beside his breakfast plate on top of the neatly folded morning paper. It was from Mary, Gabriel saw. She had received his own letter, then, which he had sent with Simon Norton, the man he had hired to be his steward. He had been obliged to take Norton into his confidence and had sent him to Derbyshire, not to displace Manley Rochford's steward at Brierley, but to do some discreet information gathering. Gabriel had told him about Mary and instructed him to make sure she was secure in her cottage for the present and had sufficient money upon

which to live. He had written to her himself to tell her he
was back in England and she need worry no longer about
her home and livelihood.

She had shed tears when she learned that he was so
close, Mary had written in her letter—not unhappy tears,
Gabriel must understand. She was still under notice to leave
her cottage, and her allowance had been cut off, though Mr.
Manley Rochford surely had no authority to do that yet. She
was grateful that Gabriel had been thoughtful enough to
send her money with Mr. Norton, whom by the way she
considered a very pleasant, respectful young man. She did
not need it, however. Through the years she had managed
to put a little aside whenever she could for a rainy day and
would be able to feed herself and the animals at least until
Gabriel came home. Did he know that Mr. Norton had been
taken on at Brierley as a gardener? And did he know that
Mr. Manley Rochford was planning to leave for London
soon with his wife to celebrate his elevation to the rank of
earl? Did he know that Mr. Anthony Rochford was already
there?

Gabriel knew. And when he opened the paper and came
to the society pages, he read that the handsome and charming Mr. Anthony Rochford, son and heir of Mr. Manley
Rochford, who was expected to become the Earl of Lyndale
in the very near future, had been seen driving in Hyde Park
at the fashionable hour yesterday afternoon with Lady Jessica Archer, sister of the Duke of Netherby. And this had
happened the very day after he had danced and sat at supper with her at Lady Parley's ball. Was the heart of the
lovely and elusive heiress about to be snared at last?

Not if he had anything to say about it, Gabriel thought.
Not by Anthony Rochford, anyway. One thing had been
clear from Mary's letter. There was no chance that she had

misunderstood the eviction notice. Rochford had not had any change of heart since moving to Brierley. Without any right to do so, he had cut off the allowance her brother-in-law, the late earl, had made her. No matter what else he was doing at Brierley or planning to do—there had been no report yet from Simon Norton himself—Manley Rochford's treatment of Mary was enough to seal his fate. And Gabriel's too. There was to be no miraculous reprieve, and therefore no return to his life in America.

Let the courtship begin, then.

The front doors of Archer House opened as he drew his horses to a halt outside at almost precisely one o'clock. Someone must have been watching for him. Netherby stepped out as Gabriel was descending from his high seat and handing the ribbons to his groom.

"A neat sporting rig," Netherby said, looking the curricle over unhurriedly. "And a fine pair of matched grays. You have a good eye."

"I believe I do," Gabriel agreed. Bertie Vickers had recommended a pair of chestnuts when he had accompanied Gabriel to Tattersalls, but to Gabriel's eye they had seemed all show and no go.

"Lady Jessica is of age, as you are surely aware," Netherby said, patting the neck of one of the horses and running his hand along it. "She is also independent of spirit and likes to insist upon making her own decisions regardless of what anyone else thinks or advises. It is quite unexceptionable for her to choose with whom she drives out, of course, even when the destination is a little more distant than Hyde Park. Her mother, however, is not happy that your choice of vehicle prohibits either her or a maid from accompanying her."

Gabriel was amused. "I have no intention of abducting Lady Jessica or of taking her anywhere inappropriate for a delicately nurtured female," he said. "But even if I did, I doubt very much she would allow it."

"Quite so," Netherby said agreeably, standing back and turning to watch his sister come down the steps, pulling on one of her kid gloves as she did so.

She was wearing a long-sleeved, high-waisted carriage dress of dark blue velvet, with a high-crowned, small-brimmed bonnet of pale silver gray. She looked startlingly lovely. Also haughty and perfectly self-possessed. She stopped on the bottom step to look over his rig.

"Impressive," she said. "I am happy to see that it is a sporting curricle, Mr. Thorne. I like to be high enough off the ground to see the world when I am on a pleasure excursion." She turned to her brother. "I suppose you are threatening Mr. Thorne with dire consequences if he veers as much as an inch from the beaten path, Avery?"

"You do me an injustice, Jess." Netherby raised his eyebrows and the quizzing glass he wore on a black ribbon about his neck. "Have you ever known me to have to resort to *threatening* anyone?"

She appeared to give the matter some thought. "Not in words, no," she said, and smiled so dazzlingly at her brother that Gabriel was almost rocked back on his heels. Good God! But the smile disappeared without a trace as she crossed the pavement and turned her haughty gaze upon him.

"Your hand, if you please, Mr. Thorne," she said, stepping up to the curricle and gathering her skirts in one hand as she prepared to climb to her seat.

"Good afternoon to you too, Lady Jessica," he said.

She gave him a measured look before setting her hand in his, but she did not comment upon his veiled reproof. She climbed to her seat and arranged her skirts about her.

A servant who had followed her from the house handed up an umbrella. Or was it a parasol?

They were on their way a few moments after that, while Netherby stood on the pavement, his hands clasped at his back, watching.

"I suppose," Gabriel said, "I ought to have applied to your mother for permission to drive out with you."

"No," she said. "You ought to have applied to me. As you did."

"It is not easy, I daresay, to assert one's independence when one is a lady," he said as he turned his curricle out of Hanover Square.

"But one must persist," she said, "or at the very least choose one's battles. I suppose you could not avoid noticing the ridiculous cavalcade of carriages and servants and outriders my brother deemed necessary to convey me from my cousin's home in Gloucestershire to London a few weeks ago."

"I might have failed to do so had it not been for the livery," he said. "It was, er, eye-catching, to say the least."

She turned her head to look at him with a gleam of something that might have been amusement in her eyes, but she did not smile as she had at Netherby.

"Why did you ask me to accompany you all the way to Richmond Park?" she asked him.

"I might say it was because I would not enjoy making the journey or seeing the beauties of nature alone," he said. "But instead I will answer your question with one of my own. How else am I to get to know you?"

Her eyebrows arched upward. She kept her head turned his way for a long, silent moment. "Most gentlemen who wish to pursue an acquaintance with me dance with me at balls or engage me in conversation at soirees and garden parties or ask to drive me in Hyde Park during the fashionable hour of the afternoon," she said.

"They join your court, in other words," he said. "It is an impressively large one, if Lady Parley's ball is anything to judge by. Has Rochford been added to the number?"

"Ah," she said. "You can read, then, can you, Mr. Thorne? Yes, he drove me in the park yesterday afternoon. Avery uses the same word you chose to describe my admirers. *Court*, that is. Time will tell if Mr. Rochford chooses to become a part of it. Will you?"

He looked at her appreciatively before giving his attention again to maneuvering his horses through the busy streets of London. "The answer is a resounding no," he said.

"Indeed?" She sounded more amused than chagrined as she watched a young crossing sweeper scurry out of the way of the curricle and scramble to pick up the coin Gabriel tossed down to him. "I suppose that explains why you did not ask me to dance two evenings ago. It would also explain why you did not invite me to drive in Hyde Park yesterday, where the whole world—and at least one newspaper reporter— would have seen you pay court to me. But why, pray, did you have Lady Parley present you to me? She did say, if I recall correctly, that you asked for the introduction. And why did you call upon me yesterday? Why did you ask me to drive to Richmond Park with you today?"

"All three questions have a single answer," he told her. "It is because I intend to marry you."

That brought her head snapping his way again. She gazed at him with wide eyes, he saw at a glance. Or perhaps *glared* would be a more accurate word. And her chin was up. He wondered irrelevantly if young Timms, his groom, was enjoying himself.

"You *intend* to marry me?" she asked, putting considerable emphasis upon the one word. "You are presumptuous, sir."

"I suppose I might have chosen a more abject verb," he conceded. "*Hope*, perhaps. Or *wish*. But *intend* is the most accurate."

"You do not *know* me," she protested. "I do not know you. I believe you must have windmills in your head."

"But you cannot be sure I do," he said. "By your own admission you do not know me."

He seemed to have rendered her speechless. She continued to stare at him for several moments though he did not turn his head again to look at her. Then she laughed unexpectedly, a low sound she probably did not intend to be as seductive as it was.

"I still believe it," she said. "You, sir, have windmills in your head if you believe I will marry you simply because you *intend* it. Or even hope or wish for it."

"You do not intend ever to marry, then?" he asked her.

"That is none of your business, Mr. Thorne," she said, her laughter forgotten, to be replaced by icy hauteur.

"How old are you?" he asked her.

*"Mr. Thorne!"*

"Twenty-four?" he suggested. "Twenty-five? Twenty-six? No more than that, I believe. But surely well past the age at which most ladies marry. Yet I cannot believe no man has ever asked or hinted that he *would* ask with the smallest encouragement. You are the daughter and sister of a duke, after all. I would be surprised if you are not also extremely wealthy. Besides all of which you are easy on the eyes."

There was a pause. "And you, sir," she said, "are impertinent."

"For speaking the truth?" he said. "Do you encourage your court to cluster about you, Lady Jessica, because you do not want to marry? Safety in numbers and all that? It seems altogether possible."

"If you do not change the subject immediately," she said, "I must ask that you take me home, sir."

"My guess," he said, "is that you have given up hope."

"Oh really," she said, sounding severely annoyed. "Are these American manners, Mr. Thorne?"

"It would be somewhat alarming," he said, "if a whole nation was to be judged—and presumably condemned—upon the words and behavior of one man who has only lived there for a number of years. But back to my point. I believe, Lady Jessica, you have given up hope of finding that one man who can distinguish himself from the crowd and renew your interest in matrimony and a new life, quite independent of your mother and brother—*half* brother, I believe that is."

"Well," she said, "you have certainly distinguished yourself from the crowd, Mr. Thorne. But if you believe that you have also aroused in me any eagerness to marry you, you are sadly mistaken. To put the matter mildly."

"Perhaps," he agreed.

"There is no *perhaps* about it," she retorted.

They lapsed into silence after that while Lady Jessica faced forward and raised her parasol. It was definitely a parasol rather than an umbrella. It was made of a pale silvery gray lacy fabric that would not offer much protection from rain. She twirled it vigorously behind her head for a few moments before lowering it again with a snap. He had discomposed her, Gabriel could see, though she maintained a stiff dignity and did not carry through on her threat to demand that she be taken home.

When they approached Richmond he directed his horses to one of the gates in the high wall that he had been told surrounded the whole of the park. Perhaps he would find somewhere inside later to leave the curricle so that they could walk. But first he wanted to find and drive along the Queen's Ride he had heard about, a grand avenue that ran between woodland on either side.

There were other people in the park, enough, anyway, to satisfy the Dowager Duchess of Netherby when she questioned her daughter later, as she surely would. Generally speaking, though, there was an agreeable sense of rural quiet here, a heightened awareness of trees swaying and rustling in the breeze, of birds singing, of blue sky above with small white clouds scurrying across it in a breeze that was hardly apparent on the ground. Once or twice they spotted deer, which apparently roamed free here in large numbers. There were the smells of greenery and soil and fresh air. Gabriel felt an unexpected wave of pleasure at being back in England. He had forgotten . . .

"I miss the countryside," she said, breaking a lengthy silence.

"You do not live in London all year, then?" he asked. Most of the upper classes did not. He knew that much from when he had lived in England himself.

"No," she said. "I grew up at Morland Abbey in Sussex, my father's home and now Avery's. I still live there with my mother. And with Avery and Anna and their children, of course."

"Your mother did not move to a dower house after your father's passing?" he asked. "Is that not what most dowagers do?"

"*Most?*" she said. "I do not know. My mother and I have our own apartment in the abbey. It is very large. The abbey,

I mean, though our apartment is spacious too. We are not confined there, however. We live freely with my brother and sister-in-law."

"You do not long for your own establishment?" he asked.

She turned her head. "Are we returning to that subject?" she asked. "My own home, you mean, as a wife and mother?"

"Yes," he said. "Are not most young ladies eager to get away from their mothers and their brothers in order to be mistresses of their own establishments?"

"I cannot speak for most ladies," she said.

"Then speak for yourself," he told her, acknowledging with a nod a couple of riders who were cantering by in the opposite direction.

"I have never been tempted," she said.

"Because you cannot be?" he asked her. "Or because it has just not happened?"

"Oh," she said, sounding cross again, "we *are* back on the subject. What about you, Mr. Thorne? You must be considerably older than I am. Thirty, at a guess? At least that. Have *you* never been tempted to marry?"

"Yes," he said without hesitation. "It happened a couple of weeks or so ago, soon after I had disembarked after a long voyage from America. I was relaxing in the private parlor of the inn at which I had put up for the night, reading and minding my own business, when I was interrupted by the landlord, who had come to beg me to relinquish my claim upon the room, for which I had already paid handsomely. A lady had arrived unexpectedly at the inn and was demanding it. A *very important lady*. He dared not say no. His business might be forever ruined. When I followed him from the room, prepared to argue the point, I came face-to-face with the lady herself, though I do not doubt I was not intended to do so. Almost instantaneously I gave in to the temptation to give up not only the parlor but also my single state. I decided that Lady Jessica Archer, sister of the Duke of Netherby, would be my wife."

"What nonsense you speak!" she exclaimed. "You *decided* that I *would be* your wife. How dared you then? And how dare you now?" She looked at him sharply. "How did you know who I was?"

"The landlord was obliging enough to provide the information," he said. "I daresay he thought that knowing who you were would the more readily persuade me to relinquish my claim upon the room."

"That was *unpardonably* indiscreet of him," she said.

"Yes, was it not?" he agreed. "That dour-looking major-domo you had with you would doubtless have had his head if he had known."

"Mr. Goddard?" she said. "He is Avery's secretary."

But it was time to change the subject. He had wanted to shock her, to make it clear to her that he had no interest whatsoever in dallying with her and thus becoming just one more member of the court for which she obviously cared not a fig. He had definitely ruffled her feathers.

"I believe the Pen Ponds are worth a look," he said. "Shall we find them and then leave the curricle somewhere and enjoy the scenery on foot?"

"Very well," she said after appearing to consider the matter. "We will walk. We will also talk, Mr. Thorne. If you are to expect that I will even consider your preposterous *intention* of marrying me, you must answer some questions. You know about me. You knew who I was the very first time you set eyes upon me. I daresay that would account for your interest. All vanity aside, I know I am extremely eligible despite the fact that I am *twenty-five* years of age. I know nothing whatsoever about you except that you are a kinsman of Lady Vickers and have recently returned to England after spending thirteen years in America. I do not even have more than a nodding acquaintance with Lady Vickers, though Avery has a great deal of respect for Sir Trevor."

"They are my godparents," he told her.

"Even that fact does not arouse any great passion for you in my bosom," she told him. "I doubt any further facts will either, but I like the Pen Ponds, and it would be a shame to have come all this way and not see them."

"As soon as we are on foot, Lady Jessica," he told her, "we may enjoy our surroundings at greater leisure while you interview me."

*"Interview?"* she said. "As though for employment? As my husband? Very well, Mr. Thorne. Prepare to make yourself irresistible to me. This may be your only chance."

He could not decide if he liked her or not. Her manner was cold and haughty and had been almost from the moment when she had stepped out of Archer House and looked over his rig while virtually ignoring him. But she had used the word *passion* a few moments ago and it had set him to wondering if she was capable of feeling any. Something told him she might be. Not that he had thought of his choice of a countess in terms of passion.

And there had been that smile she had leveled upon her brother before she crossed the pavement to his curricle. For a brief moment she had been transformed before his eyes into someone quite different. He had a hankering to see that smile again, but directed at him this time.

Perhaps it was too soon, however, to decide whether he liked Lady Jessica Archer. Or if it would make any difference either way.

He needed a countess rather more than he needed a wife.

# Seven

*P*en Ponds was a rather unfortunate name, Jessica had always thought, for what was in reality two sizable lakes separated by a causeway right in the heart of Richmond Park. One might almost be led to expect a couple of muddy watering holes with a few dejected ducks bobbing in them. They were actually very picturesque. If the Queen's Ride gave the dual impressions of grandeur and deep seclusion, the Ponds gave more the impression of open countryside, of the elemental intermingling of earth, water, and sky. The birds did not remain hidden here as they did on the Ride, pouring out their songs from the green depths of the woods, but rather called them out with freer abandon as they swooped over the water in pursuit of one another or glided and swam upon its surface.

She ought not to have agreed to walk here. She was not in the right mood for it. She ought to have demanded to be taken back home. Mr. Thorne was quite unpardonably presumptuous.

He was very different from Mr. Rochford, who had called upon her yesterday afternoon an hour after Mr. Thorne left and asked very properly if he might have the honor of driving her in the park later at the fashionable hour. He had even come into the house again when he returned for her, to ask her mother if he might be permitted to do so—Mama had been home by then. Jessica had been a bit annoyed at his doing so, of course, as she was no young girl and it was quite unnecessary, but even so, he had erred on the side of correctness. He had conversed pleasantly with her before they got caught up in the exchange of greetings and chitchat with acquaintances they met in the park, and he had been unfailingly charming. He had smiled without ceasing, as he had done the night before, but really it was a handsome smile, and it was far better than a scowl.

She did not find Mr. Thorne nearly as amiable a man. If Mr. Rochford hoped to marry her, as he very well might— he was, after all, about to become heir to an earldom and she would be a brilliant match for him—he had not so much as hinted that he *intended* to do so, just as though she were a commodity to be purchased at his will.

The seat of Mr. Thorne's curricle was narrow enough that her shoulder or elbow or hip had constantly been nudging against him during the journey here as the vehicle swayed around bends or bounced over uneven patches of road that were all too numerous. But somehow she was far more aware of him now that they were walking side by side, not touching. *Physically* aware—of his height, of the breadth of his shoulders, of the muscular shapeliness of his long legs encased in tight pantaloons and Hessian boots, of his aura of masculinity, whatever that was supposed to mean. Good heavens, he was not the first handsome gentleman with whom she had ever walked. She could not recall being aware of any of those other men to the point of discomfort, almost suffocation. She had not been uncomfortable yesterday with Mr. Rochford, despite the admiration in his eyes whenever he looked at her and the speculative glances with which they had been generally regarded in Hyde Park.

She was markedly uncomfortable with Mr. Thorne.

No other man had ever *told* her he was going to marry her. No other man had ever asked her age or suggested that she kept her court about her as a sort of shield against taking any man's courtship seriously. No other man had informed her that she was *easy on the eyes*. What a ghastly, vulgar expression! No other man had ever suggested that she had given up hope of finding the one man who would distinguish himself from the crowd. No other man . . .

Oh, bother. She was not enjoying these teeming thoughts one little bit. She was not enjoying his company either. She did not like him and resented her physical awareness of him.

They paused at the midpoint of the causeway to watch a couple of swans glide gracefully, leaving V-shaped ripples behind them, across one of the ponds.

"How do they move like that without making any apparent effort?" she mused aloud.

"All the effort goes on beneath the surface of the water," he replied, "leaving the impression above of effortless grace."

They had been virtually silent since leaving the curricle. So much for her promise to interrogate him. Or to *interview* him, to use his own word. As though she were seriously considering his . . . his what? He had not actually *asked* her to marry him, had he? Rather, he had told her he was going to. What an insufferable man. What on earth was she doing walking with him like this and gazing at the lake and talking about swans? Avery would have made short work of him long ago if he had heard any part of what Mr. Thorne had said to her.

She did not *need* Avery's intervention.

Oh, she was feeling thoroughly out of sorts.

There were not many other people in the park. At the moment there was no one at all in sight, though several times she had heard the sound of distant laughter. It was hard to know exactly from which direction it came.

She wished he was not standing quite so close. Yet when she half turned her head in his direction as though to caution him to keep his distance, she could see that there was at least a foot and a half of space between them. And a sudden thought popped into her mind, as though from nowhere.

Was *this* how Abby had felt when she met Gil? Or how Cousin Elizabeth had felt when she met Colin, even though she was nine years older than he? Was this—oh goodness— was *this* how Aunt Matilda had felt when she met Viscount Dirkson, or, rather, when she met him again?

Jessica recalled a day spent at Kew Gardens two years ago with a party of other young people, chaperoned, oddly enough, by Aunt Matilda and Viscount Dirkson. Two of the younger gentlemen had been Jessica's cousins, but two had not. One of those had been Mr. Adrian Sawyer, the viscount's son. He was a good-looking young man. She had liked him then and still did. But there had been nothing between them except mutual amiability on that occasion and since then.

Had it been different for Aunt Matilda on that day? She and Viscount Dirkson, Jessica remembered, had stayed at the top of the pagoda for a while after the rest of them had clattered down the winding stairs and gone off to see one of the temple follies. Jessica had not thought much of it at the time, but not long after Aunt Matilda had shocked the family to its core by announcing that she was going to marry Viscount Dirkson.

Was *this* how she had felt at Kew? This . . . this *awareness*?

Abby had not liked Gil when she first met him. Jessica could remember that. Yet soon after . . .

Enough.

"What were you doing in America, Mr. Thorne?" she asked.

"Getting rich," he said.

Money. Always money with him. He behaved like a cit even if he was not one. He continued unprompted.

"Partly through sheer chance and largely through hard work," he said. "A kinsman of mine owned a prosperous import-and-export business. He employed me as a lowly clerk until I proved that I was worthy of greater responsibility. He was a widower without children of his own. When he died at far too young an age in an accident, he left everything to me. In the years after his death I managed to grow the business and become even wealthier."

"What happened to the business when you returned to England?" she asked.

"My right-hand man was also a trusted friend," he told her. "I offered him a partnership and left him in charge. I feel confident that everything will continue to prosper under his management."

She had not been entirely wrong in her first impression of him, then. He *was* a businessman. A prosperous one, apparently. He was also a British gentleman.

"Why did you go to America?" she asked.

"For adventure?" he said. But he phrased his answer as a question, suggesting that that had not been his real reason.

She turned to glance at him and had to prevent herself from taking a step backward when she saw that he was looking very directly at her. She always found his eyes disconcerting. They were dark and intense and did not waver when she looked back into them. They were blue at their heart, she saw, but a deep navy blue on their outer edges.

"Why did you go?" she asked again, frowning.

"Let us say I had a falling-out with my family," he said. "It is a common enough reason to send a young man scurrying off to seek adventure and fortune. I was nineteen."

Her mind inevitably did the calculation. He had been away for thirteen years. He was thirty-two, then. Seven years older than she.

"And you did indeed find fortune," she said. "Where? America is a rather large place."

"Boston," he said.

"Why did you come back?" she asked. "If you had a prosperous business, why did you not stay to run it yourself? After thirteen years, America must have seemed almost as much like home as England. You more or less said as much two evenings ago."

"You are quite right," he said. "I was happy there."

"Then why return to England?" she asked again. This must not be just a brief visit. He wanted to marry her. He would hardly do so merely to take her back to America with him. There must be plenty of single young ladies there. And his American acquaintances were unlikely to be impressed by the daughter of a duke. Why should they?

"An inheritance brought me back," he said, and his expression grew strangely hard. "And a family situation that necessitated my being here in person."

"An inheritance," she said. "In the form of property? And fortune?"

"Both," he said curtly. "I am doubly wealthy, Lady Jessica. One might say I am the most fortunate of men."

"A family situation?" She raised her eyebrows.

"Yes."

In the distance, perhaps a little closer than before, there was a sudden burst of laughter. He was not going to explain, Jessica realized after a few moments of silence. He looked beyond her along the causeway.

"Shall we continue?" he suggested, and she turned to walk onward.

"Perhaps," she said, "I began my questions in the wrong place, Mr. Thorne. You were nineteen when you ran off to America as the result of some falling-out with your family. What was your life before that? Tell me about yourself. And tell me why the heir to property and fortune would run away and stay away. Was it your father who died recently?"

"My uncle," he said.

They had left the lakes behind before either of them spoke again. He had answered only the last of her questions. She should know better than to ask more than one and expect to have them all answered.

Lawns of high-scythed grass rippled in the breeze to either side of them. An impression of slightly tamed wildness had been aimed at, and it had succeeded. There was another, smaller lake ahead to the left and a line of trees beyond the lawn on the right that hid the Queen's Ride from view. It was an idyllic place in which to stroll. With anyone else she might have found her surroundings wonderfully relaxing. But there was still a mystery surrounding this man, and she needed to have it explained. Good heavens, he wanted to *marry* her.

"Start at the beginning," she said. "Tell me about your first nineteen years, Mr. Thorne."

"I lived with my father until I was nine years old," he told her. "My mother died giving birth to a stillborn daughter when I was two. I have no conscious memories of her. My father was always inclined to be sickly. He was a clergyman, devoted to his books and his parishioners. And to me. He was far less devoted to his health. There was very little money, but I was unaware of being poor. I was never hungry and I was always adequately clothed. I had a happy enough early boyhood. He taught me all a boy should learn at a young age and gave me a lasting love of books. He died after neglecting a chill he had taken from visiting an ailing parishioner in a distant cottage during a rainstorm. After, I was taken to live with his elder brother, an uncle I had never met before he turned up for the funeral. I lived with him for the next ten years."

"Just him?" she asked.

"And my aunt too," he said. "All four of their children were considerably older than I. One of their daughters was already married and living some distance away. The other two married soon after I went there and also moved away. Then it was just my uncle and aunt and their son. And my aunt's sister."

"You had some companionship, then," she said. "Were you close to your cousin, your uncle's son?"

"No," he said. "He was ten years older than I."

*"Was,"* she said. "What happened to him? I assume this is the uncle who has recently died and left you property and fortune. Your cousin must have predeceased him, then?"

"By one day," he said. "There was an outbreak of typhus. My aunt died too."

"Oh," she said. "I am so terribly sorry. You really had no expectation of inheriting, then, did you? But if your cousin was ten years older than you, he must have been in his forties when he died recently."

"He had no sons," he said.

This was the *family situation* that had forced him to come home, then? But he did not offer further explanation, and she did not ask. He was not wearing mourning. But despite the family falling-out that had sent him running off to America, he must surely be feeling some pain at such a sweeping loss. She had intruded enough upon his privacy, however. It was not, after all, as though she intended to marry him.

Yet she had vowed to herself that she would marry *someone* this year. Mr. Rochford, perhaps? He would be a good match for her. And he was young, perhaps even younger than she. He was handsome and personable.

Or perhaps after all she would marry no one. Now that it had come to the point, she found that it was not easy to make a rational, purely practical choice when she would be stuck with it for the rest of her life. As all women were when they married.

Could Mr. Thorne offer something more attractive? But what?

They had paused to look at the smaller pond a short distance from the path, but they walked on after nodding to a group of six people, who were in a merry mood and acknowledged them with smiles and greetings and comments upon the loveliness of the weather. It must have been their laughter Jessica had heard several times in the last half hour. The group continued on its way toward the Pen Ponds.

There were many other questions she could ask. What exactly had happened to cause him to run away and stay away? Had he had any contact with his family since? But if not, how had he discovered recently, thirteen years after leaving, that his uncle and aunt and cousin had all died, leaving him to inherit property and fortune? Why did he feel it necessary to marry? And why her in particular?

"It must have been distressing for you when you heard about your loss," she said.

"I did not wish any of them dead," he said. "I did not want to return."

There was something a bit chilling about his response. It was as though he had grieved not for his three dead relatives but only for the obligation their passing had put upon him to return. The trouble with questions, of course, was that the answers merely aroused more.

"Perhaps," she suggested when they came to a fork in the path, "we should make our way back to the curricle." The sun had dipped behind a rather large cloud and the air had cooled as a result.

They turned onto a path that would eventually circle back to where he had left the curricle. It wound through trees, with an occasional glimpse of the lakes.

"Why have you not married before now, Mr. Thorne?" she asked him. "By my estimation you must be thirty-two."

"I have never felt any strong inclination to give up my freedom," he told her. "And I have been busy. I have had an active social life too, but I have never met that one woman who stands out from the crowd." He was almost smiling when he glanced at her, no doubt remembering what he had said to her earlier about her court of admirers.

"Yet," she said, "almost immediately after you set foot upon English soil you saw a stranger at an inn where you were putting up and decided that you would marry her?"

He thought about it for a moment. "Yes," he said.

"Why?" she asked. "Did you fall violently in love with me at first sight?" She lifted her chin and frowned at him.

She was feeling angry, because the answer was very obviously no. She did not even wait for his answer. "I know why. You have come into an inheritance that cannot be ignored. Property. A house? An estate? A stately home, perhaps, situated within a park? And a fortune upon which to live there in some luxury?"

"All of those things, yes," he admitted.

"So," she said, "you came back to England in order to live the privileged life of an English gentleman. You came to take on the responsibilities of running your estate and tending to the needs of all who are dependent upon you. I daresay there are a number of servants and laborers. And tenant farmers, perhaps?"

"Yes," he said. "All of those."

"And you decided that all this could be far more effectively accomplished if you had a wife," she said. "Someone to see to the smooth running of your home, someone to manage the indoor servants and to be an accomplished hostess to your neighbors. Someone to ensure that there are sons to inherit your property and fortune when you die. Someone with the experience you lack because you have been gone so long. Someone whose lineage is impeccable and whose consequence will not be questioned by those with whom you must deal after a thirteen-year absence."

There was nothing so abnormal about what he had set out to do. She felt chilly, almost as though the blood were running cold in her veins. Would that cloud never pass over?

"Yes," he said.

Had his vocabulary been reduced to one word? But at least he was not trying to beat about any bushes. He was not trying to pretend that he really had fallen violently in love with her.

"You have approached the issue as you would any business matter, in other words," she said. "In a measured, dispassionate way. In a typically masculine way." She ignored the fact that she had been contemplating marriage in just such a way herself. "What was your aunt like, Mr. Thorne?"

"My aunt?" His eyebrows rose at the apparent non sequitur. "She was quiet, sweet, unassuming, and unassertive."

"And totally dominated by the men in her life, I suppose," she said.

He thought about it. "It would have been hard not to be dominated by my uncle," he said.

"As I thought," she told him with a curt nod. "Your life has been very lacking in females, has it not, Mr. Thorne? Your mother died when you were no more than a baby. Your aunt was unassertive. Your female cousins married and moved away soon after you went to live with your uncle. Your kinsman in Boston was a widower without children. Your business partner is a man."

"You are right," he said after thinking again for a moment.

She would have loved to ask if he had had mistresses, but there were some subjects no lady would touch upon. Ladies were not supposed to know even that such persons existed or that many men used their services. Ladies *did* know, of course. They were not stupid. At least, most of them were not.

"You know exactly what you are looking for in a wife, then," she said. "You have a list of attributes in your head. You may even have written them down—perhaps during the voyage here."

Again there was that suggestion of amusement she had detected in him on a number of occasions, though he did not smile. "I have a good memory, Lady Jessica," he said. "I believe it is women who like to make written lists."

How did he know that? But of course he was quite right. How else could a woman plan a party?

"But there is a mental list, is there not?" she insisted. "Or was. You looked at me back at that inn and mentally checked off every point. I was even *easy on the eyes*. I wonder what number on the list that requirement was. Close to the bottom, at a guess, if not right at the bottom. And were there any qualities of character on the list at all? Or are women not supposed to have qualities of character?"

"You are offended," he said.

"Yes, I am offended." She looked up to see that the sun was about to break free of that big cloud. At last. "At your presumption and your arrogance in assuming that I will marry you merely because you are prepared to condescend to marry me. And also—"

"It is hardly condescension to decide to marry the daughter of a duke," he said. "I am not myself a duke or a royal prince or a king. I am therefore somewhere below you on the social scale."

"I am the *daughter of a duke*," she said, sketching a few circles in the air with one hand. "And that sums it all up, does it not? But that daughter of a duke, Mr. Thorne, is also a person. When you looked at me—at that inn, at the ball two evenings ago, in Avery's drawing room yesterday, here today—did you see a *person*? Did you see *me*? I very much doubt it. You saw and you see the daughter of a duke."

He clasped his hands behind his back and tipped his head slightly to one side. His eyes and the upper part of his face were half hidden in the shade cast by the brim of his tall hat. He looked awfully . . . appealing. Which fact annoyed her more than anything else. She did not know him either.

She knew things about him, more now than she had known half an hour ago, but she did not know *him*. Why should one find another person appealing based entirely upon physical attributes? He might be an axe murderer for all she knew. Or a miserly businessman who cheated his clients and mistreated his employees and spent his evenings counting his cash.

He obviously had nothing to say in reply to her outburst. Perhaps he did not even know what she was talking about.

Did she?

And when had they stopped walking?

"I am not a commodity," she told him, "to be bought and sold on the exchange. Have I used the right terminology? Do you not think you should *hope* to marry me rather than *intend* it? Do you not think you should work a little—no, that you should work *hard*—to win me? There must be all sorts of deals you have to work hard to achieve as a businessman. Should not I be at least as big a deal as any of them?"

She did not know quite what she was saying. But she had worked herself into a state of considerable agitation, rare for her. She was angry at the arrogance of this man, who had made a list, even if it was only in his head, found that she suited all his requirements, and decided without further ado that he would marry her. The presumption! How dared he?

Perhaps he might not have irked her so much if she did not find him *appealing*. And that fact infuriated her even more. How *could* she? Was she that shallow?

"You wish to be wooed, then, Lady Jessica?" he asked her.

Did she? She thought about it. "With a view to marriage?" she said. "That is the end for which a man *woos* a woman, is it not? It is sometimes a necessary but rather tedious step a man must take in order to persuade her to say yes. As though she lacked the intelligence to demand more?"

He still had his hands clasped at his back. She was still rooted to the spot. She wished she had brought her parasol from the curricle. She could twirl it about her head and give her hands something to do.

"No," she said before he could answer. "I do not want to be *wooed*, Mr. Thorne. I am not at all certain it would accomplish its desired aim anyway. Indeed, I am almost certain it would not. But if you want a chance with me, then you will . . . Oh." She circled the air with her hand again. Where were the right words when one most needed them? "You will *romance* me."

His eyebrows rose. His eyes, darker than ever in the shade of his hat, were as intent upon hers as always. "Is it a verb?" he asked. *"To romance?"*

She stared at him, stupefied. "I have no idea," she said. "I am no grammarian, Mr. Thorne. But it perfectly expresses what you must do if you wish to persuade me even to consider falling in with your *intention*."

"I must romance you," he said. "How does it differ from wooing?"

She had no idea. Or, rather, she did, but how could she find the words to explain?

"Its end, its whole purpose, is not necessarily marriage," she said. "It is about . . . oh, about persons. About feelings. About getting to know another person. Not just facts, but . . . getting to know the person behind the facts. And showing that person that you know and understand and like the whole person, regardless of imperfections. It is . . ."

"Falling in love?" he suggested when she struggled for further words. His eyebrows were still up.

"Oh," she said, frustrated. "Not necessarily. It is about making the other person feel appreciated. It is about making her feel that she is a person, that she matters, that she is more precious than all the cold *facts* in her favor. It is about making her understand that she is more precious in your sight than all other women. It is making her feel that she is . . ."

"Loved?" he said when she was lost for words again.

She sighed deeply and audibly. "There are really no words," she said. "No, it is not about falling in love or about loving. How can one do or feel either of those things in advance? You do not know me, just as I do not know you, Mr. Thorne. It is about the possibility of love. The possibility of friendship and laughter and . . . oh, and something more. Something bright and beautiful. Something that will transform life and fill it with color and . . ."

This time he did not end the sentence for her. Not immediately, anyway. They stared at each other.

"Romance," he said at last.

What a prize idiot she had just made of herself. And she had *no idea* where it had all come from. Just an hour or two ago she had been planning a marriage for herself that was every bit as passionless and calculated as the one he proposed. And then she had got angry and . . . and *this* had happened.

*Romance?* She was twenty-five years old. Any man looking at her and considering her as a wife would have everything but romantic love in mind. She was horribly, hideously eligible. How could she expect any man to look beyond the facts that she was the daughter and sister of a duke, that she was wealthy, and that she had the upbringing and education and accomplishments of her rank? Romance at her age? Or at any age? It was laughable. It was pathetic.

Except that she was not just Lady Jessica Archer. She was . . . She was *her*. She was the being that was inside her and far more meaningful to her than any of the outer trappings of birth and rank.

It was a strange time to be having all these thoughts, which she could not recall ever having before. Not consciously or coherently, anyway.

He turned to stroll onward, and she walked beside him, leaving two feet of space between them. She could see the curricle in the distance. Thank heaven. Though the ride home was going to seem endless.

But she was not sorry, she thought, lifting her chin. She was *not*. How dared he, or any man, decide that he was *going to marry her*?

"Very well, Lady Jessica," he said as they drew closer to the curricle. "I will romance you. *Not* with a view to matrimony, but as an end in itself, to see where it leads."

Jessica licked her lips. Oh goodness, what had she started now? "Thank you," she said, her words cold and clipped.

"But I do hope," he said as he offered his hand to help her up to her seat, "that you will not expect a bouquet quite as large as the one that was in your brother's drawing room yesterday."

He spoke the words in all seriousness. But . . . A joke from Mr. Thorne? Really?

She settled her skirts about her as he climbed to his place and took the ribbons from his young groom.

"Oh, I will not," she assured him, raising her parasol and twirling it behind her head. "I shall expect a far larger one."

He did not laugh. But when she looked at him out of the

corner of her eye, she could see that he was actually and definitely smiling.

He looked different when he smiled. He looked handsome. Not *almost* handsome, but the real thing.

Not that looks mattered. At all.

# *Eight*

G abriel sent Lady Jessica Archer a single long-stemmed
pink rose the following morning.

He ought to have turned his eyes and his mind elsewhere, of course, as soon as it became obvious she was
going to make him work to win her, with no guarantee that
the prize would be his at the end of it all. He needed a wife
soon. And there was no reason to believe he would have
any great difficulty finding one even if the *ton* knew no
more about him than it already did. For some reason he had
captured the public's imagination. Yet he had set his sights
upon the very lady whose imagination had not been captured.

He had no time to *romance* Lady Jessica just because
she had taken offense at his saying he intended to marry
her. What the devil did it mean, anyway, to *romance* a
woman? He was still not convinced there was any such
verb. Though her meaning would stand even if the word did
not. She wished to be flattered, to be fawned over, to be

sighed over with open adoration, to be sent flowers, and generally to be treated like a goddess.

Gabriel was gazing out of his sitting room window upon rain—the drizzling sort that only England seemed able to produce in such depressingly copious quantities. He had intended to call at Archer House this afternoon to invite her to drive in the park with him later. It was what the *ton* did in large numbers, apparently, in the late afternoon. It was where they went to see and be seen, to pick up the latest gossip and to spread it, to ogle the opposite sex and to flirt.

It was not going to happen today, however. Even if the rain let up right at this moment it would be damp and miserable out there. Chilly too, or at least it had been chilly when he went to White's Club this morning with Bertie Vickers.

No. He was being unfair—perhaps because he was feeling frustrated and therefore irritable.

Everything he had just thought was almost certainly *not* what Lady Jessica had meant by the term *romancing*. It was unfair to think she was so shallow. Indeed, he knew she was not. He just could not imagine her being susceptible to any sort of flattery. She would stare right through him, her chin and her nose in the air, as though she could see the hairs on the back of his head. No. What had offended her was her assumption that he saw her as a commodity rather than as a person. *Did* he? He very much feared she might have a point. She wanted him to see her for what she really was—or perhaps that should be *who* she really was, quite independent of all the attributes that made her one of the most eligible ladies in England.

He had been taken aback by her outburst. She had been seriously upset with him. Not so much with his presumption in informing her that he intended to marry her as with the fact that it was not *she* he wished to marry, but rather the titled, wealthy Lady Jessica Archer, sister of the Duke of Netherby. Just as though they were two quite separate entities.

*Were* they?

Strangely, stupidly, the possible truth of that had not struck him until she said it. He had assumed that the Lady Jessica he saw was the whole person, that there was no more to her than the appearance she presented to the world, of beauty, elegance, poise, arrogance, and entitlement. She would perfectly suit his purpose, he had decided almost the first moment he saw her. Even her beauty would suit him. One of his first duties as Earl of Lyndale, after all, would be to produce sons. She would be an attractive bedfellow, he had thought, if perhaps a trifle cold.

Which of them, then, had been the arrogant one?

He had been taught by Cyrus and his own instincts to identify what he wanted and to go after it. He had been taught to expect success so that he could the more easily achieve it. What if those admirable traits in a businessman did not apply to a lover?

They almost certainly did not.

Gabriel drummed his fingers on the windowsill and called himself all sorts of an idiot.

Her outburst had dispelled any notion he had had that she was cold to the core. And it had done strange things to his resolve. It had not lessened it as it ought to. He had found himself *wanting* to waste time and energy romancing her, with no assurance of success. His fingers stopped drumming as he frowned in thought. *I am not at all certain I want to marry you. Indeed, I am almost certain I do not.* Those, he believed, had been her exact words. Would his time and effort be all for nothing, then? Was he willing to pin all his hopes upon that one little word—*almost*? She was *almost* certain. And what the devil *did* romancing a woman entail?

*It is about the possibility of love,* she had said when he had pressed her on the point. *The possibility of friendship and laughter and . . . oh, and something more. Something bright and beautiful. Something that will transform life and fill it with color and . . .*

She had been talking about love. Romantic love, though she would not admit it.

The Lady Jessica Archer he had thought he knew, because really there was not a great deal to know, had been transformed before his eyes into someone of mysterious depths. And he had promised that he would indeed consider the possibility she had spoken of. *Very well, Lady Jessica. I will romance you. Not with a view to matrimony, but as an end in itself, to see where it leads.*

Was he mad?

Would he keep that promise? Madness was something he did not indulge in. Madness cost time. And efficiency. And money. Time, in particular, was not something he could afford to waste in this instance. He needed a bride so that he could move on to the next stage of his homecoming.

Nevertheless he had sent her a rose this morning, wondering as he did so what she would make of it. Did she receive many gifts of a single rose? Would she be offended at the paltriness of it? Or would she be amused, as he hoped she would be, at the contrast with that ostentatious bouquet that she had seemed to find a bit objectionable? Would she make the connection?

Would she like it? Was pink her color? But she had worn it to the Parley ball.

He turned impatiently from the window. If he went now

to call at Archer House, even assuming she was there, he would probably find himself having to make labored conversation with her mother and her sister-in-law and possibly Netherby himself. And perhaps other visitors too, members of her court, of which he would appear to be the newest addition. Perish the thought. He would not do it. Instead he snatched up the pile of invitations that had accumulated upon the table by the door and summoned Horbath to bring him outdoor garments suitable for London drizzle. He would see if Lady Vickers was at home instead. He would ask her advice upon which invitations he ought to accept. Invitations had always come singly in Boston, and not daily either.

Lady Vickers was at home, having decided not to proceed with the round of afternoon calls she had planned. "I hate rain, Gabriel," she told him. "It makes me cross and lazy. But now I am glad I did not go out. I would have missed you, and that would have been a pity. Come and sit by the fire while we wait for the tea tray."

They conversed amiably until she had poured their tea and handed him his cup and saucer with two generously buttered scones on a plate. Then she got down to the serious business of reading through all his invitations.

She recommended that he attend all the balls. "You have told us one of your principal purposes in remaining in town is to select a bride," she said. "Where else are you to see all the most eligible young ladies in one place? Though Bertie reported that you did not show any particular interest in any of the young ladies I recommended for the first ball. Next time I will have to be sure to be there myself to oversee your choices. On the evening of the Parley ball I felt obliged to attend a very tedious political dinner with Trevor."

She also advised him on which soirees and garden parties and Venetian breakfasts and such like he ought to attend and which invitations he would be better off declining. "For one cannot go to everything," she said. "One must be discerning."

"And that one?" he asked. She was getting toward the bottom of the pile.

"An evening party at the home of Lord and Lady Hodges," she read aloud. "In honor of the arrival in town of the Earl and Countess of Riverdale—Lady Hodges's brother and sister-in-law. Ah, and *Lord* Hodges's sister and brother-in-law. A brother and sister married a brother and sister. I see the party is described as a select one. That means it will not be a great squeeze. I daresay most of the guests will be family. The Westcotts are a sizable and close lot."

"You believe I ought to refuse the invitation, then?" he asked her.

"Oh, by no means," she said. "This is one you must definitely accept, Gabriel. Lady Hodges is paying you a considerable compliment, given the fact that it is a small party and she does not know your full identity." She tapped the invitation card with the back of one knuckle. "The Westcotts are extremely well connected—Lord Molenor, the Marquess of Dorchester, the Duke of Netherby, Viscount Dirkson, Lord Hodges. And the Earl of Riverdale himself, of course—head of the family and a very handsome and distinguished gentleman. Let me think. There must be some young, unwed ladies among them too. It might be a good thing to meet them in a more intimate setting than a ball. Yes, of course. Lady Estelle Lamarr is Dorchester's daughter. Bertie told me you danced with her at the ball. A waltz, I believe? You do not need me to tell you that she is very eligible. Ah! And Lady Jessica Archer is the duke's sister. Her mother was a Westcott. So were

Lady Molenor and Lady Dirkson and Lady Hodges herself. The marchioness was once married to . . ."

But Gabriel was no longer paying full attention. The party was in two days' time, and the invitation, he remembered Horbath explaining to him when he returned to his hotel from White's this morning, had not come in the post but had been delivered by hand. The messenger had even wanted to take a reply back with him but had been persuaded to leave without one when he was warned his wait might be a lengthy one. *A select party.* And Lady Jessica Archer, whose mother was a Westcott, was almost certain to be one of the select persons.

"Thank you for the advice," he said. "I will certainly go."

"Lady Estelle would be a very good match for you," Lady Vickers said. "So would Lady Jessica. In the years since they left the schoolroom, however, neither young lady has shown any inclination to choose a husband. They do not need to be in any hurry, of course, as so many young ladies do. They have the wealth and the connections—and the beauty too—to marry whenever they choose. Now there is a challenge for you, Gabriel, especially if you insist upon remaining stubborn and not making it known that you are the Earl of Lyndale." She looked hopefully at him.

"I would rather it not be known yet," he said, and picked up one of the remaining invitations from the pile. "This one is for a masquerade. A costume party. Ought I to attend? And must I acquire some sort of costume if I do?"

She read it. "Ah," she said. "Yes, this will be a respectable one. Some masquerades are not, you know, but are merely an excuse for vulgarity or worse. But everyone loves a masquerade. This is bound to be well attended. And you must certainly dress up. You will stand out like a sore thumb if you do not."

"Perhaps," he suggested, "I can go as a sore thumb?"

Lady Vickers laughed heartily. "You would certainly be noticed," she said. "Let me put another scone on your plate."

Jessica was looking forward to Elizabeth and Colin's party, which they had arranged to welcome Alexander and Wren back to London. She expected that it would be a small gathering, primarily for the Westcott family and their close connections. But it would be a pleasant change from the rather hectic pace of the more crowded social events she had been attending almost daily since the Parley ball. There would probably be a few other guests from outside the family, otherwise the event would hardly be called a party, but they would be friends, people with whom she would almost certainly be familiar and comfortable.

Mr. Rochford was already showing a marked preference for her. He had stayed by her side for rather longer than was strictly polite at a soiree she had attended two evenings ago, the day after the visit to Richmond Park. He had engaged her in exclusive conversation almost the whole time, making it difficult for anyone else to join them and form a group. He had come to Avery's box at the theater during the intermission last evening to pay his respects and had ended up paying them almost exclusively to her, though he had bowed to everyone else first and had kissed both her mother's hand and Anna's. He had remained until the play was actually resuming. Avery had got to his feet with all the appearance of indolence and held the door of the box open as a hint for him to depart. He was handsome, charming, and . . . oh, and all those other things she had noticed from the start. She ought to be delighted by his attentions, given the fact that this year she was supposedly looking in earnest for a husband. She *was* delighted. She just wished he would not try quite so hard.

Which was totally illogical of her. Had she not accused Mr. Thorne of not trying hard enough? She had not set eyes upon that gentleman since he handed her down from his curricle outside Archer House on their return from Richmond and she had swept inside without a backward glance. She had embarrassing memories of that afternoon and was quite happy not to have seen him again since. What on earth had possessed her to challenge him to *romance* her if he wished to have a chance with her? He was obviously not going to accept the challenge—thank heaven. Except that each morning since, he had sent her a single long-stemmed pink rose.

She had laughed aloud the first time. The rose had been lying across her linen napkin when she arrived for breakfast, a small card tucked beneath it with the single word *Thorne* scrawled boldly across it.

"Oh, do not laugh at the poor man, Jessica," Anna had urged, though she had been laughing too. "There is something impossibly romantic about a single rose."

And that, of course, had been the whole point. But it was a sort of ironic romantic gesture, for of course it was meant to be compared with the gigantic bouquet Mr. Rochford had sent her the morning after the Parley ball.

"The man has a sense of humor," Avery had commented—though he had seemed not to make the connection with the bouquet. "He is drawing attention to the fact that he is the thorn to your rose, Jess. I hope you are suitably affected."

"Oh, I am," Jessica had assured him, picking up the rose by the stem, careful to avoid the thorns, and bringing the bud to her nose. She closed her eyes briefly as she inhaled the heady summer scent of it.

She had not expected him to have a sense of humor. Except that there had been that smile . . .

"Mr. Thorne is said to be a wealthy man," her mother had commented. "He must also be a miserly man, Jessica, if all he can send after you honored him with several hours of your time yesterday is one rose." But she had been laughing too.

When the second rose arrived the day after and the third this morning, Jessica had taken them to her room without comment. She had already pressed the first one between two heavy books without waiting for it to bloom fully. It was too perfect to be allowed simply to bloom and die.

He had not come to the house again or been at either the soiree or the theater. She wondered how long he would keep sending her pink roses. Why was he doing it? Was this his idea of romancing her? Was it working? She would be very happy to learn that he had left London. It would be embarrassing to meet him again.

In the meanwhile there was the family party, at which she would be safe from the determined courtship of Mr. Rochford and the elusive romancing—if that indeed *was* his motive in sending the roses—of Mr. Thorne. Goodness, life had not been this complicated for years.

Elizabeth and Colin's large drawing room was already half full when Jessica arrived with her mother and Anna and Avery. She greeted them with hugs, hugged Alexander, and took both Wren's hands in her own and squeezed them.

"Every time I hear of you going to Staffordshire to check on your glassworks, I am inspired," she said. "And envious. It is why you were late coming to London, Elizabeth told us. You look wonderful. The work must agree with you."

"It is lovely to be back here," Wren told her, "and to see everyone again. Christmas seems forever ago."

Jessica spotted her grandmother and Great-aunt Edith sitting side by side across the room and went to hug them both. She smiled at Miss Boniface, Great-aunt Edith's companion, who went everywhere with her on the strength of the fact that she was a relative of Great-aunt Edith's late husband. Cousin Boris was chatting with them too, as was Adrian Sawyer, Viscount Dirkson's son. Jessica hugged her cousin and greeted Mr. Sawyer with a warm smile. She hugged Peter, Boris's younger brother, when he joined them and asked him if he had had any waltzing lessons lately. Estelle, she saw when she looked around, was over by one of the windows in a group of young people that included Bertrand, Estelle's twin brother, and Charlotte Overleigh, formerly Charlotte Rigg, Estelle's friend, and . . .

Oh.

And Mr. Thorne.

Oh dear.

Whoever had thought of inviting him? Elizabeth? He was still being talked about wherever one went, of course, though Jessica was not quite sure why. Yes, he was a kinsman of Lady Vickers and also her godson and Sir Trevor's. But did anyone know for sure that he really had acquired wealth during his years in America and was not in reality a lying adventurer? From whom exactly had he recently inherited property and fortune here in England? And *where* in England? In retrospect, Jessica realized he had been very vague in his answers to her questions. Or perhaps she had not asked the right questions or enough of them. Nevertheless, the *ton* appeared to be accepting him at his word even though everyone was also still intrigued by the mystery surrounding his sudden appearance in London. They were enchanted by him.

And he was *here*. At Elizabeth and Colin's supposedly select party. He caught her eye across the room and inclined his head in greeting.

Her evening was ruined.

*But if you want a chance with me, then you will . . .* romance *me*.

If her cheeks turned any hotter, they would surely burst into flames.

Fortunately Cousin Althea, Elizabeth and Alexander's mother, moved into her line of vision and cut out Mr. Thorne. She was smiling as she kissed Jessica's cheek. "You do look lovely in that particular shade of green, Jessica," she said. And it was only at that moment that Jessica noticed she had a young gentleman with her. "You know Mr. Rochford, I believe?"

Oh. Oh, oh, and oh again. An evening doubly ruined—which was a strange thought to be having under the circumstances.

"I do." She smiled. "How do you do, Mr. Rochford?"

"Considerably better than I did a minute ago," he said, making her his usual elegant bow and favoring her with the full force of his dazzling smile. "And Mrs. Westcott took the words out of my mouth. You should always wear green."

"Thank you," she said. She would gain fame as a walking tree.

"I see that Matilda and Charles have arrived," Cousin Althea said. "Do please excuse me."

And Jessica was left alone with Mr. Rochford. Again.

"I was exceedingly gratified when Lady Hodges invited me to her party," he said. "The invitation card described it as a *select* gathering to welcome the return to town of the Earl and Countess of Riverdale. You would not have received a formal invitation, of course, Lady Jessica. You are a Westcott through the Dowager Duchess of Netherby, your mother, I understand. I believe most of the guests here this evening are either Westcotts or have a direct familial connection to them. I am deeply honored to have been included among those who are neither. I wonder to whom I am indebted." He gave her an arch look that was clearly meant to be significant.

Jessica could hazard a guess. He was a young and handsome man. He was about to be very well connected indeed. Before the summer was out his father would almost certainly be the Earl of Lyndale, all the formality of declaring the incumbent earl officially deceased over with. He had been determinedly singling her out for attention. The Westcotts, many of whom she knew were concerned about her continued single state, could always be depended upon to intervene whenever it occurred to them that one of their number might need a helping hand. She would almost wager upon it that they had decided to do some active matchmaking. She could just picture the usual committee—Grandmama, Aunt Matilda, Aunt Mildred, her mother, Cousin Althea, possibly Aunt Viola and Great-aunt Edith—convening over tea somewhere and putting their heads together to decide what could be done to prod dear Jessica into marriage with this extremely eligible and personable young future earl who would surely turn his attentions elsewhere if she did not snatch him up before it could happen.

"I would imagine," Jessica said in answer to his implied inquiry, "it is my cousin Elizabeth herself—Lady Hodges, that is—whom you have to thank."

"I have already expressed my gratitude to her," he said. "I cannot imagine anywhere I would rather be this evening than just precisely where I am."

His tone made it clear that *just precisely where he was* meant not Elizabeth and Colin's house in general or even the drawing room in particular, but this precise spot in the drawing room, alone with Jessica, space all about them even though there were enough family and guests to more than half fill the rest of the room. Even Grandmama and Great-aunt Edith, surrounded by people who had come to greet them, seemed to be some distance away, though Jessica could not recall moving away from them. But this was not going to happen again, she decided, not as it had at the soiree a few evenings ago. She had no wish to spend the whole evening virtually alone with Mr. Rochford in plain sight of a couple of dozen or so interested family members and others tactfully keeping their distance. If she was going to allow the courtship of Mr. Rochford, it was going to be on her own terms. She was not going to let her family and the whole *ton* start to see them as an established couple and then find that she had been backed into a corner from which there was no easy escape.

She reached for a glass of wine from the tray held by a passing servant, though she did not really want it, and at the same time took a few steps to her right, bringing herself into the orbit of a group that included Alexander and Elizabeth and Cousin Peter and . . . oh, and Estelle and Mr. Thorne. Mr. Rochford moved with her.

So much for her relaxed evening with family and close friends, she thought rather crossly before seeing the funny side of the situation. It was as though some malicious fate had learned of her decision to choose a husband this year and had sent her two candidates, both of whom had shown interest in her without any effort to attract on her part and both of whom made her want to run for the hills or some deep, dark cave or her bedchamber with an extra bolt added to the door.

It seemed she was not ready for marriage after all—and perhaps never would be.

She caught Mr. Thorne's eye over the rim of her glass, and he raised his eyebrows. Why was it she had the feeling he had detected her inner amusement—albeit a *rueful* amusement? There was no hint of a smile on his face.

"I cannot tell you," Mr. Rochford was saying, addressing Elizabeth, "how honored I am to have been included in your guest list in what I can see is essentially a family gathering. I suppose I must grow accustomed to being treated with such deference. It still seems much like a dream that soon my father will be Earl of Lyndale in name as well as in fact. And that I will be his heir."

"We are delighted you were able to come," Elizabeth said, smiling warmly at him.

"In *fact*?" Mr. Thorne asked. "Your father will be earl in name *as well as in fact*?"

"Ah, yes," Mr. Rochford said. "Brierley Hall was falling into chaos and disrepair in the absence of a firm-handed master. Servants, neighbors, hangers-on—they were all taking advantage of the fact. Much as my father wanted to cling to hope, even after all hope was realistically gone, that my cousin would be found alive and would return to take responsibility for his inheritance, he was eventually forced to acknowledge that it was not going to happen. Much against the grain, and knowing he might be accused of doing what he was not yet legally entitled to do, he took up residence at Brierley a while ago and began the difficult task of putting the estate to rights. It has all been very distressing for him—for all of us. Yet he *still* holds out hope that at the last moment Gabriel will reappear to lift the burden from his shoulders."

"Ah," Mr. Thorne said. "Gabriel, was he? That is my name too. I have never encountered another, though I am not encountering one in person now, alas, am I? Unlike your father, you are sure he is dead?"

"There can be little doubt," Mr. Rochford said, shaking his head sadly. "Though I hope I am wrong. I am afraid my cousin was ironically named, however. He was very far from being an angel."

"Oh, he was a rogue, then, was he?" Peter asked, grinning, his interest noticeably piqued.

"One hates to wash one's family linen in public," Mr. Rochford said with a sigh, and then proceeded to do just that. "I am afraid he was a severe trial and disappointment to the late earl, his uncle, who had taken him in out of the kindness of his heart after his father died. A little wildness in a boy, especially an orphaned lad, is to be expected, of course, and is not a bad thing in itself. But as he grew older he grew increasingly wild and unmanageable, even vicious at times. My father's cousin, the earl, hushed up some of the worst of his excesses in the hope, I suppose, that he would learn from his mistakes and grow to a more sober maturity. Finally, however, there was a scandal that could not be silenced. It involved the daughter of a neighbor and ended up with the death of her brother. There could, of course, be other explanations than the obvious ones, but Gabriel fled the very same night as the death and no one has heard from or of him since. Would an innocent man flee instead of remaining to clear his name or do the decent thing?"

"It sounds to me, then," Estelle said, "as if it might be

better for all concerned if he *is* dead. Did you know him well, Mr. Rochford?"

"Well enough," he said with a sigh. "He was a likable boy. I was fond of him. It grieved me to see his wildness turn into vice—if indeed that is what happened. I do not wish to judge him despite all the evidence. I certainly do not wish him dead. People do change, after all. And perhaps there was an explanation he did not stay to offer. Self-defense, perhaps? I would rather give him the benefit of any small doubt there may be than condemn him. Like my father, I wish even now he would reappear to claim his inheritance."

No he did not, Jessica thought, opening her fan and plying it before her face. The return of the legitimate earl from the dead would be disastrous for Mr. Rochford. It would kill all his expectations. And it was clear for all to see that he was eagerly anticipating those expectations. If he hated to wash his family linen in public, why had he done so? She felt intensely uncomfortable.

"After seven years it does seem unlikely," Alexander said briskly. "Your father is coming to London later in the Season, I understand, Rochford? I shall look forward to making his acquaintance. I do not believe I have had the pleasure of meeting him anytime in the past. And you have recently arrived in London, Thorne? From America, I have heard? I trust you had a decent voyage?"

"Thank you. I did," Mr. Thorne said. "There were no severe storms to put me in fear of my life. Or any cutthroat pirates either. It was all, indeed, rather tedious, which is the best one can hope for of any lengthy journey."

"You lived in Boston?" Elizabeth asked, smiling. "I suppose you left friends behind you there. They must have been sorry to see you leave."

"I was happy there for a number of years," he said, and went on to describe some of the social life of Boston.

Jessica was grateful to Alexander and Elizabeth for so effortlessly turning the conversation away from a topic that ought not to have been aired for public consumption. She felt oddly guilty for Mr. Rochford's questionable manners, as though she was responsible for his being here—as perhaps she was in a sense.

His name was Gabriel, Jessica thought. Mr. Thorne's, that was. He had spent thirteen years in America, having fled there after some upset with his family. He had come back, reluctantly, to claim a recently acquired inheritance. How long ago was it that the other Gabriel, Gabriel Rochford, had fled after presumably assaulting a neighbor's daughter and then murdering her brother? Though *murder* might be too strong a word if there had been a fair fight. Or a duel. Or, as Mr. Rochford himself had allowed, it had been self-defense. If Mr. Gabriel Rochford did not appear within the next few months, he would be declared legally dead and his kinsman would become the new earl.

*An inheritance brought me back. And a family situation that necessitated my being here in person.*

She could remember his saying those words at Richmond.

Surely . . .

"Lady Jessica," Mr. Rochford said, speaking low in her ear, "would you do me the honor of presenting me to the Dowager Countess of Riverdale and the lady beside her, who I believe is her sister?"

But as he was about to offer his arm, Anna came to join the group and he turned to compliment her on her appearance and bow over her hand, which he raised to his lips.

Grandmama, Jessica saw when she turned her head, was

nodding in her direction and smiling even as she was saying something to Aunt Edith. It looked as though they approved of what they saw.

Mr. Rochford had known his cousin well—or *well enough*, to use his exact words. Surely even after thirteen years a cousin one had known *well enough* would not have become totally unrecognizable.

Besides, Gabriel was not *that* uncommon a name. She would surely be able to think of one or two others if she set her mind to the task.

# Nine

It had not taken Gabriel long to understand that he had been invited to Lord and Lady Hodges's party as a possible suitor for Lady Estelle Lamarr, while Rochford was being matched up with Lady Jessica Archer. He was seeing the less than subtle hand of the Westcott family at work, if he was not greatly mistaken, or at least of its female members. Both young ladies, extremely eligible, must be a bit of a worry to their fond relatives, for both were almost certainly past the age of twenty yet remained unmarried, unbetrothed, and seemingly unattached.

What the family had perhaps *not* taken into account, at least in the one case, was the character of Lady Estelle. She had a winning smile and an air of open candor. *And* a twinkling eye. He had noticed all three as well as her prettiness at the Parley ball.

"I wonder if you understand, Mr. Thorne, that we have been thrown together to discover if we *like* each other," she had said to him when he already *did* understand after Lady

Molenor had made a point of presenting him to her—again—and then disappearing at an imagined call from another family member.

"I am flattered," he said, smiling back at her. "I am considered an eligible connection, then, for the daughter of a marquess?"

"Oh, I do not doubt that your supposed American fortune and your connections here in England would be looked at very closely indeed if you were to make an offer for me to my father," she said. "I am his only daughter and he is *very* protective. I also have a twin brother who would check your credentials just as thoroughly even if Papa did not. But you are Lady Vickers's kinsman, and she and Sir Trevor are your godparents. Sir Trevor Vickers is a prominent member of the government and is held in high esteem."

"Ah," he said. "Then I can aspire as high as to your hand, can I?" He was rather enjoying himself, he realized.

"Well, you *can*," she agreed. "But you would be foolish to do so."

"I am devastated." He set one hand over his heart and she laughed. "Is it something I said?"

"Hard as it is for my family to understand," she told him, tapping her closed fan against his sleeve, "I am not ready for marriage yet, Mr. Thorne. Eventually, perhaps, but not now."

"And I cannot sway your resolve?" The twinkle in her eye told him that she fully realized he was *not* devastated.

"You cannot, alas," she said. "This coming autumn the lease will come to an end on the house—my father's house—where Bertrand and I spent much of our childhood. The tenants will be leaving. Once the house is empty, Bertrand intends to take up residence there, and I plan to go with him. We are twins, you know, and enjoy a close bond. I do not doubt he will wish to marry eventually, and I am quite sure I will too. But first I want to go home. I want to spend time there. With my brother. And with myself."

"Leaving home, going home," he said. "They are pivotal, emotionally charged moments in life." He knew something about them. "I must look elsewhere, then, for a bride."

They continued to smile at each other, but with a little less amusement than a few moments before. He understood her, and perhaps she knew he did.

"Perhaps Jessica?" she suggested, and laughed. "Now *she* is eligible. Even more than I am. Though I do pity the man who has to face Avery to ask for her hand. He can be terrifying."

"I may have to decide if I am willing to take the risk, then," he said just as they were joined by her twin and a friend she introduced as Mrs. Overleigh.

If he had been invited here as a possible suitor for Lady Estelle, Gabriel thought, then his continued presence here was redundant. Rochford was fawning all over Lady Jessica. How the devil was he going to use this occasion to some advantage in order to *romance* her? He had not set eyes upon her for three days, and though she might have seen the humor of the pink rose the first day, the joke might have worn a bit thin on subsequent days. Besides, he did not suppose a joke was romantic. But what else was he to do? He found it difficult, even impossible, to be ostentatious. He would feel downright embarrassed about sending a bouquet. The next thing he might find himself doing was kissing his fingertips and blowing her a kiss or gazing soulfully at her.

He discovered as the evening progressed that this was not the sort of party at which one spent the whole time in the same place with the same set of fellow guests. These people were adept at moving about, aligning themselves with different groupings, keeping the conversation fresh and touching upon any number of topics. No one dominated any conversation, though Gabriel suspected Rochford would have done so if he had been allowed. But almost immediately after he had divulged that damning and astoundingly inaccurate information about Gabriel Rochford and his relationship with him, both Riverdale and Lady Hodges deftly turned the subject without being at all obvious about it. Both had perhaps felt that such conversation was not appropriate to the occasion, though young Peter Wayne, one of Molenor's sons, had been agog with interest.

It was a strange tale Rochford had told. He had been just a boy when Gabriel went to America—a boy he had never met and had known next to nothing about. Yet there had been the story about his own wildness and its gradual development into vice and rape and murder. Had all these lies come from Anthony Rochford's father? After thirteen years, without any contrary story being told, were the details now etched in stone? Had Rochford told the story tonight with the sole purpose of blackening the name of a cousin he assumed was not alive to speak for himself? So that no one would question the moral as well as the legal right of his father to take over the title?

Lady Hodges had moved to include Viscountess Dirkson and another lady in the group, and Lady Estelle had turned away with her friend when two young men, Dirkson's son, Gabriel believed, and the friend's husband, drew their attention. The Duchess of Netherby had approached to say good evening to Rochford. He was bowing over her hand and raising it to his lips.

"Lady Jessica," Gabriel said, seizing the opportunity, "do you play the pianoforte?" There was a grand pianoforte in one corner of the drawing room, though no one had yet gone near it.

She raised her eyebrows in that haughty way of hers. "Well," she said, "I *do*, but I do not lay claim to any great talent. My music teacher told me one day when I was still a child that I played as though I had ten thumbs instead of just two and eight fingers. All my governess could say in my defense was that it was unkind of him to speak so candidly. And when I ran to Avery to complain, all *he* did was look at me with that pained expression he is so good at and ask me what my point was."

Everyone in the group laughed.

"We love you anyway, Jessica," her aunt, Lady Dirkson, said, her eyes warm with merriment. "And that *was* a cruel thing to say, and not at all accurate."

"Definitely not ten thumbs, Jess," Peter Wayne, her cousin, assured her. "More like eight thumbs and two little fingers."

"Perhaps you would care to tackle a duet," Gabriel suggested.

"You play?" Lady Jessica asked.

He did. He had never had lessons and no one had ever encouraged him, though his aunt had come quietly into the room a few times at Brierley while he was playing and quietly listened and quietly went away again. Cyrus's late wife had had a pianoforte in Boston, sadly out of tune. Gabriel had had it tuned after Cyrus's death and had played it for his own entertainment.

"A little," he admitted.

"You must certainly play for us, then," Lady Hodges said with her characteristic warm smile, and she raised an arm to summon her husband. "There is some sheet music inside the bench."

He had never learned to read music.

"Shall we?" he asked, reaching out a hand toward Lady Jessica.

"Oh dear," she said, eyeing his hand with obvious misgiving. But she set her own in it and allowed him to lead her toward the pianoforte. Lord Hodges had opened the cover over the keys and was propping open the lid. Lady Hodges was removing a pile of music from inside the bench and setting it on top.

"There," she said. "I am sure you can find something you know, Jessica. And anytime I have heard you play I have found your performance quite competent."

She smiled at them both, took her husband's arm, and went off to mingle with their guests.

Lady Jessica looked through the pile of music while Gabriel stood half behind her, his hands at his back.

"Thank you for the roses," she murmured.

"I have always considered a single rose more lovely than a whole vaseful," he said.

She paused over one sheet of music, opened it, closed it again, and set it on top of the pile of discards.

"It enables one to concentrate the whole of one's attention upon the beauty of a single bloom," he said. He was sounding pompous.

"That reminds me of the poem that begins, *To see the world in a grain of sand*," she said. "Do you know it?"

"By William Blake?" he said. "Yes. Another of the lines, I believe, is, *Hold infinity in the palm of your hand.* It is the same idea in a different image. And a single rose can be more breathtaking than a whole garden."

"I could never quite understand Mr. Blake's point when I was a girl," she said. "A grain of sand is merely a grain of sand, I used to think."

She played a ballad, "Barbara Allen," though she did not sing the words. She played competently and even made a key change halfway through without stumbling. The guests had not stopped their conversations, but there was a smattering of applause nevertheless when she had finished.

"Let me see your hands," Gabriel said, leaning slightly over the keyboard. She spread her fingers and turned her hands palms up while she looked inquiringly at him. "I see four fingers and one thumb on your left hand and four and one on your right. Your music teacher *was* cruel. And quite wrong."

"I was ten years old," she said. "And he actually did me a favor. I was so furious with him and with my governess and with Avery that I was determined to show them how wrong they were. After that I practiced twice as long as I was required to instead of half as much, as I had been doing. I wanted all three of them to eat their words."

"And did they?" he asked.

"Not to my knowledge," she said. "But I did learn to play well enough not to make an utter cake of myself in company. You have not chosen *your* music, Mr. Thorne. I shall not let you escape, you see, after you've admitted to being able to play." She got to her feet, folded her sheet of music, and set it on top of the pile.

"My music is here," he told her, tapping a finger against his temple. Though that was not strictly true. He had to think, yes, in order to bring a tune to mind, but the *music* was not in his mind. And when he sat at the pianoforte, he had to rid his mind even of the tune so that it would not interfere with his fingers as they played. He did not know where the music itself came from after that. He did not know how his fingers hit the right notes or how they knew what other notes to play in order to create the full melody and the accompaniment. It all came from some unknown *somewhere* inside him, yet it seemed too vast to fit within his frame. It was a good thing he had never tried to describe the process to anyone.

"You have memorized it?" she asked as he sat on the bench and arranged the tails of his coat behind him. "That is impressive."

He very rarely played in company, and when he did, it was usually merely to entertain. Fortunately there was a hum of sound as people continued their conversations. This corner of the room actually seemed like an oasis of quiet. Of which Lady Jessica Archer was a part.

He gazed at the keyboard, not quite seeing it. He listened to the melody of Bach's "Jesus bleibet meine Freude"—*Jesus shall remain my joy*—in his head. Then he set his fingers on the keys, let them find the ones he wanted, emptied his mind, and played. Perhaps, he thought for the first few moments, he ought to have chosen something lighter, something simpler, something more obviously entertaining. He was very aware of Lady Jessica standing beside the bench, watching his fingers.

And then the music took possession of him. He closed his eyes, tipped back his head, frowning, as the main melody, stately and dignified, asserted itself through his left hand while his right hand after the first introductory moments continued with the ripple of joyful accompaniment. It was a soul wrenching contrast, part of his mind thought, between deep emotion and exuberant joy. He had heard it played on the organ in the church at Brierley when he was a boy, and the music had been a part of him ever since.

His eyes were closed again as he finished and listened to

the echo of the final notes receding to wherever the music lived when it was not being played. He was not aware of the silence in the room until it was shattered with applause.

"That was exquisite."

"I say. Bravo, Thorne."

"How absolutely lovely."

"What *was* that?"

"You really ought to be on a concert stage, Mr. Thorne."

"Beautiful."

"Oh, do play again."

A number of voices spoke at once.

"Well," Lady Jessica said after a rather lengthy pause. "I am very glad I went first. Wherever did you learn to play like that?"

"I did not," he said.

"You are self-taught?" She opened her fan and plied it before her face.

"I do not read music," he told her.

This was a party, a soiree, not a concert. He felt embarrassed and was very glad to see that conversations were resuming and servants were circulating with trays of drinks and dainties.

"I wish I could play like that," she said softly.

He got to his feet, moved the pile of music to the floor, and gestured to the bench. "Come and sit beside me," he said, "and we will play something together."

"Without music?" she said.

"I will teach you," he told her. "You can play the lower notes. They are really quite simple, but they set the tempo, the bass upon which the melody is set."

She eyed him doubtfully and then eyed the bench before seating herself and sliding along it to make room for him.

He had done this at parties in Boston. It had always been good for some light entertainment.

"You are Gabriel," she said, turning her face toward his. "But the angelic connotation is somewhat marred by your other name. Mr. Gabriel Thorne."

"A rose is spoiled by the thorn on its stem, then?" he asked, turning his head to look into her eyes.

"Are you indeed an angel, then?" she asked him. "Mr. *Thorne*?"

And it struck him that they were no longer talking about roses. It occurred to him that she knew, or at least suspected.

"By no means," he said. "How tedious life would be."

"The other Gabriel is no angel either," she said.

"Apparently not," he said. "If one is to believe Mr. Rochford's story, that is."

"And you do not?" she asked.

He shrugged. "Does it matter?"

She shook her head slightly, set down her fan on the bench between them, and rubbed a finger over one of the white keys as though she had spotted a dust mote there. "Let us discover how good an instructor you are, then, Mr. Thorne," she said. "My guess is that I am about to make an idiot of myself in front of almost my whole family as well as some distinguished guests."

"Impossible," he said. "With me as your teacher?"

They turned their heads at the same moment—a massively uncomfortable moment as it turned out. Their faces were only inches apart. Her cheeks were slightly flushed, her eyes wide. He had not really noticed before how thick and dark her eyelashes were or how her upper lip curved slightly upward when her lips were parted, as they were now. Or how pearly white her teeth were. He had not noticed how very kissable a mouth she had.

It was *not* a thought he cared to pursue at this particular moment. And yet . . . He had promised to romance her. Was that what he was attempting to do now? In full view of a roomful of people? By coaxing her to do something she was reluctant to do?

The flush in her cheeks deepened before she looked back to the keyboard. He was no accomplished lover. How did one romance a woman in a way that would speak to her heart? Unfortunately, it seemed that women thought with their hearts, while men thought with their minds. Or with another part of their anatomy equally distant from the heart. He had feelings. Of course he did. Often they came close to overwhelming him. But they were something he had always carefully guarded. Even the deep affection he had felt for Cyrus had not been fully apparent to him until after the accident, when it was too late to show it.

Agreeing to romance Lady Jessica Archer had been little short of madness.

"We will keep it simple," he said. "You will need to use just your left hand."

"Wonderful," she said. "I am right-handed."

He showed her how to play a simple rhythm with a pattern of notes that could be repeated endlessly though they could be varied with tempo changes. He did not burden her with that possibility, though. He played the rhythm with her, an octave higher, until she had it, then added a melody above it with his right hand. She turned her head to smile at him, a flashing brightness of an expression that almost made him falter. She *did* falter and had to search for both the notes and the rhythm again while he adjusted the melody to hide the gaffe. Eventually he stopped parroting her rhythm with his left hand and played a variation on it while he changed the melody with his right hand.

She flashed that smile at him again, and he smiled back at her.

"It is permitted," he said, "to play at a tempo slightly above that of a tortoise crawling across a beach."

"Oh, is it, indeed?" she said.

And she changed the tempo so suddenly that he had to scramble to keep up. And then she sped it up again. They played for a minute or two in perfect time with each other until she missed a note, exclaimed with dismay, tried to correct herself, and got hopelessly entangled with wrong keys, lost rhythm, and wayward fingers.

She bent her head over the keys and laughed. Actually, it was more like a peal of giggles while he ended his contrived melody with a grand flourish and laughed with her.

There was a ripple of laughter and applause from the rest of the room, but they both ignored it.

"Thumbs," she said. "All thumbs. Indeed, at the end I would swear there were six of them just on my left hand. It must have borrowed from my right."

And he wondered how he could ever have thought she was all cold hauteur. Oh, she could be that and often was, but it was not *her* to the exclusion of all else. Perhaps these flushed cheeks and bright eyes and gleeful laughter were not her either. But how foolish of him to have assumed that anyone was one or two things and nothing else. *He* was far more than just a successful businessman and Earl of Lyndale. *Far* more. Labels helped identify a person, perhaps, but they did not define him. Or her.

What she had said or tried to say at Richmond suddenly made all the sense in the world.

"Tell me about Lady Jessica Archer," he said.

Her smile faded, but it left her eyes softer than they usually were, and it left the flush of color in her cheeks.

"That is a request that always has the effect of completely tying my tongue," she said.

"Tell me about your childhood, then," he said. "What about your father?"

"I was fourteen when he died," she said, in a quiet voice. "He was very different from Avery. He was the sort of man to whom children are the mother's domain. I did not see a great deal of him. He was never unkind when I did, but he took no real interest in my upbringing or in *me*. I have always believed that when he married my mother he hoped for another son. A spare, so to speak. Though he never expressed open disappointment. Not in my hearing, at least. And there were no more children after me."

"You did not complain to him about your music teacher?" he asked.

"Oh good heavens, no," she said. "I would not even have dreamed of it. I am not complaining about him. It never occurred to me that a father could be affectionate or that he might wish to spend time with his children until I saw Avery with *his*—the three girls as well as the lone boy. If he feels any disappointment that he has only the one son so far, he has certainly never shown it. And indeed, I do not believe he does. He adores them all. One would not suspect it from looking at him, would one?"

Gabriel glanced about the room until he spotted Netherby, immaculately elegant despite the rings on almost every finger of both hands and the jewels that winked from the folds of his neckcloth and the handle of the quizzing glass he wore on a black ribbon about his neck. The expression on his face suggested slight boredom, though he was actively involved in a conversation with Dirkson and the

Countess of Riverdale. No. One could not quite imagine him adoring his children. Or anyone else for that matter. Yet his duchess seemed a warm, happy woman.

"I had a contented enough childhood," Lady Jessica said. "It was rather solitary, but there were children in the neighborhood of Morland Abbey with whom I was allowed to play quite often. And I was always close to my mother. I lived for the times, though, when I could stay with my cousins or they came to stay with me."

"Are they here tonight?" he asked her.

"Boris and Peter are," she said, "two of my aunt Mildred's sons. The third, Ivan, is at university. They are all quite a bit younger than I, though. They were fun and full of mischief and I loved them, but I never had a particularly close friendship with them. The other three cousins were Aunt Viola's. She is here. She is the Marchioness of Dorchester now. Estelle and Bertrand Lamarr are her stepchildren, though they were already very close to adulthood when she married their father. Harry, my cousin, Aunt Viola's son, was very briefly the Earl of Riverdale after his father, my uncle Humphrey, died. I adore him—Harry, I mean. He was three years older than I and always my hero. It was devastating for him when the discovery was made soon after Uncle Humphrey's death that his marriage to Aunt Viola had always been a bigamous one. His first wife, whom no one even knew about, was still alive when he married for the second time, and his daughter—his *legitimate* daughter—was put into an orphanage, where she remained until the truth was discovered when she was already grown up."

"What happened to her?" he asked.

"Oh," she said. "She is here too. She is Anna. My sister-in-law. Avery's wife."

Gabriel could only imagine the drama this family must have lived through after that discovery was made only to be followed by that marriage.

"My cousin Camille was older than Harry," Lady Jessica told him. "Abigail was younger, just a year older than me. We were more like sisters than cousins. We were the very best of friends. We shared dreams for our future. I suppose it would be very wrong of me to claim that I suffered as much as she did when she lost everything, including her very legitimacy, just before she was to make her come-out here in London. But . . . I suffered. I wanted to die. Foolish, was it not? I was seventeen. One's emotions tend to be very raw at that age."

"What happened to her?" he asked. "And to her older sister?"

"Oh," she said. "Camille surprised everyone by marrying an artist and schoolmaster who grew up at the same orphanage as Anna. They live in a big house in the hills above Bath, and they have a large family. Some of the children are their own and some are adopted. They use the house as a sort of artists' school or gathering place. One could never have predicted it of Camille. She was so very . . . correct, so very stiff and humorless. She was betrothed to a man no one liked, including her, I do not doubt. I am not sure many people liked *her*. Then, at least. But she's a different person now. She is very happy. No one seeing her could doubt that."

It was strange, Gabriel thought, how one could look at an aristocratic family and assume that their lives were lived on an even keel with no significant troubles. With the Westcott and Archer families, it seemed nothing could be further from the truth.

"And Abigail?" he asked.

"For several years," she told him, "she retired within herself. There is no other way of putting it. She was quiet, dignified, withdrawn. She would not allow anyone in the family to help her. She would not allow me to suffer with her. And then two years ago she met and married a lieutenant colonel who had brought Harry home from an officers' convalescent home in Paris, where he had been since the Battle of Waterloo. She married him privately, with no one else but Harry present. No one even knew she *liked* Gil. She certainly did not at first. They live now in Gloucestershire with their two children—Gil already had a daughter by a previous marriage. And she is *happy*. She did not settle for anything less. She is *happy*."

A possibility struck him. "Is *she* why you have never married?" he asked her.

She sat straighter on the bench, though her fingers rested on the keys of the pianoforte. Some of the haughtiness had returned to her manner. "I have not married, Mr. Thorne," she said, "because I have not chosen to do so."

"Did you feel somehow betrayed," he asked her, "by the sudden marriage of your cousin?"

She turned her face toward him. "I am *happy* for her, Mr. Thorne," she said. "More happy than I can say."

Which did not answer his question.

"I am sure you are," he said, and he moved his left hand across the keyboard until his little finger overlapped hers. He rubbed the pad of it lightly over the back of her finger.

He fully expected that she would snatch her hand away. Instead she looked at their hands and he thought he heard her swallow.

"A single rose," she said softly. "The touch of a single finger. Is this your idea of romancing me, Mr. Thorne?"

It would be a bit pathetic if it were true.

"If you expect grand gestures," he said, his voice low to match hers, "perhaps it is Rochford whose attentions you ought to encourage."

Her eyes came slowly to his and held there for a moment. And Lord, he thought, if he had a knife he would surely be able to cut through the air between them. It seemed like a tangible thing, fairly throbbing with tension. Then she sighed softly.

"And perhaps, Mr. Thorne," she said, "it is time we mingled with the other guests. I am going to see if there is anything my grandmother needs. Or my great-aunt."

She got to her feet, walked behind the stool, and made her way across the drawing room toward the Dowager Countess of Riverdale. Anthony Rochford met her halfway there, and they approached the dowager together.

Gabriel lowered the cover over the keys, got to his feet, and looked around before moving toward the closest group. Strangely, he had not even been thinking of romance when he had caressed the back of her finger.

He had only been feeling it.

# Ten

There was a letter among the usual invitations beside Gabriel's plate when he sat down to breakfast the following morning. It was a report from Simon Norton at Brierley. Gabriel read it while he sipped his coffee.

Manley Rochford was spending lavishly on new furniture and draperies inside the house and on new arbors and follies and other new ventures in the park. These included a wilderness walk over the hills behind the house and a lake in the southwest corner of the park.

Gabriel's eyes paused there. The southwest corner was where Mary had her cottage.

Manley and his wife were entertaining on a grand scale—teas and dinners and evening parties. There were plans in the making for a grand outdoor fete and evening ball during the summer, after their return from London as the Earl and Countess of Lyndale.

All the money that was being spent, Norton had discovered, had been borrowed on the expectation of the fortune

Mr. Rochford was about to inherit. That was something, at least, Gabriel thought. Manley had obviously not been able to get his hands on the fortune that was not yet officially his.

The next section of the letter was more disturbing, especially to a man who had made a bit of a name for himself in Boston for treating every last one of his employees well. There was some distress in the neighborhood affecting those servants who had lost their positions to the men Manley had brought with him to Brierley. In some instances their homes had also been confiscated and given to the new staff. Some of the dismissed servants had families, a fact that multiplied the suffering.

A few had been hired and accommodated elsewhere in the neighborhood. Others, notably those who were young and unattached, had moved away to look for work elsewhere. A few had been rehired at Brierley as farm laborers—at a wage not only below what they had earned in their previous positions but also below what the other farm laborers doing comparable work were earning. Some had found no work at all. Rumor had it, though Norton had not been able to substantiate it, that all wages were to go down once Manley became the earl. And, incidentally, Norton's own wages were lower than those of any of the other gardeners, though he was *not* complaining, he had added, since Mr. Thorne paid him well indeed for the steward's job he was not yet doing.

Norton had discovered that the newly installed steward, the one Manley had brought with him, had paid a call upon Miss Beck and, without a by-your-leave, had tramped through her cottage, upstairs and down, in muddy boots, peering into every room and cupboard and nook and cranny while ignoring her completely and kicking one of her cats out of his way and cuffing one of her dogs, which had been yapping at his heels. He had informed Miss Beck that she must clear out all her junk and get rid of all the strays without further delay. The cottage was to be converted into a rustic shelter to add a picturesque touch to an island that would stand in the middle of the new lake.

*Mary.*

Gabriel slammed one hand down on the report, closed his eyes, and concentrated upon breathing through the fury that tempted him to sweep all the unoffending dishes off the table around him for the mere satisfaction of hearing them smash on the floor.

And not just Mary. Innocent servants and their families had lost their employment for no just cause. Some of them were now homeless. Yet they were his. His people. Good God, they were his responsibility. For perhaps the first time he understood the selfishness of his own behavior in remaining in America for six years after learning that he had inherited the title, just because he was happy there and did not wish to upend his own life by returning to England. Yet sometimes duty ought to outweigh inclination. He should have known—and surely he had deep down—that Mary was not the only one who had suffered from his absence.

He was greatly to blame for the way things were.

There was one more section in the report. It contained information Norton had gathered while imbibing pints of ale at the village tavern during the evenings—*painfully slowly, sir, because I did not want to be too obvious with my questions and arouse suspicion.*

Mr. and Mrs. Ginsberg, once tenants on a farm owned by the late Earl of Lyndale, had moved away with their daughter, Miss Penelope Ginsberg, soon after the death of their son.

*It was said by someone who knew someone who knew*

*someone else . . . You know how gossip works, sir,* Norton had written, *that Mrs. Ginsberg died of grief not long after and that Miss Ginsberg has since married a man by the name of Clark. The couple is said to be living with her father and Mrs. Clark's son, now twelve years old, to whom she gave birth before her marriage.*

Norton could not vouch for the truth of the story, he admitted, since he had not yet had a chance to check it out for himself. He was a new employee at Brierley and could hardly ask for a three-day leave so soon. It would probably take him that long to get to Lilyvale, where they supposedly lived, do his investigation, and get back. The village was at least thirty miles from Brierley.

*It is generally, though not universally, believed by those who drink regularly at the tavern,* Norton had gone on to report, *that Gabriel Rochford—you, sir—is the father of the twelve-year-old boy. You were believed to be stepping out with the mother at the relevant time. There is much less agreement among the locals upon how Orson Ginsberg, the young lady's brother, came to his death. A duel gone wrong? Accident? They all have their proponents. The only thing everyone seems agreed upon is that young Ginsberg was shot in the back the same day Miss Ginsberg confessed to her parents that she was with child. There is also disagreement about who fired the fatal shot even though two men claimed to have witnessed you doing it, sir. Everyone I talked to, without exception, was adamant in his belief that if it was you, it was an accident and not murder. You just did not have it in you, one old-timer assured me, and there were plenty of other assenting voices. It is believed by almost all, sir, that you fled Brierley in order to avoid the hangman's noose, but opinion is divided upon whether it was an act of cowardice or prudence. There are a few—*

*pardon me for mentioning it, sir, but you did direct me to give you the full truth—who say you fled more to avoid taking responsibility for what you had done to Miss Ginsberg than out of fear of a noose.*

Gabriel folded the pages and set them aside. They left him with much to think about and a far greater sense of urgency than he had felt thus far. Also a new sense of guilt. How could he possibly have assumed that Mary was the only one who faced hardship and suffering from Manley Rochford?

He glanced through the small pile of invitations—another ball, a concert featuring a famed contralto, a garden party, an evening at Vauxhall with a party being put together by the Marquess and Marchioness of Dorchester. He paused over that last one. Dorchester was Lady Estelle Lamarr's father. Was there still a push on, then, to match her with him? It was surprising, if it was true, since she had made it clear she was not interested in him—or in any other man. Who else would be in the Vauxhall party? Lady Jessica Archer? It seemed a distinct possibility.

He thought about the evening before, particularly about the half hour or so he had spent virtually alone with her at the pianoforte. Something had happened in that short time. Something had changed. He was still determined to marry her, and still for the same reasons. But he had been thrown a bit off balance by the glimpses of humanity she had shown him—her flashing smiles, her laughter, her helpless giggles when she completely bungled their duet. And he had been oddly disturbed by that finger-touching incident. It was absurd enough to be embarrassing that that incident alone had kept him awake for at least an hour after he lay down last night. It was not, after all, as though he had stolen a kiss or fondled her in inappropriate places.

He had touched her finger, and for a few moments—not even long enough to allow him to catch the thought that had flitted into his mind and on out again—he had come close to understanding what romance was.

And perhaps what lay beyond romance.

*Would* she be at Vauxhall? Would Rochford? Gabriel's jaw tightened. That man, his second cousin once removed, was ambitious as well as conceited. His behavior was larded with false charm. Conceited men were often merely shallow, with nothing specifically vicious about them. Anthony Rochford was a malicious liar. And like a true coward, last night he had directed his malice at a man he supposed dead and unable to speak up for himself.

*Well enough,* he had said when Lady Estelle had asked him if he had known Gabriel Rochford. *He was a likable boy. I was fond of him. It grieved me to see his wildness turn into vice.*

Yet Anthony Rochford had never met him until very recently. Gabriel Rochford's behavior had always been as far from wild as north is from south. Any hard edges he had now were acquired in America. He remembered his boyhood self as quiet, studious, rather dull, too plagued by conscience and concern for the feelings of others to get into any real mischief. He had been his father's son, in other words. His first nine years had shaped his character and sensibilities.

*He was a likable boy.* Not only had Anthony Rochford never come to Brierley with his father while Gabriel was there, but he was also eight or nine years younger than Gabriel. He would have been only ten or eleven years old when Gabriel went to America.

There were two things he must do without further delay, Gabriel decided. He must marry Lady Jessica Archer—if she would have him. But first he must make a journey. It was time to take some action—almost seven years later than he ought.

He would accept the invitation to Vauxhall. It would probably be an enjoyable evening even if Lady Jessica was not of the party. He had heard that Vauxhall was a place one must see when one was in London. But he hoped she would be there. He could no longer indulge in social activities for the mere pleasure of them—not that he had done so from the beginning, of course. But he must develop a stronger sense of purpose.

He had arranged to spend the morning with Bertie Vickers. They were going to spar at Jackson's boxing saloon. Bertie was not an early riser, however. The breakfast things having been removed from the table, Gabriel sat down to write a letter to Simon Norton with instructions not to leave the estate. He would take care of further investigation himself. He wrote also to Miles Perrott, his partner in Boston, thrusting aside the wave of homesickness that threatened to engulf him as he did so. Boston was no longer home. It was regrettable, but he might as well grow accustomed to the new reality. He informed Miles that he would not be returning, at least not in the foreseeable future. He also wrote an acceptance of the invitation to Vauxhall.

This afternoon there was a garden party to which he had promised to escort Lady Vickers since both Sir Trevor and Bertie had other commitments. He would keep his promise.

Would Lady Jessica be there?

There was a long-stemmed pink rose beside Jessica's breakfast plate again. Beneath it, resting on her linen napkin, was a card that was a little different from usual. It had two words instead of one. *Gabriel Thorne,* he had written in the bold black handwriting she had come to recognize as his. The rose too was a little different. It was a darker shade of pink, very like the color of the ball gown she had worn to the Parley ball. She picked it up and held it to her nose for a few moments before taking her seat and nodding to the butler when he came to pour her coffee.

"Good morning, Jess," Avery said, lowering his paper far enough that he could see her over the top of it. "I had almost given up hope of seeing you this side of luncheon."

"I slept late," she told him, smiling at her mother as she spread her napkin across her lap. It was not a lie, but she had slept late only because she had been late going to sleep. Dawn had already been graying her room. Both Avery and her mother had finished their breakfast, she could see, but were reading over a final cup of coffee. Her mother was looking through the morning post. She set it all aside, however, after Jessica had sat down.

"Mr. Thorne plays the pianoforte extremely well," she said. "Where did he learn to play, Jessica? In America? Did he say?"

"He did not learn at all," Jessica said. "He plays by ear."

"Astonishing," her mother said. She nodded toward the rose. "I wonder if he sends a rose each day to other young ladies too. To Estelle, for example. Or is it just you?"

"I have no idea, Mama." Jessica laughed. "I could hardly ask him, could I? And I could hardly ask Estelle."

"Do you . . . *like* him?" her mother asked, half frowning. "He has certainly caught the imagination of the *ton* for some largely inexplicable reason. He is invited everywhere. But it is a bit puzzling, considering how little is known about him. Yes, he is Lady Vickers's kinsman and godson. But all families have a few ramshackle members one would not wish to see one's daughters marrying. How do we even know he has a fortune or where it comes from? Do we have any evidence but his word? And do we have even that? I have not heard that he has boasted of being wealthy. Which is to his credit, of course."

"I know no more about him than you do, Mama," Jessica said, not quite truthfully. "But does it matter? I am not about to elope to Gretna Green with him."

Avery set down his paper. "What a very tedious waste of time and effort that would be," he said, "when you are twenty-five years old, Jess, and could merely toddle along to the nearest church with a special license anytime you chose—just as Anna and I did once upon a time."

Jessica laughed again. "You must not worry, Mama," she said. "I have no intention of toddling along to the nearest church with Mr. Thorne any more than I have of running off to Scotland with him."

Anna came into the breakfast parlor at that moment. She was holding Beatrice, whose head was burrowed into the hollow between her shoulder and neck while she sucked loudly on one fist and cried with soft grizzling sounds. Her only visible cheek was bright red.

"I do apologize for being so late," Anna said. "Poor Bea really is cutting four teeth at once. We were quite right, Mother. And she will not let go of me, though Nurse tried several times to take her. Bea would only scream."

Avery had got to his feet, but it was Jessica's mother who was first to move around the table. "You are spoiling her, Anna," she said. "Let us see if she will allow her grandmother to spoil her instead so that you can eat. I have finished already. Come, chicken. Come and tell Grandmama what is wrong. Yes, I know. The whole world is against you, is it not?"

She eased the baby from Anna's arms into her own as she spoke, and miraculously Bea snuggled into her and even stopped grizzling for a moment.

"The magic touch," Anna said. "You have had it with all four of the children, Mother. Thank you."

"On behalf of my valet," Avery added, "a million thanks, Mother. He has a way of *not* complaining when I arrive in my room with one half of my neckcloth limp and soggy that I find quite unnerving."

Jessica's mother remained on her feet and rocked the baby against her shoulder, murmuring nonsense as she did so. Beatrice, still sucking on her fist, seemed to be falling asleep.

"Ah," Anna said. "Another rose. I do like Mr. Thorne's style. I assume the rose *is* from him? A bouquet was being delivered as I was coming through the hall just now. A very large one. I am guessing it is for you, Jessica, and that it is from Mr. Rochford again. He is paying quite determined court to you. He scarcely left your side last evening except when you were at the pianoforte with Mr. Thorne."

"It was very gratifying," Jessica's mother murmured. "And he was very deferential to Mama and Aunt Edith."

"A little too deferential?" Jessica said, and her eyes met her brother's across the table. He raised his eyebrows. "What do you know of his cousin, Avery?"

"His cousin?" he said. "The missing earl, do you mean? Next to nothing except that he is missing and presumed dead."

"His name was Gabriel," Jessica said—and, when his eyebrows remained aloft, "It is Mr. Thorne's name too."

"Ah," he said. "Are you seeing some intrigue at work, Jess? Are they one and the same, do you suppose?" He waggled his eyebrows at her.

"I do not suppose it for a single moment," she said. "*Gabriel* is hardly a unique name."

"Quite so," he said, but his eyes remained thoughtfully upon her while Anna talked of Mr. Thorne's playing last night.

"I could listen to him for a whole evening without growing weary," she said. "Did you notice, Jessica, that his eyes were closed much of the time while he played Bach and there was a slight frown between his brows? It was clear he felt the music right down to the depths of his soul."

"I did notice," Jessica said. "I was very glad I had played first."

"Until now," Anna said, "you have resisted all attempts to pay you serious court, Jessica. Is this year to change all that? With Mr. Rochford and his charm and his lavish compliments and large bouquets, perhaps? Or with Mr. Thorne and his mysterious silences and single roses and heavenly music? With both?"

"Or perhaps with neither," Jessica said. "Are you tired of having me forever underfoot, then, Anna?"

"Oh heavens," Anna cried, reaching across the distance between them to squeeze Jessica's hand. "Never. Oh, absolutely not, Jessica. I could never have too much family. Nor could I love the one I have more deeply than I do. That was not my meaning *at all*."

"I know it was not," Jessica assured her, squeezing her hand back.

Anna had spent twenty-two of her first twenty-five years at an orphanage in Bath, knowing herself only as Anna Snow, Snow being her mother's maiden name, though she had not known that either. When she had discovered that she was Lady Anastasia Westcott, the legitimate daughter—and only legitimate child, as it happened—of the late Earl of Riverdale, it might have been expected that she would be bitter, that she would resent the family ties and the life of privilege all the other Westcotts shared. Instead she had loved them resolutely and fiercely almost from the first moment, even while some of them had resented her.

Jessica had hated her—she had come, seemingly from nowhere, to wreck Abby's life as well as Camille's and Harry's, and to destroy her own dreams. It had taken her a long time to accept Anna as part of the Westcott family, then as Avery's wife, her own sister-in-law and cousin. It had taken even longer to love her.

Avery's eyes were resting upon Anna across the table. It often shocked Jessica to note that despite the almost bored expression her brother wore habitually in company, there was something in his eyes whenever he looked at his wife that spoke of fathomless depths of . . . Of what? Love? Passion? *Passion* seemed too strong a word to use of the indolent Avery, but appearances could be deceptive, Jessica thought. She was sure there must be a well of passion in him that very few people would suspect.

Oh, she thought with a sudden wave of unexpected yearning, how could she possibly be planning this year merely to *settle* for an eligible match? She wanted what Avery and Anna had. She wanted what Alexander and Wren had and Elizabeth and Colin. And Abby and Gil.

She wanted love. Even more than that, she wanted *passion.*

And she thought of that silly little detail that had kept her awake through most of the night, tossing and turning in her bed, punching and reshaping her pillow. She thought of Mr. Thorne's little finger caressing hers upon the pianoforte keys, very lightly, very deliberately. Very briefly. How idiotic in the extreme that such a thing could have robbed her of a night's sleep. If she were to tell anyone, she would be laughed off the face of the earth. She had felt that touch sizzle—yes, it was the only appropriate word—through her whole body, warming her cheeks, setting her heart to beating faster, creating a strange ache low in her abdomen and down along her inner thighs to her knees. Her toes had curled up inside her evening slippers.

She had wanted to weep.

She had asked him to romance her and had expected—if she had expected him to take up the challenge at all, though he had said he would—lavish gestures, similar to what she was getting from Mr. Rochford. Instead, in all the days since, she had had a pink rose each morning and a touch of his little finger to hers last evening.

It *was* laughable.

But she still, even after a few hours of sleep, felt like weeping.

She wanted . . .

Oh, she wanted and wanted and wanted.

What Avery had.

What Alexander had.

What Elizabeth and Camille and Abby had. And Aunt Matilda.

She *wanted*.

"Mr. Rochford has asked to take you rowing on the Thames this afternoon during the garden party?" her mother asked, speaking softly so as not to wake the baby.

"Yes," Jessica said, "I promised that I would go out in one of the boats with him."

"It is going to be a lovely day," Anna said. "It already is."

Jessica wished it were raining. She really did not like Mr. Rochford, she had decided last evening. He tried too hard to be charming and deferential. He smiled too much.

All of which she might have ignored or at least excused on the grounds that he had not been to London before and was new to the position of prominence with the *ton* into which his prospects had thrown him even though his father was not yet officially the Earl of Lyndale. What had turned the tide against him last evening was the story he had told about the supposedly dead earl, his cousin. It might be perfectly true. She had no reason to believe it was not. But it included serious charges, involving even debauchery and murder. Ought he to have volunteered that information to a group of strangers in the middle of a party? About his own family? He had shown poor taste at best. At worst, he had been deliberately smearing the name of his father's predecessor in order to make himself and his father look better by contrast. More legitimate, perhaps. How unnecessary. The law itself was about to make them legitimate.

Would she have been so offended if his dead cousin had not happened to have the same name as Mr. Thorne?

*Gabriel?*

Yes, of course she would. She did not like to hear people blackening the reputation of someone who was incapable of defending himself—or herself. Especially that of a relative. She could not imagine any of the Westcotts doing such a thing.

"You are right," she said in answer to Anna's comment. "It is not even windy. It is going to be a perfect day for a garden party."

After a few hours spent at the House of Lords, Avery Archer, Duke of Netherby, and Alexander Westcott, Earl of Riverdale, had a late luncheon together at White's Club.

They were not natural friends. At one time Alexander

had viewed Avery as little more than an indolent fop, while Avery had considered Alexander a bit of a straitlaced bore. But that was before Harry was stripped of the earldom and his title and entailed properties passed to Alexander, a mere second cousin. It was before Avery married Lady Anastasia Westcott, the late earl's newly discovered and very legitimate daughter. The crisis, or rather the series of crises that arose from those events and subsequent ones, had thrown the two men together on a number of occasions, not the least of which was a duel at which Avery fought—and won—and Alexander acted as his second. Their encounters had given them at first a grudging respect for each other and finally a cautious sort of friendship.

They spoke of House business and politics and world affairs in general while they ate. Once Avery discouraged a mutual acquaintance from joining them by raising his quizzing glass halfway to his eye, bidding the man a courteous but rather distant good day, and pointedly *not* asking for his company.

After their coffee had been served, Avery changed the subject.

"To what do I owe this very kind invitation?" he asked.

Alexander leaned back in his chair and set his linen napkin beside his saucer. "Jessica is giving serious consideration to settling down at last, is she?" he asked.

Avery raised his eyebrows. "If she is," he said, "she has not confided in me. Nor would I encourage her to do so. That is a matter for my stepmother to worry her head over. Or not. My sister is of age and has been for several years."

"What do you think of Rochford as a suitor for her hand?" Alexander asked.

"Do I have to think anything?" Avery sounded pained. "But it seems I must. You invited me to have luncheon with you for this exact purpose, I suppose." Avery sighed, and then continued. "He is perfectly eligible and will be more so very soon unless the missing earl should suddenly drop down from the heavens into our midst at the last possible moment like a bad melodrama. Rochford has obviously set his sights upon Jessica. Equally obviously, the usual family committee has decided to promote the match and throw them together at every turn. Why else would he have been invited to your sister's supposedly exclusive party last evening? I understand Jessica is to go out with him in a boat small enough to allow for only one rower and one passenger at a garden party this afternoon. One would hope his manners are polished enough that he will volunteer to be the rower."

"Do you like him?" Alexander was frowning.

"I do not have to," Avery said as he stirred his coffee. "Jessica would be the one marrying him. But as far as I am concerned, the man has too many teeth, and he displays them far too often. He also has abysmal taste in waistcoats. But he may have myriad other virtues to atone for those vices. And I would not be called upon to look upon either the teeth or his waistcoats with any great frequency if Jess were to marry him. Do I assume you do *not* like him? On the slight acquaintance of one evening spent in his company?"

"What do you know of Gabriel Rochford?" Alexander asked. "The missing earl."

"Nothing," Avery said after taking a drink and setting his cup back in its saucer. "Except that he *is* missing and that he shares an angelic first name with Thorne. But the world, I must believe, contains a fair smattering of other Gabriels."

"How long has the earl been missing?" Alexander asked. "Do you know?"

"I do not," Avery said. "Is the question relevant to anything?"

"Rochford told a story last evening," Alexander said. "Jessica heard it. So did Elizabeth and a few other guests. Estelle was part of the group. So was young Peter. It was not a suitable story for such an audience and such an occasion. Both Elizabeth and I turned the conversation to other topics as soon as we could, but we could hardly interrupt him midsentence. Of course, if you had been there with your quizzing glass and your ducal stare, he would have been muzzled far sooner."

"Dear me," Avery muttered.

"He told a story of his cousin's wild ways," Alexander said, "culminating in what he hinted was the rape of a neighbor's daughter and the murder of her brother. After which he fled to escape the hangman's noose."

"Who would not, given the opportunity?" Avery said. "And all this was recounted in my sister's hearing? And in your sister's? Perhaps there will now be more to my distaste for the man than his teeth and his waistcoats."

"As head of the Westcott family," Alexander said, "it concerns me that Jessica may be considering marriage to a man of . . . shall we say questionable good taste? Perhaps even spite, since the missing earl was not present to speak for himself. Of course, she is also a member of the Archer family, of which you are the head."

"You are begging me to exert myself, I understand, while assuring me that *you* will exert *yourself*," Avery said. "How very tedious life becomes at times. Is it known how long ago the alleged rape and murder happened?"

"No," Alexander said. "But it should be easy enough to find out. It should be possible also to discover how long Gabriel Thorne was in America before returning recently for a reason so vaguely explained that really it is no explanation at all."

"You have been busy for a man who returned to London only a couple of days ago," Avery said. He nodded to a waiter, who refilled his cup.

Alexander made a face at his own cup, with its cold coffee, and the waiter replaced it. "I probably have a foolishly suspicious mind," he said. "That is what Wren told me last night anyway. She pointed out that Rochford is an extraordinarily handsome man—her words. She also added, however, that if he were applying for employment at her glassmaking works, she would reject him even before studying his credentials. Any man who smiles so much, she said, must be assumed to have a shallow, even devious, mind."

"I must be careful not to smile overmuch in the presence of the Countess of Riverdale," Avery said with a shudder.

Alexander laughed. "I cannot imagine," he said, "that Wren would ever accuse you of having a shallow mind, Netherby. Or of smiling too much. She admires you greatly. But what of Thorne? If he is not making a play for Jessica too, I will eat my hat."

"Not the gray beaver," Avery said, looking pained again. "It sounds like a recipe for indigestion."

"What do you know of him?" Alexander asked.

"Next to nothing," Avery told him. "Little more, in fact, than I know of the missing earl. He has good taste in horses and curricles. He is of that rare breed of mortal that can produce exquisite music from a pianoforte without any formal training at all, or even any informal training, if Jessica is to be believed. He favors single-flower tributes to ladies he admires rather than bouquets so large it apparently takes two of my footmen to convey them to the drawing room. I believe, before you can demand an answer of me, that I must like him. Though being asked to express any sort of affection for someone outside my own family circle has a tendency to bore me."

"Ah," Alexander said. "But if Thorne has his way, Netherby, he will be a part of your inner family circle, will he not? And a Westcott by marriage."

"But not yet," Avery said softly. "Drink your coffee, Riverdale. You have already allowed one cup to develop a disgusting gray film."

Alexander picked up his cup and drank. "There is one detail, I must confess," he said, "that would appear to throw cold water on my suspicions. Rochford knew his cousin, the missing earl. Yet he showed no recognition of the man who admitted to having the same first name as the earl."

"Ah," Avery said. "But have we established that Rochford is a truthful man?"

# Eleven

L ady Vickers had gladly accepted Gabriel's offer to escort her to a garden party in Richmond that she wished to attend and to which he had also been invited.

"The house overlooks the river," she explained to him in the carriage, "and the garden is glorious. Far more so than the interior of the house itself, which I always find surprisingly gloomy. One would think that whoever designed it would have thought to insist upon large windows facing the river, would one not? And that the occupants would not have chosen to cover what windows there are with gauzy curtains to preserve their privacy? Privacy from what, pray? The ducks? The hothouses alone are worth every mile of the tedious drive, however. You must not miss them, Gabriel. Or the rose arbor, which is built on three tiers. If you like rowing, there are several boats. And the food is always plentiful and delicious. The lobster patties are as good as any I have tasted anywhere."

"You have persuaded me that I will enjoy myself," he

told her. "But I would be delighted to escort you, ma'am, even if the garden were a scrubby piece of faded grass abutting on a marsh, with only stale cake and weak tea for refreshments."

"Oh, you shameless charmer," she said, laughing as she slapped his arm.

He did not see much of her once they arrived. She introduced him to their hostess and a few other people, some of whom he had met before, and was then borne away by a couple of older ladies to join friends who had found seats in the shelter of a large oak tree down by the river.

"You will not wish to sit with a group of old ladies, Gabriel," Lady Vickers informed him. "Stay here and enjoy yourself."

He bowed to her and winked when the other two ladies had turned away.

Over the next half hour he was drawn into a few groups of fellow guests up on the terrace, most notably one that included a mother and her three young daughters, one of whom had her betrothed with her, a thin and chinless young man who looked as though his neckcloth had been tied too tightly. The other two simpered and giggled and blushed and had no conversation whatsoever beyond monosyllabic answers to any questions he posed them.

Gabriel found himself smiling at them in fond understanding while he conversed with their mother and the fiancé. He noticed that avuncular feeling coming over him again. Was he seriously considered husband material for girls who were only just beginning to leave their childhood behind? All upon the strength of an undisclosed American past and an unconfirmed fortune—and the fact that he was Sir Trevor Vickers's godson?

Lady Estelle Lamarr, strolling past on the lawn below

with her brother, must have assessed the situation at one glance. "Mr. Thorne," she called, beckoning with the hand that was not holding a parasol over her head, "do come walking with us. We are going to look at the boats to decide if they are safe to ride in."

"*You* are going to decide, Stell," Bertrand Lamarr said as Gabriel approached them. "You are the one who is so afraid of water it is a wonder you ever even wash your face."

Lady Estelle linked her arm through Gabriel's. "The trouble with having a twin brother, Mr. Thorne," she said, "is that he will blurt out one's deepest, most mortifying secrets to the very people one is most trying to impress."

"You are trying to impress me?" Gabriel asked.

"But of course," she said. "I am intended for you, am I not, by all the aunts and cousins from my adopted family? Oh, you need not look so aghast, Bertrand. Mr. Thorne and I had a frank chat about the whole thing last evening and understand each other perfectly."

Her brother and Gabriel exchanged grins over her head.

"I did not initiate that conversation, I would hasten to add," Gabriel told him.

"Of course you did not," Lady Estelle said. "You are too much the gentleman. But everyone with eyes in his head—or hers—ought to have been able to see last night that it is Jessica and you, Mr. Thorne, not me and you."

"*Stell!*" her brother scolded. "You will be putting Mr. Thorne to the blush, and all because he and Jessica played a duet together on the pianoforte last evening that ended in disaster and laughter. And—to change the subject—you see? I count five boats, and none of them have capsized. None of them are sinking or rocking out of control. No one in them looks anywhere close to panicking."

"But how do we know," she said, "that there are not sup-posed to be *six* boats out there? Where, oh where is the sixth?"

Gabriel laughed.

And rowing one of those five boats, he saw, was An-thony Rochford. Sitting facing him, her posture graceful and relaxed, was Lady Jessica Archer, the picture of sum-mer beauty in a flimsy-looking dress of primrose yellow with a matching parasol that was raised over a straw bon-net. She was smiling and saying something. Rochford—it hardly needed stating—was smiling back with dazzling intensity.

Lady Estelle had seen them too. "Do you think, Mr. Thorne," she asked, "that the missing earl is really dead? Or has he remained in hiding because he fears the conse-quences of making himself known?"

"If he is dead," Gabriel said, "he must have died young. Of what? one wonders. And why should he fear if he was an innocent man? Perhaps he had nothing to do with what-ever happened to his neighbor's daughter or with the death of her brother. Or perhaps he was guilty in both instances and was the blackest-hearted of villains. Perhaps he simply died of his sins. Perhaps we will never know the answers. Would that be so very bad?"

"Indeed it would," she said. "Curiosity demands satis-faction."

"But as Papa remarked last evening on our way home, Stell," her brother said, "it was not at all the thing for Roch-ford to tell such a story concerning his own family. And with ladies present. I can only applaud Alexander and Eliz-abeth for pointedly changing the subject, though I know you wish they had not."

"But it was such a fascinating story," she protested. "A

wronged woman. Her irate brother. Imagine if it were you and me, Bertrand. A killing—a shot in the back. And his supposed killer fleeing for his life and disappearing off the face of the earth only to become in future years a missing earl. An earl about to be declared dead and replaced by another, more virtuous candidate. A new earl with a handsome son who is pursuing Jessica with all the charm he can muster. I have not been so well entertained in years. And that is nonsense, what you implied about a woman's sensibilities being so delicate that she cannot hear about death and mayhem without swooning. It is no wonder our lives are often so dull. Leave it to men to decide what is good for us."

They were met at the riverbank by other guests, who were either waiting for a boat to be free or watching those who were already out or simply enjoying the scenery and the sunshine. Viscountess Dirkson and Mrs. Westcott, the Earl of Riverdale's mother, engaged them in conversation. The former looked thoughtfully from Gabriel to Lady Estelle as they talked, while the latter beamed at them rather complacently as though she were solely responsible for their being together. A Mr. and Miss Keithley, also brother and sister, came to talk with Lamarr and Lady Estelle and were introduced to Gabriel.

"Ah, the American," Keithley said as he shook hands. "I have been hearing a lot about you. A pleasure to make your acquaintance, Thorne."

His sister blushed.

Over to one side, under the broad shade of a giant oak, Lady Vickers sat with four other ladies. She smiled and waved to Gabriel, and he raised a hand in return.

"Mr. Thorne," the viscountess said, drawing him a little apart. "Charles and I are planning a soiree of our own this year, as we did last year. It gave us so much pleasure. It was a bit of a concert too, though nothing very formal. We had a tenor soloist, one of Charles's friends, who always insists quite wrongly that he has no particular talent, and a harpist who played and sang some traditional Welsh tunes and reduced me to tears though she sang in Welsh and I did not understand a word. There was also a chamber group— pianoforte, violin, and cello. Charles and I spoke about you after Elizabeth and Colin's party, and we were both agreed. Mr. Thorne, *will* you come this year, and *will* you play for us? The Bach piece you played the other evening and maybe two or three more?"

Oh good God.

"Ma'am," he said, "I am honored. But I do not normally play in public, you know. And I have no formal training. I do not even read music."

"Oh, I know," she said, beaming at him. "That is part of your appeal. You have a . . . How did Charles phrase it? Ah yes. You have a raw and rare talent. Do please share it at our soiree. You will make me very happy."

She was a Westcott, Lady Jessica Archer's aunt, if he remembered correctly, her mother's sister. She lacked the inherent haughtiness of demeanor of the rest of the family. There seemed even an anxious sort of humility about her. She also had a smile that went deeper than mere sociability. He instinctively liked Lady Dirkson. But at the present moment he wished like the devil he did not.

*Play* at a soiree? As a featured artist in an impromptu concert that would not be impromptu at all? He would not get a wink of sleep between now and then. And how would he practice? Was there a pianoforte at the hotel? If there was, he had not seen it. But when had he ever practiced? Would not practice invite disaster, since he would be preparing with his head? His music did not come from his head.

The viscountess was looking at him with what he could describe to himself only as naked hope.

"It would be my honor, ma'am," he said. "But do not expect great things. I might ruin your whole evening. You must have heard how my duet with Lady Jessica Archer ended. You were there."

"Oh, *thank* you," she said, clasping her hands to her bosom. "You have no idea . . . I composed four separate letters to you this morning, and I tore all four to shreds. Charles laughed at me, but he would not try writing one himself. I shall find him immediately and tell him of my triumph. I shall even gloat. But he will be as delighted as I." She turned to summon Mrs. Westcott but spoke to Gabriel again before she moved away. "And you and Jessica were doing very well with your duet until you decided to challenge each other by playing faster and faster. You had me laughing, the two of you."

A couple of the boats had come in. One of them had already been taken, and Lamarr was persuading Miss Keithley to go out in the other with him. The viscountess and Mrs. Westcott were moving off in the direction of the house, presumably to find Charles, who Gabriel assumed was Viscount Dirkson. Lady Estelle, in conversation with Keithley, broke off what she was saying to hail Lady Jessica Archer and Rochford.

"You must tell me, Mr. Rochford," she said, "what it feels like to be out on such a broad expanse of water in such a frail craft."

"But it is not frail at all," he told her. "And I have some skill at the oars. Lady Jessica was perfectly safe with me, I assure you. If this gentleman is planning to take you out—"

"Lady Jessica," Gabriel said, turning to her. "I have been told on no account to miss the hothouses while I am here. Have you been inside them yet?"

"I have not," she said, twirling her primrose parasol like an extra little sun behind her straw bonnet. "Am I about to?"

"Yes," he said, offering his arm. "We will see you all later on the terrace for tea," he told the others.

For a moment it looked as though Rochford was going to come with them, but Lady Estelle had not finished with him. Her feet firmly planted on the riverbank, she asked him a further question about the boats. At the same time, she threw Gabriel a blatantly mischievous glance and waggled her fingers at him in farewell.

That was one very interesting young lady, he thought.

He could feel the heat of Lady Jessica's hand through his sleeve. He could smell her perfume, or was it soap? It was a warm, pleasant scent, whatever it was. He had noticed it last evening too when he had sat beside her on the pianoforte bench.

"Can you swim?" he asked her.

She looked at him in apparent surprise. "Well enough to keep myself afloat if a boat I am in should capsize within sight of land," she said. "If that was what you were asking."

"It was," he told her. "All too many people think it wondrously picturesque and romantic to be rowed about on a lake or river without even considering the very real danger of drowning."

"Is this your roundabout way of saying I looked both romantic and picturesque out on the water just now?" she asked. She was playing the haughty grand lady again. Or perhaps there was no playacting involved. This outer demeanor seemed to come naturally to her.

"No," he said. "It is my way of saying I am glad you are able to swim."

"My safety matters to you, then, does it?" she asked him.

"Since I intend to marry you," he told her, "of course. I can hardly marry a dead bride."

"Ah. That is still your intention, then, is it?" she said. "But are you not afraid Mr. Rochford will snatch me from under your very nose?"

"No," he said.

"He is very attentive," she said, "and very charming. Not to mention handsome."

"I have a higher opinion of your intelligence," he said.

"But he will be an earl one day," she said.

"Perhaps."

There was a brief silence before she spoke again. "And you, Mr. *Gabriel* Thorne," she said. "What do you have to offer the daughter and sister of a duke? Will *you* be an earl one day?"

Was he mistaken or had she put a slight emphasis upon his first name?

They met Boris Wayne, one of Lord Molenor's sons, and Adrian Sawyer, Viscount Dirkson's son, at that moment. Each had a young lady on his arm—the very two with whom Gabriel had tried and failed to make conversation earlier. There was a merry exchange of greetings. The four of them were on their way down to the river to see if there were any boats free.

"We are going to see the hothouses," Lady Jessica told them.

"I would not bother if I were you, Jess," Boris Wayne advised. "We were just there and they are very hot inside and very full of people. Who wants to be jostled by the multitudes just for the pleasure of cooking as one gazes at row upon row of orange trees? We stayed for three minutes total."

"Two," the young lady on his arm said. And giggled.

"And a half," her sister added—and giggled.

"There is a floral clock through there," Adrian Sawyer told them, pointing to a high privet hedge to his right, "and an impressive fountain. And there is the rose arbor up beside the house. Someone told me there are a thousand blooms there, but I did not stop to count."

The sisters thought that deserved another burst of glee.

"The air is cooler out on the river," Lady Jessica said. "Enjoy the boats."

The four of them went on their way, chatting and laughing.

"They were mute when I met them earlier with their mother and eldest sister," Gabriel said. "Giggling, but otherwise mute."

"Doubtless they were intimidated by your solemn grandeur," Lady Jessica said. "And your advanced age."

"Do you think?" he asked.

"I think," she said.

"I suppose," he said, "I ought to have realized that if the hothouses were recommended to me, they would be recommended to multitudes of others too. Shall we forget about them? Go to the rose arbor instead?"

"To see a thousand roses?" she said. "By all means. It will make a change from gazing upon a single one."

"Are you offended by those?" he asked her.

She turned her head to look at him again. Her parasol made a lacy pattern of sunshine and shade across her face beneath the brim of her bonnet. She was very beautiful. It was not an original observation, but her good looks were a constant source of wonder to him.

"No." She hesitated. "Quite the contrary."

Crowds seemed to be gathering on the terrace and the reason became obvious as they drew closer. Tea was being set out on long tables covered with white cloths, and it did indeed look like the veritable feast Lady Vickers had predicted. Servants were setting up small tables and chairs on what was left of the terrace and on the lawn below.

"Are you hungry?" Gabriel asked.

"I would rather go to the rose arbor," she said.

Interesting. She might have lost him easily enough among the crowds gathering about the food tables—if she wished to do so, that was. Apparently she did not.

He expected that the rose arbor would be crowded too, and probably it had been until a short while ago. Now there was only one group of people on the lower tier, deep in animated conversation. The second and top tiers appeared to be deserted. Tea had been deemed of more interest than roses.

It was an impressive part of the garden, running along the whole width of the house as it did. There were trellises, archways, hedges, flower beds, low walls, the wall of the house itself, all of them loaded with roses at various stages of blooming. A high hedge, cut with geometric precision, extended all the way down the side of the arbor farthest from the house, giving the impression of deep seclusion and the reality of breathtaking beauty. Even the sounds of voices and laughter seemed muted here.

"I think," Lady Jessica said, "this is what heaven must smell like." She closed her eyes and inhaled slowly.

"We will have to be very virtuous for the rest of our lives, then," he said, "so that we may enjoy it together for eternity."

"Which might be an embarrassment," she said, opening

her eyes, "if I should end up with a different husband and you with a different wife."

"Impossible," he said.

"Do you always get your own way, Mr. Thorne?" she asked, cupping a yellow rose in both hands, though she was not quite touching it, he noticed.

"Only in the important things," he said.

"And I am important?"

"Yes."

She looked around until she saw a wrought iron seat close to the wall of the house, with its climbing rose plants, and went to sit on it. She left room for him beside her. The floor of this top tier was paved with pinkish brick. There was a small fountain in the middle, its granite basin shaped like a fully opened rose.

"Is Thorne your real name?" she asked him.

Ah.

"Yes," he said.

"Not Rochford?" she asked.

"No."

She closed her parasol and set it down on the seat beside her. "I believe you are lying," she said.

"You think I am the long-lost earl, then?" he asked her. "Just because I share a first name with him?"

She looked up at him as he stood by the fountain, his hands clasped at his back, and her eyes roamed over him. "*Are* you?" she asked, her voice so soft it was hardly audible.

He gazed back. Secrecy had not been his original plan when he decided to come to London rather than go direct to Brierley. He had merely wanted to be better prepared to go there. He had wanted to look like an English gentleman for starters. He had wanted to hire a good lawyer and agent

and acquire an experienced, reliable steward. He had
wanted to find out what he needed to do to verify his identity and establish his claim. He had wanted, perhaps, to find
out if there might be any trouble awaiting him—legal trouble, that was—though he did not believe there would be
anything he could not handle. He was no longer the frightened boy who had fled England thirteen years ago. Too
many details were circumstantial at best, and he had a decent though not infallible alibi. But there might be some
sort of trouble facing him anyway, in the form of resentment, even outright hostility, from the people living in the
vicinity of Brierley. He had always had a decent relationship with almost everyone, but things might have changed
at the end and been perpetuated by his absence. He had felt
it wise to find out what he could before he went there so that
he would know exactly what he was facing. Mary could not
be expected to know everything. She lived the life of a near
hermit.

He had not intended any great secrecy, then. If he had,
he would surely have changed his first name, which, though
not unique, was not common either. He wondered if Lady
Jessica was the only one who had guessed the truth. Several
other people, including Anthony Rochford himself, had
heard him own to the name *Gabriel* last evening.

But he had been asked a question. And a lie was point-
less. Lies usually were.

"Thorne was my mother's name," he told her, "and that
of her cousin in Boston. He officially adopted me as his son
after I had lived there and worked for him for six years. His
wife was dead and he had no children of his own. My name
was legally changed, with my full consent. I had used it
when I took passage to America, and I had used it there.
I would rather be a Thorne than a Rochford, though I do

regret any disrespect that shows to my father, who was a decent man."

"You are the Earl of Lyndale," she said. She appeared to be speaking more to herself than to him.

"Regrettably," he said.

"Why do you regret it?" She frowned.

"I was happy in America," he said. "I was never happy at Brierley."

"Why have you returned, then?" she asked him. "Why have you not just let everyone continue to assume you are dead? Or perhaps you still intend to do so. Perhaps you have come here to amuse yourself before returning to the life that makes you happy. But no, that cannot be your intention. Why would you hope to marry me if you intended to resume your life as Mr. Thorne, wealthy businessman from Boston? Your wishing to marry me makes sense only if you intend to be the Earl of Lyndale."

He moved closer to her and stood looking down at her for a while before setting one booted foot against the edge of the seat beside her and resting one forearm across his thigh. "Why have I returned?" he said. "And why have I decided to stay? Call it duty, if you will, to those who work—or worked—at the house and on the estate."

"Have you known all this time that your uncle and cousin were dead?" she asked him.

"For most of the time, yes," he said. "Letters are slow in crossing the Atlantic, especially in winter."

"So why now?" she asked him. "Just for the sheer satanic pleasure of raising hope in the man who believes he is about to become the earl and owner of Brierley and any fortune that goes with it? And in his son? And then of dashing those hopes at the last possible moment?"

"There is one person at Brierley," he said, "who is and

always has been very dear to me. She lives in a small cottage in the park that surrounds the house. She has been threatened with eviction when the new earl comes into his inheritance. He plans to have a lake created out of the land around her cottage. He plans to use the house itself as a picturesque sort of folly on an island in the middle of it. She has nothing beyond the cottage itself and the small allowance my uncle made her. That has already been stopped, though there is no one at Brierley with any legal right to have made that decision. She is about to be destitute, with no way of providing for herself. It is for Mary I returned, Lady Jessica."

She was gazing up at him, her eyes wide, her lips slightly parted.

"She is my late aunt's sister," he told her. "She was born with a deformed back and foot and hand. She takes in stray cats and dogs and any troubled wild creatures that come her way. The gardeners occasionally bring her wounded birds and she mends their wings and sets them free. She has a garden that rivals this in beauty." He gestured at the arbor around them. "I have never known anyone so contented with her life or anyone so . . . *good*. I love her. Not in *that* way. I honor and love her and would die for her."

Good God. Where were such words coming from? He felt suddenly foolish. But Mary *deserved* to be honored.

"But as it happened," she said, "you were not called upon to die for her but simply to come home. To give up everything you held dear for her sake. A sort of death in itself."

"For the only time since I have known her," he said, "she asked something of me. She asked me to come. And here I am."

He was astounded suddenly when her eyes, still riveted

on his face, grew bright with unshed tears. She caught her upper lip between her teeth.

"I would rather keep my anonymity for a short while longer," he said. "I would like to gather a little more information than I already have. Mary, it seems, is not the only one who has been made to suffer. I blame myself for not having realized the danger of that before I came here—or perhaps of refusing to consider the possibility of it. I am indeed no angel, despite my name. I believe too I would like to meet my cousin again before divulging the truth. The one who is about to be earl."

She released her lip. "Why has Mr. Anthony Rochford not recognized you?" she asked him.

"He has never seen me before now," he said. "He was just a young boy when I went to America. Whenever his mother and father came to Brierley, which happened quite frequently, he was left at home."

He watched her draw a slow breath. "I will not give away your secret," she said.

"Thank you."

She looked down at her hands spread on her lap for a few moments and then at the fountain and then back at him. He held her eyes with his own.

"I would have to be a dreadful slowtop to waste an opportunity for a little romance in such idyllic surroundings," he said.

He gave her time to turn her head away or get to her feet and suggest they go for tea on the terrace. She did neither. She licked her lips in what was surely not meant to be a provocative gesture, though it brought his eyes to her mouth. He moved his own closer and raised his eyes to hers again. She gazed back.

And he kissed her.

It was a mere touching of lips. A lingering touch. He had sensed from the moment she had demanded that he romance her if he wanted a chance with her that she would scorn any aggressive moves to take her heart by storm. Her heart was not easily taken, he had judged. Hence the single rose sent to her each morning and the music he had played for her last evening and the duet. And the touch of his little finger to hers, though there had been nothing deliberate or planned about that.

And hence this kiss, which was hardly a kiss at all except that it did things to his body and his heartbeat and his mind that far more lascivious embraces with other women had never done. It moved him somehow into a physical space that was neither his nor hers but something else without a name. It was shockingly, inexplicably intimate.

And he wanted more. By God, he wanted more.

He did not take more, except that he set his fingertips against her jaw, and when he drew back his head and gazed into her eyes again, he ran his thumb lightly over her slightly parted lips.

She smiled fleetingly and moved her own head back.

"You have a strange idea of romance, Mr. Thorne," she said. But she did not say what she meant by that and he did not ask.

"If we do not go for tea soon," he said, "the food will be carried back indoors and we will go hungry."

"That would be a ghastly fate," she said. "Let us go by all means. I daresay my mother is wondering where I am."

"Especially if she has seen Rochford and you are not with him," he said. "I gather your family is trying to promote a match between the two of you?"

"Just as they are trying to promote one between you and Estelle," she said. "Being a member of the Westcott family can be a severe trial. And a great joy. Frequently frustrating and endlessly entertaining."

"I look forward to becoming a part of it," he told her, removing his fingertips from her jaw and returning his foot to the ground.

"And there you go again," she said. "Making assumptions." But she did not sound annoyed with him this time.

# Twelve

M r. Rochford was expected at Archer House. He had begged for the honor, and it had been granted. Jessica was wearing one of her new dresses, a sprigged muslin she thought would be more suited to a garden party like the one she had attended the day before yesterday. But her mother had suggested it for today. Her mother had also come to her dressing room in person to suggest that Ruth dress her hair in its usual upswept style, but a little fussier than usual for the daytime, with perhaps a few curled tendrils to trail over her ears and along her neck. Ruth had done a perfect job of it, as usual.

Anna had gone with Cousin Elizabeth and all their children except Beatrice to visit Wren and her children. Jessica was sitting in the drawing room with her mother when they heard Mr. Rochford arrive. But she did not listen for footsteps on the stairs. He was not coming to call upon her. Not yet. He had asked to wait upon Avery.

Last evening at a literary evening Jessica had attended

because it was given by one of her friends, Mr. Rochford had seated himself beside her for the first reading and refused to be dislodged afterward. It was customary at such events to circulate, to move about the room between each reading of a poem or story, discussing its merits and conversing upon other literary topics with one's fellow guests. Mr. Rochford had followed Jessica wherever she went and had seated himself beside her whenever she settled for another performance, even though she chose a different chair each time.

She had found it irritating and did not doubt it had been observed and commented upon. She had also felt a bit sorry for him, for she knew that what was facing him was going to be a disappointment of colossal proportions. But then he was a liar. He had pretended he had known Gabriel Rochford as a boy when he had not. And if he had lied about that, could he be trusted on any details of the story he had told?

This morning Mr. Rochford had sent a formal written request that the Duke of Netherby grant him half an hour of his invaluable time at two o'clock in the afternoon.

"He is very handsome, Jessica," her mother said now. "And personable. And charming."

"Yes," Jessica agreed. "He is all three, Mama."

"And eligible," her mother added.

"Yes." It was hard sometimes to hang on to a secret.

"And young," her mother said.

Four other gentlemen had reached the point of calling formally upon Avery in the past six years or so. The last one had been close to fifty years old—older than her mother. Avery had observed in that aloof, bored way of his after she had refused him that if she had accepted, he would have locked her in her room and fed her bread and water until her wedding day.

"Yes," she said now. "He is probably about my age. Maybe even a little younger."

"You are twenty-five years old, Jessica," her mother said. She sounded a bit despairing. "This would be a very good match for you even though it may be years before Mr. Rochford succeeds to his father's title. You could be happy. Surely."

"We do not even know for certain that an offer is about to be made, Mama," Jessica said.

"Oh, come now." Her mother laughed. "Are you *nervous*, Jessica? Do you *like* him?"

"I do not *dislike* him," Jessica said, and hoped she was not lying outright. It would be unfair to hate him. He was trying very hard. If he lacked something in town bronze, it was understandable. This was his first visit to London, after all. It was his first taste of life lived in the bosom of the *ton*. He was doing his best. And he would surely learn. But . . . he was a liar. And it had been such an unnecessary lie if he believed, as he no doubt did, that his cousin was dead.

"I hope," her mother said, "you are not dangling after Mr. Thorne, Jessica."

*Dangling* after? She had never openly flirted with anyone in her life.

"I am not," she said. But she thought of today's pink rose in its narrow crystal vase upstairs beside her bed and of yesterday's—yellow, probably as an echo of the dress she had worn to the garden party or of the rose she had cupped in her hands in the rose arbor. And of all the others, in varying shades of pink, pressed so that they would not turn brown about the edges and wither and die. And she thought of that kiss, which only afterward had she realized was not remotely lascivious, though every part of her body, from the crown of her head to the tips of her toes, had melted with the sheer sensual intimacy of it. "I am not *dangling* after anyone, Mama, and can safely promise never to do so."

"It was the wrong word," her mother admitted with a sigh. "Of course you are not. There is no need. I can think of a dozen men without even taxing my brain who would fall to their knees with one glance of encouragement from you. But do you . . . *favor* Mr. Thorne?"

Jessica feared she was going to marry him.

*Feared?*

He might be a ravisher and a murderer. She had not asked him, and it seemed strange now that she had not. Had she been afraid of the answer? It seemed strange that after shrugging off so many worthy candidates for her hand she was finally giving serious consideration to the suit of a man who might have committed two of the worst crimes imaginable. But . . . Oh, but he had returned from America, not because he was the Earl of Lyndale and owner of what was probably a grand home and estate and a sizable fortune. In the more than six years since the death of his uncle he had not been tempted by those things. He had been happy in America. He had actually used that word—*happy*. He had returned because a hermit of a woman who had been born with severe physical challenges was about to be turned out of her modest cottage by the man who would be earl if Mr. Thorne did not come back. He had given up everything that was dear to him, perhaps forever, for the sake of that one woman. Because he loved her—though not in any romantic way.

Could such a man be a ravisher? A murderer?

But she had only his word . . .

And she had only Mr. Rochford's word . . .

Which did she believe? She had not even asked Mr. Thorne the important questions.

"I like him, Mama," she said rather lamely in answer to her mother's question.

"We know nothing of his lineage," her mother said, "apart from the fact that he is somehow related to Lady Vickers. We cannot even be certain that he is wealthy, though he patronizes the very best tailors and boot makers and is apparently putting up at an expensive hotel. But he may be deep in debt for all we know. And if he made his fortune in *trade*, he may not be quite up to snuff even if he is a gentleman. Not for your father's daughter at least."

"Mama," she said, smiling, "it is not Mr. Thorne who is downstairs with Avery."

No, it was not. She had thought perhaps he might come yesterday after kissing her at the garden party. Oh, not to make a formal offer, perhaps, but maybe to take her driving or walking in the park. She had thought when Avery first mentioned this morning that some gentleman had requested the favor of half an hour of his time that perhaps it was Mr. Thorne. She was getting a little tired of roses and silences. Though there had been the magical interlude with the pianoforte at Elizabeth and Colin's party. Yes, magical. And there had been the rose arbor at the garden party, and that kiss. Not quite her first, but . . . Oh, wherever *was* the man? She did not want just to be romanced. She wanted . . .

Oh, she wanted her heart to be besieged.

"You are quite right," her mother said, laughing. "And if it were, I daresay Avery would make short work of him. He would not willingly allow you to marry a cit, even one who is a gentleman by birth. Not that you need his permission, of course, but it would be as well to have it when you *do* decide to marry. Avery has his funny ways, but I would never question his judgment."

The drawing room door opened as she finished speaking and Avery stepped into the room. He raised his quizzing glass to his eye as the butler closed the door behind him, and he surveyed Jessica through its lens. A pure affectation, of course. There was nothing wrong with Avery's eyesight.

"You are looking remarkably well turned out, Jess," he said.

"Thank you." She made to get to her feet. She must go down and get this over with. But Avery raised a staying hand and lowered his glass.

"Rochford asked for half an hour and was granted exactly that," he said. "His mission might have been accomplished sooner, but he has a tendency to wrap up the kernel of what he has to say in florid language. He wishes to convey a countess's title upon you at some future date, Jess."

"Yes," she said. "I will go down and speak with him."

"Ah," he said. "I would have detained him if I had known you were eager to speak to him. Alas, he has gone."

"Gone?" Jessica's mother said. "You did not refuse him, Avery, surely."

He raised his eyebrows. "I do not have the power to do any such thing, Mother," he said. "My duty as Jess's guardian came to an end four years ago, a fact that afforded me as much relief as it did her. But men who wish to marry her seem to feel obliged to seek out my blessing if not my permission. That is what Rochford came to get. He failed and left. I did offer to bring him up to pay his respects to both of you anyway, but he seemed to be out of sorts and went away instead. Your efforts to look your best have been all for naught, Jess. Perhaps I had better take you and Mother to Gunter's for an ice."

"Avery," Jessica's mother said. "You are being deliberately tiresome. Why, pray, did you withhold your blessing from Mr. Rochford's suit? You must know that it is what all of her family has been hoping for."

*"All?"* he said, frowning. "Am I not at least an honorary member of the Westcott family, Mother, as your stepson? And as Anna's husband? You wound me."

"In case neither of you has noticed," Jessica said rather tartly, "I am here. I would be obliged if the two of you would not continue to talk about my business as though I were not. Why did you withhold your blessing, Avery?"

He turned his attention upon her. "I cannot in all honesty say, Jess, that he would have my blessing under any circumstances," he said. "Not unless he can lose a few teeth. But that might involve some painful extractions and I would not wish that upon my worst enemy."

Jessica's mother tutted and tossed her glance at the ceiling. Jessica, despite herself, smirked.

"I did inform him," Avery continued, "that he will have my official blessing at least to speak to you in my house when he can offer in fact what he offered this afternoon merely in theory. The Earl of Lyndale still officially lives. When he is officially dead and Rochford's father is confirmed in the title, then Rochford himself will be an eligible suitor for the hand of my stepsister. But before you can stamp your foot in anger over my presumption, Jess, may I remind you that I know very well you do not need my permission? It is merely my hope that you will listen to advice."

"Do you believe, then," she asked him, "that the Earl of Lyndale still lives?"

"I neither believe nor disbelieve," he told her. "I speak merely of facts, and the fact is that the present earl lives until he has been pronounced dead by the appropriate authority."

He was looking very directly at her, Jessica saw, his normally sleepy eyes unusually keen. *He knows,* she thought. *Or if he does not know, he suspects. And if he suspects, he will ferret out the truth.* Avery had a way of doing that.

"I am not about to turn down an offer of an ice at Gunter's," she told him.

He sighed. "I was afraid of that," he said.

Her mother looked from one to the other of them and tossed her glance at the ceiling again.


The day after the garden party, Gabriel made arrangements to keep his suite of rooms at his London hotel, though he did not expect to be there for the next week. He arranged to have pink roses, accompanied by signed cards, sent to Archer House each morning for the coming week. He informed Sir Trevor and Lady Vickers and Bertie that he would be away from town for up to a week. And he took his curricle and pair, his valet, and his groom and drove north.

The village was called Lilyvale, Simon Norton had informed him, and was thirty miles or so southeast of Brierley. Ginsberg lived there with his daughter and son-in-law on a tenant farm he had leased more than twelve years ago. The information was secondhand, even thirdhand, by the time it had reached Norton's ears, but Gabriel had decided to trust it. If it proved false, he would have wasted a few days. It would not be the end of the world.

The information turned out not to be false. Ginsberg lived in a fair-sized house on what looked to be a well-run farm. There was a neat garden about the house, sporting both flowers and vegetables as well as an expanse of freshly scythed lawn. Two young children, a boy and a girl, were roaring about the lawn when Gabriel arrived, involved in some noisy game. An older boy, nominally in charge of them, perhaps, was stretched out on his side on the grass, propped on one elbow, his head upon his hand. He was reading.

The children stopped to stare, and the older boy looked up from his book. "Good morning, sir," he said.

"I have come to call upon Mrs. Clark," Gabriel said. "Is she your mother?"

The boy sat up and crossed his legs. "Who shall I say is calling, sir?" he asked.

But the younger boy, less concerned with the niceties of hospitality, had turned tail and gone dashing toward the house. He opened the door, crashing it against a wall inside, and yelled. "Mama," he cried. "Someone to see you."

The little girl went tearing after him.

The older boy laughed and scratched his head. "I do beg your pardon, sir," he said as he pushed himself to his feet. "They are like a pair of wild animals today. It comes of having been cooped up in the house all day yesterday because of the rain."

Gabriel knew all about the rain. He had driven his curricle through it.

"I am an old acquaintance of your mother's," he explained. And yes, he thought, the boy must be about twelve years old. "I am staying not far from here for a day or two and came to pay my respects. Ask her if she has time to see Gabriel Rochford, if you will."

"Yes, Mr. Rochford." The boy turned to lead the way toward the house.

Before they reached it, however, a woman appeared in the doorway. She was a bit on the plump side, noticeably older than when Gabriel had seen her last—she had been seventeen then. But she was still fair haired and pretty. The little girl was clinging to her skirt and peeping about it at Gabriel. The little boy came bouncing outside again, jumping two-footed down the steps.

"Penny," Gabriel said, removing his hat.

She stared blankly at him for a few moments, and then one hand crept to her throat. "Gabriel?" she said, her voice almost a whisper. "Oh dear God, it is. I heard you were dead."

"Who is he, Mama?" the little boy asked, jumping on the spot.

She looked down at the child and blinked, almost as though she had forgotten who he was. "You will mind your manners, Wilbur," she said. "Make your bow to Mr. Rochford and go up to the schoolroom. Amelia, you go too. Kendall, take them up, if you please, and stay with them there until you are called."

"Aw, Mama," the little boy complained. "Can't we just play outside?"

"You will do as you are told," she said firmly.

"Come on, nippers," the older boy said. "I bet I can beat you both at spillikins."

"Cannot," they both chorused together, and the little girl reached for his hand.

As the children made their way toward the staircase that was visible over their mother's shoulder, an older man approached the door. He stopped abruptly when he saw Gabriel, and his gaze narrowed and then hardened upon him.

"Mr. Ginsberg." Gabriel nodded to him.

"We heard you were dead," he said. And then, with flared nostrils and barely leashed fury, "Would that you were."

"Papa, please," Penelope said. "Wait until the children are upstairs."

None of them moved until a door closed and they could no longer hear the children's voices. A flush moved up Penelope's neck and into her face. Her father's nostrils remained flared.

"Come into the sitting room, Gabriel," she said. "And I named you wrongly to the children, did I not? You are the Earl of Lyndale."

"I will not have that man in my house," her father said. "I will send for a constable if he does not leave my property immediately. He belongs in a jail cell while a gallows is prepared."

"Please, Papa," she said, closing her eyes briefly. "Let us talk about this in private."

"I did not kill your son, sir," Gabriel said. "He was my friend."

Ginsberg, white haired and straight backed, old for his years, glared at him for a long, silent moment and then turned to stalk away in the direction of a room that turned out to be the sitting room. Gabriel followed Penelope inside it and shut the door. Her father went to stand by the window, looking out, his hands clasped behind him.

"Gabriel," Penelope said again, "we heard you had died."

"I did not," he told her. Neither of them sat down. "You too probably wish I had."

Ginsberg growled but did not say anything. Penelope raised her hand to her throat again.

"I went away," Gabriel said. "I had been thinking about leaving for some time, but I was spurred on by what happened. I was a frightened boy, and it seemed to me that there was real cause for fear. You might perhaps have cleared up one misperception if I had stayed, Penny. I believe you did not do it, though, after I was gone."

She clutched her throat and closed her eyes again. Ginsberg turned sharply from the window, his face a mask of fury.

"You are not going to try denying—" he began, but his daughter cut him off.

"Please, Papa," she said.

It occurred to Gabriel that he might have tried to insist upon speaking to her privately. But he was not sorry he had not done so. His own anger had been suppressed for years, only to be aroused again now. They had been sweethearts, he and Penny—and yes, it was the most appropriate word to use of two young innocents who had rarely been alone together and had never done anything more daring than hold hands when they could and twice share a very brief, chaste kiss. She had been seventeen, for the love of God, he nineteen. They had been children.

"The boy you called Kendall is your son?" Gabriel asked. "Who is his father, Penny?"

She made a sound of distress deep in her throat. Ginsberg took a menacing step forward, only to be stopped by her raised hand.

"I never said it was you," she told Gabriel. "I let it be assumed that it was. It seemed . . . preferable. I thought Papa would persuade you to marry me, and I did not believe you would really mind. I thought you liked me and would do that for me when I explained."

Good God!

"What the *devil*!" Ginsberg bellowed. Again, her raised hand stopped him.

"And then everything got out of hand," she said. "Orson went stalking off in a rage to find you and hold you to account—or what he thought was holding you to account. And then you killed him. Oh dear God, I was beside myself.

I did not know what to do. I was *seventeen*. Barely that
even. Did I cause my own brother's death, Gabriel, as
surely as if I had fired the gun myself? I have always believed I did and that I was responsible for you becoming a
killer. But I know it must have been an accident. He was
shot *in the back*. There is no way you would have done that
deliberately. Oh dear God."

"I did not kill Orson," Gabriel said.

She looked at him with eyes suddenly grown wild, her
teeth sunk deep into her lower lip.

"What—" Ginsberg began.

"Who is your eldest child's father, Penny?" Gabriel
asked again.

She huffed out a breath, closed her eyes again briefly,
and spoke. "I was going to Brierley with a cake Mama had
baked for your aunt," she said. "She had been feeling
poorly. *They* were in the park too. I think they must have
been coming from the tavern. They looked . . . drunk. They
were weaving and laughing and . . . I could not hide fast
enough. One of them . . . He tried to flirt with me, but when
that did not work, he started to kiss me while the other one
laughed and told him I was your girl—*Gabe's girl,* he said.
And then the first man laughed and told me what I needed
was a real man. And then he . . . And the other one would
not stop him. He just laughed. He was married. I mean the
one who . . . He would not have been able to marry me."

"His name?" Gabriel asked softly. But of course he
knew.

His cousin Philip had been a man of loose morals and a
frequent drunk all the time Gabriel had known him. It was
said—and Gabriel believed it—that no female servant or
farm girl was safe from him when he was in his cups.

Manley had been just such another. He was all of five

years older than Philip, but they were friends and he had come to Brierley frequently and stayed, often for weeks at a time.

By the time Gabriel went to America, both men were married, with children, but those facts had not changed them. Manley's child had been left at home whenever he brought his wife to Brierley, and the two wives had been left at the house to amuse each other while the men drank in the village and went shooting out of season and ogled the local young women, married and single, and generally made nuisances of themselves. Lords of the manor. Entitled to whatever or whoever took their fancy.

Gabriel had always heartily disliked both of them, a sentiment they had made no bones about returning. They had always derived great pleasure from blaming him for some of the idiotic things they had done—grown men acting like bully boys. And his uncle, stern and autocratic, but as thick as a brick, Gabriel had often thought, had been unable or unwilling to see his son and his cousin's boy for what they were. He had been ready enough to take their word and punish Gabriel.

"His name, Penny?"

Ginsberg looked as though he were about to explode, but he held his peace and stayed where he was, staring at the floor.

Penelope drew a deep, ragged breath. "Mr. Manley Rochford," she said.

Ginsberg's head snapped back as though he had been punched hard on the chin. His eyes were fast closed, his face chalk white. "He came to Orson's funeral," he murmured.

"You have told no one this until now, Penny?" Gabriel asked.

"Yes," she said. "I told Mr. Clark—my husband—before I married him."

"But he did not deem it necessary to have Manley Rochford taken into custody and charged with ravishment and probably murder too?" he asked.

She frowned. "But you killed Orson," she said. "It was you he went to confront."

"He did not find me," he told her. "I was with Mary Beck. She had been brought a fawn with a broken leg, and I was helping her set and bind it. When I finally arrived home, I was confronted with three things. You were with child. Orson was dead, shot in the back. And I was guilty on both counts. You had admitted the first, and Philip and Manley had witnessed the second from a distance. They had been too far away, of course, to prevent the shooting. My uncle, his house threatened with terrible scandal, advised me to run while I could. And I fled before I could give myself time to think. It was not the wisest thing to do, of course, but I was nineteen. And there were people to swear that I was guilty of each charge—you on the one hand, Manley and Philip, my own cousins, on the other."

Ginsberg had groped his way to a chair and sat down heavily upon it.

"I am so sorry, Gabriel," Penelope said. "So very sorry. But they *saw* you kill Orson."

"Two men," Gabriel said. "One of whom had raped you, the other of whom was present when it happened but did nothing to stop it. Yet you took their word for what happened to your brother—and *my friend*? You have believed ever since that I *shot him in the back*?"

"You ran away," she said. "What was I supposed to think? I have always believed it must have been an accident, that you did not mean to kill him. But . . . you ran away."

"I am going home to Brierley," he told her. "Not immediately, but soon. I may need you to tell this story to other people, Penny. At the very least I may need to tell other people that they can confirm the truth of my story by speaking with you."

She was shaking her head, her eyes wide.

"I am guilty neither of ravishment nor of being the father of your son," he said. "I am innocent in the death—or murder—of your brother."

Ginsberg moaned softly into the hand he had spread over his face.

"The story must be told in some form," Gabriel said. "It has become imperative that I go home to Brierley. I have work to do there, and I do not wish to find myself hampered by old assumptions and old charges that might after all require me to fight for my life in a court of law. I do not wish to have to deal with the hostility of skeptical neighbors. I do *not* want Manley Rochford to continue living at Brierley and throwing his weight about there, destroying innocent lives. You ought not to want it either, Penny, surely. I am putting up at the posting inn two miles or so from here. I cannot for the life of me remember what it is called, but you must know the one I mean. If you choose to write out the story you have told me this morning and send it there, perhaps it will save you from having anyone else come here to question you in person." He waited through a brief silence.

"I will ask Mr. Clark what I should do," she said. "No. I will do it. I will send a servant."

He nodded curtly to her and turned to her father, who was still sitting slumped on his chair, his hand shielding his face.

"Good day to you, sir," he said. "I did not come to stir

up trouble. I came only to discover the truth and build my defense, should one become necessary."

Mr. Ginsberg did not reply. Penelope had nothing more to say. Gabriel found his way out of the house and along the garden path to where young Timms was walking the horses back and forth while they waited.

He knew now who had got Penny with child, Gabriel thought as he drove his curricle back to the inn. But who had killed Orson Ginsberg? Manford? Philip? One of them had surely done it. But only one of them was still alive to provide the answer. And he was a liar.

He tried to forgive Penny. She had been a frightened girl—just as he had ended up being a frightened boy. She had silently assented to the story she had thought most beneficial to herself. She had believed he would be persuaded to marry her. And perhaps she had been right. Things had not turned out the way she had hoped, however. Instead she had been forced to live ever since with the ghastly and disastrous consequences of her implicit lie in not correcting the assumption her father and brother had made.

It was hard to forgive her. Except that he was himself in need of a great forgiveness. There were people in and around Brierley who were suffering today because for the past six years and more he had ignored them. He had done it because Brierley had brought him very little happiness and some misery when he was a boy. Yet it was not they who had caused his unhappiness. He had neglected his duty, and it was not for him now to take the moral high ground and condemn a woman who had once been frightened by an unbearable crime that had been committed against her.

# Thirteen

There had been only the one yellow rose, the day after the garden party. Since then the rosebuds had been pink again.

The romantic gesture no longer meant anything to Jessica. Quite the contrary. She was angry. Quietly furious. For the flowers were the *only* evidence that the Earl of Lyndale, alias Mr. Gabriel Thorne, still existed somewhere on the face of this earth. And even they were not proof positive. He might have ordered them in advance and left a little pile of signed cards to be delivered with them. He might be anywhere by now, even six feet underground. He might be on the high seas, making his way back to Boston to count his piles of money while he was being declared dead in England. She hoped there was a ferocious storm in the middle of the Atlantic Ocean, tossing him about, breaking his limbs—preferably both arms and both legs. And his head. She hoped it would turn him a bilious green at the very least.

How dared he.

How *dared* he toy with her affections and make her begin to think that perhaps, just maybe, there was a possibility she might marry him and expect something like happiness with him? How dared he pretend that he intended to marry her, only to desert her when she was starting to lose her common sense? How dared he send her roses and play the pianoforte for her until she felt he had sucked her very soul into wherever it was the music came from? How dared he stroke her little finger? And kiss her among the roses, his booted foot on the edge of the bench beside her, his fingertips resting against her jaw, making her want to burst with . . . with *desire*?

Wherever he had disappeared to, she hoped he stayed there—forever. And she hoped it was a nasty place, overrun with snakes. And rats. If she never saw him again it would be too soon. No, that was a silly overworked expression. She never wanted to see him again. Full stop. Shoulders back, chin in air, *nose* in air, and all the rest of it. Lady Jessica Archer, ice maiden, unapproachable, unassailable—or something like that.

And then there was Mr. Rochford—that smiling liar. Far from being discouraged by Avery's refusal to give his blessing to a proposal of marriage, the man was bearing his disappointment with tragic fortitude. He had come the very next day—much to her mother's delight—to beg her to drive in the park with him, and she had gone because she did not want to admit to herself that she was disappointed it was not Mr. Thorne who had come. He had sighed and smiled and smiled and sighed and declared that the end of the seven years since his cousin the former earl's unfortunate demise could not come fast enough for him.

"For His Grace, your brother—or ought I to say half

brother?—assured me, Lady Jessica," he had told her, "that he will welcome my suit with open arms once my father is officially the Earl of Lyndale. *Then* you may expect to see me upon bended knee, setting my heart at your feet."

The thing was, though, he had not *asked*. Therefore, she had been unable to refuse. She had come to dislike him quite heartily. It was hard to understand what it was about him that so enchanted virtually every other lady in London, old and young alike, those of her own family not excepted.

And really, could one imagine Avery welcoming any man with open arms? It was such a ludicrous idea that she had been hard-pressed not to laugh aloud.

Oh, this Season was turning out to be one huge disappointment. She had launched herself into it with such high hopes for her future. And what had she got? Her usual court of admirers, all of whom were amusing and endearing, but really not husband material: Mr. Rochford, who was dazzlingly handsome and relentlessly charming but really a bit of a bore—not to mention the fact that he was a malicious liar; and Mr. Thorne, about whom the less said, the better. Who cared that when he had stood before her at the garden party, one booted foot propped against the seat upon which she sat, one arm draped over his thigh in its skintight pantaloons as he mentioned romance and then kissed her, he had exuded such raw masculinity that she could easily have suffocated—or swooned—from the sheer physicality of it? Really, *who cared?*

At least now, tonight, she was on her way to Vauxhall Gardens—her favorite place in all of England, with the possible exception of Bath, where Cousin Camille lived with Joel and their large family. But Bath was a whole city, while Vauxhall was a pleasure garden on the south bank of the river Thames, and stepping into it at night was to step into a magical world, a sort of paradise. One could not possibly remain depressed when one was going to Vauxhall. At least, she hoped one could not.

She was mortally tired of being depressed.

It promised to be a warm evening and she had been able to wear the gauzy dark peach–colored gown she had been saving for a special occasion, with the fine cashmere wrap that was only a shade or two lighter in color. Aunt Viola had invited her with the promise of an enjoyable evening with a small party, mainly family members, in a private box, from which they could listen to the orchestra and watch the dancing and even dance themselves. There were even to be fireworks later.

She was in a carriage with Boris and Peter Wayne, her younger cousins, who had assured both their mother and hers that they would guard her with their lives and bring her home in one piece sometime after midnight, when all the fireworks had been shot off. Really, though, they had wanted her as a sort of chaperon for the other occupant of the carriage: Alice Wayne, a young cousin on their father's side, who had recently arrived in London and was about to share a come-out ball with the two daughters of a friend of her mother's. Her eyes had been sparkling from the moment she stepped into the carriage with them. Jessica felt eighty years old.

She wondered who else would make up the party. Was she doomed to be the eldest, apart from Aunt Viola and the marquess? There would be Estelle and Bertrand, of course, and the four of them who were in this carriage. Perhaps one or two more. But they were bound to see other acquaintances there. They were sure to have a good time. She felt desperately in need of a good time. She wanted to be appreciated, admired, flirted with. She wanted to appreciate, admire, and flirt—something she almost never did. She wanted to dance and laugh and stroll along the main avenue through the gardens, reveling in the wonder of colored lanterns swaying in the branches of the trees on either side. She wanted to be a part of the gaiety of the crowds that would be there. She wanted to feel young and attractive.

Oh, she had waited too long to seek her own happiness. She was twenty-five years old. Ancient. Abby had married two years ago at the age of twenty-four. She was happy and in love. She had children and a home and a garden and neighbors and a husband who, for all his dour outer appearance, was absolutely besotted with her. As she was with him.

Self-pity clawed at Jessica's insides. And she had no one but herself to blame. She gave herself a mental shake and joined in the burst of laughter that followed something marvelously witty Boris had said, though she had not heard what it was.

Aunt Viola and the Marquess of Dorchester were already sitting in the open box they had reserved on the lower level of the rotunda, close to the orchestra and overlooking the dancing area. So were Estelle and Bertrand and Miss Keithley, the sister of Bertrand's friend, and another young lady whom Jessica believed to be Miss Keithley's younger sister. And . . . Mr. Rochford.

*But of course,* she thought the instant her eyes alit upon him and he got to his feet, having spied her at the same moment. He made her an elegant bow while he smiled dazzlingly at her. Of course he was here. Aunt Viola was one of the Westcott aunts, was she not? And in the few days since Avery had withheld his blessing on Mr. Rochford's suit, her mother had gone visiting twice without Jessica— once to Grandmama's and once to Aunt Mildred's. To rally the troops, no doubt.

Well, she was not going to let his presence spoil her
evening, Jessica decided as they all exchanged effusive
greetings and she succeeded in seating herself between
Bertrand and his father. She would just be very careful not
to allow him to monopolize her company. Let Estelle entertain him or Miss Keithley or someone else.

So there were six ladies and five gentlemen. That was
unusually careless of Aunt Viola. But of course again! This
party at Vauxhall had been planned more than a week ago.
She had probably invited Mr. Thorne too, for the family
committee had a two-pronged matchmaking goal. Perhaps
Aunt Viola had not yet realized that he had disappeared,
apparently without a trace. Or, if she had realized it, maybe
it had been too late to invite another gentleman in his place.

But then . . .

Well, but then he came, tall and broad shouldered and
immaculately elegant as he strode purposefully toward the
box. He bowed to Aunt Viola, shook hands with the marquess, and nodded to everyone else, Jessica included.

"I do beg your pardon, ma'am," he said to Aunt Viola.
"A cart had overturned on the bridge, completely blocking
it, and it took several minutes to clear the roadway after it
became evident that all the shouting and gesticulating was
not going to accomplish the task."

Jessica wished the cart had been full of rotten cabbages
and that it had overturned onto his head.


Since he had not warned the Marquess and Marchioness of
Dorchester that he might not be able to attend their gathering at Vauxhall Gardens and undoubtedly they had arranged it so that there would be an equal number of ladies

and gentlemen, Gabriel had made a push to be back in London in time. He had made it with three hours to spare, just time enough to bathe the grime of the road from his person and to dress appropriately for such an evening. Then had come the frustration of the spill on the bridge across the river Thames that had made him late arriving after all. It vexed him, as he had long made it a habit never to be late for appointments or social events to which he had been specifically invited.

Lady Jessica Archer looked very lovely and very haughty indeed, though she unbent sufficiently to joke with her cousins while they dined upon a meal that included the thin slices of ham and the strawberries for which Vauxhall was famous, according to Lady Vickers. Lady Jessica also played gracious hostess to a steady stream of men who came to pay homage after they had finished eating. She came close to flirting with a few of them. She danced with Dorchester and with her cousin, the elder of the two Wayne brothers.

She studiously ignored Gabriel. He might have thought he was invisible to her except that she had a way of not looking at him that involved a raised chin and a supercilious expression that disappeared as soon as she looked at someone else.

So she was annoyed with him. Because he had left town for almost a week without telling her? If that was the reason, it was encouraging.

She was doing her best to ignore Rochford too. That was not always easy to do. When the man was going through all the motions that indicated he was about to ask her to dance, she turned pointedly to the other of her young cousins and informed him that this was the dance for which he had asked earlier. Young Peter Wayne looked a bit surprised, as

well he might, as undoubtedly this was the first he was
hearing of it. But he jumped to his feet, the perfect gentleman, and actually thanked her for remembering.

And when the marchioness suggested after that dance
that they all take a walk along the main avenue in order to
work off some of the effects of the rich foods they had
eaten and had begun to suggest that her niece take Rochford's arm, Lady Estelle jumped in with an objection.

"Oh," she said, "but I am about to tell Mr. Rochford
about that bonnet I almost purchased yesterday, Mother—
the one that had what looked very much like a bird's nest
perched upon the crown. Do you remember it? It is such a
funny story. You will laugh, Mr. Rochford." And she threw
a mischievous glance Gabriel's way, smiled engagingly at
Rochford, and slid an arm through his while her stepmother
half frowned at her and glanced almost apologetically at
her niece.

"Lady Jessica," Gabriel said. "Perhaps you will give me
the pleasure of your company."

By then her young cousins had paired up with the
Misses Keithley, and Bertrand Lamarr had taken the wide-
eyed little girl on his arm—she was apparently a cousin of
the Wayne boys and must surely be eighteen if she was at
such a party, though she could easily pass for fourteen.
Short of grabbing her uncle's arm, Lady Jessica had no
choice but to take his.

A small crowd had gathered to watch the dancing. They
had to weave their way through it to reach the avenue beyond. By the time Gabriel got there with Lady Jessica, the
others were already walking ahead.

"I was told when I first arrived in town that I absolutely
must not miss spending an evening at Vauxhall," he said. "I
was told there was something particularly lovely about the

combination of trees and avenues and colored lamps swaying from the branches and the good food and music and
dancing. And fireworks. The person who told me did not
exaggerate."

"It is a pleasant place at which to spend a few hours," she
said.

"We are particularly fortunate to have been invited on
an evening when the weather conditions are perfect," he
said.

"Yes, indeed," she agreed.

"Cool but not cold," he said. "Not windy but with
enough of a gentle breeze to set the lanterns moving in the
branches and their colors to forming patterns that are a
feast for the eyes."

"It is a pleasant evening," she conceded.

"You are cross with me," he told her.

She raised her eyebrows but kept her eyes on the avenue
ahead, while all around them revelers moved at different
paces and in both directions, talking, laughing, calling
ahead or behind to others. The music was still quite audible.

"Cross, Mr. Thorne?" she said. "Whyever would I be
cross with you?"

"For apparently abandoning you," he said. "It was not
real abandonment, you know. I had every intention of coming back. I came as soon as I possibly could."

"You are mistaken, Mr. Thorne," she said. "You have
overestimated your importance. *Have* you been gone somewhere? I had not noticed."

"Had you not indeed?" he said. "I am crushed."

He moved her and himself to one side of the avenue,
where they would have to do less weaving past other couples and larger groups. There were trees on either side of
the avenue, their branches almost meeting overhead in

some places. It was even more picturesque than he had imagined. Not quite real. The pastel lamplight made the trees seem something other than what they were. It was no wonder these were called pleasure gardens.

"I needed to leave town on urgent business," he said.

She had no answer to that. She opened her fan and waved it slowly before her face—quite unnecessarily. There was a cool breeze.

The rest of the party had got some way ahead of them, he could see. Her aunt would not worry about her, though. She was of age, unlike some of the other young ladies of the party.

He did not try to keep the conversation alive. He had been merely teasing her, anyway, with the banal remarks he had been making. She looked as haughty as she had on his first encounter with her. He was no longer deceived, however. At the moment, in fact, he guessed she was boiling inside. She was severely annoyed with him. Had she considered their kiss some sort of declaration? Had she expected him to follow up on it with a visit to her brother the next day, perhaps? Just so that she could refuse him?

*Would* she have refused?

"Mr. Thorne," she said at last when they were halfway along the avenue. "*Did* you . . . assault your neighbor's daughter?"

Ah. So that was what was bothering her, was it?

"Are you asking if I raped her?" he asked.

She turned her head away to gaze through the trees. He did not suppose that word was used often, if at all, in her hearing. She was probably blushing, though it was impossible to verify his suspicion in the colored lantern light.

"The answer is no," he said.

"It was consensual, then?" she asked. "Was there a child?"

"There was a child," he said. "A boy, now twelve years old. He is not mine. There was never any possibility that he might be."

She thought that over for a minute.

"Her brother died?" she asked.

"Yes," he said. "The day he discovered his sister was with child. He died from a bullet in his back."

Their steps had slowed but not quite stopped.

"Did you kill him?" she asked.

"No," he said. "He was my friend."

"Friends kill friends," she said, "when one of them does something to kill the friendship."

"I had done nothing to kill ours," he told her. "And I did not kill him."

"But you ran away," she said. "You even took another name to throw off any pursuit. You stayed away for thirteen years. Even now you have not revealed your identity to anyone but me—and perhaps to Sir Trevor and Lady Vickers?"

"To them, yes," he said. "I ran away because I was a frightened boy of nineteen and I was about to be arrested for a murder I had not committed. My uncle urged me to go, and I went."

"Does not an innocent man stay to clear his name?" she asked.

"In a work of fiction, perhaps," he said, "when one can take comfort from the assurance that good will prevail and evil will be punished. In the real world innocent people hang as often as the guilty."

"He is a complete and total liar, then?" she said. "Mr. Rochford, I mean."

"I am prepared to give him the benefit of some doubt," he said. "He was about ten years old at the time. He did not know the situation. He did not know me. He had never been to Brierley. It would be quite understandable for him to believe the story his mother and father took home with them."

"Took home?" she said. "His parents were there at the time, then?"

"Yes," he said.

"Did they too urge you to run away?" she asked.

He thought about it. "Manley did," he said. "His wife and my cousin Philip's wife were comforting my aunt, who was in frail health to start with and had apparently collapsed with shock. They were all afraid I would be arrested and convicted. Manley and Philip did not believe my alibi would be credible."

"They all believed you to be guilty, then," she said.

"I did not speak with the women before I fled," he said. "But the three men implied that they believed it."

"Who was the father of the child?" she asked. "And who killed the mother's brother and your friend? Do you know?"

"Yes," he said. "I know."

This was a bizarre conversation to be having in these magical, festive surroundings.

"But you are not going to say," she said after a minute's silence.

"No."

Not yet, anyway.

He had noticed a few narrower avenues branching off the main one. Another of them was just ahead. He needed to give the two of them a chance to recover from this conversation. He had had other plans for tonight. Or other hopes, perhaps. He had never been as confident of success with Lady Jessica Archer as he had pretended to be. And it seemed he knew pathetically little about romancing.

"Come," he said when they reached it, and he turned her and himself onto the path he had seen.

He was a bit surprised when she did not put up any resistance. He was even more surprised when he, finding that the path was narrower than he had expected and drawing her closer to his side, disengaged his arm from hers to set about her waist, and she made no protest and did not try to put more space between them.

There were fewer lamps strung from the trees in here. The path was not totally dark, but it was dim. The sounds of voices from the main avenue and of music from the rotunda seemed immediately more remote. An illusion, no doubt. He could smell the trees and the earth and foliage in here. He was more aware of nature and less of man-made magic.

"You are not afraid of me?" he asked her. It had occurred to him that she might be.

"Why would I be afraid of you, Mr. Thorne?" she asked, the sound of chill hauteur back in her voice.

"Perhaps," he said, "you do not believe me."

"I believe you," she said. "But I do not want to talk any more about that tonight."

"What *do* you want to talk about?" he asked her.

"Do you still *intend* to marry me?" she asked in return, putting emphasis upon the one word.

"I do," he said,

"I think it had better be soon," she said.

He was not sure for a moment that he had heard her correctly. But she had spoken clearly enough, and there were no sounds close enough to distract him.

"By special license?" he asked her.

"Yes," she said. "I think so. You have no idea how my family will fuss otherwise."

"Over the fact of our marrying?" he asked.

"Oh no," she said. "They will come around to that. They have clearly deemed you worthy of Estelle, after all. No, Mr. Thorne, they will fuss over the wedding—if they are given half a chance, that is. They will expect nothing less than a ceremony at St. George's on Hanover Square with all the *ton* in attendance."

He winced inwardly. "But do you not want to be fussed over?" he asked her.

"No," she said. "I want to be married. And I believe you *need* to be married."

The conversation between them had taken a bizarre turn after all. Unless he was much mistaken, he had not even asked her to marry him yet. Had he? No formal application to her brother or her mother. No prepared speech. No bended knee. No single rose, presented in person this time.

No romance. Not really.

The path opened up ahead of them to reveal a miniature garden, with a semicircular flower bed on each side, each surrounded by a strip of grass, and each with a wooden seat behind the flowers. There were more lanterns here, all of them a pale pink. It was a little haven of unexpected loveliness. Even Gabriel recognized it as a romantic spot.

They stopped, though they did not step off the path to sit down.

"Why do you want to be married?" he asked her. "More specifically, why do you want to marry *me*?"

"You were right," she said. "I felt left behind when Abby married Gil. When I went there for the christening of their baby just before Easter and then stayed for a more lengthy visit, I even felt a bit resentful, as though she had owed it to me to remain single and unhappy. I felt a little humiliated when I realized which way my thoughts were tending. I decided that when I came back here for the Season this year, I would marry at last."

"You have legions of admirers," he said. "Why not one of them? Why me?"

"I like them all," she said. "I am even rather fond of most of them. Perhaps of all of them."

"You do not like me?" he asked her. "You are not fond of me?"

She looked at him for a long time, with something of a frown. The light of the lanterns gave a rosy glow to her complexion and her forearms, which were not covered by her wrap. It made her dress look more like a deep rose pink. A reminder of his first sight of her after he arrived in London.

"To be honest, I do not know the answer to either question," she said at last.

"Why *do* you want to marry me, then?" he asked her.

She drew breath and closed her mouth again. He waited.

"I think," she said at last, "it is because I want you."

Well, that was an unexpected answer. He guessed that she thought so too. He wondered what her cheeks would look like if the light were not already pink. It was clear she was talking about sex.

"In bed?" he said.

She turned her head away for a moment as though to examine the flowers, but she looked back into his face before she spoke. She had some courage, this woman he wanted to marry.

"Yes," she said. "Virginity becomes tiresome, Mr. Thorne, when one is twenty-five. You have had a strange way of romancing me, if that is what you have been doing.

It has been curiously effective, however. Now, though, I want you to take it a stage further. I want you to *make love* to me."

"And you think I can do it better than any other man of your acquaintance?" he said. "You think I can give you pleasure?"

"Yes." Her eyes wandered over him, across the breadth of his shoulders, down over his chest and even lower. She lifted her hands and spread them very lightly, very tentatively, over his chest. She took a step closer.

The evening air between them fairly sizzled. He had to remind himself of where they were, and, God damn it, it was far too public a place. The sounds of human revelry were not far distant.

"And in return," she said, raising her eyes back to his, "you will have a duke's daughter and sister for a countess, Mr. Thorne. Someone who has learned from a master—her own brother—how to use her aristocratic identity and upbringing to command respect and obedience. Someone who has learned from her mother how to run an aristocratic home and how to manage a houseful of servants and how to lead and entertain neighbors. Someone who knows that her primary duty as a wife, at least for the first few years, is to give birth to sons and raise them to know their duty and their place in society. It is what you want, is it not? And why you chose me?"

"Yes," he said.

"Then you can have me," she said. "And I can have what I want. But answer something else first. Am I *just* an aristocrat with all the right qualifications in your eyes, Mr. Thorne?"

He thought about it. He did not need long. "No," he said.

"What else am I, then?" she asked. Her hands were still against his chest, though they were sliding higher, toward his shoulders.

"I want you," he said. "In bed. Very much in bed. I want you naked. I want to arouse every inch of you. And I want to be inside you and to pleasure you until you cry out with the sheer pain and wonder of it."

Well, she had asked.

He set his hands on either side of her waist. It was a very small waist through the loose folds of her gown. He could feel the flare of her hips below it. Very nice.

"Pain?" she said.

"Pain," he said again. "Or what will feel very near to pain until it bursts into something quite different. If it is done right, that is."

Her hands were on his shoulders. Her thumbs were caressing the sides of his neck. "You must promise to do it right, then," she said.

He tipped back his head and drew a deep breath before looking down into her face again. He had not expected this tonight. Good God, he had not. Not ever, actually. He noticed as he had on a previous occasion that when her lips were parted the top one curled slightly upward, seeming soft and moist and irresistibly kissable.

He lowered his head and set the tip of his tongue to that lip. Her hands clenched hard about his shoulders.

He moved his tongue lower and slid it into her mouth. She gasped and then made a low sound in her throat, and his arms came hard about her and hers about him and his mouth covered hers and she sucked his tongue deeper. He moved his hands down her back to cup her bottom and snuggle her against his growing erection. She gasped cool air around his tongue, and he was as sure as he could be that she had never done anything like this before.

For a while, after all, he had forgotten how close to being public this seemingly secluded spot was. They might be interrupted at any moment. Reluctantly he loosened his hold on her and drew back his head.

They gazed at each other.

"Do you wish me to apply to the Duke of Netherby for your hand?" he asked. "Or to your mother? To both?"

He watched amusement creep into her eyes. "To Avery," she said. "It is not necessary, but I cannot resist finding out how he will receive you."

"And if he does not receive me kindly?" he asked.

"I will marry you anyway," she said.

"Would that cause a rift between you?" he asked.

"No, not at all," she said. "He knows he has no authority over me. He does not *want* to have any. But if someone applies to him for an audience, he will grant it, and afterward he will give his opinion. Then, as like as not, he will yawn."

"I begin to like the man," he said.

"I love him," she told him.

"And do many men apply for an audience with him?" he asked her. "With the object of asking for your hand, that is?"

"There have been some," she said. "Most recently, it was Mr. Rochford."

"Ah," he said. "And how was he received?"

"With courtesy," she said. "Avery withheld his blessing but not his permission. I do not need his permission. He told Mr. Rochford he would grant the blessing at least upon his proposing marriage to me after Mr. Rochford Senior is officially declared Earl of Lyndale."

"You believe your brother wishes for the match?" he asked. "As your female relatives seem to do?"

"Avery rather hopes I do not marry Mr. Rochford," she said. "He believes he has too many teeth."

He grinned at her and then threw back his head and laughed aloud. "I *do* like your brother," he said. "I wonder what he thinks of me. I tremble at the thought."

"We will find out," she said. "Gabriel."

"Jessica," he said softly. "Jess. Jessie."

"No one has ever called me Jessie," she said.

"Then it will be my name for you," he said. "Unless you abhor it."

"I do not. Not when you say it," she said. She drew breath but paused briefly before continuing. "Gabriel, who raped your neighbor's daughter? Who killed his son? Was it the same person?"

She was going to marry him. Soon. By special license. She had a right to know. There was much to be confronted in the coming weeks and months.

"Yes, I believe so," he said.

"Who?"

"Manley Rochford," he said.

She closed her eyes and inhaled slowly and exhaled before opening them.

"I am sure in the case of the rape," he said. "I went to call upon Penelope Ginsberg—Mrs. Clark now—and her father while I was away."

"It was they who were your neighbors?" she asked.

"Yes," he said. "It was Manley Rochford, while my cousin Philip Rochford looked on. They were both drunk, though what happened was not out of character for either of them. She was not their first victim. I am less sure about the murder, though I have no doubt that it was one of them."

"He is coming to town soon?" she asked.

"Almost certainly within the next few weeks," he said.

"And he will recognize you?"

"Again," he said, "almost certainly. I cannot imagine I will have any difficulty recognizing him."

"How long does it take to acquire a special license?" she asked.

"I have no idea," he said, "never having needed one before now. I will find out and take care of it tomorrow."

"There are going to be fireworks," she said. She smiled fleetingly. "Here at Vauxhall, I mean."

"We will go back to the box," he told her. "It would be a pity to miss them."

"Gabriel," she said before they moved, "let us not say anything to anyone. I would like my mother to be the first to know, and then Anna and Avery."

He rather suspected her relatives back at the box would take one look at her and find themselves making a very shrewd guess.

"My lips are sealed," he said.

"Thank you."

He set an arm about her waist again and drew her against his side as they made their way back along the path to the main avenue.

# Fourteen

Jessica had been quite correct. Gabriel applied for permission to call the following morning—or for an audience, as she had put it last night—and the Duke of Netherby had returned a prompt, affirmative reply.

Being ushered into the ducal study a few hours later was an intimidating experience. Netherby, as he rose from the chair behind a large oak desk, was neither particularly tall nor broad. He was dressed with an elegance that bordered upon, but somehow did not cross the line into, dandyism. He wore several rings upon the well-manicured fingers of the hand he extended to shake Gabriel's. Yet somehow he exuded power and the unspoken warning that one might be very sorry indeed if one attempted any sort of impertinence. Gabriel, who was adept at summing up men upon very little acquaintance, was at a loss with the duke.

"Thank you for granting me some of your time," Gabriel said, clasping his hand and shaking it firmly.

"Not at all," the duke murmured, indicating a chair for his guest before resuming his seat behind the desk.

A man's time was precious. It ought not to be wasted upon small talk except on social occasions. This was not one.

"I have asked Lady Jessica Archer to marry me," Gabriel began, though he was still not sure he *had* asked. "She said yes. We plan to marry by special license within the week. She does not wish for a large *ton* wedding. Neither do I."

If Netherby was shocked, or even surprised, he certainly gave no indication. "Congratulations are in order, then," he said. "You may have a fight on your hands with her mother over the nature of the wedding. But that is no concern of mine. Was there anything else you wished to discuss with me?"

He was a cool customer, Gabriel thought, especially in light of what Norton had had to say in the report that had arrived from Brierley this morning.

"Yes," Gabriel said. "Is your secretary at work this morning?"

The ducal eyebrows rose, and for a moment Gabriel could see a faint resemblance between him and his half sister. Or perhaps it was just that they had both perfected that haughtiness of manner that froze pretension.

"Edwin Goddard?" the duke said. "I pay him to work during the mornings. I trust he is at it now and not playing truant."

"Here at Archer House?" Gabriel asked.

A very brief smile curved the duke's lips for a moment. "It is doubtful," he said, "unless he can ride like the wind, which is extremely unlikely. He is a commendably efficient secretary, but in some instances he might be fondly described as plodding. He is not blending unnoticed into his surroundings, I take it?"

"Not as well as my man does," Gabriel told him. "Norton is a gardener at the house by day and a frequenter of the local tavern by night."

"Ah," His Grace said. "For all his many talents, one cannot imagine Edwin wielding a scythe. Or, for that matter, *blending*. When I next see him, he will give me a pained look and not quite inform me that he told me so. He *did* tell me so. How was a stranger going to park himself for a week or more at a godforsaken inn in a godforsaken village in the middle of nowhere, he told me—actually he did not say it aloud, though his manner implied it—and discover a sudden and insatiable curiosity about its inhabitants without arousing suspicion from all and sundry, even the village idiot, if there is such a person? I advised him when I saw that look on his face to do his best. For once in his illustrious career it would seem that his best was not good enough. As a matter of purely personal interest, will Jessica's name become Thorne or Rochford when she marries?"

"Thorne," Gabriel said. "My name was legally changed in Boston when my cousin adopted me as his son."

"Your mother's cousin, I presume," the duke said. "It was her maiden name too. Edwin Goddard is very good at many things, you see, though admittedly that was something I might have ferreted out even without his aid if I had chosen to exert myself. Edwin is bad for me. He enables me to be lazy."

Gabriel very much doubted His Grace allowed anyone or anything to make him lazy.

"You see," Netherby continued, "I would quite possibly have approved of your suit, Lyndale—I may call you that?—even if Jessica had needed my permission. An earl is a good match for her. I would, of course, have required detailed information about your American business and your personal fortune. Poor Edwin would have been very busy indeed. I would also have required—no, I would have demanded—a full explanation of certain events that happened just prior to your leaving for America. I trust you have been able to satisfy Jessica on those points?"

"I have," Gabriel told him. "I am innocent of both rape and murder. I can offer proof on the first and a witness, or rather an alibi, on the second."

"Quite so," the duke said with a dismissive gesture of one hand. "Miss Beck, I assume. You need not proceed to bore me with all the sordid details."

Gabriel did not doubt that he knew them already. But good God, his man had spoken to Mary, had he? Norton had spotted him in the environs of Brierley. And from the description he had given in his report, Gabriel had concluded that he and the majordomo who had been guarding Lady Jessica Archer at the inn on the road to London a few weeks ago were one and the same.

"Perhaps," he said, getting to his feet, "I may have a word with my betrothed now?"

"I do not doubt she awaits you with bated breath," Netherby said, also rising from his chair. "You may discover, however, that her mother will want more than a single word with you. You may expect to find her severely disappointed, since she and her sisters and their mother appear to have pinned their hopes upon another man who expects to be Earl of Lyndale one day."

"Jessica informed me that you withheld your blessing from him when he asked for it," Gabriel said, "because he has too many teeth."

And he was suddenly treated to the rare sight of the Duke of Netherby smiling.

Jessica was sitting in the drawing room with Anna and her mother. Her mother had not given either her or Ruth any special instructions this morning. As a result, Jessica was wearing her favorite—but not new—blue morning dress and had her hair dressed simply, without any artfully wayward curls to trail her neck or temples. She sat with a book open on her lap, a ridiculous affectation, since she could not have read a single sentence if she tried. Indeed, she had to check to make sure it was the right way up.

Her mother was *not* pleased. The fact that she had not uttered a word since Jessica joined her and Anna in the drawing room proved the point. She had not said anything or looked up from her embroidery frame even when the door knocker sounded downstairs and the heavy doors could be heard opening a short time later.

Anna was holding her peace too, though she regarded them both with kindly smiles from time to time when she looked up from the bonnet she was knitting for Beatrice.

"Mr. *Thorne*?" Mama had said when Avery had mentioned at breakfast that Gabriel had requested an audience. "But whatever for?"

"If he had included that information in his note," Avery had said, "he would hardly need to come here too, Mother."

"It cannot be," Mama had said, frowning. "He surely cannot be coming here to make an offer for *Jessica*, Avery!"

"I seriously doubt it," Avery had said. "He must know he does not need my permission."

"Avery!" she had cried. "You will surely say a resounding no, whether Jessica needs your permission or not. It is Mr. *Rochford* whose suit we must encourage. He has prospects. Viola is hoping Mr. Thorne will persuade Estelle to choose a husband at last, though she is perfectly well aware that Marcel may object to her choosing an untitled man about whom so little is known. She is bound to be upset nevertheless if it turns out he has set his sights upon Jessica. Perhaps we can avoid mentioning it to her."

Avery had simply looked pained.

"Jessica?" Anna had asked. "Did you know about this?"

Finally someone had thought to include her in this conversation. "Yes," she had said, touching the pink rosebud beside her plate.

*"Jessica?"* Her mother had looked at her in astonishment.

Jessica had got to her feet, set her napkin beside her plate, and left the room, remembering to take her pink rosebud and the card with her. This morning the card read simply *Gabriel.* Had the daily rose not been a warning to her mother? Had she really thought he was sending one to any number of women, perhaps Estelle included? Or had she merely assumed that Jessica disdained his interest as she had disdained everyone else's during the past six or seven years?

Was Avery going to come to the drawing room alone this time too, she wondered now, as he had done after Mr. Rochford called, to explain why he had withheld his blessing though he could not refuse his permission? What had Gabriel told him? The full truth? They had not discussed it last night, though she believed he wished to keep his secret for a little longer, until he had somehow dealt with the problem of Mr. Manley Rochford and his son.

Jessica closed her eyes for a few moments. It was Manley Rochford who had raped the neighbor's daughter and probably murdered her brother. Gabriel was sure on the first, almost sure on the second. If the murderer had not been Manley, then it had very probably been Mr. Philip Rochford, Gabriel's cousin, his uncle's son, who was no longer alive to admit or deny the charge.

The door opened suddenly—she had not heard footsteps on the stairs—and Avery ushered Gabriel inside before stepping in after him. Jessica's stomach performed an uncomfortable flip-flop. The events of last night—all of them—seemed somehow unreal this morning. The fact that he was standing here now proved that they were not, however. But she had never been kissed as she had been last night. She was not even sure he had initiated it. She was the one who had stepped up close to him and set her hands over his chest—because the need to touch him had been overwhelming. It had felt . . . breathtaking. She had admitted to wanting him, and he had admitted to wanting her. *Wanting*—such an inoffensive word. But he had mentioned bed, and all sorts of shocking images had filled her mind, and far more than just her mind. And then he had kissed her . . .

Now here he was, looking elegant and behaving very properly for a morning visit. He was bowing to her mother and to Anna.

"Your Grace," he said as a sort of collective greeting to both.

He merely smiled at Jessica.

"Mr. Thorne has informed me," Avery said, "that he and Jessica are betrothed and intend to marry by special license within the week."

Anna set her knitting aside and got to her feet. Jessica's

mother froze, the hand holding her embroidery needle suspended above the cloth.

"I have given my blessing," Avery added.

Anna hurried across the room, her right hand extended, a warm smile lighting her face. "I am very happy for you, Mr. Thorne," she said. "I am sure I shall love having you as a brother-in-law." She shook his hand and turned to Jessica. She leaned over the love seat upon which she sat and hugged her. "I am so happy for you, Jessica."

Jessica's mother was methodically threading her needle through the cloth stretched over her embroidery frame. She looked up, first at Jessica and then at Gabriel. Both of them were looking back at her. So was Anna. Probably Avery too, though Jessica did not look to see.

"I must trust my stepson's judgment, Mr. Thorne," she said at last. "However, I must also have your assurance before I give *my* blessing that you do not intend to take my daughter back to America to live. Frankly I would find that intolerable. And unforgivable."

"I have no such intention, ma'am," he told her. "Circumstances necessitate my living here in England."

"I am relieved to hear it," she said. "And why, Mr. Thorne, are you insisting upon a hurried, almost clandestine wedding within the week? My daughter is the only daughter of the late Duke of Netherby. She is the sister of the current duke. It would be more appropriate for her to have a far grander wedding. The *ton* will expect it of her. Her *family* will expect it."

"I do not want a grand wedding, Mama," Jessica said. "I told Gabriel so last evening at Vauxhall. I have always loved the account of the *very* private wedding Avery and Anna had, with only Cousin Elizabeth and Mr. Goddard as witnesses. And that of Abby and Gil's wedding in the village church at Hinsford two years ago, with only Harry in attendance apart from the vicar and his wife."

"Mr. Thorne," Anna said, her gaze still upon Jessica's mother, "will you allow at least my mother-in-law and Avery and me to attend your wedding? And perhaps Sir Trevor and Lady Vickers? It would mean a great deal to us."

"Jessica?" Gabriel was looking at her with raised eyebrows.

"And . . . perhaps Grandmama?" she said.

"Aunt Edith will want to come too, then," her mother said. "She lives with your grandmother, after all, and will be hurt if she is excluded. And my sisters—Viscountess Dirkson and Lady Molenor," she explained for Gabriel's benefit. "And their husbands, of course. I will be hurt if they are not invited. And Viola, who was my very dear sister-in-law for twenty-three years—the Marchioness of Dorchester, Mr. Thorne. And her husband the marquess. All three husbands, in fact."

Gabriel had on his face the amused look that Jessica was beginning to recognize even when he was not outright smiling. "And I believe, ma'am," he said, "Lady Estelle Lamarr and Viscount Watley, her twin, are the marquess's children. And the Earl of Riverdale is head of the Westcott family. The lady who arranged a party to welcome him and the countess back to London and was kind enough to invite me is his sister. Their mother was present at the party too."

Jessica could see that her mother's cheeks had turned rather pink.

Anna laughed. "Is your head spinning on your shoulders yet, Mr. Thorne?" she asked. "Do come and sit down next to Jessica while I ring for a pot of coffee. What you should have done if you wanted a swift, quiet wedding, you know, was what Avery did with me once upon a time. He came to

Westcott House on South Audley Street, where I was living at the time, told me to fetch my bonnet, and whisked me away to marry. It was the most romantic wedding in the world."

"I have never quite forgiven either of you," Jessica's mother said bitterly. "We were all planning the grandest of grand weddings for you. You were the long-lost heiress, Anna, and Avery was a *duke*. My stepson."

"That is precisely why we did it, Mother," Avery said, sounding slightly bored. "I would do the same again if I were ever called upon to marry Anna a second time. Have a seat, Thorne, while my stepmother tells you about your own wedding."

"Avery!" she scolded.

Gabriel did not move from where he stood. He looked hard at Jessica and then transferred his gaze to her mother.

"There is something you need to know about me, ma'am," he said. "And something Her Grace the duchess ought to know too, though I am still hopeful it will not become general knowledge just yet, as there are matters I need to settle first. I was born with the name Gabriel Rochford, though Thorne is now my legal name."

"Rochford?" Jessica's mother said, frowning. "You are related somehow to Mr. Anthony Rochford, then?"

"Yes, ma'am," he said, but Anna was already making the connection.

"Gabriel Rochford!" she said. "That was the name of the cousin who—"

She had not been part of the group that had heard the story Mr. Rochford told at Elizabeth and Colin's party. But clearly that story had been passed on.

"Yes, ma'am," Gabriel said. "My father was the younger

brother—the only brother—of Julius Rochford, the Earl of Lyndale, who died with his wife and only son almost seven years ago. I had gone to America six years before then and settled into a happy, prosperous life in Boston with a cousin of my mother's. Thorne was her maiden name. Before I left England at the age of nineteen I was involved in an innocent flirtation with a neighbor's daughter. Her brother had been my close friend for many years. When it became known to her father that she was with child, she allowed the assumption to be made that I was the father. She was afraid to admit that she had been the victim of violence. When her brother came after me, presumably to demand that I do the decent thing, he ended up dead, shot in the back. I was elsewhere at the time and knew nothing of either catastrophe until I returned home. All the evidence pointed to my being guilty of both crimes. My uncle, his son, and another cousin urged me to run in order to avoid arrest and an almost certain hanging. I took fright and ran."

Jessica's mother had both hands against her cheeks. "You are the Earl of Lyndale," she said, her voice almost a whisper. "You are not dead after all."

"No, ma'am," he said.

Anna had resumed her seat. Her hands were clasped, white knuckled, in her lap. Avery had moved up behind her and set a hand on her shoulder. "But why," she asked, "did you not return seven years ago, Mr. Thorne? Or as soon as you heard that your uncle and cousin had died?"

"I had no interest in returning," he said. "I had made a new life and I was both busy and happy. I grew up at Brierley from the age of nine, when my father died. I was never happy there."

"Why have you returned now?" Jessica's mother asked.

"There was one particular reason," he said. "But it has grown into several reasons since I came back and learned more."

"This will be very disturbing news to Mr. Manley Rochford," she said. "And to his son, who came here to Archer House not many days ago to ask for Avery's blessing on a marriage proposal he wished to make to Jessica—and on the expectation that he was about to become heir to an earldom."

"They will certainly not be happy," Gabriel agreed.

"Mr. Thorne," Anna said. "Who was the other cousin who urged you to run away after your friend's murdered body was discovered?"

"Manley Rochford," he said.

She frowned.

"My love," Avery said, "since you did not after all ring for coffee, and the sun is still shining outside despite dire predictions I heard during my morning ride of rain on the way, perhaps we ought to take the children to Hyde Park for an hour or so. Mother, would you care to accompany us?"

"But there is so much to be talked about," she said. "I . . . feel as though my brain must have frozen."

"Quite so," Avery agreed. "Come and thaw it in the park. Jessica and Thorne have a wedding to discuss and might make better headway if they are left alone. My advice, Thorne, is that you wait until we are out of sight, and then instruct my sister to fetch her bonnet before taking her off to the nearest church. But I daresay you have not yet acquired a special license."

"I have, actually," Gabriel told him.

"Jessica?" Her mother had set aside her embroidery frame and got to her feet. She sounded alarmed.

"You may relax, Mama," Jessica told her. "I shall flatly refuse to fetch my bonnet, and no lady can be expected to set foot outdoors without one."

Avery was holding open the drawing room door. Soon it closed behind the three of them, though her mother had looked very reluctant to go.

Jessica could not remember being alone in a room before with a man who was not a relative—oh, except when someone had come to ask for her hand in marriage. But on those occasions Avery had not gone off to stroll in Hyde Park with Anna and her mother and the children. This whole thing suddenly felt horribly real.

*Horribly?* It struck her how little she knew this man or *of* him. She had only his word for almost everything he had told her. One thing struck her as a bit odd, though.

"Why was Avery willing to give his blessing?" she asked. "Did he . . . know? Before you came up to the drawing room, that is?"

"He did," he said. "But not because I told him. Apparently he is too lazy to find things out for himself, but discovering that Thorne was my mother's name was well within the capabilities of his secretary."

"Avery is far from lazy," she told him.

"Yes," he said. "I have concluded that for myself. That man of his is at Brierley, finding out what he can while trying unsuccessfully to look inconspicuous."

"Avery told you he had sent him there?" Jessica asked.

"No," he said. "But *my* man at Brierley reported that a stranger has been asking pointed questions. It seemed to me from the description he gave that the stranger was almost certainly the same man who had the charge of you on the road to London."

"It seems to *me*," she said, "that there are definite similarities between you and my brother. You have a man at Brierley? Spying, you mean? Do you really have a marriage license?"

"I do," he said. "Do you still want to marry me?"

"Yes," she said. "Yes, I do."

If Avery had given his blessing, it would not be just because he had discovered that Gabriel was the Earl of Lyndale. Avery was certainly high in the instep, but he was not shallow. And if Mr. Goddard was at Brierley, trying, poor man, to look inconspicuous, Avery himself must have been very busy here. She was not surprised, however. It would always be a mistake to be taken in by Avery's studied indolence.

Gabriel had come to stand in front of her. He held out one hand, and she put her own into it and allowed him to draw her to her feet.

"Now?" he asked her. "Or would you rather wait and allow your mother to arrange a family wedding?"

She could in all reality go and fetch her bonnet *now* and go and get married? She felt suddenly breathless. And very tempted.

"I believe," she said, "it broke Mama's heart when Avery thwarted the plans of the whole Westcott family and took Anna off to marry her privately. I think maybe the family wedding, then. But within the week. And not the grand event they will try to press on us. I do wish, however, you also had family."

He looked at her rather wistfully, she thought, and she remembered that he *did* have family here in England. Family members who lied and committed rape and possibly murder and tried to blame an innocent man. Family members who would be far from happy to see him again.

"I do have Sir Trevor," he said, "and Lady Vickers. They are in truth my godparents. And there is their son, who has become my friend in the past few weeks. Shall we decide upon Friday for our wedding, then? I would rather not wait longer than that."

It was Tuesday already. By Friday she would be a married lady. She would be Lady Jessica Thorne, Countess of Lyndale.

"You would wait that long," she asked, "just so that Mama—and doubtless Grandmama and the aunts—would have time to arrange some sort of family wedding? Because it is what I want?"

"Yes," he said.

And she wondered. Oh, she wondered. Last evening he had admitted that he wished to marry her only because she had all the qualifications he felt he needed in a bride. He had also admitted that he wanted her. But wanting her did not necessarily mean he felt any tender emotion for her. *Did* he care for her? Just a little bit?

And did she care for him? Had she agreed to marry him just because she had decided she wanted to be married and because she wanted him? Was there anything else? It would be wise not even to think of the possibility.

"Thank you," she said, and he drew her into his arms and kissed her. Slowly and thoroughly, holding her right against the full length of him, though the kiss was not as urgent as last night's.

It was good even so. Better than good. He felt solid and dependable. Masculine. Desirable.

He already had a marriage license. Mama and Anna and all the other females in the family were about to be let loose upon wedding plans.

She was glad.
She was going to be married.
With her family about her.
She was going to be *married*.
And then she would have to face his family with him.

# *Fifteen*

I wish to say something," Lady Estelle Lamarr said to the roomful of ladies, none of whom were related to her by blood but all of whom had welcomed her into the Westcott family as one of their own when her father married the former Viola Westcott, Countess of Riverdale.

The chatter ceased abruptly, and everyone turned to listen to her with identical expressions of surprised inquiry. They were gathered in the drawing room of the dowager countess's home, it being easier for all of them to travel there than to expect her to travel elsewhere.

"You are all tiptoeing about one point," she said. "It is to spare my feelings, I know, and I do appreciate your kindness. It is, however, unnecessary. I like Mr. Thorne exceedingly well. I was never for one moment interested in marrying him, however, even though I know you all did your best to promote a match between us. *He* was never for one moment interested in marrying *me*. It ought to have been obvious to everyone that he had eyes only for Jessica—

and that she had eyes only for him, though I know you were all hoping for a match between her and Mr. Rochford. Please believe me. I am *not* nursing a broken heart. I am not even in search of a husband yet. I am only twenty-three. I am going to live in the country with Bertrand for a year or two when the summer is over. We are both agreed upon that plan. Meanwhile I am *very* happy for Jessica and Mr. Thorne."

"*Only* twenty-three," the Dowager Countess of Riverdale said, throwing up her hands. "Whatever has happened to girls these days? It was very different in our day, Edith, was it not? Any girl not married by the time she reached her twentieth birthday was very firmly on the shelf."

"It is a relief to hear that you are not upset, Estelle," Wren said, smiling kindly at her. "That would have been very unfortunate."

"I am surprised at Avery, Louise," Mildred said. "You told us only a short while ago that he had withheld his blessing upon Mr. Rochford's suit until after his father has been officially declared Earl of Lyndale, though that is a mere formality. Yet he gave it yesterday to Mr. Thorne, about whom we know far less. He is said to have inherited property and a fortune somewhere to the north, and he is said to have brought a fortune with him from America. It is all very vague, however. He has Sir Trevor Vickers to vouch for him, of course, but really I would have expected Avery to investigate more thoroughly, to make absolutely sure that Mr. Thorne will be a worthy husband for Jessica."

"You can rest assured," Louise said, "that Avery has investigated very thoroughly indeed, Mildred."

"Then where *is* this property of his?" her sister asked.

"Mr. Thorne wishes to go there in person and settle a few issues before he makes any public announcement, Aunt," Anna said. "He wants to go soon, but he also wants

Jessica to be with him when he does. That is why they have decided to marry the day after tomorrow."

"We must be thankful, then," Matilda said, "that they have not decided upon a wedding exactly like yours and Avery's, Anna. Yes, I know, Elizabeth. You are about to remind us all that it was the loveliest, most romantic wedding you have ever attended—with the exception of your own, no doubt. But you were there. The rest of us were not. Perhaps we will forgive you in a decade or two, Anna." Her eyes twinkled at her niece. "The wedding breakfast is to be at Archer House, then?"

"Oh, of course," Louise and Anna said almost simultaneously.

"We must discuss flowers," Althea Westcott said briskly. "What do you have in mind, Louise? Elizabeth and I will look after those, if you wish."

"And me too, please, Mother," Wren said. "I will provide all the vases—from the new collection at my glassworks."

"Predominantly roses," Anna said. "Mostly pink. Mr. Thorne has been sending a pink rose to Jessica every day for the last few weeks—except once when it was yellow. I would like to know the story behind that one."

"He has been sending her roses? Daily?" Edith said. "What a very romantic young man he is. It is a love match, then?"

"But of course," Anna and Wren said together.

"We have been blind," Mildred said, shaking her head. "All of us. We made our plans and we forged onward with them and saw none of the signs. That half hour they spent over at the pianoforte during your party, for example, Elizabeth. We were annoyed that Mr. Thorne had drawn Jessica away from Mr. Rochford."

"And the church, Louise?" Matilda, always the most disciplined planner of family events, asked. "Will we be able to decorate that with flowers too? I will see to that. You too, Viola? Do we know *which* church?"

Wren came to sit beside Anna while the room was buzzing with happy plans for the wedding, small though it was going to be.

"Anna," Wren said, keeping her voice low, "I suppose you *know*—do you?"

"Well, I do," Anna said, "and so do Avery and Mother. If you mean what I believe you mean, that is."

"Alexander was part of the group at Elizabeth and Colin's party when Mr. Rochford told his story," Wren said. "He was uneasy about it. He had a word with Avery."

"Ah," Anna said.

"The valet Avery's secretary took with him to Brierley was able to—"

"Mr. Goddard took a valet?" Anna said, frowning.

"He was one of our men," Wren explained. "Not really a valet at all. He was able to relate far more easily with the local people than poor Mr. Goddard, who cannot blend at all well. I am not sure what Avery was able to tell you this morning after they returned, but if you and Cousin Louise are at all worried, Anna, as I daresay you are, I believe I can relieve your minds. Mr. Rochford said at the party that his cousin Gabriel Rochford was a wild young man, even vicious as he grew older. That is not at all how the local people remember him. He had a reputation as a quiet, studious, sweet-natured boy."

"I am so glad," Anna said.

"Miss Beck, a lady who lives the life of a hermit in a small house on the estate, is quite adamant about the alibi she can offer Mr. Thorne for the afternoon when that un-

fortunate young man was killed," Wren said. "She under-
stands that she may not be believed because she had a very
close friendship with Mr. Thorne, but she was able to name
a groom from the house who had brought her the injured
fawn she and Mr. Thorne were tending at the time. Apparently the groom stayed to watch. And he still works at
Brierley—and is willing to testify."

Anna smiled. "I can remember a time," she said, "when
Avery and Alexander did not particularly like each other.
Then Avery fought a duel—it was for the honor of Camille
against that horrid man who used to be betrothed to her—
and Alexander was his second."

"Alexander has told me the story," Wren said. "If he told
it as it was and was not exaggerating, Avery felled his very
large, boastful, and contemptuous opponent with one bare
foot to the chin and almost gave Alexander an apoplexy. I
*wish* I could have been there."

"I was," Anna told her. "With Elizabeth. We hid behind
a tree."

They both dissolved into laughter, their heads almost
touching.

"Now what is amusing you two?" Elizabeth asked.

"Avery's duel with Viscount Uxbury," Anna said, and
Elizabeth joined in their laughter.


There was no betrothal announcement in the morning papers. There were no banns. Life proceeded as though nothing of any great moment had happened or was about to
happen.

Jessica drove in the park with Mr. Rochford the day her
mother and Anna went to her grandmother's to discuss
wedding plans with the rest of the Westcott ladies. On the

evening of the following day, her wedding eve, she attended a ball and found herself surrounded by her usual court. She danced with a number of them. She was relieved to discover that Mr. Rochford was not there. That was unusual for him.

She intended to leave before supper since she did not wish to arrive home in the early hours of her wedding day. But the dance before supper was a waltz, and she looked around her court, wondering which gentleman she could encourage to ask her to dance it. Lord Jennings again? Someone touched her arm, however, and she turned to find herself looking into Gabriel's face.

"Lady Jessica," he said, "may I have the honor?"

Her court had fallen into a rather sullen silence.

"You are late, Mr. Thorne," she said.

"Rather," he said, "I am hoping I have arrived just in time."

He had told her he would probably not attend the ball. He wished to leave for Brierley the day after their wedding—the day after tomorrow, that was—and wanted to be sure he had tied up some loose ends of business first. It was still difficult for Jessica to believe that two days from now she would have left London and family and everything that was familiar behind her and embarked upon a wholly new life in new surroundings and with new challenges to face.

There was nothing unusual about a woman having to give up everything when she married, of course. In this case, however, it was what they would both be doing. Gabriel had given up the life with which he had been happy in Boston. They were both about to embark upon a new world, a world full of uncertainty and difficulty.

"You have, sir," she said, placing her hand in his. "I have not promised the set to anyone."

A protesting murmur rippled through her court. She wondered if they would miss her. She wondered if she would miss them, if she would soon be nostalgic for this life she had lived since she left the schoolroom.

Elizabeth, she could see, was going to waltz with Colin, and Anna with Avery. Mr. Adrian Sawyer, Viscount Dirkson's son, was leading Estelle onto the floor, and Bertrand was smiling down at a young girl Jessica did not know. Aunt Matilda was going to dance with Viscount Dirkson, a lovely thing to see when very few older people danced at *ton* balls, especially with their spouses. And they were smiling at each other, seemingly unaware of anyone else. Even Aunt Viola and Marcel, Marquess of Dorchester, were stepping onto the floor and looking at each other like a couple of people half their age.

What was it about the waltz that made one think of romance?

Jessica felt a momentary pang. But she had known for several years now that she was not going to find that deep, romantic sort of love that so many members of her family had found. She had decided very sensibly this year that at last she would marry anyway, that she would settle for a good man and a good match. And that was what she was doing. She was happy with her choice, for surely she had not *just* settled. She looked up into Gabriel's face as he placed one hand behind her waist and clasped her right hand with his other. She really did want to be married to him, to face with him the unknown adventure that lay ahead. And she really did *want* him.

Tomorrow night . . .

She placed her left hand on his shoulder. He was gazing steadily at her with those dark blue, intent eyes of his, his look inscrutable. She wondered if he was having similar thoughts and coming to the same conclusion. She hoped it was not a *different* conclusion. She hoped he was not regretting this hasty marriage with someone he scarcely knew. He had not wanted to come back from America. He had not wanted to be the Earl of Lyndale or to return to Brierley. He was taking a bride out of sheer necessity. He had chosen the very best candidate available—she could think so without conceit. She had once told him—at Richmond Park—that when he looked at her, he saw only Lady Jessica Archer, daughter and sister of a Duke of Netherby. She had told him that if he wished to have a chance with her, he must come to know *her*, the person beneath the aristocratic veneer. Did he know her any better now than he had known her then?

Had she sold herself too easily?

The music began. And she discovered that he waltzed beautifully. She did not have to think of the steps. She did not have to fear missing one or treading on anyone's toes or having her own trodden upon or crashing into any other couple. She did not have to fear getting her feet tangled up with each other during the twirls. She was soon unaware of the other dancers around her and of the people standing watching. She was unaware of the ballroom and the chandeliers and the long mirrors and the flowers decked everywhere, of their heady scent, all of which she had admired before he'd arrived.

She smiled into the eyes of her partner and felt a little as she had felt when he'd played Bach on Elizabeth and Colin's pianoforte, as though she were being drawn into the soul of the music. But this time it filled her body too, and sound mingled with color and light. Yet all she was *really* aware of was the man with whom she waltzed.

He gazed steadily at her throughout. She lowered her

eyes after a while to avoid being mesmerized, but when she looked back, his eyes met hers with a smile that did not quite make it to his face.

"Jessie," he said. Just that.

That name on his lips somehow sent shivers down her spine.

"Gabriel," she said.

And that was the full extent of their conversation.


Bertie Vickers came to Gabriel's hotel suite the following morning in time to go to church with him. Gabriel had asked him to be his best man.

"I say, Gabe," he said, looking his friend over from head to toe, "you look as fine as fivepence. It is a shame you are not getting married at St. George's on Hanover Square with all the *ton* to gaze upon your splendor."

Gabriel had decided upon knee breeches and stockings and buckled shoes and a lace-edged neckcloth. Even the sleeves of his shirt were edged with lace rather than plain starched cuffs. His breeches and waistcoat were silver gray, his tailed coat a darker gray. His stockings and linen were snowy white. Horbath had excelled with the folds of his neckcloth, and he had placed a diamond pin in just exactly the right place. He hoped he had not overdone the outfit, but Horbath had assured him he had not.

"A man has only one wedding day, sir," he had said.

"It is quite enough," Gabriel said now, "that I will have all the Westcotts and your parents in attendance, Bertie. Weddings are an abomination."

"Ah. You had better not let your bride hear that, old chap," Bertie advised. "Weddings are the breath of life to females. M'mother bought a new hat. M'father will have to sit three feet away from her on the church pew so that he don't get clipped over the ear every time she turns her head."

Gabriel chuckled, though he was feeling a bit too bilious for proper amusement. Who could have predicted that he would be *nervous* on his wedding day? He was horribly afraid that he was doing the wrong thing. All night he had been remembering snippets of what Jessica had said to him in that rather impassioned outburst at Richmond Park. She was really two persons, was what she had been saying—the very aristocratic Lady Jessica Archer, sister of the Duke of Netherby, and the person who lived within that aristocratic outer shell. She had wanted him to find that person, to romance that person. She had wanted him to fall in love with her, even if she had not used that term and had even, in fact, denied it.

She had wanted to fall in love herself, as her cousin had done, the one who had been more like a sister to her, the one for whom she had sacrificed her own expectations of happiness. And good God, it had seemed to Gabriel during the past few weeks that that family of hers on her mother's side, the Westcotts, set great store by romantic love. They were a family of what looked like closely bonded couples. A goodly number of them had been out on the ballroom floor last night, waltzing. With each other. It must be almost unheard of. Husbands did not often dance with their wives. Husbands did not often *dance*. At least, not in his experience.

Yet despite what she had said to him there at Richmond, he was marrying her—in rather a hurry—because of her outer self. Because she was a duke's daughter and as aristocratic as it was possible for a lady to be. Her natural public demeanor was hauteur itself. She was not the sort of woman who was likely to crumble before anyone who tried to intimidate her. Rather, she would draw herself to her full height, peer at her assailant along the length of her nose, and reduce that person to the size of a worm about to be trodden upon. He would feel comfortable going back to Brierley with Jessica as his wife and countess. No. *Comfortable* was not the right word. There was no comfort to expect from what was facing him. She gave him *courage*, then. Not that he had the smallest intention of leaning upon her.

It was time to go and get married. He shook out the lace that covered his hands to the knuckles and looked around for his hat and gloves and cane, which Horbath had of course set out neatly by the door.

He did *like* her, he thought. And he certainly wanted to bed her. She was a beautiful and appealing woman. The prospect of making love to her tonight, in fact—here in his hotel suite—quickened his breathing. He just wished there had been more time to romance her, to give her more of what she had wanted. He was cheating her of that. Perhaps after they were married . . .

"Oh, I say," Bertie said. "I almost forgot. Message from m'mother, and m'father told me to be sure not to forget to tell you, though he can do so himself later, at the wedding breakfast, of course. Rochford arrived in town last night."

Gabriel stood very still, one kid glove half on his hand, as he looked back at Bertie. "*Anthony* Rochford?" he said. "Did he go somewhere?" Now that he thought about it, the man had not been at the ball last night. That was unusual for him.

"No, no," Bertie said. "His father. And his mother too. Come to celebrate being the new earl, I daresay. You will be missing all the fun, Gabe, if you insist upon leaving town tomorrow. Can't think what your hurry is with the

Season in full swing. I don't know why m'mother was so particular about that message. Perhaps she hopes you will change your mind and stay a while longer."

"Manley Rochford," Gabriel said.

"That's the name," Bertie said. "Makes one hope he is not small and puny with a name like that, don't it? He would have been ragged mercilessly at school. Slipped my mind to tell you. M'mother would not have been pleased. She already thinks there is no one on this earth more shatter-brained than I am. Are you going to finish putting that glove on, Gabe? A lot of young women are going to go into mourning after today, you know."

Gabriel pulled on his gloves and adjusted the lace over them. Horbath had appeared from nowhere to hand him his hat and cane and to hold the door of the suite open for them and bow them on their way.

So, Gabriel thought as they made their way downstairs. This news was going to change a few things.


There had been a dress at the back of Jessica's wardrobe for two years. It had never been worn, though it had gone back to the country with her each summer and returned here with her each spring. She had always loved it, but she had never been able to decide what occasion was suitable for it. It was not quite an evening gown, but it was a bit too fussy for afternoon visits or even garden parties. It was, she sometimes feared when she looked at it—and she often drew it out to hold it against herself and admire it—too young for her. It was white, a color she had avoided since her first Season, when white had been almost obligatory. But it also had pink rosebuds embroidered all over it, spaced widely over most of the dress, clustered in greater profusion about the scalloped hem and the edges of the short sleeves. A silk sash to tie beneath her bosom added a splash of color. It was pink, one shade deeper than the rosebuds.

This week she had understood why she had never worn it before. She had been unconsciously saving it for her wedding day. Not that it would have been suited to just any wedding day, it was true. But for *this* one? It was more perfect than perfect. Oh dear, her former governess would wince if she heard *that* logical impossibility spoken aloud. She had held the dress against herself the night their wedding day had been set, after Ruth had left her dressing room, and she had twirled before the full-length mirror and known that nothing else would do.

She was wearing it now, and she felt like a bride. How was a bride supposed to feel? She did not know about other brides, but she felt—euphoric. Was she being foolish? There was after all nothing truly romantic about her proposed marriage with Gabriel. She must not make the mistake of believing that a daily rose, the touch of his little finger to hers on the keys of a pianoforte, a light kiss in a rose arbor, a deeper kiss at Vauxhall, equated romance. Or, if they did in a way, they did not equate *love*. This was not a love match on either side. It would be unwise of her to deceive herself into thinking that perhaps it was.

She felt euphoric anyway. Because she *liked* him and found him knee-weakeningly attractive. She felt quite breathless when she thought about tonight. She was a virgin, of course, but she was not going to be a *shrinking* virgin. She wanted it, whatever *it* turned out to be. She wanted it very badly. With him. Not with anyone else. There could *be* no one else. Not after Gabriel.

She did not stop to analyze that thought. She wanted to

go to Brierley with him and help him sort out whatever mess was awaiting him there. She could do that. It was the sort of thing she had been raised to do with ease. She could be *very* lady-of-the-manorish when she chose. Goodness, was there such a term? She had learned the effectiveness of a remote sort of haughtiness from Avery and, to a lesser degree, from her mother.

Her mother came into her dressing room now, looking very elegant in deep blue—not quite royal and not quite navy but something of both. Ruth was placing Jessica's new straw bonnet over the coiffure she had been working on for almost an hour, and then tying the wide pink ribbons to one side of her chin before taking a step back to look critically at her handiwork. She made one adjustment.

"You will do, my lady," she said—a lengthy speech for Ruth.

"Oh, you will do very nicely indeed," Jessica's mother said, a bit teary eyed as she held her arms wide to hug her daughter. "I wish your father could see you now."

Jessica had often wondered if her mother had loved her father. She rarely spoke of him. Yet she had never shown any interest in remarrying.

"I must not crush you," she said after a brief, warm hug. "Jessica, you *are* doing the right thing, are you, dearest? You are not marrying Mr. Thorne *just* because he is the Earl of Lyndale? You do love him? Love is so important in marriage. I loved your father, you know. Very dearly. Even though he was a duke and I was an earl's daughter and love ought not to have mattered. And he loved me." She brushed at a tear that threatened to spill over onto her cheek.

Ah.

"I am doing the right thing, Mama," Jessica assured her, and she felt that surely, surely she was speaking the truth.

Liking could be love too, could it not? A certain kind of love?

"Well," her mother said. "We must not keep Avery waiting. He is downstairs now. So are Anna and Josephine."

The younger children were to remain at home. But Josephine had learned to sit still, even for an hour-long Sunday service.

Jessica suddenly felt a pang of regret that Abby would not be at the church. Or Camille. Or Harry. She had written a long letter to Abby, a shorter one to each of the other two. She did not know when she would see them again—a melancholy thought. But such was life, she supposed, when one grew up. Today, however, was not for melancholy. Today was for her and Gabriel. Today was their wedding day.

She pulled on her long white gloves, hesitated a moment, and then drew the single rose from the vase on her dressing table and dried it off with a napkin. It was yellow today, as it had been the morning after the garden party, where he had kissed her for the first time. She had worn primrose yellow on that occasion, and in the rose arbor she had stood for a few moments, cupping though not quite touching a yellow rose between her hands.

He had remembered, she thought. For today, their wedding day.

She took the rose with her, holding it by the long stem, careful not to touch the thorns.

# Sixteen

They had chosen a small, insignificant church on a long, quiet London street—the very church, in fact, where Anna and Avery had married eight years ago.

This wedding was better attended than that had been. Indeed, this particular street had perhaps never seen so many grand carriages all at once, not just moving along it but also stopping, one behind another. They waited, all of them, after the passengers had alit, liveried coachmen and footmen polishing off the small stains of travel and tending the horses. Passersby, intent upon their daily business, stopped to gawk and, if they were in pairs or trios, to wonder and speculate. The flower-bedecked carriage that stood directly outside the church was an indisputable clue, however, that a wedding was taking place inside. Several people settled in to wait, any urgency they had felt when they set out on their various errands forgotten. It was not often there was any grand spectacle to behold in this part of London.

All the Westcotts then in town and those with family

connections to them were there. So were Sir Trevor and Lady Vickers. And Albert Vickers, their son, of course, was Gabriel's best man.

The pews, even in so small a church, were not filled, but there was a feeling of warm intimacy, something Gabriel found a bit intimidating as he awaited the arrival of his bride. All the guests must be wondering—except the very few who knew the truth—why Jessica was marrying a mere Mr. Thorne from America, who had been rather vague about the inherited property and fortune that had brought him home to England. Certainly all must wonder why the formidable Duke of Netherby had given his blessing to such a seemingly unequal match. But all had come regardless, to celebrate with one of their own, who was old enough to make her own decisions and had decided to marry him, title or no title, mystery or no mystery.

The Duchess of Netherby with her eldest daughter and the dowager duchess were the last to arrive, a sure sign that Jessica and the duke were not far behind. The two ladies and the child took their places in the front pew, across from Gabriel and Bertie. The duchess smiled, the child looked at him wide eyed, and the dowager nodded graciously. Then the clergyman appeared from the vestry, dressed in simple white vestments, and lit the candles on the altar before turning to look back to the door of the church. There was a rustle of new arrivals and Gabriel got to his feet and turned.

Netherby, like him and unlike anyone else as far as Gabriel could see, was formally clad in knee breeches and evening wear. But Gabriel scarcely noticed him. Jessica was almost simply dressed in contrast with her brother—and him. She was all delicate in white and pink, and the yellow rose he had sent this morning. In the cool semidarkness of the church interior, with its slightly musty oldchurch smells of stone and prayer books, candle wax and incense, she looked nothing short of gorgeous. Her posture was proudly erect, her chin was raised, and her expression was stern and haughty. She was looking at him seemingly along the length of her nose.

But she was not *just* the aristocrat he had wanted and chosen almost at first glance. She was also *Jessica*. It was a reassuring thought. He smiled.

Her chin came down by half an inch, her eyes widened, her lips parted—and she smiled back.

After that he more or less missed his own wedding, Gabriel thought later when he looked back upon it and tried to remember details. It was very brief. There was no music, no ceremony, no full service. Netherby gave him Jessica's hand and took the yellow rose, and the clergyman addressed everyone gathered there as *dearly beloved*. Jessica in a clear voice promised to love, honor, and obey him. He promised to love and cherish and keep her for as long as he lived. Bertie almost dropped the ring and muttered something not quite appropriate for the place or occasion as he juggled and caught it and handed it over with a flashing grin. Gabriel slid the ring onto his bride's finger. The clergyman pronounced them man and wife.

And all the while Gabriel had gazed into her face, wondering if it could possibly be true that he was *getting married*, that his life was irrevocably changing. And all the while too he had waited for uncertainty, even panic, to grab him by the throat. It did not happen.

He *wanted* to be married. To her. To Jessica.

And suddenly—but surely she had only just arrived in the church and taken his hand—suddenly *he was married*.

*They* were married.

And she was smiling at him a little tremulously. The clergyman was gesturing with one arm toward the vestry, where they would sign the register, and Netherby got to his feet to join them and Bertie there as a witness. The dowager duchess came with Netherby. Then the congregation chuckled as the little girl—Netherby's daughter—spoke aloud.

"Grandmama," she said, "Papa forgot to take Aunt Jessica's rose. You take it. Be careful not to prick your finger."

And they laughed into each other's eyes, he and Jessica, and tears brightened hers before she blinked them away and bit her upper lip.

They were married and she seemed happy about it.

He would make this work, Gabriel thought. He would make a success of it. He had done it before, though in an entirely different way and under different circumstances. When he went to America, he had no experience of earning a living and certainly no experience with the sort of labor Cyrus offered him. But he had done it. He had worked hard—mostly hating it at first—and had succeeded. He had kept on striving and had come to love his employment before Cyrus died. He had kept on succeeding afterward, but only because he had never slackened, had never taken his success for granted. He would make his marriage a success in the same way—by working hard on it every day of his life. It was what he had promised a few minutes ago, was it not?

The dowager duchess hugged both her daughter and Gabriel after they had signed the register. Netherby hugged his sister and gave Gabriel a firm handshake. Bertie wrung his hand and bowed to Jessica and called her *Mrs. Thorne*. And it was time to go back into the church to greet her family and his godparents. There was to be no formal procession out. They had decided that it would be a bit ridiculous. Only smiles and greetings wherever they turned, and endless handshakes and back slappings and a few hugs.

"I thought," Lady Hodges told him, "that Avery's wedding here to Anna could not be surpassed in loveliness, Mr. Thorne. And I was quite right. It has not been. But it has been equaled today."

"Thank you, ma'am," he said. "But I must be Gabriel, please."

"Elizabeth," she said, smiling kindly at him. "Welcome to the Westcott family, Gabriel."

Jessica, he saw, was locked in the arms of a tall, thin young man, who was rocking her on the spot and laughing.

"I came yesterday," he was saying as Gabriel approached, "because Mama had been pestering me to stop being a hermit for five minutes. I came just for a week, just long enough to be measured for a new coat and boots. And what should I discover when I got here but that you were getting married today, Jess? Abby is not going to be happy to have missed it. Nor is Camille."

"Oh, but Harry," she protested, drawing back from him, "Abby did not wait for any of us to attend *her* wedding. Only you did because you were already there at Hinsford. But how simply wonderful that you are here today of all days. I would have had a tantrum if you had arrived tomorrow. And you are looking well." For a moment she cupped his face with both hands, having set her rose down on the end of a pew, but then she saw Gabriel standing slightly behind her.

"Gabriel," she said. "Look who has come. My cousin Harry—Harry Westcott. He never goes anywhere, but I am going to pretend he came especially for my wedding. This is Gabriel, Harry. My . . . husband."

"Yes, I sort of gathered that, Jess," he said, and the two men shook hands and took each other's measure as they did so. This, then, was the cousin who had once, very briefly, been the Earl of Riverdale after his father's death, only to have both the title and his legitimacy ripped away when it was discovered that his father and mother's marriage had been bigamous.

How did one recover from such a life-changing catastrophe? Though perhaps he had experienced something not too dissimilar, Gabriel thought.

"It was a fortunate coincidence I came when I did," Harry said. "I understand you are going to whisk Jessica off up north somewhere tomorrow, Thorne."

"I believe," Gabriel said, "our plans must change. We will be staying for a while longer after all."

Jessica looked at him in surprise, but her grandmother and her great-aunt had come up and she turned to hug them.

Viscount Dirkson had come to shake Gabriel's hand. The viscountess hugged him and kissed his cheek.

"Weddings are invariably romantic occasions no matter where they take place or what the size of the congregation," she said, beaming at him. "This one is no exception, Mr. Thorne. No, *Gabriel*. You are one of the family now. I am Aunt Matilda."

Her husband grinned at him. "If you should ever call me *Uncle Charles*," he said, "I do believe I would have to deck you, Thorne."

Aunt Matilda was the first to laugh merrily.

They exited the church a few minutes later to bright sunshine instead of the high clouds that had covered the sky when Gabriel arrived. A small crowd of curious pedestrians gathered outside murmured and even applauded and cheered a bit self-consciously when it must have become apparent to them that this was the bride and groom. Jessica smiled brightly at them and waved her free arm, her yellow rose clutched in her hand. Gabriel lifted a hand in acknowledgment. And then they were showered with rose petals, hurled by Lady Estelle and Bertrand Lamarr and by the Wayne brothers—and the little girl, who was giggling helplessly.

"Oh goodness," Jessica said as Gabriel handed her into the flower-decked carriage that would take them to Archer House. "That has happened at every wedding I have ever attended. Why was I not expecting it with my own?" She sat and gazed at him. "You do look gorgeous, Gabriel."

He brushed himself off before taking his place beside her and the coachman put up the steps and shut the door. "You could not have left that line for me, I suppose?" he asked.

"Do I look gorgeous?"

The brim of her straw bonnet was trimmed with tiny pink rosebuds. The wide silk ribbons that were tied in a bow to the left side of her chin were a richer shade of the same color. Her dark hair was gleaming. Her flushed, wide-eyed face was pure beauty.

"You, my dear wife," he said, "look scrumptious."

She laughed. "Scrumptious?" she said. "Well, that is something new. No one has ever called me that before."

"I am glad of it," he said.

And somehow she was not smiling any longer. Neither was he.

"I made you certain vows," he said. "I do intend to keep them."

"Oh," she said. "And I will keep mine."

He hesitated, set an arm about her shoulders, touched one side of her jaw with his fingertips, and kissed her.

"A mere promise for tonight, Mrs. Thorne," he said against her lips.

There was a faint cheer from their guests, who had spilled out of the church to see them on their way, but it was totally obliterated when the carriage rocked on its springs and moved away from the church, dragging an impressive array of noisy metal items that had been tied beneath.

She grimaced. And laughed. And then shouted over the din. "Gabriel, why has there been a change of plan? Why are we staying in London a little longer?"

"Manley Rochford and his wife have arrived in town," he told her.

Her mouth formed an O, but if sound accompanied it, it was impossible to hear.

So much for their quiet wedding.

The large hallway beyond the front doors of Archer House and the dining room looked and smelled like a rose garden. And the long table in the dining room had been set with all the very best, rarely used china and crystal and silverware. Someone—or, rather, some persons—had been very busy indeed in the relatively short while since she left for her wedding, Jessica thought.

After one peep into the dining room she ran upstairs to remove her bonnet and have Ruth make some repairs to her hair. Yes, she really did run. Her old nurse and her former governess would have had an apoplexy apiece.

A couple of large trunks and hatboxes stood in the middle of her bedchamber, ready to be loaded onto a baggage carriage tomorrow for the journey to Brierley—now delayed. Because Mr. Manley Rochford and his wife had arrived unexpectedly early in town. Jessica's stomach lurched.

Whatever was it going to mean? But she refused to think of all the implications of that just now. Not on her wedding day.

Had there ever been a lovelier, more romantic wedding? Not that she was biased or anything, but he had not taken his eyes off hers throughout the brief service, not even when Mr. Vickers almost dropped her ring and had been forced to perform a few very inelegant twistings and lungings in order to save it—not to mention his language, which fortunately had probably not been too audible beyond their little group. That episode, she supposed, had been rather funny, but she had continued to gaze at Gabriel the whole time and observe it only from the corner of her eye.

It had seemed almost like a love match. Perhaps all weddings did to the two people who were marrying. For a wedding made everything change. The future that stretched ahead was full of possibility, full of hope, full of dreams. Not that one must believe in happily-ever-after. One would be foolish to do so even if the marriage *was* a love match. But one could believe at least in the possibility of more happiness than misery. If that was what one wanted. If it was also what one's spouse wanted. Ah, so many *if*s. So much uncertainty.

"Ruth," she said after her hair had been restored to her maid's satisfaction, "I am Lady Jessica Thorne." *Countess of Lyndale,* she thought, hugging that secret knowledge to herself. "Does that not have a lovely sound?"

"Yes, my lady," Ruth said as Jessica caught up the sides of her dress and twirled once about, just like a young child on her way to a party. Like something Josephine would do. Or four-year-old Rebecca.

Her eyes rested upon the trunks again. A few bags would

already have been taken over to Gabriel's hotel, where she would spend the night and perhaps more than one night if indeed they were to stay longer in London. Either way, she would not be coming back here. She might visit Archer House any number of times in the future and perhaps even stay here occasionally. She might and probably would visit Morland Abbey. But after a lifetime of thinking of both houses as home, she could no longer do so. She did not belong here now. She belonged wherever Gabriel belonged.

And where was that?

Brierley Hall? He had lived there for only ten of his thirty-two years. And they had not been happy years. By contrast, the thirteen he had spent in Boston had been happy. But duty and his concern for a lady who was about to be turned out of her home had brought him back—to stay. Yes, they would live at Brierley Hall, Jessica thought. A house she had never seen, in a part of the country with which she was unfamiliar. Far from either London or Morland Abbey. Far from her mother and Avery and Anna. Far from Abby and Camille and Harry. Far from everyone except perhaps Aunt Mildred and Uncle Thomas.

She would make it into a home. For herself. For Gabriel. For any children they would have—oh please, please, dear God, let there be children. At least one son for the succession and a few other children just because. She would make it a happy home. It was what she had been raised to do. It was what she could and would do. She was Lady Jessica . . . Thorne. She was the Countess of Lyndale.

There was a light tap upon the door of the bedchamber and it opened before Ruth could reach it. Gabriel stepped inside, and Jessica's breath caught in her throat at the realization that he now had every right to do so. She had sacrificed privacy an hour ago as well as name and home and the little freedom she had insisted upon asserting since her twenty-first birthday.

"Everyone is awaiting the bride," he said.

"And that would be me." She took a few steps forward and linked her arm through the one he offered and stepped out of the room that was no longer her bedchamber without looking back.


There was feasting and conversation and laughter. There were speeches and toasts and more laughter. There were stories told of Jessica's childhood, some touching, some funny, a few embarrassing to her. There were stories told by Sir Trevor and Lady Vickers of the week they had spent in the small vicarage where Gabriel's father had had his living, celebrating the christening of young Gabriel. They had told about how the baby had smiled sweetly and widely and toothlessly in Lady Vickers's hold, waving his little arms about as he did so, and how she had threatened to take him home with her and never return him.

"I believe that was the moment when he vomited all over your best dress, Doris," Sir Trevor said, and everyone laughed again.

"Oh, it was not, Trevor," she protested. "That was a different time. You were very well behaved at your christening, Gabriel."

Gabriel smiled at her. He knew so little of his early childhood. He had had no one after the age of nine to reminisce about it.

"He lived up to his angelic name, did he?" the Marquess of Dorchester said.

"Don't I always?" Gabriel asked, and Jessica touched the back of his hand.

"I just wish," her grandmother said, "you were not taking my granddaughter so far away, Gabriel. And so soon. Tomorrow is too soon."

"It is," Jessica's mother said with a sigh. "However, it is what happens when a woman marries, Mama."

Some of the laughter had faded from the gathering.

"Perhaps you will be happy to know, then, ma'am," Gabriel said, addressing the dowager countess, "that we will not be leaving tomorrow after all. Or even the day after. We will be remaining in town for a while. I do not know for quite how long."

A few faces noticeably brightened.

"Oh," the dowager duchess said. "That *is* good news. What made you change your mind, Gabriel?"

He got to his feet and looked down briefly at Jessica beside him. She nodded almost imperceptibly. "Something happened last night that I learned of this morning," he said, "and it is time I shared some information that only a few of you already know. I am aware that most if not all of you have been curious about me and have wondered why, even though his permission was not necessary, the Duke of Netherby nevertheless gave his blessing on my marriage to his sister."

"I believe we are all very glad he did," Aunt Matilda said. "You do not owe us any explanation, Gabriel. If you have satisfied Avery, then we must all be satisfied."

"Speak for yourself, Matilda," Aunt Mildred said— Gabriel had been instructed by most of the family to learn and use their names. "I have been dying of curiosity."

"That is kind of you, Aunt Matilda," Gabriel said, and

smiled briefly at both sisters. "I would hope this information will remain within the family for at least a few days
longer, until I have settled some matters, but that will be up
to you. But what I want to tell you now, as my new family,
is that my legal name is Thorne. However, it is not the name
with which I was born. That was Rochford. Gabriel Rochford. I am the Earl of Lyndale. Sir Trevor Vickers has had
that fact officially confirmed. He was able to tell me that
just before we sat down to eat."

For a few moments the Westcotts were silenced.

"The *long-lost* earl?" Great-aunt Edith said, breaking
the silence. "Well, bless my soul."

"I say, this is splendid stuff," young Boris Wayne said
with youthful enthusiasm. "Rochford is not going to be at
all happy, though, is he, poor fellow? Nor is his father, at a
guess."

"I think I decided to come up to London at just the right
time," Harry said. "This beats rusticating at Hinsford."

"But what—"

"But why—"

Cousin Althea and Uncle Thomas began speaking at the
same time. Gabriel held up a staying hand.

"It is a long story," he said. "If you wish, I will tell it. But
the reason Jessica and I will not after all be leaving for
Brierley tomorrow is that Manley Rochford, my second
cousin, who expects to have my title within the next few
weeks, arrived in London last night with his wife."

"Oh my," Wren said. "We did not know that, did we,
Alexander?"

"We knew he was coming soon," he said.

Netherby, Gabriel noticed, did not look at all surprised.

"We *do* wish," Estelle said, leaning eagerly forward
across the table. "To hear your long story, that is, Gabriel.

Please do tell it. But I would wager—if it were genteel for ladies to lay bets—that what Mr. Rochford said of you at Elizabeth and Colin's party was not true at all. But how *priceless* that you were there to hear him and he did not know you. I suppose he had never seen you before in his life until you appeared here a few weeks ago."

"Let the man speak, Stell," her twin said.

"No," Gabriel said, "those stories were not true. Neither was Anthony Rochford's supposed familiarity with me. He was about ten years old when I went to America. He had never been to Brierley, where I lived for ten years after the death of my father. Let me be as brief as I can. This is a wedding breakfast, my own and Jessica's, and I would not wish to shift the focus too far from celebration."

He told the story with which some people at the table were already familiar.

"I wished to marry before returning to Brierley Hall to take up my position and the responsibilities there that I have neglected for almost seven years," he said at last. "I wanted the moral support of a countess and the practical support of someone who had had the upbringing and training to run a home that has been without a mistress for a number of years, and to cope with a situation that is sure to be a challenge for a while. And I wanted a wife for whom I felt an affection. I hope I will be a worthy member of this family."

"I have just realized," Cousin Althea said, "that Jessica is the Countess of Lyndale."

After the tense minutes that had preceded her words, everyone laughed.

"I expected and hoped to deal with Manley Rochford at Brierley," Gabriel said. "It might have been less dramatic. And perhaps less . . . humiliating for his son. However, he has come here with his wife, and I must decide how best to break the news to him that I am alive and back in England."

"Tell me," Colin, Lord Hodges, said, "was Manley Rochford involved in any of those things of which you stood accused, Thorne?"

Gabriel had minimized details of the whole nasty episode that had sent him running off to America.

"Yes," he said now after a brief hesitation.

"I suppose he was the guilty party," Colin said. "Of one or both charges?"

"Definitely one," Gabriel said, "probably both. Almost certainly he was implicated, at least as an accessory to the second."

Uncle Thomas whistled. "Is there any proof?" he asked.

"On the first, yes," Gabriel said. "I have spoken to the woman who was involved. She has given me a letter that may suffice as evidence. She will testify in person if further confirmation is needed, I believe, though understandably she is reluctant to do so. I would protect her from that if I can."

"She *will* do it," Riverdale said. "Her husband has persuaded her that she must if it becomes necessary."

Gabriel leveled a look on him.

"And there are two witnesses who will give Lyndale a solid alibi for the time when the murder was committed," Netherby said.

"Two?" Gabriel raised his eyebrows.

"Miss Beck, of course. But you have perhaps forgotten," Netherby said, "that the groom who took the wounded young fawn to her remained there for most of the time she and you were setting its broken leg. He is still employed at Brierley."

"Ah," Gabriel said, trying to remember. But yes, he seemed to recall that the young groom had been too squeamish to watch but too concerned to go away. He had hovered outside the cottage until the deed was done. "My man fell a bit short on that one, Netherby. Yours apparently did not. But yes. That is quite right. I had forgotten."

"What we need now," Aunt Matilda said, "is a plan. Our house, tomorrow afternoon. You will not mind, Charles?"

"Not at all, my love," he said with great good humor, "provided you do not require my presence. In my experience plans are better left with the ladies."

"Wise man," Elizabeth said, twinkling at him. "I will be there, Cousin Matilda. So will Mama."

"I will indeed," Cousin Althea said.

"Another toast," Riverdale said, getting to his feet and raising his glass. "To the Earl and Countess of Lyndale's remaining in London for a while longer."

There was a prolonged clinking of glasses and a chorus of voices.

"Jessica," Gabriel said soon after that, "shall we be the first to leave? With many thanks to everyone who has made this such an unexpectedly festive day, considering the fact that we had decided upon a quiet wedding."

She set her hand in his and got to her feet. "Yes, thank you all," she said. "And now, if you will excuse me, I am about to get a little emotional."

Gabriel tightened his grip on her hand and led her from the room while Netherby, with the mere lifting of one eyebrow and one finger, sent a servant scurrying to call up their carriage—minus all the flowers and all the hardware, Gabriel hoped, for the short journey to his hotel.

Jessica was a bit teary eyed, as she had warned. But he

did not believe they were unhappy tears. He hoped not. All their wedding guests streamed out of the dining room after them to wave them on their way. It did not help her composure.

It had been an eventful wedding day. And it was not over yet.

# Seventeen

The carriage Gabriel had purchased for his wedding day and the journey to Brierley Hall had indeed been denuded of its floral decorations and metallic noisemakers before it left Archer House. Even the remaining traces of the flower petals with which he and Jessica had been showered outside the church had been thoroughly removed. Those facts saved them from attracting undue attention on their way to his hotel. They did not, however, save them from a grand reception at the hotel itself, where Gabriel had been putting up since his arrival in London.

He had informed the manager that Mrs. Thorne would be joining him to spend the night here. Perhaps that bare announcement had raised an alarm, for during the weeks of his stay he had given no indication that he was a married man. Perhaps the manager, who had bowed to him with the utmost respect this morning, had feared that the hotel was about to fall into disrepute. Whatever the reason, he or his minions had done some swift research and had come up with the astonishing news that Mr. Thorne, a wealthy gentleman late of Boston, America, had that very day married the sister of no less a personage than His Grace, the Duke of Netherby.

The red carpet was out. Literally. It had been rolled down over the wide, shallow steps outside the main doors and across the pavement. It was in such pristine condition when Gabriel's carriage rocked to a halt at the curb beside it that it seemed probable no other guest had been allowed to set foot on it but had been put to the inconvenience of using a side door.

The ornate brass handles on the outer doors had been polished until they rivaled gold in brightness. The manager and footmen, whose jobs respectively were to register newly arrived guests and carry in their baggage, were suddenly resplendent in uniforms so stiff and spotless that they must be reserved for the most special and rare of occasions. The owner of the hotel, who looked as if he had dressed for an audience at court, stepped out through the doors and executed a bow that would not have shamed him had he been making it to the Prince of Wales himself. As soon as the newly arrived guests had stepped down from their carriage, he delivered a brief, pompous speech, which had been either written inaccurately or memorized poorly. He welcomed to his humble hotel Lady Jessica Archer and Mr. Archer. With one practiced sweep of his arm he invited them to step inside.

And there in the gleaming foyer waited two straight lines of hotel employees, also clad in their special-occasion best, smiling and, at a cue from the manager, applauding. At another cue, the clapping stopped abruptly, the men bowed, and the women curtsied.

They must have spent all day rehearsing, Gabriel

thought. They would have done a military parade proud—
except for the smiles. He ought to have taken a suite at the
Pulteney instead of at this perfectly comfortable but obviously second-tier hotel. At the Pulteney they must be accustomed to the aristocracy and foreign dignitaries flitting
in and out. There would have been no fuss or fanfare at all
there but, if anything, an even greater discretion than usual
to preserve the privacy of their guests.

For the first time Gabriel saw the results of his careful
reasoning about the choice of a bride. He had thought to
choose someone who would fit into the role of Countess of
Lyndale at Brierley as a hand would fit into a glove. He had
chosen Jessica within half an hour of his first encounter
with her. At the time it had not occurred to him that she
would also ease his way back into his London hotel on his
wedding day.

She had sat beside him in the carriage on the short journey from Archer House, her hand in his, her cheeks flushed,
her eyes bright as the two of them looked back over the past
few hours and commented upon several details they had
found particularly memorable or touching. She had been
Jessica.

But the moment the carriage door was opened outside
the hotel and she summed up the situation at a glance, she
became a different person—the one he had met at that inn
on the road to London. She became the haughty yet gracious daughter of a duke that she was. She became Lady
Jessica Thorne, Countess of Lyndale.

She waited for Gabriel to alight first and then set her
hand in his and descended to the red carpet with regal
grace. She ignored the two footmen who stood on either
side of the carpet—it was, Gabriel realized, a serious faux
pas to acknowledge their existence, as he did with a brisk

nod for each—and ascended the steps as the owner delivered his speech. She afforded him a gracious inclination of the head and a murmured thank-you—similar to the one she had given Gabriel on their first encounter—while she offered her hand at the end of a fully extended arm to discourage the man from moving any closer. Then she swept inside while Gabriel was giving the owner a more conventional—and less aristocratic—handshake.

The applauding lines of servants did not throw her off stride for a single moment. She stopped walking, waited for the performance to come to an end, and smiled down the length of her nose while she looked unhurriedly along the women's line and back along the men's before nodding to both lines and speaking.

"Thank you," she said. "What a lovely welcome."

And to a man—and woman—they almost melted with pleasure at her words, all six of them. They could not have looked more gratified had she presented each of them with a gift.

And she looked unerringly toward the manager, who jumped forward, bowed, indicated the wide staircase with a sweeping arm gesture, and then led the way up to Gabriel's suite as though he would not be able to find it unassisted. Gabriel meanwhile nodded and smiled at the employees, most of whom looked familiar to him by now, and followed his wife.

She was extraordinary.

"Thank you," she said again as the manager, his chest puffed out with importance, paused outside the suite and opened the door—somehow it was unlocked.

And she swept inside, turned toward Gabriel as the door closed behind him, and . . . became Jessica again. And the thing was, he thought, she seemed unaware of the two roles she had played in the last ten minutes. Being Lady Jessica Archer—or, rather, Lady Jessica Thorne—was so much second nature to her when she was in a public setting that she did not even have to think about it.

"I am sorry about that," he said. "I did *not* announce this morning that I was off to marry the daughter of a duke. And I do not believe Horbath would have announced it either—my valet, that is."

"Gabriel." She laughed. "You must have been in America too long. Servants, employees, often know things about their employers or paying guests before those people know those things for themselves. There is no keeping anything secret from one's servants, you know. That is why it is important to engage their loyalty and even affection. It is why it is important to treat them well."

He was not sure it was quite the statement of equality for all that was so touted in the New World, even if it was not a perfect reality there. But he was in England now, where the class system was still alive and well and perhaps always would be, and where it would work comfortably for all, provided there was mutual respect along the spectrum. It was not perfect. But what was? And these were not thoughts he needed to be having at this precise moment.

"Horbath?" he called. He was not sure whether his valet was in the suite or not.

"Sir?" Horbath stepped out of his bedchamber.

"You may take the rest of the day off," Gabriel told him. "Until after dinner anyway. Let us say half past nine?"

"Yes, sir," Horbath said. He bowed to Jessica. "Does my lady wish me to take my lady's maid with me?"

"Ruth is here?" she asked. "Yes, by all means, Mr. Horbath. Thank you."

Horbath disappeared. There was the murmur of his

voice and a female's before another door to the suite that was outside the sitting room opened and closed, and there was silence.

"Perhaps," Gabriel said, his eyes moving over Jessica's wedding dress and straw bonnet, "I ought to have consulted you before sending your maid away. Perhaps you will need her sooner than half past nine tonight."

"I can manage without," she told him.

"And," he said, "I can be an excellent lady's maid. Not that I have had any experience, I hasten to add. But I can brush hair and I can undo buttons on a dress that are inaccessible to the wearer."

Her cheeks flushed. "Thank you," she said. She did not add, he noticed, that she could manage without.

He looked at the clock that was ticking on the mantel. It was half past four. An awkward time. Three and a half hours to dinner. A little too late to plan anything. Too late to go out. Besides, if they went out, they would probably throw the downstairs staff into consternation. It was too early to—

He stepped forward, took her in his arms—one about her waist, the other about her shoulders—and kissed her. Hard and deep. Her mouth opened and he pressed his tongue inside. Her hands, still gloved, came to rest just below his shoulders. She made an inarticulate sound in her throat.

"It is still afternoon," he said when he lifted his head. "Daylight."

"Yes." The color in her cheeks had deepened. She was still wearing her bonnet as well as her gloves.

"Will you consider it in very poor taste," he asked her, "if I take you to bed now, rather than wait until tonight?" Waiting would be a severe trial. What else was one to do in three and a half hours with a new wife whom one found damned attractive, to say the least?

"I think perhaps," she said, "that in some part of the world it is night, Gabriel."

"Where?" he asked. "India? China? Where shall we imagine we are?"

"Either," she said. "But we had better both decide upon the same place. It would be too bad if you were in China and I were in India. Join me in India, if you will."

"Done," he said. He was still holding her against him. He could feel the warm, slender shapeliness of her from the shoulders to the knees. The soft femininity of her. He could smell the same subtle perfume she had worn when they sat together on the pianoforte bench at her cousin's party.

"There are two bedchambers," he told her. "Will you come with me to mine? Will you allow me the pleasure of brushing out your hair and unclothing you?"

He watched the color deepen yet more in her cheeks as her teeth sank into her lower lip, leaving the upper to curl upward very slightly—and very enticingly. He watched her consider her options and glance briefly at the window, through which the sun was beaming from a clear blue sky, still very far from sinking over the horizon.

"Yes," she said, and even in speaking the one word she sounded breathless. But quite decisive.

"Come." He took her by the hand and led the way.

Jessica had imagined a nighttime consummation with darkness and bedcovers and the white silk and lace nightgown, only very slightly daring, which she had purchased for the occasion. She had imagined Ruth getting her ready and leaving her room a discreet five minutes or so before the

appearance of her bridegroom in his nightshirt and bro-
caded dressing gown belted at the waist. She was eager for
the experience. She was hardly nervous at all except for a
bit of anxiety that she would be awkward and not know
quite what to do. But that was a foolish fear. Though she did
not know for sure, she would be very surprised if Gabriel
did not have a good deal of experience. She hoped he did,
though she did not—thank you kindly—want to know any
details.

But now it was to happen in the daytime with bright
sunshine beaming through the rather large window of the
bedchamber into which he took her. He did not even cross
to it to draw the curtains.

It was a large square room with another door. But that
must lead into a dressing room only large enough for essential private functions. There was a dressing table in here
as well as a great marble washstand.

The masculinity of the room struck her immediately.
Two pairs of large boots—riding boots and Hessians—
stood neatly beside the wardrobe. There was shaving gear
spread out on the washstand, a set of man's brushes on the
dressing table as well as a neat pile of starched neckcloths.
The room smelled faintly and enticingly of something dis-
tinctly male—his shaving cream, perhaps, or his cologne,
which was in a dark glass bottle on the dressing table. It
was something she smelled whenever she was close to
him—something that always made her want to burrow
closer. There were three leather-bound books on one of the
bedside tables, a handkerchief folded in the top one, presumably to keep his place.

There was no sign of any of her things. They must be in
the other bedchamber. Ruth probably had everything laid
out ready in there.

There was no Ruth either, she thought, not until half past nine tonight. She had left the suite with Gabriel's valet.

There were just the two of them and this room and bright daylight. And a large, high bed.

She was still wearing her gloves, Jessica saw, looking down. And her bonnet. And her wedding dress.

She drew off her gloves and looked around for somewhere to put them. He took them from her, dropped them—oh dear—on the floor, and came to stand directly in front of her. He pulled loose the bow beneath her chin and removed her bonnet, using both hands. He looked into her face the whole while, those dark eyes of his roaming over it. He dropped the bonnet. Her hair must be squashed.

"My hair must be squashed."

His eyes came directly to hers. "I will give myself the pleasure of withdrawing the pins and brushing it out," he said. "The first part may not be as easy as it sounds. It is a work of art."

"Ruth is good with hair," she told him.

"We will have to see," he said, "if I am better."

His voice was low. She seemed to hear it less with her ears than with some location low in her abdomen. What a foolish thought to be having. And now something down there was aching and pulsing and she swallowed.

"Perhaps," she said, "I ought to have hired you as a lady's maid instead of as a husband."

"Ah," he said, "but you did not *hire* me as a husband, did you, Jessie?"

And why did the sound of that particular variation on her name almost take her knees out?

"Besides," he added, "we are not sure yet, are we, that my skills surpass those of Ruth."

"Are you good at ironing?" she asked him.

He gave her a look that implied a clear *no*. "Come," he said.

He seated her before the dressing table, and she watched in the mirror as he removed all the pins from her hair. He placed them in a neat pile on the dressing table, she was relieved to see, rather than sending them to join her gloves and bonnet on the floor.

He was in no hurry. But something struck her. He was already making love to her. His fingers untangled each curl as it was freed of its pins, and his knuckles caressed her scalp each time. He kept his eyes on what he was doing rather than on her image in the glass. He had a brooding look on his face. No, wrong word. But she did not know what the right word was. He looked wholly intent, wholly engrossed. He was in no hurry at all.

And then all the pins were gone and her hair was in a riot of untidiness about her shoulders and she swallowed again. Strange men ought not to see one with one's hair down. But he was not a stranger. He was her husband.

For the first time he looked into the mirror.

"It is horribly untidy," she said.

"Gorgeously disheveled," he said.

"Is that not a contradiction in terms?" she asked.

"No." Just the one word.

He picked up his own brush from the dressing table and began to draw it through her hair with long, slow strokes from the roots to the tips. Smoothness replaced the riot and her hair shone in the sunlight, which was beaming directly on them. He was still fully dressed in his wedding finery. Lace half covered his hands. There was a strangely enticing contrast between the femininity of the frills and the masculinity of the hands. He might have been a businessman, but she doubted he had spent all or even most of his working days behind a desk.

He put the brush down and drew his fingers through her hair at the temples to draw it back behind her shoulders. He held her eyes with his own before he dipped his head and kissed the side of her neck. Her toes curled up in her slippers. His hands closed about her upper arms, and he drew her to her feet, still facing away from him. Then he swept her hair forward over one shoulder and unbuttoned her dress down the back, from her neck to her hips. He moved it off her shoulders and down her arms. It whispered down her body and pooled about her feet and he left it there. Ruth would have a fit.

Her stays went next. He untied the laces and let the stays fall on top of her dress. Only her shift and her stockings— and shoes—remained. As well as her pearl necklace.

Oh my. It was a short shift. It did not even reach her knees. Neither did her stockings from the other direction. Her knees were bare. He turned her and looked her over without even trying to respect her modesty. He seemed very fully clothed in contrast to her. Apart from the lower halves of his hands there was not the merest hint of bare flesh from his chin on down.

She was going to die. Of mortification? Or . . . of something else?

His eyes were heavy lidded. Even when they looked back up into hers. And then—oh goodness me—he went down on one knee before her and began to draw off one garter and roll down one silk stocking to the ankle. He lifted her foot—she braced herself with one hand on his appealingly solid shoulder—and removed first her shoe and then her stocking with the garter. They landed on top of her dress and stays. The other garter and stocking and shoe joined them in the next minute or so. He really was in *no* hurry. He stood up.

And while she watched, he shrugged out of his coat. It was a tight fit. It was more like a second layer of skin, she thought, than a garment. His silk waistcoat followed it to the floor. Was his valet the sort of man to have a fit? He removed his neckcloth. Then he pulled his white shirt free of his knee breeches, crossed his arms, and drew it off over his head to drop onto the heap of their combined garments. And . . .

Oh my and goodness me.

And heaven help us.

He was *magnificent*. He definitely had not spent the past thirteen years sitting behind a desk wielding a pen. His upper arms, his shoulders, his chest, all rippled with firm muscle.

Jessica licked her lips, and his eyes dipped to watch the progress of her tongue. One hand came beneath her chin to hold it in the cleft between his thumb and fingers while the other hand spread over the back of her head. And he kissed her with open mouth while no other part of his body touched hers.

She would surely explode. And somehow not knowing what to do did not matter any longer, for he clearly *did* know. She was glad it was daytime, with sunshine and nothing of her own in the room except her person and her wedding clothes, all but her shift of which were on the floor. She was standing barefoot in the middle of them. His tongue was moving inside her mouth, stroking surfaces, tangling with her own tongue, and somehow—oh, how did he *do* that?—making her whole body sizzle with pain that was not pain at all and . . . Ah, and with a terrible longing for something else. Something more. Something she wanted. And wanted. She wanted *him*.

"Gabriel," she said when he lifted his head. It came out on a gasp. Her arms, she realized, were at her sides. But she could *feel* him—his body heat, his masculinity—though he touched her nowhere except beneath her chin and against the back of her head.

Those heavy-lidded eyes gazed into hers. "Come to bed," he said.

Yes. Oh yes, please. Please, please. She was not speaking the words aloud, she realized.

He waited until she was beside the bed and he had pulled back the bedcovers before grasping her shift at the hem and lifting it upward. She raised her arms, and the next moment there was a little pile of shift on the floor. He watched as she lay down on the bed, strangely unselfconscious about her nakedness, for he was clearly liking what he saw. He kicked off his shoes, peeled off his white stockings and then his breeches.

She closed her eyes briefly. Not out of fear or modesty or shock, though she certainly felt at least some of that last. She closed them because for the moment the desire she felt was more than she could bear.

He was on the bed with her then and raised on one elbow and leaning over her, his free hand touching now far more than her chin and the back of her head. It was touching her everywhere, exploring, caressing, pressing, even scratching lightly. And his mouth kissed her mouth and then her throat and then her breasts, drawing her nipples, one at a time, into his mouth and suckling them before he opened his mouth and exhaled warm air on them. His hand meanwhile had moved down to secret places to explore, to touch, to tease, to reach inside her with one finger. Shock hit her even as her own hands, without her quite knowing it, were moving over his upper body, feeling all those warm, powerful, rippling muscles as she breathed in the cologne and shaving soap smell of him.

"Jessie," he murmured, his voice so low that everything from her toes on up curled just with the sound of it.

And he was on her and spreading her legs with his. And—ah, dear God, he was coming into her. Slowly, stretching her, bringing a sting of pain that was soon pain no longer but shock as he pressed deep. Wonderment. Happiness.

She considered irrelevantly, even though thought was not dominant at this precise moment, if theirs was a love match after all. Surely, oh surely, it was more than just a convenience for them both. She would think more on it later. Perhaps this, whatever it was, was enough.

He lifted some of his weight off her then and began to move in her, deeply, thoroughly, slowly at first while her body adjusted as she slid her legs up the mattress, first to brace them on either side of his, then to twine about their hard-muscled strength. And his movements quickened, rocking her, laying her bare seemingly to the soul, building that ache of not-really-pain until she heard someone moan to the rhythm of it and realized it was her. He gave her his weight again then and pounded into her until something exploded inside her and she went slack with pain become pleasure too intense for words, even mental words. He held deep and she felt a gush of heat at her very core.

The marriage, she thought needlessly as she listened to the beat of her heart slowing and felt his slow with it, was consummated. She was Gabriel's wife. He was her husband. Until death did them part. It seemed a lovely, lovely thought. Not so much the death part of it, but the sense of eternity. That they belonged together forever and ever.

He withdrew from her and moved off her after a few minutes, and she regretted it even though he was a heavy man. But he had an arm about her shoulders and turned her against him. He was hot and sweaty. So was she. The sunlight from the window slanted warm across their bodies, just missing their faces.

She was so, *so* glad they had done this in daylight. She wondered if the family, the wedding party, was still at Archer House. She was almost sure they would be. How strange that life was proceeding normally there.

"Did I hurt you?" he asked.

"No." He had, but it had not really been pain. Not as other pains were. That was impossible to explain in words, however. "No, Gabriel."

He turned onto his back, his arm still about her, and bent one leg to set his foot on the mattress. He rested the back of his free hand over his eyes. And he slept, his breathing becoming deep and even.

It was almost—oh, not quite, but *almost*—the loveliest moment of the consummation. They were husband and wife in bed together, and he had made love to her and then fallen asleep.

Jessica smiled, turned her face to rest against his shoulder, and closed her eyes.

One's wedding day was supposed to be the happiest day of one's life.

She had just become the quintessential bride. For in her case it was surely true.

# Eighteen

Gabriel was gazing up at the ceiling, thinking about his father. There was a time—it went on for years after he had been taken to Brierley to live—when his grief had been a raw wound, a daily ache of longing, an almost nightly anguish, with sleep elusive. How could his papa have been so very different from Uncle Julius, he had wondered then, and from Philip? His uncle had not been unkind to Gabriel, just . . . indifferent. He had been an abrupt, autocratic, impatient man who seemed to lack all finer feelings, even with his wife. Especially with her, perhaps. It had been difficult for Gabriel to believe that Uncle Julius and his papa had been brothers.

The intensity of that early grief had faded over time. But he had never forgotten how much his father had loved him, how much he had loved his father. When he had gone to America, he had transferred some of that love to Cyrus.

He missed them both today. But for his father he felt some of the raw ache his childhood self had felt when he was led away from the cemetery beside the vicarage where they had lived, and he had understood, perhaps for the first time, that he would never see his papa again. Never. Never had seemed an unfathomable expanse for his nine-year-old self. It still did today.

His father had not been at his wedding.

Or his mother. But he had known her only through the stories his father had told of her—and those Cyrus had told him. The rawness of loss had not been so immediate with her. His father had once told him that he had cried inconsolably for a whole week after her death.

"A penny for your thoughts," a soft voice said from beside him, and he turned his face toward Jessica's.

It was very close. His arm was about her. Her head was nestled against his shoulder. Her eyes were dreamy with sleep. Her dark hair, which he had so thoroughly brushed not long ago, was spread about her in a disordered mass. He had pulled the top sheet over them, but beneath it they were both still naked—except for her pearl necklace, he realized for the first time. He could feel her, soft and warm, all down his side.

And now someone else belonged to him. Just to him. She was his wife. This was their wedding day. It still seemed unreal.

"I was thinking about my father," he told her.

"Tell me," she said.

"I think," he said, "I never quite forgave him for dying. It was unnecessary, you see. He neglected a chill because it was more important to him to serve his parishioners than to live for me. I blamed him for that, for loving them more than he loved me. But he didn't, I understand now. He loved everyone. I had a very special place in his heart—I was his son. But that did not mean he loved his flock any the less.

He was a man who had a religion—he was a clergyman. More important, though, he *lived* that religion. Maybe I should forgive him at last. What do you think?"

"I think you already have," she said.

She was gazing back into his eyes. He was going to have no alternative than to love her, he thought, and was amazed he had not really considered the matter before. He was, after all, his father's son and Cyrus's adopted son. This was a different relationship, a far more intimate one. But she was his. His wife. This morning he had vowed to love, honor, and keep her. She had given up everything today in order to spend her life with him. She would, God willing, be the mother of his children. Of course he was going to have to love her.

He had certainly enjoyed *making* love to her. And he had been right when he had thought that day at Richmond Park that despite his first impression of her she might be capable of passion.

"Gabriel," she asked him, "what are we going to do about Manley Rochford? And his wife? And Anthony Rochford?"

Yes, and there was that. It had been at the back of his mind all day. He had largely ignored it because this was his wedding day.

*We,* she had said. *What are we going to do?*

"I knew he was planning to come here soon," he said. "I was hoping, though, to get there before he left. It would have been easier to confront him there. I waited too long."

"Because I wanted a family wedding," she said. "We ought to have married on Tuesday, as soon as you came with the special license."

"Even then it would have been too late," he said. "We would probably have passed him on the road. Besides . . ."

He smoothed her hair back from her face, hooked it behind her ear, and touched his fingertips to her cheek. "I liked our wedding just the way it was. Did you?"

"I am very glad Mr. Vickers did not drop my ring," she said, and he watched a smile light her eyes.

And there, he thought. *There.* That was how he wanted her to look. For him. Because he had pleased her or amused her. Because they could share a joke. Because there was some bond between them. He smiled back at her, and there was a flicker of something in her eyes, something that took away the smile but left a lingering look of . . . what? Wistfulness? Yearning?

"I liked our wedding," she said.

But she had asked a question.

"I suppose," he said, "I should call on him. Privately. Let him know I am back. Still alive. Give him a chance to leave quietly and avoid embarrassment."

"You suppose *we* should call on him," she said.

His first thought was that he would not expose her to that. But it was for this very thing he had married her. This confrontation with Manley and the return to Brierley.

She did not wait for him to answer. "Would he give in that easily?" she asked him. "Or would he have you arrested?"

It would be a toss-up. It could go either way. Manley might simply admit defeat and creep on home, taking his wife and son with him. He might not want the humiliation of having all his hopes dashed in full sight of the *ton*. On the other hand, his disappointment would be colossal, and he might choose to fight. He had set up Gabriel as a ravisher and murderer thirteen years ago, he and Philip between them. He might well believe that the charges would stick now and take Gabriel to the gallows. Or he might try to send him scurrying back to America with the threat of arrest. It had worked before, after all.

"He might," he said. "I believe he wants very badly to be the Earl of Lyndale, owner of Brierley, possessor of a large fortune. And he is tantalizingly close to achieving his dream. I am not so easily frightened these days, however, and I can put up a good defense."

"It might be messy," she said.

He ran his thumb across her lips and then kissed her softly. Was she taking fright? Even though she had known before she married him—

"And why *should* he be given the chance to slink off home if he chooses not to fight?" she asked. "Gabriel! He ravished your boyhood sweetheart and left her with child. He murdered her brother, your friend, in the most cowardly way imaginable, by shooting him in the back. And he is just as guilty even if it was actually your cousin who fired the gun. He tried to put the blame on you. He would have let you hang. Are you going to allow him to walk away now, unpunished?"

She sounded, rather incongruously, like the Lady Jessica Archer of his early acquaintance.

"If anyone deserves to hang," she said, "it is he."

He turned more fully onto his back and draped his free hand over his eyes.

"And if anyone deserves to be publicly humiliated, Gabriel," she added, "it is surely Mr. Manley Rochford."

He had cut off Mary's allowance without any authority to do so and was about to turn her out of her home to certain destitution. He had got rid of a number of servants at Brierley, again without any right to do so, and had turned several of them out of *their* homes. He had not changed in thirteen years. Perhaps he had never again ravished anyone—though Gabriel would not wager against it—or shot anyone else in the back. But he was still a sorry excuse for a human being. Just as Philip had been. How *could* they have been related to his own father?

"Yes," he said.

She moved more fully onto her side then and spread one hand over his chest. She moved one leg between his.

"Gabriel," she said, "what are we going to do?"

*We* again.

"We are going to let things be messy," he said, using her word. "We are going to confront him, Jessie, in as dramatic and as public a way as possible."

She lifted her head, and because she could not hold it up comfortably, she came farther over him, bracing herself with both hands on his chest and moving her leg right across both of his. Her hair fell about her face and over his chest. She was smiling. And looking damned irresistible. Looking *and* feeling.

"Where?" she asked him. "And when?"

"Ah," he said, cupping her face with his hands, "those are the questions."

"We need answers," she said. "Aunt Matilda and Viscount Dirkson's soiree? You are to play the pianoforte there, are you not? Aunt Matilda is very excited about it. But no. That is not until the end of next week. Anyway, it would not be public enough. What is coming up in the next few days that simply *everyone* will be attending? Let me think."

"There is a masquerade ball on Tuesday," he said.

She stared down at him. "The masquerade," she said. "With all the drama of the unmasking at midnight. Oh,

Gabriel, it will be *perfect*. We must find out if Mr. Manley Rochford is going to be there. We must make sure he is sent an invitation—and that he accepts it. Oh, I know. The family committee is meeting tomorrow at Aunt Matilda's. I will go to it. Oh, they are going to *love* this."

"Jessie," he said, frowning a bit. He did not need to drag the whole Westcott family into what was bound to be a messy scandal, whichever way it went. If anything, her family members needed to be warned to stay away from the masquerade.

Three fingers pressed against his lips before he could say more.

"Oh no," she said. "You must not object, as I can see you are about to do. No, Gabriel. This is why you married me. Because I am an aristocrat myself and because I have the full force of a very aristocratic family behind me. We can be *very* formidable when we choose to be."

And even when they did not so choose, he thought.

"You must not forbid me," she said. "I would have to disobey, and I promised just this morning to obey you. What a foolish part of the wedding service that is. The whole of it was written by men, of course." She looked down at him and then smiled, sunshine and mischief dancing in her eyes. And then she laughed softly. "When you married me, you married into the Westcott family. Now you have to take the consequences."

"In the meanwhile," he said, "I will call upon my lawyer. I may need him."

"To deal with me?" Her eyes were still laughing. She was actually enjoying this, he realized.

"No," he said. "I think I can manage that without his help. Jessie, *did* I hurt you? I would not want—"

"Oh, but I would," she said.

And she slid her hands up his chest and cupped his face

with them, bringing her full weight down on top of him and her face very close to his as she did so.

She kissed him.

It was an invitation not easily resisted. He did not even try.

The news spread quickly, as news always did, that Mr. Manley Rochford, very soon to be the Earl of Lyndale, had arrived in London with his wife. Their son, Mr. Anthony Rochford, had been informed of their arrival soon after he arrived at a ball on Thursday evening. He had left immediately, much to the disappointment of many, in order to welcome them, as any dutiful son would.

All three attended church on Sunday—St. George's on Hanover Square, of course, the church favored by most of the *ton* while they were in town during the spring. Mr. Anthony Rochford introduced his parents to the clergyman and to as many important personages among the congregation as he could. His father received their words of greeting with an air of gracious gravity. He would, with the greatest reluctance, accept the title and the duties it imposed upon him when the fateful day came, of course. It seemed, alas, that he had no choice. At the same time, that would be a day of grief rather than unalloyed rejoicing, for it would be final confirmation that there could be no further hope of his cousin's still being alive. It would be the day he had wished fervently would never come.

The *ton* seemed deeply affected. Mr. Manley Rochford was a dignified, handsome man—an older version of his son without the smile. Nobody seemed particularly to notice his wife, who said nothing. Or, if she did, no one heard. Mr. Anthony Rochford still smiled, but there was a brave, sad tinge to it on that Sunday morning.

"It was a magnificent performance," Estelle reported to her father and stepmother at luncheon. "I almost soaked a handkerchief with my tears."

They had not been there. But Estelle and Bertrand had gone to church, as they usually did. They had been brought up by an uncle and aunt who had strict rules about worship. Though, as Bertrand was fond of saying whenever questioned on the matter, he and his sister went from personal inclination too. It was, after all, many years since they had lived with their uncle and aunt.

"He is a distinguished-looking man—I will give him that," Edith Monteith remarked to the Dowager Countess of Riverdale, her sister, as they rode back home in the carriage.

"And handsome too," Miss Adelaide Boniface, her companion, agreed. "I admire the graying at the temples that happens to some fortunate men when they reach a certain age."

"If he had been on the stage," the dowager commented sourly, "he would have been booed off it for overacting."

"Pride goeth before a fall," Mildred, Lady Molenor, said to her husband as they walked home from church. "Where is that quotation from, Thomas? The Bible?"

"The Bible or William Shakespeare," he said. "It is bound to be one or the other. I assume you are making a prediction about Rochford?"

"He is going to be hideously disappointed," she said. "I cannot wait to witness it. Our plan—Jessica and Gabriel's actually, but we all have a part to play—is quite spectacular and quite diabolical."

"I married a bloodthirsty woman," he said.

"Thomas," she said. "He is a—" She looked around to make sure no one was within earshot but lowered her voice anyway. "He is a *ravisher*. And almost certainly a murderer too."

"Are you quite sure you wish to accompany me tomorrow, Wren?" Alexander, Earl of Riverdale, asked his wife during the afternoon while she was feeding their baby in the nursery. "I will be quite happy to go alone."

"After observing his behavior at church this morning," she said, looking up at him tight-lipped, "I will go even if you change your mind. He would have let Gabriel *die* thirteen years ago. He would have watched him hang. For something *he* did. He is beneath contempt. And compassion."

He leaned across their suckling baby and kissed her hard on the mouth.

The Westcott women had held their meeting at Viscount Dirkson's home on Saturday afternoon. They had all been present, including, to the surprise of everyone else, Jessica herself.

"Because," she had explained when questioned, "it is not enough simply to confront the man privately and allow him to slink off back home to lick his wounds—though the thought even of that gives me some satisfaction. He must not be allowed to escape some sort of justice, however."

"My thoughts exactly, Jessica," Wren said. "But how are we going to bring that about?"

"It is the precise reason why we have gathered here," Aunt Matilda pointed out.

"I think we should have him arrested," Grandmama said. "And thrown into a deep, dark dungeon. A *damp* one. With rats."

"On thirteen-year-old charges?" Cousin Althea said. "For offenses that were committed a long way away? I think that might be easier said than done, Cousin Eugenia, though I do wish we could do it."

"Avery could do it," Jessica's mother said. "And make the charges stick. So could Alexander. The two of them together—"

"We need a definite *plan*," Cousin Elizabeth said. "Something we can implement even if Avery and Alex disagree on the bold move of trying to have Mr. Rochford arrested."

"I have one," Jessica told them. "It is why I am here. I would not have come otherwise." And then she wished she had not added that last, for everyone looked at her—naturally, for she had spoken—and she could feel her cheeks grow hot. She had slept last night, deeply and dreamlessly, probably for several hours, but before and after—

Well.

She probably looked like a dewy-eyed bride the day after. Which was precisely what she was.

"There is that costume ball on Tuesday evening," she continued. "I have been looking forward to it ever since I received my invitation."

"I *love* masquerades," Estelle cried. "And I am not telling anyone what my costume is to be. No one will recognize me in a million years." She laughed.

"It is bound to be a great squeeze," Aunt Viola said. "Everyone loves a masquerade—the respectable kind, anyway, and Lady Farraday's is always very respectable indeed. No one sneaks in uninvited there despite the most impenetrable of disguises. That distinctive invitation card is everything. Are you hoping Mr. Rochford—Mr. *Manley* Rochford—will be there, Jessica, even though he is such a recent arrival in town?"

"That is where all of you come in," Jessica said, glancing about the room. "We need to make sure both that he is invited *and* that he attends."

They all gazed at her thoughtfully for a moment.

"I sense a brilliant plan," Elizabeth said. "The unmasking will be a sensation. I suppose it is the unmasking you are picturing as the climactic moment, Jessica?"

"Yes," she said. "It will not take care of the meting out of full justice, it is true. We may need another plan for that when the time comes. But it will be a very public humiliation if it is well enough orchestrated. It will be talked about for the next decade. Gabriel and I will take care of that."

"Oh," Estelle cried, "why should you have all the fun, Jessica?"

And there she went again, Jessica thought, blushing to the roots of her hair and to the ends of her toes, though that was not what Estelle had meant.

"They will not, Estelle," Aunt Matilda assured her, sounding quite militant. "Not when there will be Avery and his quizzing glass and Alexander with his magnificent height and looks. And Thomas and Colin and Marcel and Charles. And Bertrand and Boris and Peter too. And *that* is to name only the men. Then there will be *us*."

"All of which," Grandmama said, "will be worth nothing, Matilda, if Lady Farraday does not send that man an invitation and if he does not attend the masquerade."

"Mama," Aunt Mildred said, sounding incredulous. "You surely do not doubt that we can make absolutely sure both those things happen."

"Who will come with me tomorrow afternoon to call upon Lady Farraday?" Aunt Viola asked.

"I will," Elizabeth and Wren said together.

"I will go too," Jessica's mother said, "even though it will be Sunday. I will go separately from the three of you. Matilda, you must come with me. You too, Mildred. I believe we make a somewhat intimidating trio. The Westcott sisters."

"I daresay," Grandmama said, "half the *ton* will call upon Mr. Rochford and his wife next week. They will, after all, be the sensation of the hour. They already are. Edith and I will call upon them on Monday."

"Charles and I will call too, Mama," Aunt Matilda said.

"And Marcel and I," Aunt Viola said. "With Estelle, if she is willing. She will be an inducement for the man to come to the masquerade, after all, and to bring his son with him. Not that Mr. Anthony Rochford has ever been reluctant to attend any entertainment, though he may be nursing a broken heart if he has discovered that Jessica has married Gabriel. It will be in the morning papers on Monday, I suppose?"

"I am almost as grand a prize as Jessica, however," Estelle said. "Daughter of a marquess and all that. Yes, I will go with you and Papa, Mother. I would not miss going for worlds."

"I believe," Anna said, "we will all wait upon the Rochfords on Monday. Avery normally avoids morning or afternoon calls rather as he would the plague, but I can dare predict he will make an exception on this occasion."

"And when we go, we will all express the fond hope that his future lordship will be at the masquerade with his wife," Wren said. "Before his cousin is declared officially dead, that is, and his grief keeps him from all grand entertainments."

Grandmama made a sound of contempt that was not quite a word, but she seemed to sum up everyone's feelings. They subsided for a few moments into a satisfied silence.

Oh, Gabriel had indeed married into a whole family yesterday!

*Gabriel!* For a moment Jessica's thoughts wandered. He had gone to find his lawyer, even though it was a Saturday and the man might not be amused to have his day off disturbed. Then they were going to dine together and compare notes and . . .

Well.

Gabriel had been looking forward to getting back to his hotel and to Jessica returning from her meeting with the women of her family. He had looked forward to dining privately with her and to retiring early to bed with her. Last night had been one of broken sleep. Not that it was just to catch up with missing sleep that he hoped to retire early tonight, of course.

Bedtime did not come as early as he had hoped, however. Neither did they end up dining alone.

Jessica was in the middle of telling him all about the meeting at her aunt's house while he removed her bonnet and kissed her throat, and she accused him of trying to distract her, when they were both distracted by a knock on the door.

They waited for Horbath to emerge from the bedchamber to open it. They listened to the discreetly hushed murmur of voices.

"I beg your pardon, sir," Horbath said with a deferential bow, leaving the door slightly ajar while he came to report to Gabriel. "There is a Mr. Simon Norton belowstairs wishing to have a word with you."

Norton? Here? Not back at Brierley? He must have assumed that his job there was completed now that Manley had come to London. Or perhaps he had come to bring that news.

"Have him shown up," he said. He smiled ruefully at Jessica. "I am sorry. Will you mind? He is the man I sent to

Brierley to find out a few things for me. I will get rid of him as soon as possible."

"Of course I do not mind," she said.

But when Norton was admitted, he did not come alone. He had Mary with him.

# Nineteen

So this was Mary Beck.

The woman for whom Gabriel had come back from America, leaving behind him the life he had made for himself there, his home and his business, his friends and his neighbors. For more than six years he had resisted the allure of an earl's title and all the honor and respect it would bring with it as well as a stately home and estate and a fortune. He had not been interested. He had been happy where he was.

She was tiny, perhaps not even quite five feet tall. She appeared to have a bit of a hump on her back and one twisted arm. She limped heavily. She wore a long, shapeless coat and no hat. Her hair, a drab mixture of faded brown and gray, was scraped back over her head and sat on her neck in a small, tight bun. She had a long, plain face. She was probably in her fifties, though that was only a guess.

And Gabriel had spoken her name with warm affection and bent over her to hug her close. He held her for a long time, his eyes tightly closed, his arms noticeably gentle.

"Gabriel, Gabriel," she said over and over in a deep, almost manly voice, patting his upper arms. She laughed softly. "Look at you. You are all grown up."

The man Jessica assumed was Mr. Norton stood just inside the door, which Gabriel's valet had closed quietly before disappearing back to the bedchamber.

"You came all this way?" Gabriel asked rhetorically, moving back far enough to look into her face, though he kept his arms about her. "Mary? What were you thinking?"

"I heard that Mr. Rochford had come here," she said. "And I was afraid he would have you thrown in jail, Gabriel. I was afraid they would . . . hang you before I could stop them. So I went to find Mr. Norton and persuaded him to bring me. Don't chastise him for coming, even though you had not given him orders to leave his post. I threatened him. I told him if he did not bring me, I would come alone on the stagecoach and you would not like it and blame him. And I meant it. I have a letter with me from Ned Higgins."

"Ned Higgins?" He frowned. "But Mary, never mind that just now. Let me take your coat and make you comfortable and introduce you—"

But Mary was not to be deterred. If she had been able to talk without stopping for breath, she would surely have done so. "Ned is the young groom who brought me that little fawn and stayed outside the cottage while you and I set its broken leg," she explained. "Not so young any longer either. He has a wife and three children, two of whom like to come and pick flowers from my garden for their mother when I pretend not to be looking. Ned is still squeamish about animals in pain, bless his heart. I wrote the letter for him, Gabriel, because he can only barely read and write. I asked Mr. Norton to be there, though, so that he could watch and make sure that I wrote only what Ned said and that I did not prompt him at all. Ned did read it over when I was finished, and then he signed it. Mr. Norton witnessed it with his signature. Something I did not know before then was that after Ned left the cottage on that day—you were still there with me—he came upon a cluster of men gathered about the dead body of that poor young man. Ned watched while he was taken up by a few of them to be carried home to his father. So. They are not going to hang you, Gabriel, or throw you in prison. I won't let them."

She was breathless by the time she finished. And the whole of her focus was upon Gabriel.

"Mary," he said, "thank you. Thank you for all this. Thank you for coming, though I am vexed that I made it necessary for you to travel all the way to me when I ought to have gone to you. Thank you for the news, for bringing the letter, for caring. But come and be comfortable. Let me introduce you to someone very special. To Jessica. She did me the great honor of marrying me yesterday."

He turned her toward Jessica and released his hold on her.

And they looked at each other, the two special women in his life.

"Jessica." Mary's hands, one terribly twisted, came up beside her face, palm out, and her face lit up with a smile. "But you are *lovely*."

And Jessica realized something that made no sense from the point of view of her eyes. Mary Beck was beautiful. It was something to do with her face—her plain face—and her eyes. She had heard it said that the eyes are the window to the soul. But Mary's eyes . . . No. One could not see her soul through her eyes. One could see it *in* her eyes and beaming out from them to light and to warm the whole world. Mary was a living soul. Which was a bewilderingly foolish thought. Especially upon an acquaintance of mere moments. It was true, though. Surely it was.

Jessica reached out both hands, and Mary set hers in them. Jessica clasped the twisted one very gently. "How very happy I am to meet you, Mary," she said, and kissed the older woman on the cheek.

Travel over English roads must *not* have been comfortable for her. And that was probably a great understatement. She had not even had the luxury of Avery's carriage to travel in.

"I beg your pardon, sir," Mr. Norton was saying to Gabriel. "But I judged you would want me to accompany Miss Beck rather than stay put, especially as Mr. and Mrs. Rochford were gone. I'll turn around and go back up there, with your permission, and see if I can find Mrs. Clark."

"It is already done," Gabriel told him. "And you did the right thing, for which I thank you. Go home, Norton—on full pay. I will send for you when I need you again."

"Thank you, sir." Mr. Norton let himself quietly out of the room.

Mary meanwhile seemed aware of her surroundings for the first time. She looked around in something like awe and then, beaming happily, turned her attention back to the two of them.

"Yesterday," she said. "You were married yesterday. Two beautiful people. And I can see that you were made for each other."

"You just missed our wedding," Jessica said. "What a

pity that is. But you must come and sit down. It will be dinnertime soon. Gabriel will send Mr. Horbath to arrange for the table to be set for three."

"Oh no, no, no," Mary said, holding up her good hand in protest. "I did not come to impose my company upon Gabriel. Even less so upon Gabriel and his *bride*. We can talk another time. I will remain in London—my, my, what a vast place it is—until I am quite certain you are not going to be thrown in jail, Gabriel. Mr. Norton—what a very polite and gentlemanly person he is—has recommended a women's boardinghouse to me. I will ask one of the kind porters downstairs to give me directions and . . . Well, perhaps I will ask him too if he will call me a—hackney cab, do you call carriages for hire here? Then I will be able to take my bag with me. It is downstairs. That very courteous manager promised Mr. Norton that he would keep it for me."

"Mary," Gabriel said, "don't be ridiculous."

She looked at him in some surprise, saw that his eyes were twinkling, and laughed her deep laugh. "Well," she said, "perhaps *you* will come downstairs and make the arrangement for me, Gabriel. I confess to being a bit overwhelmed. I will not keep him from you for more than a few minutes, Jessica. Oh, you *are* a lovely young lady. And a kind one."

"Mary," Jessica said, smiling. "Sit down. On that chair beside the fireplace. It is the most comfortable. And that is an order."

Mary threw up her hands again and laughed.

"Jessica was Lady Jessica Archer before I married her," Gabriel told her. "Sister of the Duke of Netherby, a most formidable aristocrat, Mary. He could reduce you to a dithering heap with one look through his quizzing glass. Jessica could do the same thing—if she carried a glass."

"I could indeed," Jessica said. "Come, Mary, and sit down. Gabriel will go in person to arrange for dinner and to secure you a room here at the hotel. And you shall have Ruth, my maid, to keep you company and prevent you from being too bewildered. Just do not expect her to talk. She is a woman of few words."

"Words are not always necessary, dear," Mary said as Gabriel helped her off with her coat and she sat obediently in the most comfortable chair, which came close to swallowing her up. She looked about her again. "What a very pleasant room this is. And how lovely to have arrived. And, I must confess, to be staying here. Though I would not for the world make a nuisance of myself."

"As if that were possible," Gabriel said, pouring her a glass of lemonade at the sideboard as Jessica sat down beside her.

"You must tell us about your journey," she said. "Was it a very uncomfortable experience, Mary? How brave of you to come all this way virtually alone."

"Well, I did have Mr. Norton with me," Mary said. "He made me feel very safe. And he insisted upon hiring a private parlor for me last evening even though I protested at the extravagance."

Gabriel handed her the glass and stayed for a few minutes before going to make arrangements for a room and for an extra place to be set at the table. It was very clear to Jessica that these two were indeed very fond of each other. He hesitated for a moment when he did get to his feet and looked thoughtfully down at Mary while she beamed back at him.

"Mary," he said, "have you ever wanted to go to a masquerade?"

\* \* \*

Masquerades, or costume balls, as they were often called when they were given by members of the *ton* (and were therefore assured of precluding any so-called riffraff who gave the public masquerades at the opera house such a disreputable name), were always more popular than almost any other entertainment the Season could offer. They gave grown men and women a chance to dress up, to spend a whole evening playing a role and a guessing game at the same time, though most disguises were easily penetrated, it was true. They gave an extra burst of excitement as the evening grew old, when midnight brought with it unmasking time and they could all discover whether their guesses had been correct. They gave everyone a chance to behave in somewhat less inhibited a manner than a more formal ball allowed. Young debutantes might dance with rakes and older matrons with handsome young blades. A Roman emperor might take the floor with a milkmaid, and a harlequin with Good Queen Bess.

Lady Farraday's masquerade ball was looked forward to with even greater than usual anticipation. For Mr. Manley Rochford, so soon to be the new Earl of Lyndale, had made his anticipated arrival in town just in time to attend, and attend he would with his wife. Lady Farraday had confirmed that fact by calling upon them in person the very morning of the ball, following the note she had sent late in the afternoon of the day before. She did not add, when she boasted of this considerable coup to various guests, that she had been urged to do so by no less illustrious personages than the Duke of Netherby and the Dowager Countess of Riverdale, to name but two. Everyone who had not been at

St. George's on Sunday was eager to catch their first glimpse of the soon-to-be earl, and even those who had been there anticipated pursuing a closer acquaintance with so distinguished-looking a gentleman.

But there was even more reason for excitement.

For the morning papers had carried notice of the unexpected marriage of Mr. Gabriel Thorne, that American gentleman who had so aroused the *ton*'s interest and curiosity over his recent, unexplained return to England after an absence of several years. And he had made nothing short of a brilliant marriage, his bride being Lady Jessica Archer, daughter of the Dowager Duchess of Netherby and sister of His Grace of Netherby.

The news would have been sensational enough even without one additional factor. But there *was* an additional factor, for it had been generally believed among the *ton* that Mr. Anthony Rochford, soon-to-be heir to the earldom of Lyndale, had been in hot pursuit of Lady Jessica and that she had favored his suit. And who could have doubted that? The gentleman, even apart from his prospects, was gorgeously handsome—all the ladies were agreed upon it. His smile! And exceedingly charming besides. Again, his smile! Yet Lady Jessica had confounded all predictions and married Mr. Thorne, who had rivaled Mr. Rochford in the contest for favorite of the *ton* but had never quite equaled him. Mr. Thorne, after all, was not about to become heir to anything, least of all an exalted title.

And both men were attending the masquerade—Lady Farraday confirmed it to all who asked. Indeed several members of Lady Jessica's family, not to mention Lady Vickers, seemed downright eager to pass on the information to anyone who would listen, even to those who had not asked for it. Both men were to attend the masquerade. So was Lady Jessica, of course.

Who could resist all the potential drama inherent in a love triangle? How would Mr. Anthony Rochford react to his first sight of Lady Jessica as a married lady? And how would he react to the sight of his rival for her hand? The man who had bested him.

*And would he recognize them before midnight?*

*Would anyone?*

*Would anyone recognize Mr. Anthony Rochford himself?*

Even those few people who had accepted their invitations but had half decided that they would not go to something that was sure to be a sad squeeze decided that after all they must attend.

Lady Farraday's ball had become the most anticipated entertainment of the Season.


Mary was the only one who needed a heavy disguise, for she was quite a distinctive figure to those who knew her—and presumably Manley and his wife as well as their son had seen her a time or two. She rather fancied the nun's costume that was presented for her review among a few other possibilities. It would cover all but her face from eyebrows to chin and would enable her to hide her bad arm.

"Hmm," Jessica said when Mary tried it on. "Your face is still recognizable, Mary. We must add a mask—just a half one. Full masks are horrid things. It becomes hard to breathe, especially in a stuffy ballroom. Black, I think." She added the mask to Mary's disguise and took a step back.

"The bandit nun," Gabriel said, and Mary laughed merrily.

"The bandit nun," she said. "I like it. *May* I choose this costume, Jessica?"

Surprisingly—*very* surprisingly—her face had lit up with delight when Gabriel had asked if she had ever wanted to go to a masquerade. And when he had explained to her what the plans were for Lady Farraday's ball, she had first looked very serious, and then had lit back up and looked like an excited child in anticipation of a treat, seated as she had been in that chair, which was many sizes too large for her. Her feet did not even reach the floor.

"Provided I will not have anything to do except sit and watch—until after midnight," she had said, "I will do it. Will I be able to wear a costume?"

"It is imperative that you do," Gabriel had told her, and she had smiled from him to Jessica and looked very pleased indeed with the world. "You will be quite safe, Mary. I will see to it."

"I know you will," she had said. "What an adventure I am having. Did I tell you that Ned and his elder son are staying at my cottage to look after my animals until I return? They are very kind. So is Ned's dear wife for allowing him to do it."

"Do you wonder that I love her, Jessie?" Gabriel asked that night when they lay in bed, relaxing after making love. Perhaps it was not the wisest thing to say of another woman to one's brand-new wife.

"I do not," she told him. "I think, Gabriel, she must be an angel. And what a foolish thing to say. How embarrassing." She laughed. "But she must be."

He turned onto his side and kissed her. Hard. And for

perhaps the first time since returning to England he was consciously *glad* he had come. Even with all the challenges ahead, he was glad.

Gabriel chose a black domino for his costume, with a black half mask. It was neither an imaginative nor a very effective disguise, but that would not matter. He did not care if everyone recognized him—as everyone surely would—as long as Manford and his wife did not until midnight. He did not even care if he was pointed out to them as Gabriel Thorne. It was unlikely that after thirteen years they would know him just from the lower half of his face.

"Oh," Mary, the little bandit nun, said when she saw him on the evening of the masquerade, "you do look splendidly handsome, Gabriel. Does he not, Jessica?"

"Be still, my heart," Jessica said, smiling brightly at him and fairly rocking him back on his heels. She herself had already been looking disturbingly gorgeous in her deep pink domino and matching mask even before she added the smile.

"Mine could not grow stiller if it tried," he said, his eyes fully upon her. "It has already stopped."

Mary clapped her hands and laughed with glee.

"And as for you," he said, "you look very fierce, Mary. Who has ever heard of a nun with a mask? She can only intend mischief. You must stop smiling, however, if you hope to frighten everyone."

She *did* stop smiling. Suddenly, so did all of them. For this was it. The confrontation they had planned with such meticulous care together with Jessica's family, who had insisted, against his better judgment, upon being involved. The most carefully thought-out plans, of course, often went awry. Everything depended upon Manley's being there tonight. They had all done their part to see that he would be. There was nothing else they could do on that front but wait and see.

There was a knock on the sitting room door and Horbath reported almost immediately that her ladyship, the Dowager Countess of Riverdale, awaited Miss Beck in her carriage outside the hotel doors.

"She will be kind," Gabriel assured Mary before escorting her downstairs. "She can be a bit intimidating, but she admires your courage. She told Jessie so." He worried about poor Mary, who had lived most of her life as a hermit, her companions almost exclusively of the animal kingdom. She was to sit for most of the evening between the dowager and her sister.

"But of course she will be kind," Mary said, not looking nearly as nervous as Gabriel felt and Jessica looked. "She is Jessica's grandmama, is she not?"

She had not yet seen Jessica at her aristocratic best. She probably would later tonight. But Mary would not be intimidated anyway, he suddenly realized. Her eyes would look past every barrier to the good that lay within any person she met.

Except when there was no goodness to be seen.


Manley Rochford was dressed as King Arthur, complete with a golden crown encrusted with paste jewels and a black mask. His wife—unfortunately, considering her rather plain, matronly looks, a number of guests remarked behind their hands or fans—appeared as Guinevere, also with a mask. Several people did not know them, but since most had come in the hope of catching a glimpse of them and perhaps making themselves known to them so that they would be the more assured of receiving invitations to the grand celebrations they were said to be planning, they were soon pointed out to everyone by those who *did* know.

Anthony Rochford was unmistakable in a billowing, all-enveloping domino and a mask that covered three-quarters of his face, for the entire costume was a glittering gold embellished with sequins. And who, anyway, could mistake that smile even though it proceeded from almost the only part of his body that was not covered?

Masquerades were always amusing, Jessica thought, for of course very few people went unknown to everyone else. The few exceptions were almost always those people whom almost no one knew anyway. She recognized friends and acquaintances wherever she looked. And family members, of course. And they were all here—except Harry, who had returned home to the country yesterday. Even Grandmama and Great-aunt Edith and Miss Boniface had come, partly because wild horses could not keep them away on this particular occasion, Grandmama had told her, and partly because they had undertaken the important task of looking after Mary until she was needed later, which might or might not happen. Mary sat now, resembling a mischievous elfin blackbird, between Boadicea—Grandmama—on her left and someone who was either a dragon or a giant robin—Great-aunt Edith—on her right. Miss Boniface, like many of the other guests clad in a domino and mask, hovered behind them.

Some members of Jessica's old court found her out—it was not difficult—and swore to broken hearts and other silly things like the determination to challenge Gabriel to pistols at dawn. A few of them danced with her.

One thrilling moment came when the golden domino bowed before her, solicited her hand for a dance, congratulated her on her recent marriage, and proceeded to look tragic while they danced. In other words, his smile was not in evidence except when he looked at other women, which he did a number of times. He smiled with dazzling intensity at Estelle, who was partnered with Adrian Sawyer, Viscount Dirkson's son. He smiled without ceasing when he danced the next set with Estelle and then swept her off in a flourish of gold to introduce her to King Arthur and Queen Guinevere.

A marquess's daughter would do quite nicely, it seemed, when a duke's was no longer available. The father was making much of Estelle, who made a very pretty mermaid, with feet that peeked discreetly from beneath her multicolored tail. Her mask matched it.

"I am crushed," Jessica told Avery and Anna between sets.

She waltzed with Gabriel not long before midnight. He was tense and grim faced, she could see, though he did not miss a step. She was feeling the fluttering of nerves in her stomach too.

"One could almost believe," he said, "that he is expecting to inherit a king's title."

"I suppose," she said, "he has been something of a nobody for most of his life, Gabriel. And he had almost no expectation either until recent years. Both you and your cousin, not to mention your uncle, stood between him and the title—and fortune. Does he have money of his own?"

"I think not," he said. "He was always eager to live upon the hospitality of my uncle and aunt at Brierley."

"The unmasking is to happen after this set," she told him, as though he was not well aware of that fact for himself.

"Yes," he said. "It may all come to nothing, you know, Jessie. It may be a massive anticlimax."

"But only we will know," she said. And all the Westcotts and those with family connections to them.

The music came to an end. Had that last waltz of the set been shorter than the others? It did not matter. It was over, and Lady Farraday, assisted by her husband's hand, was climbing to the orchestra dais and raising her arms for silence. She got it after a few moments of excited murmurings and hushing sounds from everyone else. She looked around the ballroom, clearly enjoying the drama of the moment, and slowly removed her own mask. The obligatory gasp of surprise was followed by the equally obligatory round of applause.

"Yes," she said when it had died down. "It is I. And this is the moment when I get to discover if I have been entertaining a roomful of total strangers and impostors all evening." She waited for the laughter to subside. "My lords and ladies and gentlemen, it is time to remove your masks and reveal your identities."

There was a great deal of noise and laughter as everyone complied and looked around at one another and pretended astonishment at discovering acquaintances they had not identified until that precise moment.

Manley Rochford, as they had hoped, aroused particular interest now that everyone could admit to knowing who he was. And he was standing, conveniently enough, almost in the center of the ballroom. Well-wishers gathered about him to shake his hand or to curtsy. He smiled graciously upon them all, a rather handsome King Arthur without his mask. His son, still glittering even without *his* mask, stood smiling at his right hand while his wife hovered at his left.

Gabriel looked steadily at Jessica and offered his arm. They approached that most dense group of guests together and a pathway opened before them, perhaps because the space had been occupied by Avery and Anna, Elizabeth and Colin, Alexander and Wren, Boris and Bertrand, and Sir Trevor and Lady Vickers.

Manley Rochford looked graciously upon the two of them, prepared to receive their homage.

"Hello, Manley," Gabriel said.

# Twenty

Manley looked somewhat startled at being so familiarly addressed. His smile faltered for a moment, but he nodded graciously at them both.

"Mr. Thorne, Papa," Anthony Rochford said. "I have told you about him. And Mrs. Thorne—Lady Jessica Thorne."

"Ah, yes." Manley's eyes rested upon Jessica. "I understand congratulations are in order. And Mr. Thorne." He made them a slight bow.

"*Gabriel* Thorne," Gabriel said. "How are you, Manley?"

Manley frowned in puzzlement. "Do I know you?" he asked—and Gabriel saw the beginnings of unease in the man.

"A long time ago," he said. "Thirteen years ago and more."

He was very aware of Jessica's hand on his arm. He knew, though he did not turn his head to look, that since

removing her mask she had become the cool, poised, aristocratic Lady Jessica. He was aware too that the loud
sounds of merriment that had succeeded the unmasking
were dying down slightly in their immediate vicinity.

Manley's handsome face, framed by becomingly graying hair upon which sat a jeweled crown, had paled. His
jaws had clamped together—to prevent him from gaping,
perhaps.

A definite quiet had fallen upon the crowd around them
now, and Gabriel sensed that other people were drawing
closer to see what was happening.

"It cannot be." The words barely passed Manley's lips.
"No."

"But yes," Gabriel said. "It can be. And it is."

Manley's wife set a hand on his arm. Gabriel could not
for the life of him remember her name. She had always
been a shadowy figure, along with Philip's wife. And his
aunt too. Women were not highly regarded by most of the
Rochford men.

"Manley," she said, her voice noticeably shaking. "He is
*Gabriel*."

Manley shook off her arm with open impatience. His
nostrils flared. His eyes blazed. "You are *dead*. This man
is an impostor." He pointed a finger at Gabriel and took one
wild look about the crowd, as though searching for an ally.
"Marjorie, we are leaving."

*Marjorie*. That was her name.

"Papa?" Anthony Rochford said. "This is Mr. Thorne.
The man from America I told you about. Mama?"

"Actually," Gabriel said without taking his eyes off
Manley, and he knew now that he had a rather large and
avidly listening audience of the cream of society, "I was

born with the name Rochford. *Gabriel* Rochford. I kept that name until I sailed for America thirteen years ago."

The reaction was worthy of any melodrama. There was a gasp followed by loud murmurings followed in turn by frantic shushing noises.

"Papa?" Anthony Rochford sounded close to panic now.

Manley ignored him. He was having a bit of an on-slaught of panic of his own, Gabriel guessed. But he mastered his emotions with a visible effort. He thrust back his shoulders and continued to point a now shaking finger at Gabriel. He looked rather magnificent, actually, with his crown glinting in the candlelight from the chandelier over-head. All he needed to complete the picture was Excalibur clutched in his hand.

"This man," he said, addressing the crowd, which must have swelled to consist of almost every guest at the ball. "*This man*, who changed his name and hid away in America, as well he ought, for thirteen years, has now been driven by ambition to consider it worth the risk of returning at the last possible moment to claim his birthright. I am here to stop him in the name of justice."

"You may try, Manley," Gabriel said. He was surprised by how little hate he felt for his cousin, who would have sent him to the gallows thirteen years ago and would do it again now. He felt only contempt.

"This man," Manley said. "This *Gabriel Rochford* is a *murderer*."

There was another wave of sound. Manley waited for it to subside, as it soon did. No one wanted to miss a word. He took a step forward, leaving his wife and son slightly be-hind him. He knew how to play to an audience, Gabriel thought appreciatively.

*"This man,"* Manley continued, "ravished the young and innocent daughter of a neighbor of the Earl of Lyndale, his uncle, and left her in disgrace and with child. When confronted by the young lady's brother and *my dear friend*, Gabriel Rochford murdered him. He shot him in the back. *I witnessed him doing so*, though I was too far away, alas, to stop him. Is there a worse or more cowardly crime than to shoot an unarmed man in the back?"

The cream of society obviously did not think so. The murmur this time was uglier. Equally ugly glances were being directed Gabriel's way.

"He escaped," Manley said, "before my cousin, the earl, could have him apprehended. A sure admission of guilt."

"Perhaps we can take this discussion elsewhere," the loud, overcheerful voice of Lady Farraday said. "Perhaps—"

Manley ignored her. So did everyone else.

"This man should be seized now," he said, "before he can escape again. Gabriel Rochford is a dangerous man and worthy only of a dark prison cell until he can hang by the neck until he is dead."

The murmurings were becoming a little louder and a little uglier. The situation was about to turn downright nasty. At any moment now, Gabriel thought, he was going to be tackled and brought down on the ballroom floor, his arms pinioned behind his back. Perhaps it was only social etiquette and the presence of ladies—several of whom looked just as outraged as their men, however—that had prevented its happening already.

"I find it a little strange, Manley," Gabriel said, and the need to hear what he had to say outweighed the urge to prevent him from fleeing. Silence fell almost immediately. "I find it strange that you saw me shoot Mr. Orson Ginsberg, *my friend*, in the back. Of course, by your own admission you were some distance away and were perhaps mistaken about the identity of the murderer. You were the only witness, were you?"

"I was not," Manley said. "My cousin was with me. *Your* cousin too. Mr. Philip Rochford."

"Ah," Gabriel said. "The *late* Philip Rochford, that would be."

"He reported what he saw," Manley said, "to a number of people, including the earl, his father, and representatives of the law. You made a grave mistake in coming back to England, *Gabriel Rochford*. If you believe your prospects will protect you—"

"I find it strange," Gabriel said, cutting him off, "because I know of two other witnesses who are willing to swear, in a court of law if necessary, that I was nowhere near the scene of the murder at the time it was committed."

"Oh yes?" Manley said. He was sneering now and looking about him to encourage his audience to sneer with him. "Produce them, Gabriel *Rochford*."

Gabriel felt someone step up behind him and tug lightly on his domino. Jessica looked back and released her hold of his arm in order to step to one side and draw Mary into the gap between them with one arm about her shoulders. The little bareheaded nun had removed her wimple as well as her mask. She looked steadily and reproachfully at Manley.

He recognized her instantly. So did his wife.

"It is Miss Beck," she said.

"Be quiet, Marjorie," Manley commanded, his voice harsh. "You are a long way from home, Miss Beck. Gabriel was always a great favorite with you, I recall. But you may wish to consider well before perjuring yourself in order to save him from the gallows."

"I never have to consider for long before telling the

truth, Mr. Rochford," she said in her calm, deep voice.
"Truth is the only thing to be told, at all times. Gabriel was
at my cottage for several hours of the afternoon when poor
Mr. Ginsberg died. He was helping me tend a wounded
fawn one of the grooms had brought me. The groom remained too and remembers. I have a letter from him in
safekeeping."

It was currently locked inside a safe in Netherby's study
at Archer House.

"I have a firm alibi, you see," Gabriel said. "You were
mistaken, Manley. It was not I who murdered Orson."

*"Alibi!"* Manley said scornfully. "It is easy to get your
friends to say anything you wish, Gabriel. I demand that
this man be arrested."

The crowd no longer seemed so eager to pounce.

"Besides," Manley cried, trying to reestablish his hold
on them, "he is a *ravisher* as well as a murderer. I daresay
he has no alibi for *that*."

"Oh, I say," someone said. "Remember there are ladies
present, Rochford."

"Even for that rape," Manley said, repeating the word at
least one of his fellow guests had found offensive, "he deserves to die."

"And I have a letter," Gabriel said, "written by the lady
herself and witnessed by her father and her husband, exon-
erating me from that charge. You were mistaken again,
Manley. It was someone else who ravished her."

That letter too was in Netherby's safe.

He waited for the renewed swell of sound around them
to die down.

"She does name that someone else in her letter," Gabriel
added, his eyes fixed upon Manley.

Manley had turned even paler, if that was possible. His lips looked almost blue in contrast.

"You brought a fortune from America with you, Thorne," Anthony Rochford blurted suddenly. "How much did you pay the strumpet? And her father and husband? How much did you pay Miss Beck? And the groom who wrote a letter— if he *did* write it? In my experience grooms do not write. Or read." He looked triumphantly about him.

But his words fell flat. And Manley seemed lost for further words. His wife set a hand on his arm again, and again he shook it off.

"We are done here. For now," he said, speaking with an awful dignity. "If no one among you is man enough to hold this man until the authorities can come to arrest him and haul him off to jail, where he belongs, then I will have to make those arrangements myself. Come, my dear. Come, Anthony."

A path opened up for him, though he did have to lead his wife and son around Gabriel and Jessica and Mary in order to reach it. They left the ballroom unimpeded. Everyone else simply watched them go.

Gabriel looked down at Mary and smiled. And he looked over her head at Jessica and . . . saw two persons combined. One and indivisible. He saw Lady Jessica Thorne at her most haughty. He saw also Jessica, the lovely, warmhearted woman he suspected had become indispensable to him for the rest of his life.

"My felicitations, Lady Farraday." It was the voice of Netherby, bored and aristocratic, not raised above the level of ordinary conversation by one iota but nevertheless commanding the attention of everyone in the ballroom. "I daresay your costume ball will go down in the annals of social history as one of the most memorable entertainments of the decade."

And a small group of ladies began a round of applause, there were a few cries of *Hear, hear*, a man whistled piercingly, and Lady Farrady almost visibly let go of the conviction that her precious masquerade was a disaster. The floor was clearing, the orchestra was readying its instruments, but still there was a cluster of persons in the middle of the ballroom.

"I believe we are done here too," Gabriel said to the two ladies beside him. "Are we ready to leave?"

"Yes," Jessica said.

"In a minute," Mary said, looking apologetically from one to the other of them. "I must first thank your grandmother and aunt, if I may, Jessica. They have been very kind to me. What lovely ladies they are."

Gabriel smiled rather grimly at Jessica as Mary moved away, and she looked back—ah, with that wide, sunny smile that always rocked him back on his heels.

Lady Farraday's guests had allowed Mr. Manley Rochford and his wife and son to leave without attempting to stop them. It was, of course, otherwise with Gabriel. It made perfect sense to Jessica.

Some wished merely to shake his hand and congratulate him, calling him *my lord* or *Lyndale* as they did so. Others wished to assure him that they did not believe for a single moment that he was guilty of what he had been accused of and were very glad that he had a solid alibi for both charges. A few were bold enough to ask him if he knew who *was* guilty. *Was it Mr. Manley Rochford himself?* No one asked that specific question, but all wondered. Or so it seemed to Jessica.

"What the devil?" Mr. Albert Vickers said, pumping Gabriel's hand, seemingly unaware that there were ladies within earshot, including Jessica. "What the *devil*, Gabe? I jolly well hope you have those letters in a safe place."

"I do," Gabriel assured him.

Jessica was not ignored. She was congratulated—upon her marriage and upon the fact that she was the Countess of Lyndale. She was assured that no one believed any of those nasty things Mr. Rochford had said about the earl, her husband. Predictably, a few people told her they had not really liked or trusted the man from their first sight of him at church on Sunday.

The orchestra was poised and ready and Lady Farraday was looking a bit anxious again. Finally Gabriel drew Jessica's arm through his and they were able to leave the ballroom to rather embarrassing applause.

Alexander was waiting outside the ballroom doors with Mary.

"Tomorrow morning, then," he said, "in a private dining room at your hotel? The arrangement has not changed?"

He and Avery were planning to meet Gabriel for breakfast tomorrow morning, to assess what had happened tonight, to discuss what ought to happen next. Gabriel had been unwilling to make plans for the latter ahead of time. They had had no way of knowing how their plans for the ball itself would turn out.

"I have reserved a room," Gabriel told him, shaking his hand. "I appreciate the support, Riverdale, even though I am such a new member of the family."

Alexander grinned. "We thrive upon such crises," he

said. "I hope you reserved a largish room. I suspect Wren and Anna will insist upon coming too, and I would not bet against a few others. Jessica, for example." He turned to her and hugged her tightly.

"Thank you, Alexander," she said. "You look very impressive as Alexander the Great."

He laughed.

And finally they left.

Mary, seated beside Jessica on one carriage seat while Gabriel sat with his back to the horses, was very quiet.

"You are tired, Mary?" Jessica asked her.

"I believe," she said, "I could sleep for a week if no one disturbed me. What will happen to him, Gabriel?"

"I am not sure," he told her. "It is what will be discussed at tomorrow's breakfast meeting. I suppose, Mary, you feel sorry for him?"

She thought about it in her serious, quiet way. "We diminish ourselves too," she said at last, "when feeling sorry for someone who has done a dreadful wrong leads us to excuse him and simply hope he will mend his ways. Feeling sorry for someone but acknowledging that justice ought nevertheless to be done is more appropriate to moral beings. Yes, Gabriel, I feel sorry for him—and I feel real sorrow for his wife and his son, who appears vain and occasionally callous, but is perhaps not really vicious. For Manley Rochford I feel pity and hope for justice. It breaks my heart."

"Even though he was intent upon making you homeless and destitute?" Jessica asked.

"Even though," Mary said, patting her hand.

None of them said anything else during the ride home— home, for the present at least, being a hotel. They both saw

Mary to her room, which was close to their suite. Ruth was waiting for her inside.

"My dear Ruth," Mary was saying as Gabriel was closing the door, "you ought not to have waited up so late just for me. You must lie down on that truckle bed right away. I hope it is comfortable."

The first thing Gabriel did when they stepped inside their own suite was to summon his valet from his bedchamber and dismiss him for the night. He went with a respectful bow and a murmured good night.

"He was not happy at being dismissed before he could perform his final duties for the day," Jessica said after the door closed behind him.

"How can you tell?" Gabriel asked, grinning at her. "I have never known anyone with a more impassive face."

"One gets to know," she said, smiling back. "Servants give subtle hints of their true feelings that they fully expect their employers to interpret."

"I suppose," he said, "your maid was annoyed with you just now even though she did not even look at you?"

"But of course," she said. "She *did not look at me*, Gabriel."

Oh, it was so lovely to see him smile, to hear him laugh. Smiles and laughter made him look downright handsome as well as younger.

And then both the smile and the laughter were gone, and he cast aside his black domino and strode toward her to remove hers. Both garments landed in a heap on the floor—his customary storage place for clothes as they were removed, it seemed. He caught her up in his arms and held her tightly and wordlessly. It was almost hard to breathe. He held her for a long time until she realized something that threatened to turn her knees to water.

He was weeping.

"Gabriel?" she whispered.

"Oh good God," he muttered. "Devil take it."

He released her and turned away from her. He went to stand facing the fireplace, one forearm resting on the mantel.

Jessica picked up their dominoes and set them on one of the chairs at the table where they dined. She leaned back against the table and looked at him. He was drawing deep breaths and releasing them a bit raggedly. Men found it so embarrassing to weep, foolish creatures. Though she was blinking her eyes more than was normally necessary and swallowing several times to quell the gurgle in her throat. She pushed herself up to sit on the table, something she could not recall ever doing before.

He took out his handkerchief, blew his nose, and put it away. And he turned his head to look at her.

"He is my *cousin*, Jessica," he said. "Second cousin, to be exact. Philip was my cousin. My uncle Julius was my father's brother. They are—*were*, in some cases—my *family*. And then consider *your* family."

Life was rarely fair, was it? She had realized that, probably for the first time, eight years ago, when life as she had known it had been shattered. Yet her family had held firm and prospered. They were always there to lean upon or simply to love.

"You were lonely, Gabriel?" she asked. Oh, surely more than lonely. His father died when he was nine, his mother years before that.

"The world is full of lonely people," he said, coming toward her. He took hold of a ringlet of hair that was hovering over the corner of her eye and hooked it behind her ear. "It must never be used as an excuse for unhappiness or self-pity. Consider Mary."

"Your aunt was her sister," she said. "Were they not close?"

"No," he said. "My aunt did her duty by taking Mary to Brierley with her after her marriage to my uncle, and he did his duty by giving her a home of her own and making her an allowance. Much can be said for duty. It ought to be done. But it is no substitute for love."

"Your uncle did his duty by you," she said.

"Yes."

"And then," she said, "you went away and worked hard and found both happiness and love—with your mother's cousin."

"Cyrus," he said. "Yes."

She felt infinitely sad. She cupped his face with her hands. How cruel it must have seemed when Cyrus died in a senseless accident. "And ultimately duty brought you back to England."

"And love," he said. "I love Mary."

"Yes." She leaned forward and set her lips softly to his. He did not immediately respond, though he did not draw back his head either.

"And now," she said, "you love everyone else at Brierley, all those who are suffering from having had Manley Rochford there for a while."

"I did not know," he said. "I ought to have. I have been derelict in my duty."

"But not any longer," she said. "You must not be hard on yourself, Gabriel. You had duties in Boston too. You dealt with those by leaving your friend in charge, confident that he will carry your legacy forward. Now you will solve *this* problem. And you have already started. Manley will no longer be there. And you and I will. I will be there by your side. It is why you married me."

"Jessie," he said. "That is not—"

She set a finger across his lips.

"And it is why I married you," she told him. "Duty and—"

"Love?" he said.

Ah, but she did not want to load that sense of guilt upon his shoulders. "Affection," she said. "You feel some for me. I know you do. And I feel some for you. It is a start, Gabriel. It is a very good start."

"Yes," he said, and they gazed at each other.

What was the difference, she wondered, between affection and love? Or between desire and affection—and love? What *did* she feel for her husband? What did he feel for her? But did it matter by what name it was labeled? It just *was*.

His hands came to her hips then and his mouth returned to hers. But open and hungry this time. And hot. Oh, so hot. *He* was hot. Whatever that meant. Words again. Words could be so stupid. Stupidly inadequate. So could thoughts.

Begone, then, thoughts.

His mouth was devouring hers. His tongue was deep in her mouth and sending trails of tingling heat right down inside her to her toes, though it concentrated about her womanly parts, those she had discovered on the bed in the next room during the past few days and nights.

But mouth and tongue were not sufficient. Not by half. Oh—

He was raising her evening gown, none too gently, and he lifted her above the table for a moment so that he could raise it up and, after he had dealt quickly with the buttons at the back, all the way off her body to be tossed to the floor. Her stays followed in short order. And then her shift. He did not touch her evening slippers or her silk stockings and the garters that held them up. He shrugged out of his evening coat, with a bit of help from her, and his waistcoat and neckcloth. He tugged at his shirt and pulled it up and off his head to join everything else on the floor. He dealt with the buttons at his waist but did not remove his breeches. His mouth ravished hers almost the whole time. And then she realized—oh goodness!

He was not going to take the time to carry her into the bedchamber. He was going to—right here, right now.

His hands came to her naked hips again and pulled her to the edge of the table. She wrapped her legs about him. And he thrust hard into her.

The table squeaked as he worked in her. The sound got all caught up with the eroticism of the moment—that and the rhythmic sound of the wetness of their coupling.

It was unbearably painful. Unbearably sweet. Unbearably—

Her forehead came to rest on his shoulder as she shuddered and then shuddered again and again before floating downward from . . . Well, there went the stupidity of words again. There never were any for the truly important things. She floated downward.

He was still pulsing and throbbing inside her though he was still and she knew he was finished.

And he was *hot*. There was really no other word that came close to describing what he was as a lover.

"I am so sorry, Jessie," he said. He was still inside her. He sounded breathless, as well he ought.

She raised her head and looked into his dark blue eyes— they were heavy lidded with the aftermath of passion.

"If you really mean that, Gabriel," she said, "I am leaving you in the morning and going home to Archer House."

He smiled slowly at her.

Oh, that smile.

# Twenty-one

The table in the private dining room Gabriel had reserved at his hotel had been set for ten. He and Jessica were down first, but they were soon joined by Riverdale and Netherby and their wives. The Marquess of Dorchester arrived next with Baron Molenor and Viscount Dirkson. Bertie Vickers came on their heels. Gabriel was rather touched to see him.

"I was not invited, Gabe," he said, shaking hands with him and nodding first to Jessica and then to everyone else. "But m'father found out about it from Netherby, and I told him I was coming, invitation or not. I was offended by that gold waistcoat of the younger Rochford a few weeks ago, and I was offended by his gold domino and mask last evening. Sequins on a man, for the love of God! The *father*, on the other hand—well, talk about smiling villains. There is a Shakespeare quote about them somewhere. Can't remember where. Did I understand correctly, Gabe? Did the man commit crimes and then try to blame them upon you?

Would he have sent you to the gallows in his place? Would he still if he could get away with it? We have to do something. And if there is something I can do to help . . . Well, it is why I came."

"I am glad you did," Gabriel assured him.

No one else came, though all the younger men of the Westcott family and a number of the women had apparently *wanted* to. But they had been persuaded to remain at home. So ten settings were exactly enough.

The English aristocracy was a remarkable breed, Gabriel discovered over the next half hour while they partook of a sumptuous breakfast—the hotel cooks and kitchen staff had probably been up half the night preparing it, he guessed with a twinge of guilt. They conversed easily and with apparent interest on a number of topics, which ranged from politics to foreign affairs, from the newest books and pamphlets to the opera, from the state of the crops on their various estates to—yes—the weather. Anyone listening in, as the manager and waiters no doubt did as they carried in an endless supply of food and removed plates and dishes and poured coffee, would have assumed that this was a mere social gathering.

It was not until the table had been cleared of all except their coffee cups and the cream and sugar and a large pot of fresh coffee that they got down to business.

"First things first," Riverdale said. "Those papers are locked up in the safe in your study, Netherby?"

"I can safely report," Netherby said, "that they are quite perfectly safe in the safe."

Bertie smirked and Dirkson chuckled.

"And Miss Beck and the groom from Brierley—Ned Higgins, I believe?—are prepared to testify in a court of law if necessary, Lyndale?" Riverdale asked. "And Mrs. Clark?"

"I would not allow Mrs. Clark to be called in person as a witness," Gabriel said. "Her letter, witnessed by her father and her husband, will have to do."

"Yes," Jessica said. "I agree."

"Oh," Anna said. "And so do I. One knows very well what would happen if she were dragged into court. Soon everything that happened would be *her* fault."

Netherby's well-manicured, beringed hand covered hers briefly on the table, Gabriel noticed.

"Mrs. Clark's letter—in her own handwriting, I assume, Lyndale?" the Marquess of Dorchester began, and paused, eyebrows raised.

Gabriel nodded.

"And witnessed by her male relatives," Dorchester continued, "is surely proof enough first that Lyndale did not ravish her or father her child, and second that Manley Rochford did—by overpowering her and proceeding without her consent. You are safe on that charge. On the second you are safe too since you have an alibi, to which two witnesses are prepared to testify. But—is there any proof that Manley Rochford committed the murder?"

"It was almost certainly either Manley or Philip Rochford, my cousin," Gabriel said. "He died seven years ago. Hence my title and my return to England. His version of events died with him, though both he and Manley swore to my uncle that they had seen me commit the crime. Both joined him in urging me to flee. Perhaps they were afraid their story would not hold up in court. But I am afraid probability would not bring a conviction in court. There were no other witnesses that I know of and therefore there is no proof beyond all reasonable doubt that one or the other of them shot Orson Ginsberg in the back."

"And so," Wren said, "even if he can be convicted on the one charge, on the other he cannot be. Which is exactly why we all came here this morning, Gabriel. If justice is to be meted out, or an approximation of justice, then it must be done in a different way."

"A bloodthirsty wife you have there, Alexander," Molenor said, but he was nodding approvingly at her.

"I like to see justice done, Uncle Thomas," she told him. "Not only is Mr. Manley Rochford a—a *ravisher* and a murderer, but he is also willing to commit a second, judicial, murder by framing Gabriel and sending him to the gallows. He must not be allowed to creep home, his only punishment being his disappointment over not gaining the earldom. And he is still the heir to that earldom. You had better watch your back, Gabriel."

"You are so very right about everything, Wren," Anna said.

"Hear, hear," Bertie said. "*Will* he creep back home?"

"He had not made any move to do so up to the time we came here," Netherby said. "My man outside his house and the one outside his carriage house had a tedious night. So did the mysterious stranger who also had an eye on the house."

"Stranger?" Gabriel frowned.

"Alas," Netherby said. "My man was unable to identify him when he spotted him. And then he disappeared—or seemed to."

"We are on it," Riverdale assured Gabriel.

"What I would like to do at the *very* least, with apologies to the ladies," Gabriel said, "is pound Manley Rochford to a pulp. Bertie, will you serve as my second?"

Jessica, he noticed without actually turning his head in her direction, clapped both hands over her mouth.

"It would be my pleasure, Gabe," Bertie assured him.

"You are right about this not being appropriate for the hearing of ladies," Dirkson said. "Remember that Rochford would have the choice of weapons if you were the challenger, Lyndale."

"Women, Charles," Anna said, "are not such delicate creatures as men believe. But . . . surely there is an alternative? Duels are not the answer to everything."

"They are not, Anna," Dorchester agreed. "Unfortunately they are the *only* answer to some things."

"How good are you with a pistol, Lyndale?" Molenor asked.

That was when Jessica's forehead thumped onto the table, narrowly missing her coffee cup. She had fainted.

By the time Jessica returned to full consciousness and convinced Ruth that she had no intention of being an invalid for the rest of the day or even for one more minute, Gabriel was no longer in their suite of rooms. Apparently the breakfast meeting was over and everyone had dispersed.

It seemed a little suspicious to her that neither Anna nor Wren at the very least had insisted upon coming with her when Gabriel apparently had carried her unconscious form upstairs. It was also *very* suspicious that he had not remained himself to hover at her bedside. Instead he had disappeared the moment she stirred but before her mind was clear enough to allow her to do anything constructive with her consciousness—like make him swear upon his most sacred honor that he would not be fighting any duels.

When Ruth had finished tidying her dress and repairing

the damage to her hair, Jessica stepped into the sitting room and found Mary waiting quietly for her there.

"Mary! Do you know what's happening? Gabriel has gone out to find Manley Rochford and challenge him to a duel and shoot him," Jessica cried in a voice that sounded frantic even to her own ears. "But instead, he is the one who will end up shot. I have to go out and find—"

"Now, dear, calm down. Gabriel had to go out on some quick business," Mary told her, sounding infuriatingly calm. "Just some very tedious business of the sort men always have to see about. He will be back here before we are, I daresay."

"Before we are?" Jessica asked, determinedly ignoring the buzzing in her ears. She was *not* going to faint again. How very humiliating that she had done so earlier, and in front of half her family, who would by now have carried the delightful news home to the other half. Anna and Wren had behaved like warriors during that meeting, while she had . . . fainted. But it was not *their* husbands who were about to have their brains blown out.

"Well, Jessica," Mary was saying, smiling, "your dear grandmama and her sister are taking me out to show me the Tower of London and Westminster Abbey, and then we are going to a tea shop, which is apparently very fashionable. And you are to come with us. This is *such* a treat for me. Who would have thought I would ever be in London and attending a masquerade ball and visiting the Tower of London with the Dowager Countess of Riverdale? All my animals will be very impressed indeed when I tell them about it."

"Mary," Jessica said, sitting down on a sofa before she could fall down. She knew just what was going on, of course. There was no way on earth Mary could be this insensitive while smiling so very placidly at her. "I cannot go."

"Yes," Mary said. "You can and you will, my dear. You are the Countess of Lyndale. You are the sister of the Duke of Netherby—and what a very formidable gentleman *he* is, by the way. I like him exceedingly well. Gabriel wishes you to accompany us. And my dear Jessica, there will be no pistols. No bullets. He assured me of that, and he asked me to assure you. He advised me to tell you that I do not lie. And he is right. I do not."

Jessica sucked in a breath and let it out slowly.

She was the Countess of Lyndale, Mary had reminded her. More to the point and from long experience, she was Lady Jessica Archer. Mary did not tell lies. But perhaps Gabriel had lied to Mary. No. Surely, surely he would not have done that if there was any risk that someone—Avery? Alexander? Anna?—might have to come here later to tell her he had been shot through the heart in a duel.

But he was without any doubt up to *something*. Something he did not want her to know about, or he would not have dashed away in such a hurry before she could question him. But it was not *that*. He would not be so rash anyway, for it must have occurred to him—and to all her family members who had been here for breakfast, and even to Mr. Vickers—that if he died in a duel, Manley Rochford would become the Earl of Lyndale after all. It would have occurred to Gabriel that it was *his duty* to remain alive at least long enough to beget a son.

She would kill him anyway with her bare hands the next time she saw him.

Unconsciously she adjusted her posture and raised her chin.

"You will love the Tower of London, Mary," she said. "And Westminster Abbey. So will I. I have not made a visit to either for at least a year or two."

As for the tearoom . . . Well, she would think of that when the time came. At the moment the very thought of food or even a cup of tea made her want to vomit.

"You are a very dear and brave young lady," Mary said. "Gabriel is a fortunate man."

Gabriel had spent a busy few hours, though it was not easy to keep his mind off Jessica. He had tried to keep her from attending that meeting, but of course she had insisted. The last thing he had expected her to do, however, was faint. And she had been out cold. Some chafing of the wrists by Anna while one of her uncles had fanned her face with a napkin had done nothing to bring her around. Gabriel had scooped her up in his arms and carried her back to their suite.

His first instinct had been to send for her mother. When Horbath had gone to fetch Ruth, however, Mary had come with her. Leaving her with Mary was leaving her in very safe hands indeed. And leave he must, before Jessica had recovered enough to interrogate him on his intentions. He waited just until she was stirring back to consciousness and both Ruth and Mary assured him that she would be perfectly fine after a little rest. Mary had come out to the sitting room with him and told him that the Dowager Countess of Riverdale and her sister had very kindly offered to show her some of London today.

"I could cancel the outing without suffering any great disappointment," she said. "But I believe it would be better, Gabriel, to go and to take Jessica with us."

"An excellent idea," he said after a moment's thought. "I will call upon the dowager and inform her of the slight change in plan and the reason for it."

"Gabriel," she said as he took his hat and gloves from Horbath, "you will remember, will you not, that all life is sacred, even that of a miscreant?"

"I will remember," he told her, looking steadily at her. "He will not die at my hands, Mary, and I cannot take the risk of dying at his. Much depends upon my staying alive, at least for a while."

No, he could not challenge Manley to a duel. As had been pointed out at breakfast, that would give Manley the advantage of having choice of weapons. And Manley had grown up with a gun in his hands. Gabriel, on the other hand, had not. Anyway, a duel was an affair of honor between two gentlemen. Manley did not deserve a duel. Gabriel regretted even mentioning it now, but it had been in the heat of anger.

He called upon Jessica's grandmother and great-aunt and gave them a brief summary of the morning's meeting. He discovered from them exactly where they planned to go with Mary and at approximately what time they expected to arrive at each place. And he told them he would be obliged to them if they would stay away from Hyde Park.

"We will certainly do so," the dowager assured him, giving him a hard look. "But do remember, Gabriel, that in a duel it is just as likely that the aggrieved party will be shot dead as the offender. I would not wish to see my granddaughter widowed so soon after she has become a bride."

"There will be no guns, ma'am," he assured her, "and no shootings. No deaths."

"I am almost sorry to hear it," she told him. "But go now. Edith and I need to get ready for a day of pleasure."

He went to Sir Trevor Vickers's house next. Bertie had told him at breakfast that his mother was going to call upon Mrs. Rochford this morning.

She had indeed gone and was already back home.

"She received me, Gabriel," Lady Vickers told him after she had asked about Jessica and been assured that she was recovering from her swoon and was in very good hands. "I sympathized with her over the ordeal she suffered last evening. My sympathy was genuine. She thanked me profusely for calling on her. No one else has. Not yet, anyway. Perhaps later. But that may be too late. I went mainly because I felt dreadfully sorry for the woman last evening. But I went also because both Trevor and Bertie felt that you needed to know if Mr. Rochford plans to leave London in a hurry to avoid any further inquiry into his own behavior all those years ago. And yes, Gabriel. Although there was nothing in the hall downstairs to suggest an imminent departure, upstairs in Mrs. Rochford's sitting room, where she received me, there was a pile of packed trunks and bandboxes outside what must have been her dressing room. And I could hear activity inside there all the time we spoke. I do believe they are planning to leave tomorrow or even perhaps today."

"Thank you, ma'am," he said, taking both her hands in his and squeezing them.

She sighed. "Why is it," she asked him, "that it is always the women who suffer? Do not make *your* wife suffer, Gabriel. She is far too young to be a widow."

"I do not know what Bertie has told you," he said, "but there will be no pistols at dawn, I assure you, ma'am. Or at any other time of day either."

"Just remember," she told him, "that only you stand between him and the earldom he has so craved, Gabriel. Watch yourself. Please."

"I will." He kissed the back of one of her hands.

Bertie went with him when he left the house. They proceeded to Archer House, as planned hastily when Gabriel was carrying Jessica from the private parlor at the hotel. While Bertie was shown into Netherby's study, however, Gabriel was asked to step up to the drawing room, where Anna and Jessica's mother were awaiting him.

"Jessica will be fine," Gabriel assured them before they could even ask. "She was conscious before I left, and she is in excellent hands. Her maid is very competent, as I am sure you know. And Mary has healing powers that extend to all living beings."

"Jessica is not a deer or a horse," the dowager duchess said tartly. "But Ruth I know I can depend upon. I have never known Jessica to faint. I daresay the prospect of your being shot dead in a duel was too much for her sensibilities. I suppose she cares for you."

She was on the verge of tears, Gabriel could see, but like her daughter—on most occasions—she had herself well under control and looked every inch the duchess.

"And I care for her," he said. "There will be no duel. No pistols. No deaths."

"There is a veritable army of Westcotts downstairs in Avery's study," Anna told him. "*We* have been excluded, of course. *We* are mere women."

"One woman fainted this morning, Anna," her mother-in-law reminded her, "because she was *included* and realized there was a possibility that her husband of less than a week could have his brains blown out before today ends."

"But as Avery pointed out to us when we got home, Mother," her daughter-in-law said, "Gabriel cannot afford to die just yet. If Mr. Manley Rochford could avoid prosecution, he would become the Earl of Lyndale after all, and that is unthinkable."

"Hmph," the dowager said. "You had better go down

and join them, Gabriel. They are all doubtless bristling with ideas. But I will tell you this. *That man* deserves to be strung up by his thumbs."

"I will keep it in mind," Gabriel said, and he grinned at them—Jessica's mother and her sister-in-law—before he left the room and went downstairs.

Good God! Every man who either was a Westcott or had some familial connection to them must be in the study. Plus Bertie. In addition to those who had been at the breakfast meeting, there were Colin, Lord Hodges; Molenor's sons, Boris and Peter Wayne; Dorchester's son, Bertrand Lamarr; and Dirkson's son, Adrian Sawyer. All of them grim faced.

"They are packed and ready to leave," Gabriel told them after nodding his greeting to the group.

"My men on the morning shift are keeping a close eye," Netherby said. "No actual movement yet."

"He has been thoroughly humiliated," Hodges said. "And masterful choreography there, may I add, Lyndale. But he has probably concluded that it is unlikely he is facing imminent arrest. He is not likely to be convicted upon a thirteen-year-old rape charge, after all. As Elizabeth pointed out to me last night, it rarely happens. Enough doubt will be cast by any defense lawyer worth his salt to suggest that the encounter was consensual or that the woman lied about the identity of her assailant. As to murder, well, all the evidence is purely circumstantial. Unfortunately. There were no witnesses."

"Proving Lyndale innocent is the easy part," Dorchester said in full agreement. "Proving Rochford guilty is virtually impossible. Even his false claim to have seen Lyndale commit the murder can be explained by the fact that he was observing from a distance and was simply mistaken. His urging of Lyndale to flee can be explained by familial fondness."

"We know what cannot be done, Marcel," Lord Molenor said. "But what *can* be?"

"He cannot be allowed to go completely free," Dirkson said. "Even though he would probably die of disappointment and live in abject misery until then. The whole business cries out for *some* sort of justice."

"I plan to beat the stuffing out of him," Gabriel said. "For what he was about to do to Mary Beck. For what he has already done to a number of the faithful servants at Brierley. For what he did to Penelope Clark. For what he did to Orson Ginsberg."

"And for what he did to you," Bertrand Lamarr added.

"And for what he did to me."

"How?" Riverdale asked. "You have an idea, Lyndale?"

"Yes," Gabriel said. "I would have written a note before leaving the hotel, but I wanted to get out of there before Jessica recovered sufficiently to . . . complicate matters. Perhaps I may write it here, Netherby. I will invite him to meet me in Hyde Park today, this afternoon, to discuss how we will proceed from here. I will inform him that I and my wife's relatives are seriously considering having him arrested for rape and murder and attempted murder—of me. I will invite him to come and tell me why we ought not to do that. I will imply that I am willing to let him go unmolested if he can come to some sort of agreement with me— to keep out of my sight for the rest of his life, perhaps."

There was a brief silence.

"Weak," Hodges said. "He will know perfectly well that no solid case can be made against him."

"But there may be enough doubt there," Riverdale said, "to make him nervous."

"I will emphasize," Gabriel said, "that there are to be no weapons, that it is not a duel to which I am challenging him."

"If he believes that," Boris Wayne said, "he has feathers for brains."

"There will *be* no weapons," Gabriel said, "except my fists."

"He would still be an idiot," Peter Wayne said, looking him up and down. "If I were in his shoes, I would bring some weapon. Probably a gun."

"So would I," his father agreed. "He has every motive to get rid of you, Lyndale, if he possibly can."

"I will not be going alone, though," Gabriel said. "If one or more of you can be persuaded to go with me, that is. There would be too many witnesses. He would not dare risk being taken up for a hanging offense."

"But what if he does?" Boris Wayne asked.

"I believe," the Marquess of Dorchester said, "there must be more of us with you than will be apparent to the eye."

"Slinking in the bushes?" Hodges asked. "Armed to the teeth, Marcel?"

"There is to be no shooting," Gabriel said. "There are to be no deaths. No violence except what I plan to mete out with my fists—and what he may choose to return with his."

"That is the ideal," Riverdale said. "Sometimes, however, reality is different. Shall we agree that there will be no unprovoked shooting?"

"I suppose that is the best we can aim for," Gabriel said. He *knew* it was essentially a weak plan. So much could go wrong. But something must be done. Of that he was determined.

There was a brief silence, during which no one came up with any more brilliant ideas.

"Write the note," Netherby said, getting up from his chair behind the desk. "I shall give myself the pleasure of delivering it in person."

"Heaven help the man," Boris Wayne said, laughing.

"Where shall I suggest we meet?" Gabriel asked as he walked behind the desk. "Hyde Park is rather large."

"There is a handy clearing among the trees on the eastern side of the park," Riverdale said. "Netherby fought a duel there some years ago. That did not involve pistols either. Or swords. Only Netherby's lethal feet. *Bare* feet, I might add."

"Mine, alas," Gabriel said, "are capable only of conveying me from place to place. I believe my fists are handy enough, however. Give me specific directions. Manley Rochford will be as unfamiliar with the park as I am."

"Will he come?" Adrian Sawyer asked.

"Of course he will," Lord Molenor said. "Netherby will be delivering the note, will he not?"

And so it was that a few hours after leaving his hotel, Gabriel was standing in a largish clearing of level grass in an area otherwise of rather dense trees on the eastern side of Hyde Park, awaiting the arrival of Manley Rochford. Bertie was with him, as was Riverdale. Most of the other men who had gathered in Netherby's study had been persuaded to stay away, though it had gone much against the grain with all of them. Dorchester, his son, Dirkson, and Netherby were somewhere out of sight. Well out of sight. Gabriel had not caught a glimpse of any one of them.

"Will he come?" Bertie asked when it was five minutes past the appointed time.

"It will be a bit of an anticlimax if he does not," Gabriel said, strolling away from his two companions to the other side of the clearing. "But if he does not come to me, then I will go to him." He peered through the trees to see if anyone was approaching from that direction.

And it was just at that moment that a shot rang out from somewhere behind him, quickly succeeded by another.

# Twenty-two

D own, Lyndale. *Down*, Vickers!" the Earl of Riverdale
yelled. "Devil take it!"

It was advice he did not immediately apply to himself.
He came hurtling across the distance between himself and
Gabriel and brought him down with a flying leap.

If he had been shot, Gabriel thought, both the warning
and the tackle would have come too late. But he did not
believe he was dead. Pain registered all over his body, and
for a few moments, while the breath was still knocked out
of him and most of the sense out of his head, he tested the
pain to discover if any of it was attributable to a bullet
wound. And, if so, if it was fatal. He did not *believe* he was
at death's door. But he was bound to be in shock, and shock,
he had heard, could delay one's reactions for a considerable
time. His ears were certainly ringing. He could hear voices
even so—neither Riverdale's nor Bertie's. Nor his own,
though he did consider the possibility that one of the voices
at least was his.

Someone was wailing in a demented sort of way. Not him.

Someone else was warning that although he was down, he ought to be careful. Neither *he* was identified.

A third voice was saying with perfect clarity, "You do not have to hold me. I have no intention of running away."

And then, unmistakably Netherby's voice—*not* his usual bored voice, but one of far greater authority. "He is dead."

The wailing voice acquired words. "You killed him. You *murdered* him. *Papaaaa!*"

Riverdale eased off Gabriel and cautiously raised his head. Gabriel pushed himself to his feet and absently brushed himself down. One detached part of his mind observed that his right boot had suffered what might be irreparable damage in the form of long scuff marks. Horbath would not be pleased.

"*Who* is dead?" Bertie was demanding of Netherby, who had just stridden into the clearing, not looking anything like his usual indolent self. Bertie was also brushing at his clothes.

"Manley Rochford," Netherby said, his words clipped, a hardness in his face Gabriel had not seen there before. "He was about to shoot Lyndale in the back. Had you no more sense, Thorne, than to move away from the other two? Had *you* no more sense, Riverdale, than to let him? Or *you*, Vickers?"

"Who killed him?" Gabriel asked, wondering if the buzzing in his ears was entirely attributable to the gunshots. "You?"

"I had no clear line of fire," Netherby said. "It looked as though he was approaching with his son in all good faith. Dorchester saw otherwise and got off a shot. Though his was not the first, and if I am not much mistaken, it merely grazed Rochford's gun hand and forced him to drop the pistol. We did agree there were to be no deaths if they could be avoided."

"Who, then?" Bertie demanded as they all strode off into the trees. "Egad, but that man has a loud voice."

*That man*, Gabriel could see, was Anthony Rochford, bent over the body of his father, and clearly distraught.

"It is time we discovered the answer to that question," Netherby said, and Gabriel looked toward three men standing on the far side of the body, two of whom—Dirkson and Bertrand Lamarr—had a firm hold upon the arms of the third man, who stood tall and proud between them, a pistol at his feet.

"Mr. Ginsberg," Gabriel said.

"I am not going anywhere," the man said, shaking off the hold of the other two men. "I will take my trial. And I will die like a man. I will die satisfied, knowing that I have been preceded from this life by the scoundrel who debauched my daughter and murdered my son." His voice was firm and distinct even though Anthony Rochford was still wailing and sobbing.

"He murdered my father," he said. "He killed my father."

"He felled a man who was about to murder the Earl of Lyndale," Netherby said in that same cold, authoritative voice. "And there were four witnesses. This was not murder, Mr. Ginsberg. This was a shot fired to save the life of an innocent, unarmed man."

"But for you, Mr. Ginsberg," Dorchester said, "Lyndale might be dead now, killed in the same way as your son was killed."

"You will not hang, Mr. Ginsberg," Riverdale said. "You will not even stand trial. After the inevitable inquiry, which will very probably not take long at all, you will be able to go home to your daughter and live in some sort of peace at last."

"Was that your man who was watching Rochford's house last night?" Netherby asked him.

"Not my man," Ginsberg replied. "Me. I spotted your man in time to duck into a better hiding place. I followed Rochford here today."

Gabriel went down on one knee on the grass beside the body of his second cousin. He spread a hand across the back of Anthony Rochford. "You will need to be brave for your mother's sake," he said. "She is going to need you, Anthony."

The wailing stopped. The sobbing did not. Gabriel patted his back, closed his eyes, and swallowed against a lump in his throat. There was Jessica's family. And then there was his own. But it included other cousins—female ones. First cousins, daughters of Uncle Julius. And his family included Marjorie Rochford. And Anthony himself. Perhaps . . .

But these were strange thoughts to be having while he was kneeling over the body of the man who would have murdered him in cold blood.

He continued to pat Anthony's back while he sobbed and hiccuped.

"I d-did not kn-know," he managed to say, "that he h-had b-brought a g-g-gun with him."


They had duly visited the Tower of London and spent all of half an hour there. They spent more time at Westminster

Abbey, partly because they sat down for a while to rest.
They conversed without stopping, commenting with great
enthusiasm upon all they saw. Mary declared more than
once that her breath was quite taken away, and Great-aunt
Edith observed that it was really quite delightful to see such
national treasures through fresh eyes that had not grown a
bit jaded from seeing them so much. Grandmama injected
a note of reality by reminding them of some of the grim
history behind those breathtaking places, especially the
Tower. Jessica agreed wholeheartedly with everything that
was said. She was having a *wonderful* time, she assured
everyone whenever she was silent too long and her grandmother looked at her with a frown.

Oh yes, everyone agreed, they were *all* having a wonderful time.

*There was to be no duel.*

*No guns.*

*No deaths.*

No one even whispered any of those things, of course.
They were too busy having a wonderful time.

And then they arrived at the tearoom, which was to be
the climax of their day out, with its fine china tea service,
its delicate crustless sandwiches, its scones and strawberry
preserves and clotted cream, and its dainty pastries and
cakes of all kinds.

"What a wonderful banquet!" Mary exclaimed. "Oh, I
*am* being spoiled."

Yes, wonderful, they all agreed. And Grandmama nodded graciously to the other occupants of the rooms, mostly
ladies.

It had perhaps not been the best choice of tearoom, Jessica decided within minutes of arriving. For of course most
of the members of the *ton* now present in London had at-

tended that costume ball last evening. And any who had not
would have read about it in the morning papers. Any few
who had missed both would have been exposed to gossip
all day. Their story must be at the very top of everyone's
list.

Everyone wanted to smile and nod at Jessica. A few
bolder souls approached their table with the same basic
message—"I will not interrupt your tea, Lady Lyndale, but
*do* allow me to congratulate you and tell you how delightful
it is that the earl, your husband, has returned as though
from the dead. I knew from the first time I saw him as Mr.
Thorne, the American gentleman, that there was something
very special, even *aristocratic*, about him."

Everyone's smiles and nods had to be acknowledged.
Everyone who approached had to be thanked. Never had
Jessica been more thankful for her *Lady Jessica Archer*
persona, though she had not even known until very recently
that such a thing existed. Perhaps she had realized it only
at Richmond Park when Gabriel had wanted to marry *that
person* and she had been upset that he had had *no idea* who
the real Jessica Archer was.

*There was to be no duel.*

*No guns.*

*No deaths.*

The mantra had run through her head without ceasing
since before she left the hotel. Her head believed it. Her
stomach knew it all to be a blatant lie.

Each of them took one tiny sandwich while Great-aunt
Edith poured the tea. Each of them looked at her tiny sandwich, and each of them dutifully bit into it.

Each of them, perhaps, was hearing that same mantra
repeat itself to the point of utter weariness.

The famed tearoom sandwich felt and tasted like cardboard in Jessica's mouth. She chewed and swallowed, half expecting to choke. She did not.

"Ah," Mary said at last, interrupting some historical feature of Westminster Abbey that Grandmama was recounting for their edification. Her face lit up with a smile. "Gabriel!"

Jessica turned her head sharply and then leapt to her feet, tipping her delicate chair to the floor as she did so. He was striding across the tearoom, narrowly missing a few tables that stood in his way. His eyes, burning hot in a pale face, were focused upon her. And he caught her up in a tight hug—or she caught *him* up. It was impossible to say which of them was the more guilty of causing such a scandalous public spectacle. For the moment she did not care—or, indeed, even think of such a triviality as propriety.

"I am all right," he murmured against her ear. "I wanted you to know that as soon as possible. I have only just been able to get away. I am safe. You can stop worrying."

She lifted her face to his. He was deathly pale. And he kissed her, very briefly, on the lips.

She was jolted back to reality by the burst of applause and laughter all around them.

"Oh," she said.

Gabriel had a little more presence of mind. He released her, looked about the room, and removed his hat. "I do beg your pardon," he said, including the whole clientele with a sweeping glance.

IIio words were met with more laughter. Someone— surely one of the few men present—whistled through his teeth.

"Gabriel," Grandmama said as he leaned down to pick up Jessica's chair—it was undamaged, she was happy to see. "Do join us."

And someone rushed up with another chair and some-one else appeared with another place setting, and within a minute at the longest he was seated at their table. The general hubbub died down, though Jessica did not doubt they were the focus of avid scrutiny from all sides and would be the subject of numerous conversations for at least the rest of the day.

"We have had a wonderful time, Gabriel," Mary said. "And now it has become more wonderful, especially for dear Jessica. You have had a good day too?" She was smiling her sweet, placid smile, giving everyone, both at their table and at all the rest, time to settle down to a semblance of normalcy.

He spoke very quietly, for their ears only, as Great-aunt Edith poured him a cup of tea. "There has been a spot of bother," he said, smiling. "Nothing for any of you to worry about. I am delighted you have had a good day. The weather has certainly been your friend."

His smile succeeded only in making him look paler.

"A spot of bother?" Grandmama asked.

"Yes," he said. "It delayed me for a while, ma'am. But it is being very competently dealt with by Netherby and Dorchester and Riverdale. As soon as I judged my presence to be no longer essential—at least for the present—I came to set your minds at rest. I hoped I would find you still here."

"With *what* are they dealing competently, Gabriel?" Jessica asked. She was chewing the second half of her sandwich. It tasted only marginally better than the first.

"Manley Rochford is dead," he said, and his hand closed tightly about hers on the table.

She lifted her chin. She was *not* going to faint again.

"Oh, Gabriel," Mary said. "How?"

"I arranged a rendezvous with him in Hyde Park," he told them. "I intended to . . . punish him before allowing him to leave London and return home. There is no proof, you see, that he murdered anyone. And the other charge would merely drag the name of an innocent woman through the mud and would probably not result in a conviction. So I knew there was really no legal recourse for achieving justice. I decided instead to confront him myself. But not in a duel. I sent him a message simply asking him to meet me in Hyde Park. I had people with me and others keeping an eye upon any route he might take to join me. I did not expect any real trouble, but unfortunately I underestimated him. He brought a gun with him and would have shot me in the back with it had not Mr. Ginsberg shot him first—and killed him. Ginsberg is the man whose daughter was ravished and whose son was murdered. I do beg your pardon. But I saw no way of *not* letting you know."

Jessica clutched his hand. And they were all silent for a long minute.

"I will say only this," Grandmama finally said, keeping her voice as low as his had been. "I am *not* sorry he is dead. He deserved to die. And I am not sorry he was killed by Mr. Ginsberg. It is fitting that he was the one to mete out justice since no court of law would be able to do it. Now." She raised her voice somewhat. "A scone, Miss Beck? With strawberries and cream? I can assure you they are always delicious here."

And, amazingly, they continued with tea just as though this were any other afternoon of social leisure.

A week later Viscount Dirkson and his wife stood just inside the open doors of their drawing room, greeting the select group of guests who had been invited to their soiree. Aunt Matilda looked so very much younger and lovelier than she had two years ago, before she met the love of her youthful years again and then married him, Jessica thought as they hugged. Aunt Matilda glowed with happiness even after the two years of marriage.

Gabriel was nervous, Jessica knew. For he had agreed to play the pianoforte for the "impromptu" concert that would begin later in the evening. He had agreed to play the Bach piece he had performed at Elizabeth and Colin's party and one or two other pieces.

"The thing is," he had explained to her, "that whenever I have played for other people in the past, it really has been an impromptu thing. I have never had to stare the ordeal in the face for days ahead of time and wonder if I was going to make an utter ass of myself."

"You will not," she had said. "Allow yourself to disappear into the world of your music, Gabriel."

He had given her a hard look. "You *do* understand," he had said.

"Yes, I do," she had assured him.

"And another thing," he had said, refusing to be fully reassured. "When I play the Bach piece, Jessie, it will be nothing like it was last time. When people use written music, they can more or less guarantee that what they play now will be identical or at least very similar to what they played in the past and what they will play in the future."

"Yours will be just as lovely this time as it was last, even if not identical," she had told him. "Better even. Because it will not be music that has been frozen onto a sheet of parchment but music that is living and breathing inside you."

He had laughed. Though he was no less nervous tonight than he had been since Aunt Matilda asked him during that garden party where he had kissed Jessica for the first time. How could he be nervous over something like this when he had lived through a nightmare of a week, starting with that moment in Hyde Park when he had come so close to being shot in the back and killed?

Jessica would have nightmares about that for the rest of her life.

Everything had been settled. There had been enough witnesses—and illustrious ones at that—to swear that Manley Rochford had been about to shoot an unarmed Gabriel in the back and had been stopped in the nick of time in the only way possible. His motive was perfectly clear to everyone who needed to be convinced. He had been deprived of the title he had so long coveted, and he was fearful that he would be charged with rape and murder. He had compounded the danger of that happening by attempting to kill the man who stood between him and what he had believed rightfully his until the night before. Mr. Ginsberg, though he had a definite motive for killing Manley Rochford, could not rightfully be accused of murdering him. He had shot to save the life of an innocent man, who, moreover, had had his back to his would-be killer.

No one had asked Mr. Ginsberg what his intention had been when he followed Manley to the park. He had returned home. So had Mrs. Rochford and her son, returning to their home and not Brierley. They took the body of Manley with them for burial.

Jessica and Anna had called upon Mrs. Rochford before she left. They had not been at all sure they would be received, but they were. Mrs. Rochford had been wan but gracious. She was *not* sorry, she had assured them, that she was not after all to be the Countess of Lyndale. She had never wanted the title. She had implied, though she had certainly not said it, that she was not sorry either that her husband was gone. She had family of her own, she had told them—brothers and a sister who all lived close by and would support her. *Not* financially, she had added, but in every way that mattered. And she had her son, who she claimed was good at heart and would grow stronger under the influence of his uncles. She had thanked them for calling.

Gabriel had called upon her too—and been received. But she would take nothing from him, he had reported. He owed her nothing. Quite the contrary. She and her son would manage. She would be able to live frugally now that they would be on their own—a statement that had spoken volumes about how Manley had lived. She had thanked him for his offer of help and sent him on his way.

"I am expecting Anthony to return at any moment," she had explained to him. "I would rather he not find you here, Gabriel."

Mary had also returned home. They had wanted her to stay until they were ready to go themselves, but she had explained to them that she was no longer needed here and was missing her home and her animals and her garden quite dreadfully.

Gabriel was sending Mr. Norton back to Brierley with Mary to take over as estate manager from the man Manley Rochford had put in place. Mr. Norton had much to do to start sorting out the mess of fired servants and the ones who had been brought in instead of them. All must somehow be found employment, Gabriel had instructed Mr. Norton, since it would be grossly unfair to make servants suffer for the perfidy of their employer. Mr. Norton had been confident that he could settle all to his lordship's satisfaction. A number of the servants could simply be sent back to Mrs. Rochford's home, for example. She would surely have need of at least some of them.

Mr. Norton and Mary returned in a carriage that was far more comfortable than the one they had come in. And, despite Mary's protests, Ruth had been dispatched with her. Jessica could manage perfectly well without her maid until she reached Brierley herself, she had assured Mary not quite truthfully. And it was unthinkable for Mary to travel alone, with only a man for company—though she had done it on the way to London, of course.

Jessica and Gabriel were to leave tomorrow. All their belongings were packed. Tonight was a farewell with the family, though Jessica did not doubt that at least a few of them would turn up at the hotel tomorrow morning to wave them on their way.

The thought of leaving, of being far away in a place she had never seen before, a place moreover that had a rather sad history as far as Gabriel was concerned, brought a lump to her throat. But she swallowed it away determinedly and smiled as she greeted her relatives and the other guests at the soiree.

She was, after all, Jessica Thorne, Countess of Lyndale.

Aunt Matilda would be very pleased with her soiree, she thought later in the evening. Her drawing room was crowded, though not packed to the point of discomfort, and it seemed that all her guests, family and friends alike, were in unusually high spirits. The past week had been a good one for the family despite the stress. They had come together, as they always did, to deal with a crisis that threatened one of their own, and they had prevailed. Jessica had married well, her husband had assumed his title, and the two of them were about to set off for the earl's home and estate and the beginning of a new life together.

"And as is perfectly clear to us all, Jessica and Gabriel," Aunt Matilda said to them at one point in the evening, "you have followed the Westcott family tradition and made a love match. *We* heard about the scene in the tearoom, did we not, Elizabeth? Mama told me even before Charles read it aloud to me from the morning paper the day after."

"And Colin and I heard it from a dozen people who thought we might be interested to know," Elizabeth said, looking from one to the other of them with her usual twinkling smile. "I only wish I had been there to see it for myself. What a romantic moment it must have been. It drew cheers."

Jessica felt herself blushing. Not so much over the reminder of that scene in the tearoom, but because Gabriel was at her side, hearing Aunt Matilda assume that theirs was a love match. She had no idea if it was true and she tried not to think of it. They were indeed embarking upon a new life, and it would be challenge enough, though not nearly as great a one as Gabriel had feared when he had chosen her as his bride. Her specifically. Not because he had loved her, but because he had judged that she had the connections and character and education and experience and demeanor to do an adequate job as his countess.

Those guests who were not family seemed as happy to be at the soiree as everyone else. The new Earl of Lyndale and his countess had achieved a great deal of fame since the masquerade ball, and they were obviously the main attraction this evening. None of which did anything to allay Gabriel's fraught nerves, Jessica suspected.

One of the guests, a thin, pale young lady who was there with her mother, opened the impromptu concert with three songs to her mother's accompaniment on the harp. She had a sweet, untrained soprano voice, which did not at all seem to go with her unremarkable appearance. She was someone else, Jessica thought, who held great beauty inside herself until it was time to release it as music.

"She sings like an angel," Grandmama said loudly enough to be heard by almost everyone after the applause had died down.

Yes, she did.

She was followed by the very young son of Viscount Dirkson's elder daughter. He played some sort of jig on his violin and got everyone's toes tapping, even though he paused a few times, breaking the rhythm, while his little fingers felt around for the note he needed in order to proceed. He favored the audience with a gap-toothed grin when they applauded, and when someone suggested an encore, he played it all over again, pauses and all, before setting his instrument down with a clatter and dashing for his grandpapa, who scooped him up and let him hide his face against his broad shoulder.

Viscount Dirkson was also Katy and Seth's grandpapa, Jessica thought suddenly—Abby and Gil's children, that was. And she felt a sudden melancholy at the thought that her cousin and best friend was so far away and soon would be farther. When would they see each other again? But that was the nature of life when one grew up, and she could not

honestly say she wished she was going to stay here, close to
her family. Not when that would mean letting Gabriel leave
without her.

But this was no time to let her thoughts wander. Viscount
Dirkson, still holding his grandson, was telling everyone
that Gabriel had kindly agreed to play for them—beginning
with Bach's "Jesus bleibet meine Freude," roughly trans-
lated to mean *Jesus shall remain my joy*, with which he had
enthralled the Westcott family some weeks ago.

There were some smatterings of applause and a buzz of
interest as Gabriel took his seat on the bench, arranged the
tails of his evening coat behind him, and looked down at
the keyboard as he flexed his fingers in his lap. He was still
horribly nervous, Jessica thought, resisting the urge to rub
her sweating palms over her skirt. She was sitting quite
close to him. The movement might distract him. Her heart
was pounding in her ears. He looked really quite, quite
gorgeous—a totally irrelevant thought to be having at the
moment. His hair needed cutting. It was curling all over his
head. She was glad he had not yet had it cut.

*Oh please. Please, please start.*

And he did. And he had been right. The music he produced was nothing like it had been the last time. And everything like it. For it was not a performance of something
that had been written down and memorized. Yet it was Bach,
surely as Bach was meant to be played. And it was music that
seemed to come from a deep well of beauty and creativity
and *rightness*. As he had done at Elizabeth and Colin's, he
closed his eyes soon after he started playing and tipped
back his head slightly, a frown of concentration between his
brows—until toward the end he bowed his head over the
keys, his eyes still closed.

Jessica found herself swallowing repeatedly so that she

would not disgrace herself either by sobbing aloud or by allowing tears to spill from her eyes down her cheeks.

When he was finished, he lifted his hands from the keyboard and made no other movement for a while. Neither did anyone else. Until Avery of all people got to his feet to applaud and everyone else followed. Except, for a few moments, Jessica.

*Oh dear God, she loved him.*

Not for his looks. Not for his sense of duty and honor. Not for the music that was in him. Not because he was still bringing her a rose each day. Not because he had hurried to that tearoom, knowing she would be beside herself with worry. Not even because his frequent lovemaking made her deliriously happy. Not because of *anything*.

She just loved him.

He was back in his surroundings, she could see, and looked acutely embarrassed as he acknowledged the applause with a smile and a curt nod of the head. His eyes met Jessica's and there was something in his, something far back within them, that caught at her breathing and surely stopped her heart for a moment before it resumed its beating, audible to her ears again.

He next played a short piece by Mozart and something else Jessica could not identify. Then he got to his feet and moved away from the pianoforte even though someone at the back of the room—the same person as last time?—begged for an encore.

And the party continued.

Aunt Matilda hugged Gabriel tightly, seemingly unconcerned about the tears that trickled down her cheeks. "Thank you, Gabriel," she said. "Thank you for playing just because I asked you to. If you want, I will adopt you. Charles will not mind."

And they both laughed as they hugged, and Jessica lost the battle with two tears.

It was only the start of an emotional hour, of course.

It was never easy to say goodbye.

Even though, as Uncle Thomas pointed out with cheerful gruffness, *goodbye* very rarely meant forever.

# Twenty-three

❧

The goodbyes had been said—inevitably a small crowd had gathered outside the hotel to see them on their way—and Gabriel's carriage had left London and taken the road north.

They had not spoken since leaving the hotel behind. Gabriel had left Jessica to her thoughts, going only so far as to take her hand in his and hold it on his thigh. Her shoulder was leaning against his. It had been an emotional leave-taking, of course. Even he had been a bit choked over the hugs and backslappings and good wishes of people he had never even heard of a mere few weeks ago. And of those from Sir Trevor and Lady Vickers. It was understandable that Jessica needed a little time to compose herself. It must be some consolation to her, though, that her mother and brother and sister-in-law had promised to pay them a visit sometime during the summer.

He looked into her face at last. "I am sorry," he said.

"Sorry?" She gazed back at him.

"For taking you away," he said. "Life is sometimes cruel to women."

"But you were taken away from your life in Boston," she said. "It was a choice you made, Gabriel. Just as it was my choice to marry you."

"I do not know quite what we are facing at Brierley," he told her. "It is a long time since I was there. And I was never happy there, you know."

"I do know," she said. "Are you fearing that your memories and perhaps the collective memories of your neighbors will wear us down and make it impossible for us to be happy there?"

He had been fearing just that, but hearing it put into words made him sound very weak. He just could not think of Brierley with any sort of joyful anticipation, though.

"I want so much to make you happy," he told her.

"Then do it."

"Very well." He smiled and glanced at the pink rosebud that lay on the seat opposite. "I may not be able to find you a rose tomorrow."

"Then pluck a daisy for me," she said. "It is not the roses that make me happy, Gabriel. It is the fact that you give them to me. That you care a little bit."

He turned his head to look out the window.

"Gabriel," she said. "We will make our own memories at Brierley. From the moment we arrive there. It is our home. The space is ours. The servants and neighbors and potential friends are ours. The future is ours. The past is gone. The future is bright if we want it to be. And the present is lovely. We are together."

"Is it lovely?" he asked, looking at her. "I have just taken you away from your family."

"You *are* my family," she said.

And, ridiculously, he felt the heat of tears prick at his eyes. It seemed to him that he had spent most of his life without family. Since he was nine years old. And only briefly had he found it with Cyrus. He had spent most of his life lonely, though he had rarely called it that.

He was not normally a self-pitying man.

Now he had a family. Jessica. The Westcotts. Sir Trevor and his wife—and Bertie. Mary.

"My uncle had daughters," he said. "They are my first cousins. They all married years ago. They probably have grown children."

"I will write to them during my first week at home," she said.

*At home.* She meant Brierley.

"I will invite them to come and visit us," she said.

"Philip had a wife," he said, "and two daughters. Mary mentioned in a letter some years ago that they had returned to her family and that she had remarried."

"I will write to her," she said. "We are almost never quite alone, you see. Not unless we choose to be."

"You will be a good countess," he told her. "It is why I married you."

"I will not disappoint you." Her tone sounded a little brisk even though she smiled.

"But I persuaded you to marry me under false pretenses," he said.

"Oh?" Her eyebrows were up. She looked haughty. It was an expression of self-defense, he realized.

"I think," he said, "I fell in love with you at Richmond Park when you scolded me for seeing nothing when I looked at you but *Lady Jessica Archer.* When you demanded that if I wanted a chance with you, I must *romance* you. I am still not sure that word is a verb. I had no idea how to go about doing it. I still do not. I am a dull fellow, Jessie. But I fell in love and have not fallen out since. Indeed, I have fallen so far in that I am quite certain I am a hopeless case."

She snatched her hand away, turned sharply on the seat so that her knee was pressing against the side of his leg, and crossed her hands over her bosom.

"Gabriel!" she exclaimed. "You *idiot!*"

"Yes, I know," he said, grimacing ruefully. "But it need not matter. We will still do a good job as earl and countess. We will still make a happy home, for ourselves and, if we are so blessed, for our children. We will—"

"Gabriel!" she said. "You are a double idiot."

He stopped talking. He looked warily at her. Had he gone and ruined everything? He had hoped she might be cautiously pleased.

She pointed a finger at his chest and waggled it as she talked.

"If you do not tell me and show me every single day for the rest of our lives that you love me," she said, "I will leave you and go home to my mother. Or else I will go about performing my duties with a permanent pout. And if I do not tell you and show you the same thing every day, then, then— Oh, stop!"

Because he was laughing, at first quietly and then helplessly.

"Stop it!" she said when he set one arm about her shoulders and the other under her knees and lifted her across him to set her on his lap. "Stop it this minute, Gabriel."

But she was laughing too, and they were still laughing when he kissed her.

"Stop it," she said against his mouth.

He kissed her more deeply, and laughter subsided as she

wriggled one arm from beneath his and wrapped the other about his neck.

"No, never, Jessie," he told her when he came up for air. "Never, ever. I plan to keep on kissing you for the rest of our lives."

"Well, there go all our other plans," she said. "There is to be only kissing all day, every day, for the rest of our lives?"

"Don't forget the nights," he said.

"You are absurd," she told him.

"I know," he said. "I love you. Kiss me."

She laughed. "You are still absurd, Gabriel. I love you too. I do. I really do."

And she kissed him.

Laughter and absurdity were both forgotten long before they stopped.

Only love remained.

# One

Despite the fact that the late Earl of Riverdale had died without having made a will, Josiah Brumford, his solicitor, had found enough business to discuss with his son and successor to be granted a face-to-face meeting at Westcott House, the earl's London residence on South Audley Street. Having arrived promptly and bowed his way through effusive and obsequious greetings, Brumford proceeded to find a great deal of nothing in particular to impart at tedious length and with pompous verbosity.

Which would have been all very well, Avery Archer, Duke of Netherby, thought a trifle peevishly as he stood before the library window and took snuff in an effort to ward off the urge to yawn, if he had not been compelled to be here too to endure the tedium. If Harry had only been a year older—he had turned twenty just before his father's death—then Avery need not be here at all and Brumford could prose on forever and a day as far as he was concerned.

By some bizarre and thoroughly irritating twist of fate, however, His Grace had found himself joint guardian of the new earl with the countess, the boy's mother.

It was all remarkably ridiculous in light of Avery's notoriety for indolence and the studied avoidance of anything that might be dubbed work or the performance of duty. He had a secretary and numerous other servants to deal with all the tedious business of life for him. And there was also the fact that he was a mere eleven years older than his ward. When one heard the word *guardian*, one conjured a mental image of a gravely dignified graybeard. However, it seemed he had inherited the guardianship to which his father had apparently agreed—in writing—at some time in the dim distant past when the late Riverdale had mistakenly thought himself to be at death's door. By the time he did die a few weeks ago, the old Duke of Netherby had been sleeping peacefully in his own grave for more than two years and was thus unable to be guardian to anyone. Avery might, he supposed, have repudiated the obligation since he was not the Netherby mentioned in that letter of agreement, which had never been made into a legal document anyway. He had not done so, however. He did not dislike Harry, and really it had seemed like too much bother to take a stand and refuse such a slight and temporary inconvenience.

It felt more than slight at the moment. Had he known Brumford was such a crashing bore, he might have made the effort.

"There really was no need for Father to make a will," Harry was saying in the sort of rallying tone one used when repeating oneself in order to wrap up a lengthy discussion that had been moving in unending circles. "I have no brothers. My father trusted that I would provide handsomely for my mother and sisters according to his known wishes, and of course I will not fail that trust. I will certainly see to it too that most of the servants and retainers on all my properties are kept on and that those who leave my employ for whatever reason—Father's valet, for example—are properly compensated. And you may rest assured that my mother and Netherby will see that I do not stray from these obligations before I arrive at my majority."

He was standing by the fireplace beside his mother's chair, in a relaxed posture, one shoulder propped against the mantel, his arms crossed over his chest, one booted foot on the hearth. He was a tall lad and a bit gangly, though a few more years would take care of that deficiency. He was fair-haired and blue-eyed, with a good-humored countenance that very young ladies no doubt found impossibly handsome. He was also almost indecently rich. He was amiable and charming and had been running wild during the past several months, first while his father was too ill to take much notice and again during the couple of weeks since the funeral. He had probably never lacked for friends, but now they abounded and would have filled a sizable city, perhaps even a small county, to overflowing. Though perhaps *friends* was too kind a word to use for most of them. *Sycophants* and *hangers-on* would be better.

Avery had not tried intervening, and he doubted he would. The boy seemed of sound enough character and would doubtless settle to a bland and blameless adulthood if left to his own devices. And if in the meanwhile he sowed a wide swath of wild oats and squandered a small fortune, well, there were probably oats to spare in the world and there would still be a vast fortune remaining for the bland adulthood. It would take just too much effort to intervene, anyway, and the Duke of Netherby rarely made the effort to do what was inessential or what was not conducive to his personal comfort.

"I do not doubt it for a moment, my lord." Brumford bowed from his chair in a manner that suggested he might at last be conceding that everything he had come to say had been said and perhaps it was time to take his leave. "I trust Brumford, Brumford & Sons may continue to represent your interests as we did your dear departed father's and his father's before him. I trust His Grace and Her Ladyship will so advise you."

Avery wondered idly what the other Brumford was like and just how many young Brumfords were included in the "& Sons." The mind boggled.

Harry pushed himself away from the mantel, looking hopeful. "I see no reason why I would not," he said. "But I will not keep you any longer. You are a very busy man, I daresay."

"I will, however, beg for a few minutes more of your time, Mr. Brumford," the countess said unexpectedly. "But it is a matter that does not concern you, Harry. You may go and join your sisters in the drawing room. They will be eager to hear details of this meeting. Perhaps you would be good enough to remain, Avery."

Harry directed a quick grin Avery's way, and His Grace, opening his snuffbox again before changing his mind and snapping it shut, almost wished that he too were being sent off to report to the countess's two daughters. He must be very bored indeed. Lady Camille Westcott, age twenty-two, was the managing sort, a forthright female who did not suffer fools gladly, though she was handsome enough, it was true. Lady Abigail, at eighteen, was a sweet, smiling,

pretty young thing who might or might not possess a per-
sonality. To do her justice, Avery had not spent enough time
in her company to find out. She was his half sister's favorite
cousin and dearest friend in the world, however—her
words—and he occasionally heard them talking and giggling together behind closed doors that he was very careful
never to open.

Harry, all eager to be gone, bowed to his mother, nodded
politely to Brumford, came very close to winking at Avery,
and made his escape from the library. Lucky devil. Avery
strolled closer to the fireplace, where the countess and
Brumford were still seated. What the deuce could be important enough that she had voluntarily prolonged this excruciatingly dreary meeting?

"And how may I be of service to you, my lady?" the
solicitor asked.

The countess, Avery noticed, was sitting very upright,
her spine arched slightly inward. Were ladies taught to sit
that way, as though the backs of chairs had been created
merely to be decorative? She was, he estimated, about forty
years old. She was also quite perfectly beautiful in a ma-
ture, dignified sort of way. She surely could not have been
happy with Riverdale—who could?—yet to Avery's knowledge she had never indulged herself with lovers. She was
tall, shapely, and blond with no sign yet, as far as he could
see, of any gray hairs. She was also one of those rare women
who looked striking rather than dowdy in deep mourning.

"There is a girl," she said, "or, rather, a woman. In Bath,
I believe. My late husband's . . . daughter."

Avery guessed she had been about to say *bastard*, but
had changed her mind for the sake of gentility. He raised
both his eyebrows and his quizzing glass.

Brumford for once had been silenced.

"She was at an orphanage there," the countess continued. "I do not know where she is now. She is hardly still
there since she must be in her middle twenties. But Riverdale supported her from a very young age and continued to
do so until his death. We never discussed the matter. It is
altogether probable he did not know I was aware of her
existence. I do not know any details, nor have I ever wanted
to. I still do not. I assume it was not through you that the
support payments were made?"

Brumford's already florid complexion took on a dis-
tinctly purplish hue. "It was not, my lady," he assured her.
"But might I suggest that since this . . . person is now an
adult, you—"

"No," she said, cutting him off. "I am not in need of any
suggestion. I have no wish whatsoever to know anything
about this woman, even her name. I certainly have no wish
for my son to know of her. However, it seems only just that
if she has been supported all her life by her . . . father, she
be informed of his death if that has not already happened,
and be compensated with a final settlement. A handsome
one, Mr. Brumford. It would need to be made perfectly
clear to her at the same time that there is to be no more—
ever, under any circumstances. May I leave the matter in
your hands?"

"My lady." Brumford seemed almost to be squirming in
his chair. He licked his lips and darted a glance at Avery,
of whom—if His Grace was reading him correctly—he
stood in considerable awe.

Avery raised his glass all the way to his eye. "Well?" he
said. "*May* her ladyship leave the matter in your hands,
Brumford? Are you or the other Brumford or one of the
sons willing and able to hunt down the bastard daughter,

name unknown, of the late earl in order to make her the happiest of orphans by settling a modest fortune upon her?"

"Your Grace." Brumford's chest puffed out. "My lady. It will be a difficult task, but not an insurmountable one, especially for the skilled investigators whose services we engage in the interests of our most valued clients. If the . . . person indeed grew up in Bath, we will identify her. If she is still there, we will find her. If she is no longer there—"

"I believe," Avery said, sounding pained, "her ladyship and I get your meaning. You will report to me when the woman has been found. Is that agreeable to you, Aunt?"

The Countess of Riverdale was not, strictly speaking, his aunt. His stepmother, the duchess, was the late Earl of Riverdale's sister, and thus the countess and all the others were his honorary relatives.

"That will be satisfactory," she said.

Anna Snow had been brought to the orphanage in Bath when she was not quite four years old. She had no real memory of her life before that beyond a few brief and disjointed flashes—of someone always coughing, for example, or of a lych-gate that was dark and a bit frightening inside whenever she was called upon to pass through it alone, and of kneeling on a window ledge and looking down upon a graveyard, and of crying inconsolably inside a carriage while someone with a gruff, impatient voice told her to hush and behave like a big girl.

She had been at the orphanage ever since, though she was now twenty-five. Most of the other children—there were usually about forty of them—left when they were fourteen or fifteen, after suitable employment had been found for them. But Anna had lingered on, first to help out as housemother to a dormitory of girls and a sort of secretary to Miss Ford, the matron, and then as the schoolteacher when Miss Rutledge, the teacher who had taught her, married a clergyman and moved away to Devonshire. She was even paid a modest salary. However, the expenses of her continued stay at the orphanage, now in a small room of her own, were still provided by the unknown benefactor who had paid them from the start. She had been told that they would continue to be paid as long as she remained.

Anna considered herself fortunate. She had grown up in an orphanage, it was true, with not even a full identity to call her own, since she did not know who her parents were, but in the main it was not a charity institution. Almost all her fellow orphans were supported through their growing years by someone—usually anonymous, though some knew who they were and why they were there. Usually it was because their parents had died and there was no other family member able or willing to take them in. Anna did not dwell upon the loneliness of not knowing her own story. Her material needs were taken care of. Miss Ford and her staff were generally kind. Most of the children were easy enough to get along with, and those who were not could be avoided. A few were close friends, or had been during her growing years. If there had been a lack of love in her life, or of that type of love one associated with a family, then she did not particularly miss it, having never consciously known it.

Or so she always told herself.

She was content with her life and was only occasionally restless with the feeling that surely there ought to be more, that perhaps she should be making a greater effort to *live* her life. She had been offered marriage by three different men—the shopkeeper where she went occasionally, when she could afford it, to buy a book; one of the governors of the orphanage, whose wife had recently died and left him with four young children; and Joel Cunningham, her life-long best friend. She had rejected all three offers for varying reasons and wondered sometimes if it had been foolish to do so, as there were not likely to be many more offers, if any. The prospect of a continuing life of spinsterhood sometimes seemed dreary.

Joel was with her when the letter arrived.

She was tidying the schoolroom after dismissing the children for the day. The monitors for the week—John Davies and Ellen Payne—had collected the slates and chalk and the counting frames. But while John had stacked the slates neatly on the cupboard shelf allotted for them and put all the chalk away in the tin and replaced the lid, Ellen had shoved the counting frames haphazardly on top of paintbrushes and palettes on the bottom shelf instead of arranging them in their appointed place side by side on the shelf above so as not to bend the rods or damage the beads. The reason she had put them in the wrong place was obvious. The second shelf was occupied by the water pots used to swill paint brushes and an untidy heap of paint-stained cleaning rags.

"Joel," Anna said, a note of long suffering in her voice, "could you at least try to get your pupils to put things away where they belong after an art class? And to clean the water pots first? Look! One of them even still has water in it. Very *dirty* water."

Joel was sitting on the corner of the battered teacher's desk, one booted foot braced on the floor, the other swinging free. His arms were crossed over his chest. He grinned at her.

"But the whole point of being an artist," he said, "is to be a free spirit, to cast aside restricting rules and draw inspiration from the universe. My job is to teach my pupils to be true artists."

She straightened up from the cupboard and directed a speaking glance his way. "What utter rot and nonsense," she said.

He laughed outright. "Anna, Anna," he said. "Here, let me take that pot from you before you burst with indignation or spill it down your dress."

But before he could say anything more, the classroom door was flung open without the courtesy of a knock to admit Bertha Reed, a thin, flaxen-haired fourteen-year-old who acted as Miss Ford's helper now that she was old enough. She was bursting with excitement and waving a folded paper in one raised hand.

"There is a letter for you, Miss Snow," she half shrieked. "It was delivered by special messenger from London and Miss Ford would have brought it herself but Tommy is bleeding all over her sitting room and no one can find Nurse Jones. Maddie punched him in the nose."

"It is high time someone did," Joel said, strolling closer to Anna. "I suppose he was pulling one of her braids again."

Anna scarcely heard. A letter? From London? By special messenger? For *her*?

"Whoever can it be from, Miss Snow?" Bertha screeched, apparently not particularly concerned about Tommy and his bleeding nose. "Who do you know in London? No, don't tell me—that ought to have been *whom*. *Whom* do you know in London? I wonder what they are writing about. And it came by *special messenger*, all that way. It must have cost a *fortune*. Oh, do open it."

Her blatant inquisitiveness might have seemed impertinent, but really, it was so rare for any of them to receive a letter that word always spread very quickly and everyone wanted to know all about it. Occasionally someone who had left both the orphanage and Bath to work elsewhere would write, and the recipient would almost invariably share the contents with everyone else. Such missives were kept as prized possessions and read over and over until they were virtually threadbare.

Anna did not recognize the handwriting, which was both bold and precise. It was a masculine hand, she felt sure. The paper felt thick and expensive. It did not look like a personal letter.

"Oliver is in London," Bertha said wistfully. "But I don't suppose it can be from him, can it? His writing does not look anything like that, and why would he write to you anyway? The four times he has written since he left here, it was to me. And he is not going to send any letter by special messenger, is he?"

Oliver Jamieson had been apprenticed to a bootmaker in London two years ago at the age of fourteen and had promised to send for Bertha and marry her as soon as he got on his feet. Twice each year since then he had faithfully written a five- or six-line letter in large, careful handwriting. Bertha had shared his sparse news on each occasion and wept over the letters until it was a wonder they were still legible. There were three years left in his apprenticeship before he could hope to be on his feet and able to support a wife. They were both very young, but the separation did seem cruel. Anna always found herself hoping that Oliver would remain faithful to his childhood sweetheart.

"Are you going to turn it over and over in your hands and hope it will divulge its secrets without your having to break the seal?" Joel asked.

Stupidly, Anna's hands were trembling. "Perhaps there is some mistake," she said. "Perhaps it is not for me."

He came up behind her and looked over her shoulder. "Miss Anna Snow," he said. "It certainly sounds like you. I do not know any other Anna Snows. Do you, Bertha?"

"I do not, Mr. Cunningham," she said after pausing to think. "But whatever can it be about?"

Anna slid her thumb beneath the seal and broke it. And yes, indeed, the paper was a thick, costly vellum. It was not a long letter. It was from Somebody Brumford—she could not read the first name, though it began with a J. He was a solicitor. She read through the letter once, swallowed, and then read it again more slowly.

"The day after tomorrow," she murmured.

"In a private chaise," Joel added. He had been reading over her shoulder.

"*What* is the day after tomorrow?" Bertha demanded, her voice an agony of suspense. "*What* chaise?"

Anna looked at her blankly. "I am being summoned to London to discuss my future," she said. There was a faint buzzing in her ears.

"Oh! By who?" Bertha asked, her eyes as wide as saucers. "By *whom*, I mean."

"Mr. J. Brumford, a solicitor," Anna said.

"Josiah, I think that says," Joel said. "Josiah Brumford. He is sending a private chaise to fetch you, and you are to pack a bag for at least a few days."

"To *London*?" Bertha's voice was breathless with awe.

"Whatever am I to do?" Anna's mind seemed to have stopped working. Or, rather, it *was* working, but it was whirring out of control, like the innards of a broken clock.

"What you are to do, Anna," Joel said, pushing a chair up behind her knees and setting his hands on her shoulders to press her gently down onto it, "is pack a bag for a few days and then go to London to discuss your future."

"But what future?" she asked.

"That is what is to be discussed," he pointed out.

The buzzing in her ears grew louder.

READ ON FOR AN EXCERPT FROM THE NEXT BOOK
IN MARY BALOGH'S WESTCOTT SERIES,

# Someone to Cherish

COMING IN 2021

Lydia Tavernor was seated in one corner of Hannah and Tom Corning's parlor, listening to the conversation of the people around her but not, at the moment, at least, participating in it. She was conscious of an inner welling of contentment as she looked about at the familiar faces of her fellow villagers and of a few people from somewhat farther afield. It was not exactly a party and was not a particularly large gathering, so Lydia was even more pleased, therefore, to have been included on the guest list for what Hannah had described as "an evening of cards and conversation with tea and cake." The card games were over, and the guests were enjoying cake and pastries and tea while exchanging news and opinions and even a bit of good-natured gossip.

Sometimes Lydia felt a little guilty about her contentment, even when it did not well up quite as abundantly as it did this evening, for she had been widowed only fifteen months ago and perhaps ought to be still prostrate with grief. It was what some of her neighbors might expect.

Her husband, the Reverend Isaiah Tavernor, had been the vicar here for only three years before his sudden death, but he had made a lasting impression upon the community, both by his life and by the manner of his dying. He had been a young man—only thirty-three years old when he died—and handsome, vigorous, and charismatic. His eyes had burned with zeal in the service of his Lord and in his duty to the sheep of his flock. Apparently he had been a great contrast to the quiet, elderly vicar who had preceded him, though Lydia had never known Reverend Jenkins. Many people had considered Isaiah a welcome change. Some, it had seemed to Lydia, had even come close to worshiping him, almost as though they had put him in place of the very God he preached about. He had worked indefatigably for his church and his people. He had died by drowning while rescuing young Jeremy Piper from a river swollen and flowing fast and furious after several days of torrential rain.

The general opinion in the days of bitter shock and grief that had followed the tragedy was that Jeremy was a bad, useless boy who had defied strict orders to stay away from the water and would surely come to no good for the rest of his miserable life. Meanwhile, he had caused the death of a man who was goodness through and through but had now been cut off from doing the work the Lord had appointed him to do. No one had thought to suggest that perhaps the Lord had appointed him to save the child's life, even at the sacrifice of his own.

Lydia's own shock and grief had been absolute. She had not collapsed or taken to her bed, but she had turned totally . . . blank, for days afterward, moving about as though in a dream. Or nightmare, rather. For her whole life had revolved about Isaiah's. He had always called her his helpmeet—almost never his wife—and that was exactly what she had been. His work had been her work. His beliefs and opinions had been hers. She had not known for days on end how she could continue without him.

Yet here she was now, continuing on. She was invited almost everywhere now that her official year of mourning was at an end. Most of the time, she supposed, she was invited for Isaiah's sake rather than for her own, as she could not be described as the life and soul of any gathering, and never had been. She far preferred to listen than to talk. Every conversation needed listeners, did it not? And in her experience, far too many people preferred to talk, pausing only long enough during a conversation to be polite while someone else spoke before launching back into speech.

Not that Lydia was overcritical of talkers, especially those who just needed a sympathetic ear into which to pour their concerns, their aches and pains, or their loneliness. She was particularly kind toward, and patient with, those people others habitually avoided if they could do so without being too obvious about it—the long-winded bores and those, usually the elderly, who liked to tell the same stories they had been telling to the same audience for many years past. Lydia could always be relied upon to listen attentively and to respond as though she were hearing the story for the first time.

No one was talking specifically to her at present. She was at leisure to listen to everyone and to look about and conclude that contentment was actually more desirable than active happiness. For where there was happiness, there was almost invariably unhappiness awaiting its turn. Extremes tended to be like that. They had a way of attracting their opposites, as though some cosmic balance needed to be restored. It was better and safer to settle for some position in the middle. Not that one could always choose, of course. Life was never that neat, nor its ups and downs that much within one's control. But . . . Well, tonight she felt as though her life had turned out well for her.

She had chosen to remain in this place after her husband's death because she liked the village of Fairfield and had grown fond of the people who lived here. She could have gone back home to her father's house. He and her brothers had certainly assumed that she would. When Papa and James, her eldest brother, had come for Isaiah's funeral and then accompanied her to his brother's home for his burial in the family plot, they had expected to take her directly home with them afterward. It was their very assertiveness, perhaps, that had pulled her out of her dreadful lethargy. It would have been so easy to allow them to take charge—of her situation, of her life, of *her*. They had been astonished—not to mention alarmed—when she had announced her intention of returning to the village and staying there.

"Alone?" Papa had said. "Lydie! It is out of the question. You are not thinking straight—as how could you be? I cannot think of anything worse that could have happened to my dearest girl. Go get the bag you brought with you and come immediately, while you have James and me to give you our company and support and to protect you on the journey. The rest of your things can be sent for. James will see to everything. You must not addle your mind over it. You know this is what Isaiah would want."

Oh yes, she had known that. And perhaps for the first time it had really struck her that Isaiah was no longer with her and never would be again. She had dug in her heels and insisted upon coming home. Home being *here*.

She could have stayed where she was, with Isaiah's brother, Bruce Tavernor, Earl of Tilden, and his wife. They had been civil enough after the burial to offer her a home with them, even to urge her to stay, since she was their last surviving link to Isaiah. She had not been ungrateful.

"Though you will no doubt be going home with your father, Lydia," her brother-in-law had said. "If, however, you would prefer to remain here to live with Ellen and me, even if just for a while, you would be very welcome. For Isaiah's sake. It is what he would expect of us, and not without reason. We must all be proud of him, you know, even though it is difficult to feel anything but raw grief at present. He died a hero."

His own grief had been profound, and Lydia had hugged him tightly and clung while Ellen wept into her handkerchief.

Both Lydia's father and Bruce lived in mansions set in large private parks and run by a host of servants, both indoor and out. Both had offered her a life of ease and security, a balm to the great bruise that was her life. She had chosen instead to come back to Fairfield, though she had moved out of the vicarage a week after her return, of course, to make room for the Reverend Bailey, the new vicar, and his wife, who had both been unfailingly kind to her ever since. She had been fortunate enough to have been left enough money to purchase a small cottage on the edge of the village, and have enough remaining with which to live modestly for the rest of her life.

Her father had declared himself lost for words, though he had somehow found plenty anyway in the letter that had arrived after she announced the purchase. How could she possibly prefer to live in a house that would surely fit into a mere corner of his own? How could she possibly choose to live *alone*? But to Lydia, her cottage soon became as precious as a palace. It was *hers*, and there, she was answerable to no one but herself. That fact, totally unexpected in her life, was a luxury surpassing all others.

Her neighbors had doubtless been as surprised as her relatives when she decided to stay and live all alone among them. She would not even consider hiring someone to be her companion, though her father—when he had understood that she was not to be budged, at least at present, when she was still clearly out of her mind with grief—had suggested an indigent female relative who would be only too happy to come and lend her some respectability. Lydia had said thank you but no, thank you. She did not invite Mrs. Elsinore, the cook and housekeeper Isaiah had hired to run the vicarage, to move in with her. While Isaiah had lived, Mrs. Elsinore had prefaced most of what she said in answer to Lydia's directions with, *"But the reverend says . . ."* After his death, she had changed that habitual response to *"But the reverend would say . . ."*

Lydia hired no one to replace her. The house was not so large that she could not keep it clean and tidy herself. She did not possess so strong a personal vanity that she could not groom herself to look decent in company. She did not have a stomach so large that she could not feed herself, though she had never in her life had to do so up until that point. She discovered that she actually enjoyed cooking and baking, once she had gathered some recipes from her neighbors and done some experimenting and made a few adjustments until she was able to produce edible and eventually even appetizing meals. Even dusting and polishing could be satisfying when she looked upon the results. For jobs like scything the grass and cleaning the outsides of the windows and running certain heavy errands, there was the blacksmith's middle son, a lad who was happy enough to earn a little pocket money.

Lydia was living the life she had hardly dared to dream about before fifteen months ago. She had relatives and in-laws of whom she was dearly fond and with whom she corresponded regularly, but she was not answerable to any of them. She had neighbors who were amiable and fussed over her in quiet, sympathetic ways while she was still in mourning, forever bringing her flowers and baked goods and produce from their gardens. Mrs. Piper, Jeremy's mother, was particularly attentive in these ways, almost to the point of being intrusive, since she always brought her offerings right inside the house without waiting to be invited and looked around with avid curiosity as she talked.

The neighbors now included Lydia in the social life of the community, both simple gatherings, such as this one tonight, and more elaborate events, like dinners at Sir Maynard Hill's and the assemblies above the village inn, where there was music and dancing. But from her neighbors—*most* of them, anyway—as much as she valued their kindness, Lydia could withdraw to the privacy of her own home whenever she wished.

She had even acquired a few real friends over the last year or so, women such as Lady Hill and Hannah Corning and Denise Franks, with whom she could visit and sit and talk and laugh. Women she could welcome into her own cottage. She had never been able to enjoy that luxury at the vicarage, where people were invited only on formal church business, organized and conducted by Isaiah and catered to by Mrs. Elsinore. Lydia had never had women friends until recently, in fact. She liked it.

There was only one thing she needed now to make her

life perfect. Oh, it was not a man. Well, not exactly, anyway. She had had a man. Indeed, she had had nothing but
men all her life, it seemed, ever since she was eight, when
her mother died a few weeks after giving birth to Anthony,
the youngest of her three brothers. She had no sisters and
no grandmothers. Her only aunt, her father's sister, was es-
tranged from him, since she had insisted upon marrying a
man he had considered less than respectable. Then, at the
age of twenty, Lydia had married Isaiah, who had one
brother but no sisters and no living mother and not even a
sister-in-law until three years ago, when Lydia was twenty-
five. She had been married to Isaiah for a little over six
years before his death.

There had been nothing but men in her life since she
was eight—*twenty years ago*—until recently. She had decided during the past fifteen months that she had had
enough of them, though none of them had ever been openly
cruel to her. But there would be no more men—not, at least,
men who would own her and have charge of her life and her
very mind and person. Freedom was a wonderful thing, she
had discovered. It was far too precious to give up. Ever.

Mrs. Bailey, the vicar's wife, was arranging her considerable bulk on the pianoforte bench, having been invited to
play by Tom Corning himself. She was by far the most accomplished pianist in the community. Unfortunately, the
instrument was slightly out of tune, as it had been for as
long as Lydia had been at Fairfield, and the key of high C
stuck whenever it was depressed with any degree of pressure and had to be manually restored to its position before
the music could continue. Everyone listened indulgently
anyway, while Mrs. Bailey played and Major Westcott
stood at her shoulder to turn the pages of the music and
lend his assistance with the sticky key.

"Tom," he called across the room when the first piece came to an end and the smattering of applause had died down. "If you do not hire someone within the next week to overhaul this instrument and repair that key, I swear I will undertake the task myself and you will be sorry."

"He will probably saw off the key altogether, Tom, and leave a gaping hole in its place for Mrs. Bailey and others to break a finger through," Dr. Powis warned. "I would not chance it if I were you, though the broken finger would be business for me. Get the dratted piano tuner here."

"You have been threatening to have the thing tuned for at least the last four years, since I came home," Major Westcott said. "Hannah must have the patience of Job to put up with it."

"I am not such a saint, Harry," Hannah said. "I have been threatening to tune *Tom* over it for at least that long."

There was general laughter. Tom Corning and the major had apparently been close friends since childhood and were grinning at each other as they bickered.

Lydia laughed with everyone else.

No, it was not a man that was missing from her life.

It was a lover.

They were one and the same thing, of course, some might argue. But those people would be wrong. A man in her life, whether father, brother, brother-in-law, or husband, would want to own her—they *would* own her. They would also want to dominate her. She would not allow herself to be owned or dominated ever again. A lover, on the other hand, could be enjoyed and sent on his way when his presence became bothersome.

Mr. Carver, one of Major Westcott's tenant farmers, who lived a mile or so beyond the village, had come to sit beside Lydia before the music began. As soon as Tom and Major

Westcott had finished calling across the room to each other, he launched into an account of the sudden and mysterious lameness of one of his horses in the right foreleg, just when there was a great deal of farm work to be done. Lydia turned her attention to him, though at least part of her mind was imagining how very deeply shocked he and all her neighbors and friends would be if they were aware of her deepest musings.

*A lover could be enjoyed and sent on his way . . .*

She had been the Reverend Isaiah Tavernor's wife and *helpmeet.* That was the word he had liked to use to describe her. It was as though she had had no identity of her own. She was only his helpmeet. For more than six years, first as a curate's wife, then as a vicar's, she had cultivated modesty and invisibility because it was what he had expected of her. Not literal invisibility, of course. Everyone had seen her, welcomed her, apparently liked and approved of her. She had forever been busy about parish business and the performance of good works, as befitted the wife of the vicar. But nobody, it seemed to Lydia, not even her closest acquaintances, had really *known* her. She had had no close friends while her husband lived. She had been too busy, all her time and attention devoted to furthering the work that was his passion. Sometimes she had had the rather dizzying suspicion that she did not know herself. Was there even a self to know? Someone quite separate and distinct from her energetic, zealous, charismatic husband?

Since Isaiah's death, she had chosen to remain more or less invisible. It had been better thus while she was still in her blacks, and it was easier now so that she could guard her fragile, hard-won freedom. She was known, she supposed, as the amiable, placid, even bland Mrs. Tavernor, the brave, tragic widow and helpmeet of their much-revered deceased vicar. She did not mind. At least for the present, she did not.

Yet here she was, seated in the midst of a number of her fellow villagers, dreaming of a lover.

Specifically, of Major Harry Westcott.

Who very probably scarcely knew she existed.

She had never flirted with him or tried in any way to engage his interest. She would not even know how to go about either one, anyway, if she wished to try. She had no serious designs on him. The chance that she would find a lover, any lover, here in this small village, was slim to none. Actually, slimmer even than that.

But a woman could dream, could she not? Dreams were often ideal pleasures, because one could make of them whatever one wished. And if they never came true, as most did not—and this one certainly never would—then what did it matter? Her real life was very nearly perfect as it was. Her dreams merely brightened it a little more.

Major Westcott was a young man, probably about her own age. He was tall and lean—*not* thin. That was too negative a word. Besides, his arms and shoulders and chest looked strongly muscled beneath the well-tailored coats and waistcoats he always wore. And his legs were long and shapely and powerful-looking under his pantaloons. They looked even more so in riding breeches and boots, she had noticed on other occasions. He was fair-haired and good-looking, even if not outstandingly handsome. He had a good-humored face, with blue eyes that almost always smiled. She was not deceived by either his face or his eyes, however. What had always fascinated her most about him was the suggestion of darkness that he kept very well hidden.

Perhaps it did not even exist. His mask—if it *was* a mask—never slipped in public, or never had when she had been present to witness it, anyway. And he was generally known as an even-tempered, sunny-natured man without a trouble in the world now that he was back home after the Napoleonic Wars in which he had fought. Lydia did not believe it. She knew very little of his past, but she knew enough to understand that there had been much suffering in his life, and that it was unlikely he had either dealt with it all or otherwise put it behind him. It was far more likely that he had repressed most of it. Lydia knew all about repressed suffering.

Once, very briefly, after the death of his father, he had been the Earl of Riverdale, with properties and fortune that had made him a very wealthy and socially prominent young man. He had been brought up and educated for just that life. But he had lost everything after the bigamous nature of his father's marriage to his mother had been discovered. It all must have been absolutely devastating to his family. And to him. Oh, he was treated here with great deference despite that huge change in his life. Most people here had known him all his life and had always liked him. He was still treated as lord of the manor, somewhat above all of them in rank. He could no longer be called *my lord* or *Lord Riverdale*, of course, but he could, and was, called *Major Westcott* as a mark of their respect, even though he was no longer a military officer.

He had been severely wounded at the Battle of Waterloo and had spent years recovering, first in France and then here at Hinsford Manor. He seemed perfectly fit now and had no visible scars, but Lydia doubted his recovery was complete, or ever would be. Perhaps there were wounds of war that were not entirely physical. She had no evidence of that, but she had always thought it. How could one fight other human beings to the death, slaughter them by the dozens, watch one's friends and comrades being slaughtered, be wounded almost to the point of death oneself, and come away from it unscathed?

How did one live with memories of hell?

Why did people speak of battlefields as fields of glory? They must be as close to hell as it was possible to get in this life.

Oh, there was surely darkness in Major Westcott. Lydia could sense it. But it served only to make him more impossibly attractive to her than his appearance and outer manner already made him.

Could something be *more* impossible than impossible?

Lydia smiled to herself, gave herself a mental shake, and focused more of her attention upon Mr. Carver, who was still speaking even though Mrs. Bailey was playing again.

"Perhaps," he was saying, "he has just grown too old and is ready to be put out to pasture. Do you think that might be it, Mrs. Tavernor?"

"Perhaps he just needs to rest for a while until his leg is better," Lydia suggested.

As soon as the music had finished, Mrs. Bartlett, Lydia's next door neighbor, approached Lydia and smiled apologetically down at her.

"Mrs. Tavernor," she said, "I am sorry to interrupt your conversation. My daughter-in-law has persuaded me to go out to the farm with her and my son to stay for a few days. There is room in the carriage for me to go with them tonight. I have things out there and will not need to go back home first. I always welcome the chance to spend some time with my grandchildren. I will not need you to walk home with me after all, then. I know you are not afraid of the dark, but I do hope you will not mind going alone."

"But we can squeeze Mrs. Tavernor into the carriage

too, Mother, and give her a ride home," her daughter-in-law protested, appearing at her side. She smiled at Lydia. "It will be no trouble at all."

"There really is no need for you to go out of your way," Lydia assured her as she got to her feet. It was indeed growing late. "I will enjoy the exercise and the fresh air after all the excellent cake I have eaten. And I really do not have far to go."

"But—" the younger Mrs. Bartlett began, while all about them other guests were also getting to their feet and preparing to leave.

"Mrs. Tavernor will not have to walk alone, Mrs. Bartlett," Tom Corning called across the room. "I'll run upstairs and fetch a coat and come with you, ma'am. I doubtless need the exercise, and you really ought not to walk on your own at night."

Lydia opened her mouth to protest. The main street of the village was not terribly long, after all, even though the Cornings lived at one end of it and she lived a little beyond the other end. A number of people between here and there would be at home, with lamplight or candlelight illumining their windows. There was absolutely nothing of which to be afraid. And then another voice spoke up from the direction of the pianoforte, where Mrs. Bailey was gathering up the music and Major Westcott was putting it away neatly inside the bench.

"I am going in that direction anyway, Tom," he called, "and would be happy to escort Mrs. Tavernor home. You will be perfectly safe with me, ma'am. I can fight off wild bears and wolves with my bare hands."

"That would be a sight to behold," Tom said derisively, grinning as he spoke. "Do you wish to take the risk that he is merely boasting, Mrs. Tavernor?"

"Since I have never in my life seen a wolf or a bear, stray or otherwise, in this neighborhood," Lydia said, "I believe it is safe to take the chance. Though I hope I am not dragging you away earlier than you intended to leave, Major Westcott."

"Not at all, ma'am," he assured her. "Tom and Hannah will probably be glad to see the back of me. And it will be my pleasure to walk with you."

He smiled at her. A sweet, quite impersonal, devastatingly attractive smile.

"Then thank you," she said.

Oh goodness.